Books should be returned or renewed by the last date above. Renew by phone **03000 41 31 31** or online *www.kent.gov.uk/libs*

Caroline Montague is the author of four novels, most recently *Shadows Over the Spanish Sun*. She lives with her husband at Burnt Norton House in the Cotswolds, a name made famous by TS Eliot's poem, the first of his *Four Quartets*. She is also a designer and mother to seven children and step-children. She divides her time between England and Italy, inspiring the setting for some of her novels.

THE
PIECES
OF US

CAROLINE MONTAGUE

ORION

An Orion paperback

First published in Great Britain in 2023 by Orion Fiction,
an imprint of The Orion Publishing Group Ltd
Carmelite House, 50 Victoria Embankment
London EC4Y 0DZ

An Hachette UK Company

1 3 5 7 9 10 8 6 4 2

A CIP catalogue record for this book is
available from the British Library.

ISBN (Paperback) 978 1 4091 9811 6
ISBN (eBook) 978 1 4091 9812 3

Typeset at The Spartan Press Ltd,
Lymington, Hants

Printed in Great Britain by Clays Ltd,
Elocograf S.p.A.

MIX
Paper from
responsible sources
FSC® C104740

www.orionbooks.co.uk

This novel is dedicated to Jemma Baskeyfield,
Burleigh historian at Middleport Pottery and my mother,
Patricia Marks, a barrister who believed women could
achieve anything.

I would say to those who mourn — look upon each day that comes as a challenge, as a test of courage. The pain will come in waves, some days worse than others, for no apparent reason. Accept the pain. Do not suppress it. Never attempt to hide grief from yourself.

Daphne du Maurier

Chapter One

2017

As Marina approached the farmhouse, she shaded her eyes. The roses were fading, their blush petals fluttering to rest beneath the cream stone walls. The oak front door was ajar, the sunlight filtering onto the terracotta floor. Later the heat would become intense, and the housekeeper, Signora Feranti, would glide through the rooms closing the doors and shutters, until the house became womblike and silent. Marina looked up, drew in her breath and as her gaze came to rest on *the* window, her step faltered. This was the room she had painted with Hugh before Francesca was born. It is where their beautiful baby girl had spent much of her short life.

She pulled her gaze away, forcing herself to join her husband on the terrace.

'It's nearly time, Marina.' Hugh placed his panama on his head. 'I'm going for a walk before we leave.' Marina watched him as he went beyond the rose garden towards the cypress trees. She waited until his slim figure had disappeared through the rusty Belle Époque gates at the end of the avenue, and was consumed by the shadows, then she entered the house. She went first through the cool hallway and up the wide staircase to the landing above. She knew it was foolish to enter the nursery, but she was pulled by an invisible thread, the primitive instinct that once caused her milk to flow.

The cot was still there, she refused to allow Hugh to remove it. The elephant mobile swayed gently as she approached. She wound it up, leant over the empty cot and, as the tinkling strands of music filled the air, she remembered climbing from her bed, stumbling across the landing for the first feed, knowing that in a moment Francesca's little arms would cling to her and her dark eyes would shine with recognition. She would run her finger over the tiny strawberry on her cheek that, at five months, was already fading to a pale smudge. Marina shuddered, recalling the hot prickle of worry down her spine as she had entered the room, the sense of foreboding and the precise second that panic beat like a hammer against her ribs. Her child had been lying on her back, but her little features were composed, immobile. There was no gentle rising and falling of her chest, no snuffling breath.

'Chessy! Chessy!' Her voice had become a scream as she picked up her daughter, looked into her face, and charged down the corridor to her husband.

'Hugh,' she shrieked '*Dio mio*. Hugh, help me.'

It was too late; Francesca's body was already cold.

Her gaze flickered around the room. The chair with the gingham cover was where she'd nursed her daughter, the small table in front of the window was where she dressed her. The cupboard was still stacked with nappies, muslins, nightdresses, the para-phernalia of a new-born child. She took the blanket from the cot and held it to her nose; the baby smell was fading fast but if she inhaled deeply perhaps...

The buggy was folded in the corner. Marina remembered pushing it along the wooded tracks, Francesca gurgling with delight as it bumped over the ruts, her little arms waving in the air. She recalled describing everything to her daughter, believing that one day in the future, Francesca would recognise the sound of wild boar rustling in the undergrowth, the buzzards mewing overhead. But she had been wrong; for Francesca, there would be no future.

Marina zipped up her suitcase and dragged it downstairs. When she reached the bottom step, she sank onto the worn stone, buried her head in her hands. How had she not sensed the danger? How had she not known of her child's struggle, her attempt to cling on to life? And why had her perfect little girl gone first?

Her shoulders tensed as she remembered the funeral, her parents helpless in the face of her grief, her grandfather trying to console her, Hugh standing apart as if he no longer belonged.

The priest she had known her entire life, who had married them and christened Francesca, recited prayers at her grave side, but his hollow words could not bring her baby back.

Later her family and friends had come to her, their voices filled with sympathy. She pretended to listen, thanked them for their kindness, but their words fell on deaf ears. She wanted to be on her own with Francesca, because her heart was buried with her daughter in the tiny white box.

Marina locked the door for the last time and put the key beneath the table leg for Signora Feranti to find. She ran her hand along the rough wooden surface, remembering Hugh making the table for their wedding breakfast, sawing the planks on the terrace, his back turning golden brown. And what a feast it had been, the guests assembled beneath the shaded pergola, Marina leaning against Hugh as he gave a speech, her warm, encompassing family sharing laughter and food. Even Hugh's mother relaxing at last. She remembered the sweet Tuscan wine from the family vineyards, the silence when Grace was given and the moment when the last guest drifted away and Hugh had led her to the apple orchard, where they had lain on their backs in the grass to look up at the stars. 'I have learnt this,' he had said in a low, sensual voice. 'A translation from the eighth-century Gaelic poem, "Máiréad Linnane", and it is for you.'

How long ago that seemed she reflected, and what a difference a year had made. She drew in her breath and without looking back she walked away. In a few hours she would be on a plane to England, and to the house Hugh had inherited from his uncle, Jeremy, three years before. She opened the car door knowing Hugh was hoping a new start would cajole her back to life, rekindle the spirit that had been extinguished. She understood these things for she has seen the regret in his eyes. Until now they had mourned separately, two individuals washed along by the tide of their own grief. If she wanted to save her marriage, she needed to think about him.

Marina checked the letter box for mail at the bottom of the hill.

'Don't worry your mother will send it on,' Hugh assured her.

'I'm not worried,' she replied, ashamed of the curt tone in her voice, the dismissal.

'Come on Marina, we'll get through this, you'll see.'

She closed the gates behind her, the dull thud of metal matching the heaviness inside. She had carried Francesca in her womb, watched her tiny heart beating on the scan, felt the first flutter in her belly and later, the pounding, insistent little feet, kicking her, demanding to be heard. She had felt the pain of delivery, the rush of love when Francesca took her first breath.

She slammed the car door, refusing to look at her husband's face. Every olive tree they passed, every field of wilting sunflowers, was taking her further away from her daughter. She opened the window, filling her lungs with her last scent of Tuscan earth. She was betraying Francesca by leaving her behind.

They were nearing Mercatale, when she banged her hand on the dashboard. 'Stop,' she yelled. 'Stop the car!' The car shuddered to a halt and Hugh turned to face her.

'Do you wish to stay?' he asked. 'Do you want me to go on alone? I have to return to Thorncliffe, Marina, the estate cannot run without me forever, it's my duty now.' Marina noticed the new gaunt angles of his face, the lines drawn from his nose to his chin and his eyes, dead like their daughter's.

'No,' she whispered. 'I'm so sorry, Hugh, just give me time.'

They remained in silence the engine ticking over, and Marina remembered the moment she had first met Hugh in Florence. She had been heading back to her office from a court hearing, when a young man rushed from a coffee shop onto the pavement. She had noticed immediately his long wavy hair and angular frame, his face that broke into a charming but hesitant smile.

'You are on television; I am sure it is you.' He tried again in broken Italian so appalling that Marina had smiled back.

'I speak English,' she volunteered, unable to keep the amusement from her voice. 'I knew they were filming outside the court, but to televise it so soon ...'

'Please come inside, let me buy you a coffee. If you say no, everyone will laugh at me.'

Marina wasn't in the habit of accepting offers from strangers, but the man in front of her looked safe, so hopelessly English, and to Marina on that April morning, extremely attractive.

She followed him into the café and the customers clapped, in a way that only Italians can, before returning their eyes to the screen.

'*Oh yes,*' she was saying in a serious but triumphant voice. '*It was definitely the outcome my client Chiara Ricci deserved. She suffered years of abuse at the hands of her husband. It was my job to demonstrate that she was the victim of a crime, not the perpetrator.*'

While she sat down, the young man darted off to the counter returning with an espresso. 'For you Avvocatessa Angelini, you see I know your name even if you do not know mine.' He put it on the table and Marina noticed his hands, long with slender fingers covered with paint.

'And you are an artist.'

'My secret is out.' His eyes crinkled at the corners and Marina felt a strange feeling in her stomach.

They had talked briefly before she had gathered up her files. '*Mi dispiace*, I am sorry, but I have to return to my office … the debriefing.'

He had got to his feet. 'It has been a pleasure; I hope our paths meet again.'

For the rest of the day Marina couldn't stop thinking about the unknown artist with the paint-spattered hands.

Two days after they had first met, and several internet searches later, she returned to the Santo Spirito neighbourhood of Florence, and the Rinaldini Atelier. When the door to the ancient building opened, she slipped inside, waiting in shadows as the students flowed past. Though her senses were attuned, she was oblivious to their chatter, listening for the one voice she would recognise. And then she found him standing at the front of the north lit studio and time stood still. The students who stepped back and forth from their easels to gauge the proportions and measurements of the muscular nude were irrelevant to her, the hypnotic scent of oil paint and turpentine, she only had eyes for the teacher with the slant of sunlight illuminating his high cheekbones and dark wavy hair. At the end of the class he came towards her.

'So you have found me?' He was gazing at her intently and her heart turned over.

'It seems so.'

'I was hoping that you would.' He brushed a strand of hair

from her cheek, his thumb lingering on her jaw. She couldn't look away.

They had lunch on the steps of the *Basilica di Santo Spirito* and the following day it was the same. It was not long before she shared his bed in the one-roomed apartment in an old palazzo, making love beneath the frescoed ceiling, running down the narrow streets to catch a taxi to work.

For a year they alternated between her stylish apartment near the Duomo and the crumbling palazzo, it seemed the idyll could never end. But the following year she was pregnant and Hugh asked her to be his wife. Marina's parents were delighted and offered them a small farmhouse on the estate. At seven months, they packed up their apartments and moved from Florence to the hills above the Niccone Valley. The house had a barn, with a loft suitable for a studio where Hugh would paint during the day, and they would watch the stars climb in the sky at night. Her mother brought her the cot crafted by her grandfather, the sculptor Davide Angelini.

'He made this in preparation for my birth,' she said. 'And now you are using it, what a gift, my child.'

Marina's eyes snapped open, and she put her hand over Hugh's, she could feel it tremble beneath her own.

'*Avanti*, to England,' she said. 'To a new beginning.'

As the engine ticked over, she wondered whether the fate that had brought them together would also tear them apart.

Chapter Two

Thorncliffe Hall

The car was approaching a pair of open wrought iron gates when Hugh slowed down.

Marina leant forward, her gaze moving between tall pillars, capped with carved stone dragons, the lodges either side. Weeds pushed their way through the gravel, and dust covered the windows in a grimy film. A feral cat stalked across the cattle grid turning its amber eyes on Marina.

'You have misled me,' Marina's tone was reproachful. 'This is not the entrance to a normal country house, not with gatehouses, not...'

'I didn't want to put you off.'

'Put me off?' Marina's voice rose a fraction.

Hugh touched her arm, but she shook it away. 'You should have warned me.'

'If I had warned you, you wouldn't have come.'

Marina realised the logic in this and was silent as he took his foot off the brake and they continued down the drive. Here the landscape was gentler than the untamed moorland outside. Sheep grazed in the parkland and a pair of red kites circled lazily above an oak tree. It was only when they had navigated the last bend and the house came into view, that she drew in her breath. This impression of tall chimneys and turrets, a bell tower rising above the roof line, the multitude of leaded windows, would stay with her, imprinted on her brain forever. But it was the length of the house, the very power of it that intimidated her.

'*Beata Merda*,' she uttered.

Hugh cleared his throat. 'Somehow "Holy Shit" sounds better in Italian.'

'This is not funny, Hugh.'

'Forgive me, I was trying to inject a little humour.'

'But you never mentioned this, no one said anything, not your mother not—'

'I asked her not to.'

He got out and Marina followed, but her footsteps were slow, tentative. She was struck by the stillness in the forecourt, the silence.

Hugh walked past the vast pillared portico towards a smaller door on the far right-hand side. Marina caught up with him. 'Our wing,' he put a suitcase down on the step. 'My uncle moved out of the main part of the house when I was a child, its much cosier in here.'

Cosy was not the adjective Marina would have used but she let it slip by. 'Will Mrs Danvers head a welcoming party?' she asked, and Hugh gave a lopsided smile.

'There will be no welcoming party.' He put his arm around her waist. 'And rest assured, there is no Mrs Danvers.'

Before he had time to ring the bell, the door was opened by the bearded retainer who hurried down the steps, followed by a tiny woman with a wide smile and immaculate grey hair.

'How good to see you.' Hugh went towards them, put out his hand.

The man's face broke into a warm smile. 'Lord Derrington, welcome, and to you, your Ladyship.'

Marina had a sudden inclination to laugh. She had known there was a title, but never really considered it. She looked across at Hugh hoping he would understand her silent plea. She was Marina, she couldn't have her identity taken away.

Mrs Crump held onto Hugh's hand. 'We are so pleased you are here, Master Hughie, I mean Lord Derrington, and you Lady Ursula.'

'Marina, may I introduce Mr and Mrs Crump, they have been at Thorncliffe for as long as I can remember.'

'I have known your husband since he was in short trousers, and I'll find it difficult getting used to the change.'

'There will be no change, Mrs Crump, for myself I would rather stay as Hugh, and I know my wife would like to be called Marina.'

'Well, that's a relief, I rehearsed it in the mirror, but I still gets it wrong. When there is company, we will address you correctly, that's what we are used to and we would like to keep it that way.'

Marina was about to speak but Mrs Crump continued. 'I knew you'd be attractive, Master Hughie being such a handsome boy.' She dropped Hugh's hand, her face turning pink.

'Mr Crump,' she instructed, her voice becoming imperious. 'Take the bags up to their room.'

'Done,' said her husband.

'And make sure there are no flies on the carpet.'

'None,' said her husband.

Hugh winked at Marina.

'What a pleasure to open up the house, I said to Mr Crump, it's been too long, much too long, you should have heard—'

'We are here now, Mrs Crump,' Hugh said, preventing any further observations, but the housekeeper wasn't put off.

'After you have freshened up, a nice cup of tea will be waiting for you in the Blue Parlour.'

Marina hated tea and knew Hugh would much prefer strong black coffee but smiled graciously not wishing to offend.

They followed Mr Crump along a wide panelled passage and up a winding set of stairs to the first floor.

'You're in Grosvenor, sir,' he deposited their luggage on the Turkish carpet. 'I hope you will be comfortable. Mrs Crump thought Shell a bit—'

'Gloomy,' Hugh finished.

'That is the word I was looking for. All those pictures of the Great War, hardly suitable for a young bride. This has such a lovely view of the garden and Lord Derrington did the furnishings. Your bathroom is Waterloo down the hall.'

'Waterloo?' Marina looked at her husband.

'Named after the battle,' Hugh explained.

'*Naturalmente*, a bathroom named after a battle, why not?'

He left them, and Marina wandered to the window. The expanse of lawn was broken by tall Scots pines and swathes of rhododendrons. In the distance she glimpsed a lake, the water glittering in the late afternoon light.

'So, do you think you can bear it?' Hugh asked, holding her close.

In any other circumstances Marina would have examined every detail of the charming bedroom, the embroidered silk curtains, the four-poster bed that could be better serviced by a stepladder, the watercolour of a young girl above the fireplace. She may have even pulled her husband with her, but today she only cast a cursory glance at the photographs on the mahogany desk.

'*Ci proverò*,' she whispered. 'I'll try.'

They had been in England for three weeks, but Marina hadn't settled. She took frequent walks – *constitutionals* Mrs Crump called them – wandering down the terraced lawns, beyond the banks of rhododendrons, to the Georgian pavilion at the head of the lake. But the busts of forgotten ancestors, sitting on their lonely pedestals, made her mourn her own family in Italy and the child she had left behind. The ornamental vegetable garden with an orangery at one end, was sad and neglected, the glass roof collapsed. It was now a dumping ground for broken statuary and discarded pots. Even the Egyptian obelisk on the fringe of the parkland, didn't stir her imagination. Once she would have pushed her way through the dense vegetation, scrambled up the bank, had a lively argument with Hugh on the rights, or in her case wrongs, of looting from other cultures, but it was too much effort.

'You could restore the garden,' Hugh had encouraged her. 'We have the funds for a new gardener, someone with your flair would bring it back to life.' Marina had agreed but, in the fog and mist of an English autumn, everything seemed grey and heavy, like her heart. She longed for the colour and vibrancy of Italy where their farmhouse seemed to grow from the land, and its vistas were the sunlit hillsides dotted with rows of cypress trees, olive groves and vines.

As she struggled to cope with her new surroundings, she realised sadly that the fire inside her had gone out. She recalled the daunting cases she had taken on in the past, the two young teenagers from Eritrea who had wanted asylum and the countless children she had fought for, but her spirit had been crushed and there was no fight left. Hugh encouraged her to go back to work. 'Take the necessary steps, practise here, I hate the thought of you being bored.'

But you needed energy, drive, the belief in your judgement and in yourself, but that had all gone with Francesca. Her response had been ugly and unkind.

'I am stuck in this huge old house while you disappear to the office leaving me on my own, yes I am bored and ...' She stopped mid-sentence. '*Mi dispiace*, I'm sorry, Hugh, that's unfair, I realise you have to run things here.'

'Whether I like it or not, it is my responsibility. Honestly, Marina, sometimes I wonder why you came here at all.'

'I didn't mean it, it's just that...'

'I know what it is,' he had replied.

Every evening Marina hurried through her routine in the old-fashioned bathroom and climbed into bed hoping that sleep would bring closure and forgetfulness, but she was wrong. She would wake in the night, her ears attuned to the creaking of floorboards, the pattering of rain on the roof. Were they footsteps she wondered, hearing a light, rhythmic beat on the floor, a child crying, could it be Francesca?

Hugh would hold her shaking body. 'It's just the wind, Marina, you'll get used to it.'

But Marina knew better; it was not the wind.

One night, she slipped from the room, walked down the dark passage, stopping at a door at the end. An indefinable scent lingered in the air. Was it herbs she wondered, hugging her dressing gown closer. She rattled the handle, but no sound came from within.

She returned to bed, curling herself into a tight ball and as light crept through the curtains she finally slept.

'Let's go to London,' Hugh suggested at breakfast.

'London?' she repeated, noticing the grey smudges beneath his eyes.

'Just for the weekend, I think we both deserve a break.'

Marina lowered her copy of *la Repubblica*. 'If you would like to.' Her voice was flat.

'I'll take you to a hotel with a spa and a great restaurant. You could have a massage, even one of those steam bath things?'

'Thank you, Hugh.'

Marina returned to her newspaper and Hugh folded his napkin and left the room. At the door he turned. 'It would help if you showed some interest, Marina. I'll be in the estate office if you need me. I'll be back late.'

Hugh was walking through the park towards his office when he changed his mind. He turned off the track towards a small enclosure beneath the overhanging trees. It was here he found the memorial to the war horse, Endymion, brought home to England by his grieving ancestor, after his son was killed in action in 1917. Hugh had always found solace there; it was where he came when his own father died.

The inscription had worn over the years, but it still resonated. *'Endymion, charger, warrior and loyal friend.'*

He brushed away the leaves and sat down, putting his head in his hands. When Francesca came on to this earth he was transformed, his confidence grew. This miracle of creation was part of him, and he loved her with every fibre of his being. He had vowed he would keep her safe, he would nurture her, yet he had failed, they had both failed and now their marriage was falling apart, and they were caught in a riptide of grief.

But it hadn't always been like that. They had been ridiculously happy, sure of themselves and their love, but the old Marina had gone, and he wanted her back. He sighed recalling the cases she had fought, the women she had helped; young girls abducted, forced into sex work and exploited. There was one incident in particular, an Ethiopian teenager selling bags near the Duomo, a man lingering nearby. Marina had noticed her immediately.

'We have to do something; the girl is here against her will.' She had pulled out her mobile phone, and in minutes the *Polizia* arrived. The girl had recovered her freedom and was now working in a children's home. Marina's superior had prosecuted the trafficker.

Hugh remembered taking Marina to the Palazzo Medici not long after they had met.

'How is it that you have lived in Florence for seven years and you haven't been to the Magi Chapel?' he teased as they stood in front of the Gozzoli frescoes of the Magi's journey to Bethlehem. 'The most beautiful fresco in the world. Look at the vibrant colours, the exquisite horses and figures, the harmonious decoration. It could have been painted yesterday.'

Marina had raised herself to her full height. 'You say that, but have you seen the Giotto Exorcism of the Demons in the Basilica of San Francesco in Assisi. The sky is positively writhing and the buildings ...' She tossed her dark hair and looked at him challengingly. 'It makes you want to walk into the painting and explore.'

'No, I haven't, but—'

'There are no buts Mr Englishman. Until you have seen every fresco in Tuscany you cannot make that assumption.'

There had followed a healthy debate on Italian frescoes, followed by a walk down to the Arno where he had kissed her and accepted he was falling in love with her.

'Will you move in with me?' he had asked. And she had laughed her infectious, deep laugh.

'You are asking me to move out of my ordered flat into your crumbling bedsit, albeit a bedsit in a palazzo?' She had looked at him beneath her lashes, her voice dropping. 'You will have to make it worthwhile.'

'And how would I do that?'

'Umm first you would have to massage my back.'

'And then?'

'*Il mio collo.*'

'And after your neck?' he had murmured.

They had got no further, running along the banks of the Arno and down the side streets until they had reached Santo Spirito and his apartment, pulling the clothes from each other until they were naked beneath the frescoed ceiling.

'I think this might be the most memorable fresco of all,' Marina had murmured before his lips had silenced her.

The following weekend they had gone to meet her grandfather at the family home near Cortona.

'Should I be terrified?' Hugh had asked, from behind the wheel of her Alfa Romeo Spider.

'Definitely,' she had giggled. 'If he doesn't approve of you, I will have to ditch you right now.' But Hugh believed he may have passed the test because he spent the entire afternoon in Davide Angelini's studio, admiring his carvings and his sculpture, talking about his exhibitions, his extraordinary career, and in turn the nonagenarian's eyes had lit up when Hugh told him about the studio where he taught.

'I gave a lecture there once,' he had said. 'A very excellent school.'

Hugh didn't ask about his life as a partisan or mention his parents who he knew had been murdered in Dachau, but he quickly discovered sculpture and his past were so much part of the man.

'This piece,' Davide had picked up a small, perfectly carved wooden horse, 'I made for a friend. He died shortly afterwards, but somehow it found its way back to me, and this bird of prey was for my beautiful wife Diana.' He had looked up and Hugh had seen the love for his wife still shining in his faded blue eyes.

Chapter Three

Hugh left for the estate office and Marina lingered in the dining room, a letter from her grandfather on the table in front of her.

'When you've finished, why don't you have a mosey, dear, just get used to things.' Mrs Crump was clearing the breakfast around her. 'There's a short history of the house on the main hall table. Mr Crump uses it when he shows visitors around.'

'Visitors?'

'Tour groups, that sort of thing. Lord Jeremy was keen on sharing the history. You might like to take over ... not at the moment of course.' She continued stacking the plates. 'Mr Crump and I are so sorry, my dear.'

Marina swallowed. 'Her name was Francesca.'

'That is a very pretty name. If ever you want to talk ... I may not seem qualified, but I always wanted children. Sadly we were not blessed.' She cleared her throat. 'I bet your Francesca was a lovely little girl.'

Marina nodded. 'I miss her, Mrs Crump,' and even as she said the words, she could feel the torrent of grief surging through her. She bit her lip; she wouldn't let go, not now. 'I ... I don't know what to do.'

Suddenly the crockery was deposited, and she found herself

enfolded in the diminutive woman's arms. 'Have a proper cry, my girl, I always say it's the tears that heal.'

'She was my life.'

'No doubt about it, and she always will be, but the pain will soften in time, you'll see.'

On the morning of their trip, they took the fast train from Stoke-on-Trent to Euston and were walking through the entrance of the Haymarket Hotel three hours later.

Hugh checked in while Marina wandered around the foyer.

'Will it do?' he asked, coming to stand beside her. 'I found the hotel online, it reminded me of—'

'My flat in Florence,' Marina interrupted, admiring the light airy spaces, the brightly coloured paintwork, the modern design. 'But this sculpture,' she stopped in front of an artwork made of polished steel. 'Though interesting it is not as good as the work of Papa Davide.'

Hugh laughed. 'Nobody could be as talented as your grandfather.'

They were in the lift when Marina took his hand, ran her fingers over his knuckles and brought them to her lips. 'I don't know how you put up with me, I have been so . . .' She screwed up her face, wondering how to name the debilitating, crushing feeling inside, but then it came to her.

'I have been so angry, Hugh, not with you, but with God, with the world for taking Francesca away from us. Does that make sense?'

'I am angry too, Marina, but I'm trying to find a way to move forward with our lives.'

'I'm not sure I want to move forward without her.' Marina looked up, her eyes pools of misery and Hugh took her in his arms.

They had supper in the dining room, an interesting mixture

of the old and the new. The quirky chairs were upholstered with a different breed of dog on the back of each one. Marina chose the poodle and as the Italian waiter fluffed out her napkin, she raised her eyebrows.

'The English and their dogs, *sono pazzi tutti quanti*, they are all quite mad.'

The waiter laughed. '*Gli inglese e il loro amici dei cani*, totally mad, excluding you, sir, naturally.'

Marina was in the bath when Hugh came in. Her hair was tied on top of her head exposing the long column of her neck. She looked vulnerable, exposed, the knob of each vertebra prominent through her pale skin. Hugh wanted to reach out and touch her, but he was afraid.

In his apartment in Florence, he would have climbed in behind her, put his hands around her waist and pulled her to her feet. They would have made love, the water splashing over the bath, their laughter echoing through the building, until Signora Maggi from the floor below would knock on the ceiling with her extendable broom. But this was not Florence, and those were different times. Marina turned her head to look at him and smiled, but Hugh could see the suffering in her dark eyes, the hollows in her cheeks.

She stood up and he passed her a towel, wrapped her in it, until she was enclosed in his arms. 'Come to bed,' he whispered, and he led her to the bedroom, unwrapped the towel and lifted her onto the bed. Marina wound her arms around his neck, pulled his face closer until their lips were touching, their breath met. His body became insistent, demanding. Marina wrapped her legs around him until they were indivisible, drawn together by passion and despair.

Afterwards they lay together, listening to the hum of the traffic outside the window, the sound of a woman's heels clicking on the pavement, laughter. Their breathing was synchronised, steady. Hugh ran his hand over her breasts, touching the silver marks scored there, a reminder.

'I'm not even pretty,' she moaned. 'Look at me.'

Hugh turned his head. 'I am looking,' he said, 'and every mark is beautiful. You are beautiful.'

Marina slept well for the first time since her arrival in England, and after a typical English breakfast – she knew Hugh had paid a lot for the room and was determined to do it justice – she put on her navy coat and cream woollen hat before going outside. Marina's experience of central London was limited, and Hugh wanted to show her around.

'First stop St James's Palace,' he suggested. 'Perhaps some shopping and tomorrow the National Gallery?'

After a brisk five-minute walk, they were standing in front of the Tudor gatehouse on Pall Mall.

To Marina it was very different from the powerful, rusticated buildings in Florence, but it had a beauty of its own.

'*Mi spieghi,*' she demanded. 'Explain to me the history,' and Hugh put his arm around her shoulders and told her of the Tudor King, Henry VIII, who had lived there. For an instant her eyes sparkled.

'The one who murdered his wives?'

'The very same,' Hugh replied.

From St James's they walked up Haymarket to Piccadilly Circus, purchasing books from Hugh's favourite shop, and after a quick lunch they found themselves in the Burlington Arcade. They were nearing the end of the nineteenth-century arcade, Marina having bought an embroidered waistcoat for Hugh and some handmade chocolates for Mrs Crump, when she noticed the antique shop. It had a large frontage with ornaments of every description filling the window. There were jugs, bowls, porcelain clocks.

'Overpriced,' Hugh murmured, coming to stand beside her.

'*Probabilmente*,' she agreed.

Spotting a china coffee pot with a charming little fox flying through a night sky, he pointed it out to Marina.

'It reminds me of a jug I have seen at home.'

'But it's enchanting.' Marina clapped her hands together, and Hugh knew he would buy it for her, whatever the cost.

They went inside and were greeted by the proprietor who introduced himself as Mr Button.

'There is a coffee pot in the window,' Hugh started. 'It has a—' He got no further.

'This one I believe.' Mr Button made a show of taking it out of the window.

'A fine piece. You have good taste, sir.'

Hugh ignored the flattery.

'Early twentieth century.' Mr Button flicked imaginary dust from the lapel of his pinstripe suit. 'The potter was a contemporary of Clarice Cliff. We have a teapot from Miss Cliff's iconic Crocus range, and a charming jug by the celebrated potter, Cleo Doyle.'

Marina had heard of neither, but she clicked her tongue, satisfying Mr Button.

When the pieces were placed together on the counter, he stood back to contemplate them. 'Magnificent,' he observed, his head on one side.

Hugh squeezed Marina's hand, his face a picture of innocence. 'But the design of the jug and the coffee pot is similar is it not?'

'Definitely not,' said Mr Button.

Marina observed the three objects. The teapot was undoubtedly attractive, the orange and purple crocuses painted on the front radiated exuberance and life, and the jug decorated with an imaginary undersea world was also beautiful, but it was the coffee pot that attracted her most.

'May I hold it?' she asked.

Mr Button handed the coffee pot to Marina who wrapped her fingers around it and closed her eyes. There was something intriguing about the piece, naïve.

Holding onto the lid she turned it over, and on the bottom, there were two tiny sets of initials EC and LD.

Hugh looked closer, 'I am sure I have seen it … perhaps the cabinet in the hall.' He took out his glasses. 'And this is the Derrington stamp.'

Marina felt her heart thrum, like an engine ticking into life. 'Are you telling me this was made in your factory?'

Hugh frowned. 'I am pretty certain …'

'You have connections with the Diligence Works?' Mr Button interrupted, with something akin to awe on his face.

'My ancestors owned the pottery until the 1980s, when the recession forced them to close.'

'Do you understand the rarity of these pieces? This was crafted by a relatively unknown young potter, Elody Cole, and her assistant, for the Lucian range.' Mr Button was sweating slightly, his face flushed. 'You don't happen to own any more?'

Hugh laughed. 'I shall be looking out for it.'

'We know so little about her, what became of her, she just vanished into thin air. That is why this piece is so sought after, so …'

'Expensive,' Hugh finished for him.

All this time Marina had been holding onto the coffee pot.

'How much is the jug, Mr Button?' Hugh asked.

'I am afraid, sir, the best I can do is nine hundred pounds. The Lucian range is the most exclusive, there is so little of it you see.'

'Done, Mr Button,' Hugh's voice grew stronger. 'Wrap it up and it will return to its rightful home.'

Mr Button wrapped up the coffee pot and put it in a box. When he saw Hugh's title on his bank card, he was almost genuflecting.

'I am so glad it's going somewhere where it will be appreciated. Thank you for finding my humble little shop, Lord Derrington.'

That night Marina leant back against the upholstered bedhead. The coffee pot was on the table beside her. She touched it and looked at her husband.

'You didn't have to buy it.'

'When I saw your face, I would have paid anything for it, but don't tell Mr Button.'

Marina ran her finger down his cheek. 'Thank you,' she said, her voice gentle. Hugh unclipped her hair so that it fell around her shoulders and buried his face in the soft waves. His wife smelt of shampoo and soap, and at once he was reminded of Francesca at bath time, gurgling as he poured the water over her head, her little legs kicking as it ran down her cheeks. Marina looked up and their eyes met.

He pulled away from her, his lashes wet with tears. 'Do you mind, tonight I just want to hold you. Please forgive me, it's nothing to do with you I just want us to feel close.' He put his arm around her shoulders and her head fell against him.

'I feel so lost. Sometimes I just don't know where I am, or where I've gone.'

'You're right here where you belong,' he murmured, 'and we will find ourselves again in time, you'll see.'

The following morning, Marina raised herself on her elbow and looked at her husband. Even in sleep his body was taut, the sheet wound through his fist. He moved slightly, a sigh escaping his lips. She wanted to put out her hand, reassure him, lessen the distance between them; instead she turned away and dropped her legs over the side of the bed. What had happened to them she wondered, where was the passion that had once united them?

She recalled the despair on Hugh's face as he recoiled from her the night before, the fear in his eyes, but in truth she hadn't wanted it either. She would have gone through the motions, but she was numb, dead inside.

She picked up the coffee pot, her fingers tracing the pattern, the movement in the sky, the outline of the charming flying fox. She was touching the same surface, feeling the same swells and curves Elody Cole and her assistant had touched so long ago. As she put it back on the table, she wondered what had happened to them and why all trace of them had gone. She had a feeling the coffee pot was somehow important. Perhaps if she could find a link between this and the piece at Thorncliffe Hall, it could bring them back together again. She knew the idea was irrational but the more it took hold, the more inspired she became.

Chapter Four

It was dusk when they arrived back at Thorncliffe. Marina sprinted up the three steps to the West Wing with some of her old energy and was about to open the door when she looked back. Hugh was pulling a weed from the gravelled forecourt, perhaps it was the vulnerability in his stance, his shoulders rounded as he leant down, or the house, which was softer, less inhospitable in the evening light, perhaps it was the three days in London, but something had shifted inside her.

She called to Hugh who pushed the hair from his eyes, his face breaking into a boyish smile, and she put a finger to her lips. 'Thank you for everything,' she murmured, hurrying through the inner hall, past the mounted hooves of a long-departed horse, the wooden rack of silver topped canes. She ran the length of the blue patterned carpet, into the Polish Vestibule, called because of the tapestry sewn for an ancestor by a grateful Polish people, stopping at the rosewood cabinet where an eclectic assortment of china was displayed. She tried the handle, it was locked.

After searching in the office, first in the paper tray, a repository for discarded items, then in a bank of satinwood drawers, she found a selection of keys in an oval tin.

'Which one?' she asked Hugh.

'Uncle Jeremy hid his keys, then forgot where he had put them. The tin was his safety net.'

Marina raised an eyebrow.

'I know what you're thinking, the eccentric English, but—' He got no further because Marina had run off with the tin.

As she tried each one, she had an image of an older version of Hugh searching for his missing keys. It wasn't long before a small silver key turned in the lock. Hugh joined her, and together they moved the pieces around. There were Dresden cups and saucers, Limoges figurines, Worcester, Chelsea, some tiny Etruscan urns, but no coffee pot.

'Perhaps my uncle sold the piece and it ended up in Mr Button's hands.'

'I feel sure it's here somewhere.' Marina shook her head in frustration. 'It has to be.'

Mrs Crump was taking the lids off the domed silver dishes when Marina arrived in the dining room the following morning.

'Your favourite black pudding, sir,' she nodded at Hugh. 'Mr Crump managed to get it at the butcher's even though it is Monday. I imagine you won't be wanting it, Marina?'

Marina shuddered. 'If you don't mind.'

'Not to everyone's taste, I agree, shall I help you to scrambled eggs?'

Afterwards, Marina presented a delighted Mrs Crump with the chocolates, then she took the coffee pot from its bed of tissue paper and handed it to her.

'Can you imagine, Mrs Crump, this was made up here at the Derrington Pottery by an unknown girl called Elody Cole and her assistant for the Lucian range.'

'Lots of things were made up here, love.'

'But it's so romantic, don't you think?' Marina gazed at the little pot, her brow furrowed.

'That's the Diligence Works, all right.' Mrs Crump squinted at the stamp.

'Hugh believes he may have seen something similar in one of the cabinets?'

'I haven't come across it, but in a house this size…'

She was about to hand it back when she took another look.

'EC and LD. I imagine the D stands for Derrington, and the L…?' she chuckled and put the jug on the table. 'Now I may not have all the examinations in the world, Marina, but my Atticus says I'm a regular detective.'

'Atticus?'

'If you had a surname like Crump, you'd want something better at the start.'

'I see.' Marina was smiling.

'If I was a betting woman, I'd say the L stands for Lucian.'

'*Dio mio*, Mrs Crump, you could very well be right.'

'Just a suggestion, but I'd take a look for your missing pot in the main part of the house. I'll fetch the key.'

Mrs Crump unlocked the door to the vestibule and let Marina into the vast, empty hall.

'Call my mobile if you need any help, or if you get lost. It's a big old place and took me years to find my way around!'

She closed the door and Marina was alone. In the distance a clock chimed, and a door closed. A whisper of breeze touched her face with the lightness of a feather, she called out, there was no reply.

Was it one of the Three Graces who had stepped from the painting to dance around the hall, or the children in the conversation piece who were playing with a clockwork train, their roller skates discarded nearby?

She continued up the stairs, and at the half landing where the staircase split into two, she took the left-hand side until she reached a gallery that looked down on the hall below. A tattered banner hung from the balustrade telling of an illustrious past, and a sedan chair waited in the corner for an occupant who would never appear. Two large trunks, studded with an intrcate pattern of brass nails, were placed against the wall. Marina was lifting the heavy lid when she drew in her breath; the noise was imperceptible, but to Marina it was footsteps, one foot, then another padding across the floor beyond a pair of double doors. Her eyes were glued to the handle, expecting it to turn, the door to creak open. 'Enough,' she whispered at last. 'Enough.' She straightened, letting the lid fall with a resounding crash, the reverberations echoing around her. She was poised for flight and yet her legs wouldn't move. She waited, seconds passed, silence returned. Perhaps it was the wooden panelling shrinking, or water running through the pipes? Perhaps it was one of the dancing girls?

Forcing herself to remain calm, she moved towards the cabinets, her eyes searching the shelves, darting over cups, plates, dinner services in different patterns, different styles, all physical records of the Diligence Works. Nothing resembled her coffee pot. She hurried down the stairs.

Marina was sitting on the sofa in the Blue Parlour, her legs curled beneath her, holding a brief history of the house. Outside the window, Atticus Crump was cleaning the ornamental fishpond while his wife was hoovering in a passage nearby. Marina felt safe now, secure, she had imagined the footsteps, they were an illusion of the past, nothing more.

She started to read and was quickly engrossed in the story of advantageous marriages and royal visits, set around the aristocratic Hamilton family whose entitlement to the land was recorded in the Doomsday Book. As the story unfolded, she was drawn deeper into the web of past suffering and lies – the

Hamilton Countess who bore a king's child and passed it off as her husband's, the Jacobite who betrayed his cousin and many of his former allies to save his own skin, the butcher's son substituted at birth to keep the Hamilton line intact.

At some point she moved beyond the illustrious and often murky history, to the end of the nineteenth century and the failing fortunes of the Hamilton family. When she came to the marriage of Ursula Hamilton to the rich pottery manufacturer, Andrew Derrington, she wondered if theirs had been a love match or just advantageous? Had their affection for each other supported them through the Great War, comforted them after the loss of eight young men from the household including their son Giles? But of course not, she thought, her throat tightening. They would have been submerged beneath a tidal wave of misery and grief, quite probably neglecting the house, the garden, the pottery and each other.

Much later Marina was making herself coffee, when the thought struck her, she had read the entire text and yet there had been no mention of the potter Elody Cole or Lucian.

It was late afternoon when Marina returned to investigate the basement in the main wing of the house.

'Another exploration,' Mrs Crump said, opening the door for Marina. 'I don't go down there myself, all those old rooms, no I leave that to Mr Crump.'

'I would like to see what's there.'

'A lot, and it's not been touched since the war.' She patted Marina's arm. 'It's a time warp this place, all those old dresses stuffed into a glass case upstairs.' She lowered her voice as if the ghosts of Thorncliffe could hear her. 'They would say they were collectors, but myself I would say they were hoarders. Did you know the fifth Earl…'

Marina made her escape, descending the stairs towards the

servants' quarters on the lower ground floor. One step at a time she entered a different world. Even the smell was different: polish, linoleum and still, after seventy years of disuse, the faint smell of food. Stopping to inspect a propaganda poster from the First World War she felt a tug at her heart. Lord Kitchener with his famous pointing finger was instructing the youth to go to war. There were photographs of princes and parliamentarians, and Marina finally understood the depth of history lodged within the walls.

At the end of a passage, a small plaque announced she was entering the housekeeper's sitting room. As she looked around the dim interior, she realised Mrs Crump was right, she was stepping back in time. A broken wicker cage was upended beside a stack of ancient magazines, a sofa with its stuffing disgorging remained beside two comfy chairs. In the staff dining room, a bench was pulled out, as if someone had left only moments before. Jelly moulds were stacked on the kitchen dresser, copper pots hung from the ceiling, even the range was there, and three Belfast sinks. A white frilled apron still hung from one of the pegs on the wall. As her hand ran over the pine table and felt the roughened surface beneath her fingers, she imagined the hands that had been here before, the cook kneading dough, a maid shelling peas…

She let the images fade and closed the door, proceeding down a wooden ramp to a wide passage, where the walls were painted pillar-box red. Was this where the brothers from the painting roller skated in the years before the war? She could almost hear their careless laughter, anticipating a future that would never be theirs. Room by room she discovered remnants of the past, the wine cellar filled with empty bottles, a footman's room for polishing shoes, a tin of dried-up polish in an old wooden box, a pair of leather hunting-boots abandoned on the floor. In the silver room she unearthed a crested spoon. She nearly missed

Toby Slatter's old bedroom and, as she read the nameplate above the door, her chest constricted. Toby was the last head footman at Thorncliffe and one of the eight members of staff who joined a Staffordshire regiment, never to return.

She switched on the light, blinking in the sudden brightness. Cobwebs hung from the ceiling and dust covered the surfaces in a thick cloud. An old metal bed was propped against the wall, the horsehair mattress sagging on the floor. A mouse ran across the skirting, disappearing through a tiny hole in a connecting door. Marina's hand closed around the tarnished handle, but it wouldn't move. She pushed harder, the wood creaked, adjusted. She threw her weight against it, the door opened, and she fell inside.

As her eyes became accustomed, her breath stilled. The room was large, suitable for a servant of standing. It had a fireplace and a sink, but it was the pottery wheel that caught her eye, the working platform. Two chairs were side by side, one for an adult, another for a child. A shaft of sunlight leaked through the window alighting on a tray of ceramic paints. A brush was on the table beside an empty bottle of turpentine. On the shelf she found an old plate, it was chipped at the edges, unfinished, but there was something fine about the fluted design, the outline of a bird. She turned it over.

'EC and LD,' she whispered, the initials on her coffee pot, the initials Mrs Crump had identified. She ran her hand down the smaller chair, over the indent in the seat, was it possible Elody's assistant was a child?

In the days afterwards, Marina went through letters, photographs, old clothes she found in a trunk in the Polish vestibule, but there was nothing to suggest a young boy called Lucian had lived at the hall. On a damp autumn morning, after a solitary walk on the moors, she took the tin of keys and returned to the door at the end of the corridor. As she fitted the largest key in the lock and turned the handle, the door opened, and she went inside. She stood for a moment absorbing the silence, inhaling the musty scent of neglect. She identified a kitchen to the right of the passage by a porcelain sink, a spiderweb of cracks in the glaze, a trail of green mould leading to the plughole below. A map of the world still clung to the inside of a cupboard, held by a solitary pin. She examined the ragged chintz curtains, the empty bookshelves, she lifted a corner of the threadbare rug. Whose room was it? she wondered, drifting back down the corridor and entering the largest room of all. '*Soggiorno*,' she murmured softly, imagining sofas, chairs, possibly a little dining table in the corner. In the bathroom, a slatted wooden platform was positioned beneath the bath. She ran her fingers along the step, imagined small feet climbing on to it, a child swinging a leg over the edge, but there were no bath toys, no pictures, nothing was left behind. The apartment was empty, desolate, a relic from long ago. She was about to leave when she noticed something lodged beneath the radiator in the hall. She dropped to her knees and peered underneath. As she pulled out the small toy engine, her hand trembled, it was the clockwork train in the painting downstairs.

Chapter Five

Outside the dining room window, the leaves were falling, carpeting the ground with gold, but to Marina, the beauty was invisible, it was just a new season, a new month without Francesca. For days she had hunted for clues about the makers of her charming little coffee pot, but as her daughter's birthday drew nearer, her interest waned. What was the point of searching for Lucian and Elody Cole, it was only a diversion after all?

She looked up as Hugh pushed the toast rack towards her, a hesitant look on his face.

She took a piece, spread the butter thickly, then pushed the plate away.

'How are you getting on with your mystery potter?'

She knew Hugh was trying to make conversation, but her words just came out.

'Oh, I don't know, Hugh, some long dead *ceramista* won't bring our daughter back.'

'Why don't you consider returning to the Bar?'

Marina's head snapped up. 'And I told you last time, I'm a foreigner in this country. It's not that easy.'

'If not the law, there is another possibility.' It seemed Hugh was determined to continue. 'There's a charity in Stafford that might interest you, the Artemis Centre. It's for victims of domestic abuse, my mother volunteered there, someone with your skills…'

He got no further because Marina stood up and walked towards the door.

'I shouldn't have asked,' he uttered, to her receding back. 'It seems we have nothing to talk about anymore.'

'We do,' she whispered, turning to face him.

He did not reply.

Marina bolted upstairs. She was lashing out at Hugh, taking out her anger and grief on her husband when it was not his fault.

She could feel the gulf between them widening, she had to make it up to him before it was too late.

'Would you like me to ask your mother to stay for your birthday?' she asked him later that evening, trying to make amends, hoping the gesture would be seen as an olive branch.

'I thought you found her difficult.'

'No, Hugh just…' She tried to think of the word. 'Perhaps a little intimidating, but I should like to know her better.'

He smiled, but his face was taut. 'Actually, Marina, my mother has never been very good at grief; now is not the time.'

Hugh arrived at the estate office, collected an espresso from the machine and sat down at his desk. As the relentless march towards winter continued, the grey skies matched his mood. He glanced at the estate map, then pushed it away. For the last few weeks, they had been deciding which farms they could amalgamate in order to make them more profitable for the tenants and therefore more secure for the landlord, but these days he had little appetite for work. Perhaps because he had little appetite for anything.

An estate vehicle pulled up outside and Michael Bagshawe, the land agent, got out, his eight-year-old son Tommy jumping down behind.

'Wait for me,' the boy called, following his father inside, and Hugh remembered his own childhood, scrambling into Uncle Jeremy's Land Rover, having escaped his great aunt's clutches.

'Hurry, young man, if you want to come with me. Great Aunt Alice will serve you up on a plate if she catches you skipping homework in favour of a day with your uncle.' Jeremy had revved up the engine purely to add an element of excitement and off they had sped. How he had loved his witty, irreverent uncle. Jeremy came to the rescue when Hugh's father died.

'Your mother wants to be with you desperately,' he had explained to the confused child. 'But right now, it is better for her to keep the Mayfair gallery open, so will you stay with me, at Thorncliffe?'

So ten-year-old Hugh had changed schools and changed lives. In those formative years, his life was centred around Jeremy, his autocratic Great Aunt, Alice, and Mr and Mrs Crump. Jeremy had given him an idyllic and secure childhood, filled with adventure combined with more than a smattering of culture. At the end of every Lent term, they went off in his 1920s aquamarine Crossland, the roof open, the luggage strapped to the back, visiting Europe like the travellers of old.

'A modern-day grand tour,' Jeremy would say, chuckling. 'Good for the soul, Hugh.'

They visited cities in France, Spain, Italy and Germany, but it was Venice Jeremy loved the most, renting rooms in the same faded palazzo off Campo Santo Stefano. For two weeks at a stretch, they would explore churches, museums, discover architectural features known only to those who were prepared to take their time.

'Don't hurry over this bridge, young man, pause at the top and look around you, tell me what you see.' Hugh had been dazzled by the carved stone doorways and ogee windows, the reflections of the buildings shimmering in the canals below. He learnt to appreciate the myriad of warm earthy colours and architectural styles, the grey days when Venice was shrouded in mist and the canals grew secretive and mysterious, or the rain-filled mornings when the clouds were mirrored in the dark and swirling waters below. Jeremy bought him a sketchbook and a set of watercolours and soon byzantine facades, baroque churches and intimate passageways, filled the pages. He painted the beautiful loneliness of the ancient *Basilica di Torcello* standing on its little island in the lagoon. He captured the light wrapping its way around the columns, sparkling on the ancient mosaic cycles, the broken statues and architectural features that littered the ground outside. He painted the news-stands, nineteenth-century gas lamps, the poignancy of the Jewish ghetto, where tall, tightly packed buildings were unadorned and bleak in contrast to the splendour elsewhere.

They became known at the finest restaurants and the smallest cherished trattorias frequented mainly by Venetians. In Harry's Bar Jeremy was always given the same table in the window upstairs, and it was here that Hugh tasted his first Bellini. 'Just a sip, we wouldn't want you drunk in charge.'

Each morning Jeremy would defer to his nephew before making the decision himself. 'Now what do you think, Hugh? Where should we go today?' he used to say, taking his various guidebooks from the shelf. 'I think perhaps the *Scuola di San Giorgio degli Schiavoni*. The Vittore Carpaccio cycle has to be part of your education.' And as they stood in the intimate *scuola*, beneath St George facing the dragon in an Italian landscape strewn with carnage, Hugh's future was clear.

As memories of turquoise waters, lagoons and Jeremy in his rumpled linen jacket and panama hat faded, Hugh remembered the other Jeremy who took him to school at the beginning of term, who came to his concerts, cricket matches and terrible school plays. It was Jeremy who prepared him for his future role.

'We don't own any of this,' he had once said, standing on top of the escarpment, looking down over the Staffordshire landscape below. 'We are just caretakers of the estate for the next generation. You are my next generation, Hugh.' At the time the prospect had seemed light years away and his uncle invincible, but it wasn't the case and he had died when Hugh was just twenty-five years old.

As he put down his coffee cup, a smile touched his lips as he recalled Jeremy's two pet Suffolk sheep Mildred and Mabel. They followed him everywhere and to Alice's dismay they were frequent visitors inside the house. At their death of pneumonia Jeremy was inconsolable.

'We shall have a funeral,' he announced. 'Only that will cheer me up.' The vicar was summoned, the service of blessing taking place in Thorncliffe church. Instead of flowers, a wreath of carrots, broccoli and turnip tops adorned each wooden crate with a Jefferson Airplane song playing through the speakers. When his musical choice was questioned, he had a ready reply. 'It's called "The Good Shepherd". I find that rather apt, don't you?'

When Jeremy died, Hugh insisted it was played at his funeral.

Hugh was the child Jeremy would never have, a fact that Great Aunt Alice found hard to accept. He had overheard her berating him. 'You will marry, Jeremy, you need children, an heir.'

'I have no intention of getting married, Mother. Hugh will inherit.'

'You will get over this temporary aberration...'

'No, Mother, I will not, and it is not an aberration, I find that extremely offensive.'

The conversation ended when they turned to see ten-year-old Hugh in the doorway. Though he didn't understand their words, it was made quite clear in a note circulated in the science class at school.

'My father said Lord Derrington kisses men.' The note reached

him, and he had known the culprit immediately, Alex Arkwright standing smugly behind his Bunsen burner. He had wanted to thump him right there and then.

His humiliation had been compounded when his great aunt marched into school prayers the following day and collared the headmaster. Apparently, she had threatened to sue the school and set her dogs on Alex Arkwright. The fact that they were two sloppy Labradors was irrelevant! Once he had recovered from his anger at the offending boy and indeed his great aunt, he grew close to her. She was as eccentric as Jeremy with a strong sense of justice and plenty of humour. Over the years she stopped trying to change her son.

Hugh drained his coffee and went to find the agent. Michael was working at his large wooden desk; his son was reading a comic on the floor nearby.

'Let's go and have a look at these proposals. Tommy, I hope you have your wits about you because we'll need your advice!'

Chapter Six

Marina was putting on wellingtons, ready to go into the garden when Mrs Crump hurried into the boot room, her face flushed, her normally immaculate hair in disarray.

'Are you all right, Mrs Crump?'

'Yes, I mean no, the thing is …'

Marina put the boots on the settle beside her.

'It's been on my mind since Lord Derrington died. When you and his Lordship arrived last month, it was my top priority, but the moment was never right and then you went to London and you had so much on your plate with Francesca, and you were moving into this house …' She tailed off.

'What are you trying to tell me?' Marina's voice was gentle.

'Lord Derrington was nearing the end and his sister-in-law, that is Hugh's mother, Mrs Derrington-Blackett had gone to London for the day … He told me where he had hidden the key to the Boulle chest of drawers, you know the fancy one in the drawing room. He said it was in a book, but I can't remember which book.' Mrs Crump twisted her fingers together. 'I'm so s-sorry, I asked Lord Derrington again, but he didn't know what I was talking about, too ill you see.' She stumbled over the words, a rarity for Mrs Crump. 'I wanted to tell your mother-in-law at the time, but she was so upset and after he died, she returned to London. My Atticus said if I didn't tell you he would do so himself.' She stopped having run out of steam.

'And you have been worried all this time?'

She nodded, chewing on her lip. 'I thought he said something about a disaster, but I couldn't be sure.'

'Disaster, nothing else?'

'I think he mentioned there were papers inside, alluding to past family history that was best forgotten. It may have been best *not* forgotten; his voice was so faint you see.'

It was as if an engine was ticking inside Marina, ready to burst into life. She got up and put her arm through Mrs Crump's. 'If we're going to find this key, we need to start at the beginning.'

'We?'

'Why not we, Mrs Crump? You know more about this family than most, and I could certainly do with some help.' She took a hunting horn from the mantlepiece, put it back down and turned around, her eyes bright.

'Supposing the family history he was alluding to was Lucian's. I think in England you would call it a long shot, but we need to find out; we need to locate that book.'

Half an hour later they were trawling through the bookshelves in Marina's bedroom.

'I knew this would be here.' Mrs Crump pounced on a faded paperback. '*Anna of the Five Towns*. Not that there are five towns in Stoke, the author got it wrong.'

'Wrong, Mrs Crump?'

'There are six. Any foreigner should read it, and in these parts me and Mr Crump are considered foreigners, just like you, Marina.'

By eleven the floor was piled with books, but there was no key. From there they moved to the Blue Parlour and last, the library in the main wing of the house.

Marina ran her hand along the spines. 'See, Mrs Crump, even books in Italian.'

Mrs Crump indicated with a nod, the row of plaster busts on the bookcases above her. 'I bet that lot could read Italian.'

'Who are they?'

'Ancestors most of them. They'd tell a story or two, particularly with the stuff and nonsense going on in this very room.'

'I'm not sure I understand.'

Mrs Crump walked across the room and pulled aside a brocade curtain. Inside was a tiny cubicle with a window seat piled high with cushions. 'It's not only reading that's happened in here. When Mister Hugh was sixteen, he was caught sitting on one of them cushions smoking exotic substances. I had never seen Lord Derrington cross before, but on this occasion, oh my lord! He took the cigarette from his mouth – spliff he called it – and stubbed it out in the ashtray. "Did you think an old fart like me wouldn't smell the stuff? Well, you're wrong. If it happens again your allowance will be cut off immediately." Hugh was dejected for a day or two, but they made it up, and as far as I know it didn't happen again at the Hall.'

Marina smiled. 'That is a wonderful story Mrs Crump.'

The housekeeper let the curtain fall. 'Now if you will excuse me, I must prepare your lunch. I wouldn't want to be in trouble with his lordship ... I mean Mister Hugh.'

When she had gone Marina wandered along the bookshelves, pulling out one volume then the next. It was one o'clock when Hugh found her on the floor surrounded by books.

'What on earth?'

Marina laughed. 'Mrs Crump has been telling me about your misdemeanours. You were not such a perfect little boy, after all.'

Hugh picked up a pile of books, marched across the carpet and put them back into their original place. 'The books were in order, Uncle Jeremy's order, this is... really, Marina.' His voice was rising.

'I thought you'd be happy.' Marina sat back on her heels, eyebrows raised. 'I'm actually enjoying myself; you've been telling me for weeks to—'

Hugh wasn't listening. 'I'll have to clean up after your mess, this is most inconsiderate.'

Marina's excitement was evaporating fast. 'Who lived in chaos in the palazzo? Wasn't it me who had to reform you?' She got up, her smile tight. 'Don't be so grumpy, Hugh. My father says a library should be used, the books stored where the air can circulate freely. If they are never moved they—'

'I don't care what your father says, Marina.'

'*Dio*, what is wrong with you?'

'Nothing's wrong with me, but I have better things to do.'

'I see.' Marina's back was rigid as she walked from the room. At the door she turned. 'Mrs Crump has prepared your lunch; you can have it on your own.'

Marina had reached the willow tree when Mrs Crump tripped across the lawn.

'Nasty things, altercations...'

'You have seen how it is, we are both...' Marina swallowed hard.

'It's my opinion Mister Hugh doesn't mean to be difficult... See, Marina, it's all about control. He couldn't prevent Francesca dying but he can control his environment. There was this programme on *Woman's Hour*, fascinating it was.'

'We're both saying things we don't mean.' Marina gave her head a tiny shake. 'Both being cruel. I am trying, but these comments just slip out. Today it was Hugh, and it was totally uncalled for.'

'I always says to my Atticus, we takes it out on those we love.

Now, I had better get my bread-and-butter pudding out of the oven, before it's burnt to a crisp.'

She was turning to leave when Marina put her hand on her arm. 'I'm not ready to tell Hugh about the key. Can it be our secret for a while longer?'

'I have kept it to myself for all this time, a few more weeks won't make any difference, but my advice, don't leave it too long.'

As Marina watched the diminutive figure pick her way across the lawn, she sighed. Mrs Crump was an exceptional woman. She had sacrificed her precious red leather shoes to comfort her and was always watching out for her. Without Mrs Crump she would be entirely lost.

Marina went into supper and before Hugh had time to pull out her chair she sat down. In the past she had loved the old-fashioned gesture but tonight she was having none of it.

'I thought...' He paused, picked up a glass and put it back down.

Marina raised her eyes, noticing the creases in his normally immaculate clothes. 'Yes, Hugh?'

'I had two thoughts actually, first we should open a bottle of your favourite Brunello to accompany Mrs Crump's shepherd's pie!'

'And the second?'

'On my birthday I would like to take you to Burgess and Leigh, a pottery in the same road as the original Diligence Works – where your coffee pot would have been made.'

'But that's a treat for me.'

'It's to make up for being mean.'

Marina smiled, the knot inside loosening. 'You are forgiven, *mio caro*, and as to the Brunello, it will enhance the flavour of Mrs Crump's delicious shepherd's pie!'

43

Hugh's birthday arrived and Marina came into the dining room with a handful of cards. She found her husband looking through the window, his hands behind his back.

'I used to love this time of year,' he murmured, turning to face her. 'So much beauty.'

'And now?' she asked.

'I'm finding it hard to see it.'

Marina followed his gaze to the flower beds where dry seed pods stirred in the wind and holly berries were red against the fading leaves. 'You'll find it again, Hugh, we both will.'

The conversation was interrupted by Mrs Crump who entered the dining room.

'I remember your uncle Jeremy always sang to you on your birthday, but I'll not be doing that.' She produced a large envelope concealed beneath her arm.

'I ordered the card online, or at least Mr Crump did, my computer skills not being so good, but I chose the photo. See it's you, Mister Hughie, when you were off to prep school for the first time. I remember sewing the tapes into those little blue shorts.'

Hugh shuddered imperceptibly remembering the day when he had been dropped off by his uncle and left to the mercy of the headmaster, Mr Sharp. He looked up at the housekeeper, his face beaming. 'Are my knees still so bony?'

'I haven't seen them that recently, sir.'

'I can confirm they are still bony,' said Marina.

'Ouch,' said Hugh.

'The card had to be special, Mister Hughie.'

'And it is, Mrs Crump, just like you.'

Mrs Crump blushed and left the room, for once lost for words.

*

An hour later Hugh turned the car off the ring road and negotiated the back streets of Burslem, past rows of Victorian terraced houses, corner shops and disused factories. When they reached Harper Street, Marina opened her window and leant out.

'So many empty buildings?'

'When the Potteries declined, so did the towns.'

'They look so sad, neglected, this is not how I had imagined it at all.'

'How did you imagine it?'

'Dark skies, chimneys and smoke.' Marina shrugged and Hugh laughed.

'The Burslem of Arnold Bennett, sadly that was a long time ago. There is more derelict land in Stoke than any other town in Britain, two thousand acres to be exact!'

Marina did a calculation in her head. '*Allora*, that is eight hundred hectares.'

Hugh followed her gaze beyond the broken-down factories, to a slag heap in the distance.

'The town is now subject to a massive regeneration project,' he tried to reassure her because it was his history he was talking about, his roots. 'One day it will all be restored.'

'But it makes me sad, Hugh, my beautiful little coffee pot made in a town that is now abandoned and forgotten.'

Hugh smiled. 'Hopefully that will soon change.'

They turned into Port Street, passing the restored entrance of Burgess and Leigh, and at the other end of the lane, Hugh turned off the engine

'*Dio*,' Marina uttered, following him from the car, her gaze taking in the dilapidated range of buildings behind a collapsed wire fence, the weeds filling the cracks in the broken concrete, the boarded windows and graffiti-covered walls. A wrought iron sign that must have hung over the entrance was propped sideways against an old stone trough. Marina tilted her head to read it.

'"*Derrington & Son*".' So this is it, your family business?' She knew she looked shocked, that her tone was wrong, but she couldn't help herself. 'This cannot be where our little coffee pot was conceived.'

Hugh put his hand on her shoulder. 'My great uncle moved the factory to Longton after a stray bomb hit the engine house in the Second World War. Instead of rebuilding, they relocated, possibly because of its proximity to the railway station – I believe they considered these premises unlucky.'

'Why?' Marina's voice was low.

'There had already been a catastrophic fire in 1925 when the pottery had to be rebuilt. Only the studios next door remained unharmed... and a horse.'

'What happened?'

'The story goes the old dray horse was discovered wandering in the road after the fire, but no one knew how it got out. I have always found it rather moving, a horse appearing through the smoke like a ghost!'

'And he was OK, this horse?'

'That, Marina is as far as the story goes, but I am convinced he survived.'

Hugh climbed through a gap in the fence and looked up at a narrow two-storey brick building. 'These workshops remained unharmed through both disasters. Perhaps this is where...' He didn't finish because Marina had run ahead of him to the outside steps and was nearing the entrance to the floor above when he sprinted after her.

'Stop, please, it's unsafe.'

Marina longed to reach her hand through the door in front of her and into the past. Was this where Elody Cole worked with her assistant? Was Lucian the owner of the clockwork train?

She lingered a second more, tried to capture their essence but they remained insubstantial and just out of reach.

They returned to the pottery next door where Becky, their guide, was waiting for them.

'May I suggest you look up.' She pointed to the brick gable above the arched entrance. 'This regal emblem of Burgess & Leigh makers of our famous Burleigh ware, will give you an understanding of our founders. You can see they had big aims and ambitions – but unlike other pot banks we are still open for business today!' She grinned and Marina was immediately drawn to the girl in a bright green boiler suit, a diamond glinting in her front tooth.

'So,' she said, pushing her hands into the deep pockets. 'Let the tour begin.' As they went over the weighbridge, and along the cobbled passageway, Marina discovered Becky's commitment to the pottery and its history.

'You will see,' she said, throwing a glance over her shoulder. 'The potters are using the same equipment and techniques they have used for one hundred and seventy years. I love to think of all the anonymous individuals who worked here, and the different skills they brought to this place. Quite something, no?'

They climbed an outside staircase, stopping in a narrow workshop, the weak sunlight filtering through the window. 'You see Mr Harris here, one of our mould makers, he is forming plaster of Paris moulds to the original designs. Stunning, aren't they?' She handed a mould to Marina. 'Do you see how beautiful this is, and to think...' Becky's voice carried through the studio and Marina was transported to a different age.

As they crossed the uneven boards moving from one workshop to the next, past men and women concentrating on their tasks, Marina observed the caster filling the moulds, the spongers, the fettlers, each an expert in their field. Becky showed them the ancient machines where traditional patterns were printed from engraved copper cylinders. She watched transfixed as the printer fixed the cylinder onto the machine, spreading the thick oil-based ink.

'The ink melts as the machine heats up,' Becky told them. 'And as the cylinder rotates, it flows into the lines of the roller. The tissue paper is drawn beneath the cylinder creating a continuous stream of pattern. You certainly won't see anything like this anywhere else.' She smiled at the printer. 'Will they, Bob?'

The printer didn't take his eye off the machine. 'Not this side of heaven, they won't.'

Marina finally pulled her gaze away and moved to the individual workstations, where women were cutting the tissue paper with extraordinary accuracy to fit the ware, before applying it.

'We are the last English pottery to use this highly skilled decorating process, Marina, but we have a lot still to see, so we'd better move on.' She grinned at Hugh. 'I think your wife would stay forever if she could.'

'You're probably right,' he agreed.

When they entered one of the now redundant bottle ovens, Marina could almost feel the heat. She could imagine the firemen, sweat pouring from their faces, labouring night and day to keep the fires burning at the correct temperatures, the bricklayers bricking up the entrances when the bottle ovens were filled.

'Every bottle oven is different, the few that are left, that is.' Becky was watching Marina, her head on one side as she stared up the brick chimney, towards a little circle of light far above them. 'You're really taken with this, aren't you?'

'It's fascinating, your tour *spettacolare*! To see the stages the china goes through before it's finished, I had thought you moulded the clay, painted it and it was done.' She laughed. 'No that is not true, I hadn't the least idea how it was made, these words, spongers, fettlers they are new to me. And these glorious chimneys, to think they were once stoked night and day.'

Becky shrugged her shoulders. 'It's the stories I like, Marina.

According to George Wade, a potter in the thirties, the chimneys all had their own temperaments and the firemen had to coax them, humour them, even love them because a change of wind, weather even humidity or fuel would upset them, with consequent loss of ware. He said it was due to nothing but bloody mindedness on the oven's part because they were female.' She grinned, the diamond glinting. 'God, men had attitude in the old days, not that it's much better now.'

Hugh gave a lopsided smile. 'Not all men.'

'Not all,' she agreed.

They had reached the canal when Marina shielded her eyes, gazing across at a large plot of uneven land on the other side.

Becky regarded her. 'That, Marina, is an old shordruck, I don't imagine you've come across one of those before.'

Marina shook her head. 'Not that I know of.'

'The waste from the Potteries needed to be tipped somewhere, so they chose poor quality land nearby. The undergrowth has taken over, but beneath that hill you will find tons of old moulds, broken ware, anything a factory wished to dispose of. It was a favourite place for kids, but as you can imagine, totally unstable and not remotely safe. Now the developers are getting hold of it and God knows what they'll build!'

'I remember my uncle taking me to a shordruck at Longton. He said it was better we dug for treasure together than I killed myself on my own.' Hugh grinned. 'We found a Toby jug of Winston Churchill; I still have it somewhere.'

'So you're from around here?'

'You could say that.'

'His family owned the Diligence Works.' Marina looked at Becky and the girl laughed.

'When you booked, I knew the name was familiar! Well, I never.'

When they reached the bath house, Hugh tried a tap on one of the old-fashioned sinks.

'Not working anymore,' Becky told him. 'The washroom is by the canteen, but back then this place was the height of modernity. They had hot and cold running water, and a proper bath. So many of the pot banks only had an outside privy and, if you were lucky, a tap. Our enlightened founders realised for good production you had to look after your workers. Remember the air was thick with pollution, so you needed to give them the facilities to keep themselves as safe as possible and clean. That meant washing your hands after working with toxic materials, keeping the floors sprinkled with water and brushed every day.' Becky frowned. 'Women and men were dying of respiratory diseases and plumbism – lead poisoning to the uninitiated, even small children, that's why the unions fought for change.'

'I can only hope my family behaved responsibly,' Hugh frowned.

'I'm sure they did, Hugh, but we're not to blame for the errors of the past.'

'Do you know about the Diligence Works?' Marina had been holding onto the question and could wait no longer.

'The Diligence Works? To be honest not really because they moved away, but there have been rumours of a remarkable boy called Lucian – an artist. It is said when he died, the range he helped to create died with him. I know little more than that I'm afraid.'

As they followed her back to the café for lunch, Marina was silent. The pieces were fitting together. Lucian was the artist whose beautiful fox flew across a night sky, but what had happened to him? Was he affected by plumbism, did the conditions at the Potteries cut short his career?

She was quiet in the car, knowing she had to find Elody and Lucian, she had to know more of their lives.

Chapter Seven

They were back in the house when Marina made an entrance with her *Torta alla Panna* and gave Hugh his present.

She watched him pull the paper from the large walnut easel.

'Apparently it belonged to John Singer Sargent.' Marina was rushing her words. 'At least the man in the shop in Leek said so, but privately, I doubt it.' She tailed off, hoping her husband would respond, that his face would light up, the fire return.

'It's handsome, Marina, a fine easel, thank you.' He turned the crank handle to adjust the height, ran his hand along the ledge where chalk could be stored.'

'Perhaps you'll start painting again?' she asked, aware that his eyes were dead. Hugh was going through the motions, nothing more.

'One day, Marina, and perhaps you'll resume your career.'

There it was, on the table. It seemed both of them had lost the will to do what they really loved. They were running away from life and each other.

Marina spent much of her time in the library. She now felt a responsibility towards the potter. 'I'll find you,' she promised. 'I'll not let you slip away.'

She pulled out one book then the next wondering as she did so, why the quest had become so important to her. Perhaps the coffee pot had reignited something inside her that was lost and the mysterious potter and her assistant made her come alive. Maybe her instinct as an attorney made her wish to solve the mystery of the elusive Elody Cole.

She was putting a book back into place when a nineteenth-century volume of Keats caught her eye. She sat with her back to the bookcase, and was instantly transported to Florence, to their carved and faded bed, the gilded church candlesticks making a halo of light around them. She remembered Hugh reciting 'Ode on a Grecian Urn', his voice, sensual, hypnotising as he caressed the side of her neck.

> *Thou still unravish'd bride of quietness,*
> *Thou foster-child of silence and slow time,*

'Keats is addressing the urn,' he had murmured afterwards, 'and the urn is the historian telling a story passed down through countless centuries.' She had turned onto her front, while Hugh ran his fingers down her spine, the concerto for Violin No. 1 by Max Bruch playing in the background, the flames from the candles flickering on the palazzo walls.

Marina closed the jewelled cover remembering buying the candlesticks in *Via del Vellutini*, taking them home afterwards and the first time they had lit the candles. She tried to catch the tenuous smell of oil paint that lingered on Hugh's skin, the scent of candle wax and incense, but they were just out of reach. She dropped her head to one side, wanting Hugh's hands on her body, longing for him. The memory faded, and Marina felt a lump in her throat. She needed all of it, the love they had felt for each other, the passion. As she read the poem again and the beautiful words travelled through time towards her, she remembered Hugh's wry sense of humour, his enquiring mind and his gentleness, all the traits that had drawn her to him. Yes, she would find her way back to him, and hopefully discovering Elody and Lucian would help her on her way.

It would take two more days before Marina found the 'Le Tragedie di Seneca'.

As her hand rested on the spine, she was aware of her heart beating faster. The word disaster could so easily have been misinterpreted by a flustered Mrs Crump. She gently removed the leather copy. She had studied Seneca at university; his works were part of Italian culture, part of their national pride. Shakespeare had been inspired by the tragedies, countless others, and this copy printed in Ferrara in 1484 by Andreas Belfortis was a work of great beauty. Hugh's Uncle Jeremy was speaking from the grave.

She opened the cover, the delicate pages, and found a silver key with a label attached. *'For the Boulle chest of drawers'.*

By the time Hugh arrived from the agency, Marina was pacing the floor. It was the right moment to tell Hugh about Mrs Crump's revelation and her discovery.

'Are you all right, Marina?'

'Yes, I've—'

She got no further because he kissed her cheek.

'Forgive me, I have an urgent call – an electrical fault in the milking parlour at Home Farm. It needs to be sorted tonight.'

He left the room, and Marina sat down. She shouldn't be deflated; this was obviously important; she would tell him when he returned.

It was half an hour before Hugh came into the Blue Parlour and fixed himself some whisky.

'Thank God that's done. I think you met Mike Bowden; it was good of him to come at such short notice. And how was your day, Marina?'

Hugh was standing in front of the fireplace, one hand on the mantel the other around the crystal tumbler. He was staring into the contents of the glass.

'You know, a naked run through Stoke, that sort of thing.'

'Oh good, well done, Marina.'

Marina could feel the anger building inside her, Hugh wasn't listening to a word.

'When you're back with us, perhaps you'd like supper. I cooked it tonight,' she held back her retort, the biting words.

'Thank you, I could do with a change.'

The following morning Marina stood beneath the drawing room chandelier, prisms of light reflecting on the carpet below. She held out her hands and watched the colours dancing on her skin. The room was silent, still. She turned her head sideways, her eyes skimming over the French furniture, the delicate gilded chairs, until they rested on the Boulle chest of drawers. She went towards it, tried the drawer, it was unlocked. Disappointment made her eyes sting. She had come this far only to have her hopes dashed. She ran her hands through the dark interior and was about to give up when her fingers settled on a small internal drawer. The key turned; the drawer opened to reveal a thick brown envelope.

Marina held it in her hands, breathed deeply and drew out a sheaf of paper. Weeks of anticipation had led to this moment, and now it was here.

My life started with the Potteries and I daresay it shall end in the Potteries. She read the spidery script slowly, savouring the words, the blots on the paper, the mistakes eradicated with a line. It was immediate, extraordinary, as if the author had been in a hurry. At last, she had found Elody Cole.

Minutes ticked by then she went in search of Mrs Crump. The housekeeper put down the rolling pin and wiped her hands on her apron.

'Just making the pastry for your...' She stopped mid-sentence, her gaze glued to the envelope.

'You have it, don't you?'

Marina nodded.

'Mister Hugh will be that pleased when you tell him, my Atticus, he always said...'

'But I'm not going to tell him, Mrs Crump, not yet.'

Mrs Crump bit her lip, her brow furrowing. 'If you say so, Marina, your secret and mine.'

Marina took the envelope and walked up the winding stairs to her bedroom. Climbing onto the bed she took out the manuscript, and as the words entered her consciousness, she became lost in the world of Elody Cole.

Chapter Eight

The Past

1925

Since the early seventeenth century, particles of black coal dust have swept north-east from the Potteries, swirling and eddying over the Staffordshire grasslands, through the villages of Bucknall and Bagnall, through Leek towards Blackshaw Moor, and it seemed to Elody Cole, as she stepped from the car on that freezing January day, it had all come to rest on the Jacobean chimneys and turrets of Thorncliffe Hall.

'Shall I take your bag miss or… your feline friend?' Elody's attention was drawn from the edifice in front of her to a thin old gentleman in a tailcoat, whose shoulders were hunched against the cold. He was looking with distaste at her cat, Rhea, who was glowering from the confines of a wicker cage.

'That will not be necessary, thank you.' Elody held on tighter.

'Then follow me. Lady Ursula will see you in the drawing room. Shaw will deal with the bicycle.'

'You can get it from the basement, miss,' a young man called over his shoulder. 'Any problems just ask for Jacob Shaw.'

They made slow progress across the gravelled forecourt, up

four wide stone steps beneath the pillared portico, through a panelled hallway the size of which she had never seen before, until he came to a stop outside a pair of double doors.

'Just remember you are in the presence of an earl's daughter,' Mr Simkins said, puffing out his chest. 'You will show respect, young lady.'

He tapped lightly and for the first time she heard *her* voice. It was clear, with an unmistakable authoritative tone.

'Enter, Simkins.'

'Yes, milady.' They crossed the threshold into an elegant room with hand painted silk on the walls and gold sconces that lit the room with a gentle glow. Lady Ursula Derrington was sitting on a gilt chair near the marble fireplace, a dachshund in her lap, her complexion saved by a needlepoint screen.

For an instant Elody was back in the parlour in Louise Street, her mother handing her a newspaper cutting of a young couple standing outside a church in their wedding finery.

'Drew, now Lord Derrington, was my best friend, until he met Ursula.'

She had looked at the photograph of the slim young man with the deadpan expression holding the arm of the woman beside him. She was beautiful, of that there was no doubt, with an oval face and abundant hair, visible beneath the diamond tiara and lace veil.

'As children we did everything together.' Her mother had shrugged her shoulders, and Elody witnessed the hurt in her soft brown eyes. 'He kept in contact with me to start with, but then it all changed. It was right, certainly, but difficult when we had been such friends. A couple of years later I met your father, we married, and you came along. Sadly there weren't other children, the pot bank saw to that...'

She had sighed touching Elody's cheek. 'When I asked Andrew to be your godfather, he accepted. I should be glad of that.'

'By why him, Mama?'

'He is my safety net in case...'

'In case what?'

She had taken her by the shoulders, looked deep in her eyes. 'Nothing, my love, nothing at all. You're unlikely to even meet him, he moves in a different world.'

Her mother had been wrong because Elody had just buried her in the graveyard in Burslem, and the Derringtons had offered her a home.

She jumped at the sound of Lady Ursula's voice.

'Miss Cole. Come stand by the fire, let me look at you.' She beckoned to Elody. 'Simkins, please relieve the girl of her bag.'

Elody let go of the battered suitcase and went towards her.

'I wasn't aware you were in possession of a cat?' On cue, Rhea hissed at the dog and the dachshund snarled.

Elody raised her chin. Lady Ursula was like the photograph, but more arresting with high cheekbones and heavy lashes above large grey eyes.

'She was my mother's cat,' Elody responded.

There was a pause as Lady Ursula smoothed the skirt of her lavender silk dress. 'I imagine she is a useful ratter?'

'She is, ma'am.'

'She may stay, but she will live outside.'

'She's an indoor cat,' Elody blurted, anxiety making her accent stronger. 'She can't—'

'I hardly think you are in any position to dictate—' Lady Ursula drew in her breath.

Simkins, who had been hovering nearby, coughed discreetly.

'What is it, Simkins?'

He leant towards her, his voice hushed.

'Very well, Elody.' Lady Ursula's fingers were strumming on her knee. 'Mr Simkins tells me the housekeeper, Mrs George, lost her cat last month. If she agrees, the animal can live in her sitting room in the servants' quarters downstairs. I do not expect to see it in any other part of the house, is that understood?'

'Yes, milady.'

'Simkins will take you to meet her, then I imagine you will wish to see your room.' Her voice was cold, distant and the hurt was severe. She didn't expect Lady Ursula to be dancing for joy, but she had hoped for some warmth, some humanity; a few words of welcome would have been gratefully received. She followed the butler but at the door she turned back. Her mother had always told her to be polite whatever the cost.

'Thank you for taking me in.'

'It is my husband you have to thank,' she replied.

In the galleried hall, a girl hurried towards a green baize door carrying a silver tray piled with an assortment of china. She glanced at the cat.

'Collecting the tea things, miss, what time would you be liking your morning pot?' The girl's vowels were soft, her r's rolling, she could only be Irish.

'Millie,' Mr Simkins admonished her. 'You do not address Miss Cole directly; I will tell you what time it is required.'

'That won't be necessary,' Elody interrupted. 'I can't have you running around after me.'

'That's my job, miss.' Millie grinned, ignoring Mr Simkins and nodded at the cat. 'What's kitty's name?'

'Rhea,' Elody responded.

'I'll see you later, Rhea, and you too, Miss Cole.'

At the bottom of the back stairs, Millie went one way, and they went another. Elody could hear her humming as she kicked open a door with her foot, and expletives from the other side.

'Millie Doyle, if you chip the paint, it's you that'll be sorting it!'

Simkins and Elody had barely entered the housekeeper's

sitting room when a stout middle-aged woman, sailed towards them, expertly navigating the furniture and piles of magazines.

'Come, do come in, the kettle is on the boil. So, who have we here?' Her face broke into a smile.

'Elody, ma'am.'

The woman laughed and her whole body shook right through.

'Ma'am, well I've never been called that before.' Her eyes alighted on the cage, and she threw up her hands.

'It's God's work that it is, Miss Elody.' She opened the wicker door and drew out the cat.

'Last week, as true as I'm standing here, there was a stirring of ashes in my dying fire, and I says to myself, "Mrs George, a stranger will come into your life, and a good one at that."'

It was obvious to Elody, the good stranger she was talking about was Rhea.

Elody took a last look at Rhea and followed Mrs George up the wide staircase, past a suit of armour – she hoped there wasn't a skeleton inside – a sedan chair, the roof all tattered and caved in, and along yet another wide passage to her new bedroom. Mrs George fussed around her as she unpacked.

'I'm guessing this is not quite what you're used to.' Her eyes narrowed as she looked at the battered case.

'Things are rather different where I come from, Mrs George.'

Elody was unwrapping a framed photograph when the older woman made a soft tut-tutting sound.

'Your family?'

Elody held out the photograph, how formal it seemed, her father in his Sunday best, her mother in a white lace shirt and stiff black skirt, little Walter in velvet bloomers. She remembered the fuss he had made to get into them.

'Aunty, I onner wearing girl's clothes,' but he had worn them anyway and Elody had played his favourite hand-print game.

'That's my father, my mother and my cousin Walter who

lived with us.' She swallowed on the last bit unable to say her parents were dead, Walter had been taken away from her, and the chances of seeing him again were nought if Aunty Jean had anything to do with it. Her little cousin who had had fallen in the canal when she had been in charge. She propped the frame on the dressing table somehow holding herself together and turned her attention to the unpacking. Her darned stockings came first, followed by flannel nightdresses and underthings. Next came two dresses of her mother's and three pinafores which she hung in the large mahogany cupboard.

She stood back surveying the contents inside. 'I reckon these are a little different from the usual garments, Mrs George.'

Mrs George chuckled, taking it as her cue to ask the question that had been on the lips of the entire household below stairs.

'Can I ask what the connection is between your family and his Lordship's?'

'You mean, what is a girl from the Potteries doing here? I dare say you've been curious.' She folded a blouse into the chest of drawers and picked up her stockings. 'Lord Derrington is my godfather. As a boy, he lived in a big house off Porthill Bank; my granddad shod their horses, and my mother went along. They became good friends.'

'I see.' Mrs George had a satisfied look on her face and Elody realised the information would soon be relayed throughout the house.

'Dinner is at eight in the dining room,' Mrs George advised as she left the room. 'You'll be sure to hear the gong.'

Loneliness was nothing new to Elody, when Walter left, her mother returned full time to the pot banks, then war came, and her father didn't come back. She was used to it, but here amongst strangers she felt the weight of isolation pressing on her chest.

'You get hold of yourself, Elody Cole,' she muttered, pacing the patterned carpet. 'Don't you let that *mardy* Lady Ursula get the better of you.' She threw herself on the bed and buried her face in the soft pillow. She had to admit it smelt nice, but it was alien, not her mother's flannel sheets, the surface made rough by washing, with darned scratchy bits that gave way when you were tucking them in. She put out her hand, touched the smooth cotton, her heart cracking. She would give everything to hear Walter's snuffling breath on the mattress they shared, to feel his hand searching for her own. She would sell her soul if it meant she could push the hands of the clock backwards and change it all.

Elody awoke to the sound of a gong echoing along the passage. She ran to the cupboard, pulled out the ankle length gown of her mother's and with fingers that couldn't get a grip on the buttons, she somehow did up the dress and hurtled downstairs.

The family was already in the dining room when she arrived. Lord Derrington was standing with his back to the fireplace, a spaniel at his feet, Lady Ursula in grey taffeta was seated, and a young man in a dinner jacket was talking to a girl with flaming red hair. Elody noticed her dress made of the softest muslin, the embroidered shawl. Lord Derrington stubbed out his cigarette and came towards her.

'Miss Cole, I hope you're comfortable in your new room?'

Elody looked into the face of her host, comparing him to the man in her mother's newspaper clipping at home. Though he was older, with streaks of silver in his dark hair, he was still handsome, with nice blue eyes and an aquiline nose.

'Yes, sir, I am that. Comfortable I mean. I ... I'm late, sorry.'

'Hester, Archie, let me introduce Miss Elody Cole.'

The girl only mumbled a greeting, but Archie detached himself from the wall where he was leaning.

'Miss Cole,' he drawled.

Elody looked up, recognising immediately the matinée idol looks, the crisp shirt against a clean-cut jaw. He was walking out with Felicity Billington, the boss's daughter at work.

'So, you are here to stay?'

Elody was conscious of his accent, his dismissive tone. She glanced at her scuffed boots, her rough hands with the nails bitten down, and pushed them behind her back.

'Apparently I am.' Heat flooded her cheeks as she faced him, but she would not be crushed by his rudeness.

He was the first to look away.

Elody got through dinner somehow. Her napkin was the size of a tablecloth and there were more knives than she could think of, more forks. She had to sneak a look at Archie's plate to see what he was doing.

He leant towards her. 'The spoon on the outside is for the soup, the knife and fork next to it are for the fish course.'

'I know.'

'Good.' His eyes were sparkling with amusement. 'Then I won't have to help you again.'

In her mind Elody could hear her mother's voice, 'Never forget you are as good as anyone Elody Cole'. But she didn't feel as good as anyone, she felt gauche, badly dressed, just a girl from the Potteries.

While Archie spoke to his father, Lady Derrington conversed with her daughter, but when she fixed her cold gaze on Elody, her stomach turned over.

'Miss Cole, do you read?'

'Do you mean, can I do my letters, ma'am? At school Mr Bartlett said I had a good understanding.'

Hester muffled a smirk behind her napkin, but Archie did little to hide his mirth.

'No, Elody, I meant do you enjoy reading because we have a library full of books which you may use.'

Elody stared at her plate wishing the floor would open up and swallow her whole. She loved books, with a passion. Her mother had a job getting her nose out of them, and yet here she was struck dumb. She could feel everyone watching her, waiting for her reply. 'Thank you, ma'am,' was all she said.

'Ma'am is not an entirely suitable address, Elody. Lady Ursula will do quite well.'

At last, it was over and while the family went through to the Blue Parlour, Elody made her excuses and fled to her room.

Opening the window wide, she leant over the sill, gulping in the cold air. A white moth fluttered through the casement, banging its fragile wings on the oak boards. Elody cupped her hands around it, curling her fingers under its body, then released it into the night.

'If only I could come with you,' she whispered as it flew towards the flickering stars.

Elody wasn't taken to self-pity but on this night, in the blank space of darkness, she let her tears soak the pillow. She was alone in the world with only her mother's cat, Rhea.

She closed her eyes trying to conjure up images of happier times, but all she could think about was the last stage of her mother's illness, running up and down the stairs with trays of food, bathing her clammy face, clearing up the vomit, because that's what lead poisoning did to you. On a particularly bad day, after changing her mother's nightdress for the second time, she had taken her hand, her grip surprisingly strong, her confused mind ordered and in control.

'Sit down, Elody, we need to talk about your future while I still have the strength and the sense to speak.'

'There's plenty of time for that. There's stuff to be done downstairs and I need to get on with it.'

'No, Elody, we need to talk now.'

Elody had sunk onto the bed beside her. 'You have to get well, there is no future without you.' She could hear the desperation in her voice, the pleading.

'Listen to me, Elody, I have written to Lord Derrington and he has promised to take you in.'

'But I don't want to live with strangers. I want to be with you.'

'They will give you a good life.'

'It's the rich pot bank owners who've caused this. If they'd provided proper facilities, stopped you licking the paintbrush to get a fine point, but they didn't, did they? It's all about money at the risk of our health.'

'At this moment there's no alternative to lead in the glazes, no substitute ... until something can be found ...' She had shrugged her fragile shoulders. 'Anyway, I feel sure the Derringtons look after their workers.'

'They're all the same, too mean to keep us safe.' Elody twisted the counterpane. 'They wouldn't let their children work in the dust and the filth.'

'You'll have standing in the community, a voice.'

'But if you're not here, what's the point?'

'Come now, Elody, remember the meeting I took you to, all women it was. You were ten at the time. Afterwards you said you were going to change things, improve conditions in the Potteries, work towards equality. I was that proud of you.'

'But we were going to do it together.' Elody squeezed her eyelids closed, forcing the tears back in.

'And now you'll have to do it without me, but you can do it in safety, away from all this.' She smiled weakly. 'With their name behind you, every door will open for you. You could be everything you ever dreamed of, fight from a position of power, even take your place in government.'

'You mean a woman Member of Parliament?' Elody brought her mother's hand to her lips.

'You may not be born to riches, but you can achieve anything you please. Look at Lady Astor, she did it, the first woman MP.'

'But if I'm to live with the Derringtons, surely I can't push against them?'

'You can, my girl, because you must. Besides, Andrew knew my position, he will see your point in the end. Anyway, enough child, fetch my bag.' She tried to pull herself up.

'Open it, Elody.'

Elody opened the battered leather handbag.

'In the side pocket are twenty florins, your father's savings. Don't use them unless you have to. Hide them well, that's a lot of money in anyone's book.'

She sank back onto the pillow with a sigh. The long speech had exhausted her, but she seemed at peace. Elody put her head on the pillow beside her.

'So, it's done, Elody,' she whispered, giving her fingers a squeeze. 'I have said everything I need to say, and all will be well.'

As the days passed Elody noticed her mother getting progressively weaker and the convulsions stronger. It was early evening on what proved to be her final day and Elody was sitting by her bed her head resting on her arms, when her mother's eyes fluttered open. She tried to speak.

Elody grabbed the sponge wetting her mother's lips.

'Hush, Mother.'

'No, Elody, it's time.'

'Please, I don't want you to go.'

'Get Mrs Atkins at number twenty-five to lay me out, there's lavender oil in the cupboard, I don't want strangers.'

Elody gulped, her nails pushing into the soft skin of her hand.

'And finally, my dearest beautiful child, I need your blessing.'

Elody choked back her tears, she had to do this for her mother, and she had to be strong whatever it took.

'You have my blessing,' she said, stroking her mother's forehead, willing herself not to scream. 'Close your eyes, I will be with you while you sleep.'

Elody remembered the days afterwards, packing up the house with her best friend Florence and her mother, Mrs Wright, putting a lifetime of memories in boxes for the Methodist chapel sale. She recalled standing at the graveside, letting the earth fall on the cheap coffin below, and the vow she made. She would honour the promise to her mother and fight for better conditions and equality for women, but she couldn't, wouldn't forget her own ambitions. Mr Asland, the foreman at the Greenfield Works had told her she had talent and she believed him, because she believed in herself. He promised her if she worked hard enough, she could create her own range.

Chapter Nine

Breakfast was another hurdle for Elody. Was she meant to help herself from the dishes on the sideboard, or would the footman serve? Lord Derrington's head was buried in a newspaper, and Hester ignored her. There was no sign of Lady Ursula or her son.

Her dilemma was solved when Jacob Shaw, the chauffeur who doubled as a footman leant over her chair.

'Perhaps Miss Cole would like to collect her own breakfast,' he murmured.

'Thank you,' she whispered in reply.

Elody was folding her napkin, when Archie strolled in, ambling to the sideboard with a grace that Douglas Fairbanks would have found hard to achieve, and lifted a silver lid.

'Cook does the best devilled kidneys in Staffordshire, have you tried them, Miss Cole?'

The dish had never appeared at home, and she had no intention of trying it now.

'No, I can't say I have.'

Archie helped himself and dropped into the chair beside her.

'Are you aware that offal is good for the brain?'

'I wasn't aware that I needed any help in that department. Excuse me, sir.'

Elody got up with what she hoped was dignity and left the room. Was he mocking her, she wondered, and Hester? They may have been born to riches, but where were their manners? In Louise Street a guest was made welcome whatever their circumstance.

She passed Lady Ursula and Mr Simkins conversing in the passage outside.

'I can see your arthritis is troubling you again, Simkins.'

'No, milady, I'm well, I assure you.'

'If you're in pain, you must rest, and we'll try and manage without you.' She had smiled at the old man and Elody speculated Ursula Derrington had a heart beneath the cold exterior. This opinion quickly changed.

'Miss Cole.' She beckoned with a slender finger. 'Did I mention that you will not be returning to the Potteries?'

'But...'

'There are no buts, it's a highly unsuitable occupation, and while you're with us at Thorncliffe, you will desist from making pots.' She nodded at Elody, and with her fox tails swinging over the collar of her narrow-waisted suit, she proceeded to the waiting car.

Elody could hear the door closing, the engine revving and as the wheels spun the gravel, she charged outside. Her life was at the Potteries, her friends, how could she live without Florrie and the girls?

Taking refuge beneath a big old oak, she slumped to the ground. Lady Ursula couldn't stop her, nineteen years old was an adult, she could do as she pleased, but as the rain started to fall, she realised this wasn't the case, she had to do as she was told.

'Why did you send me here, Mother?' she cried. 'Why did you have to die?'

It was Mr Simkins who found her huddled on the wet grass, her pinafore soaked, her hair a tangle of sodden curls.

'What do you think you're doing, Miss Cole?' he gently reprimanded her. 'I saw you from the Blue Parlour window, you will catch your death of cold, and then who will look after your cat?'

Elody sniffed. 'Rhea already prefers Mrs George.'

'I hardly think that's true, come on, young lady, let's get you inside.' Mr Simkins produced a blanket and put it around her shoulders. 'We can't have you dying on us quite so soon.'

Elody noticed the humour in his faded blue eyes and gradually her shaking subsided.

She stood up, and with the old man supporting her, she returned inside.

When she had changed, she went in search of Mrs George. She found her directing operations in the kitchen. Agatha Blunt was stirring a sauce at one end of the large range, while Millie was slicing onions on the scrubbed pine table. She dabbed at her eyes and grinned at Elody.

'They've not been beating me, and that's the truth. Lawd in heaven, what's happened to you?'

'Millie Doyle, don't you be cheeking a house guest in such a way.' Mrs George pressed her lips together and huffed across the kitchen. 'And you, Miss Cole, come and sit by the stove, I'll make you a nice cup of tea.' She passed her a magazine. 'This will keep you occupied, there are recipes in abundance inside.'

But what was the point of recipes when she wasn't able to cook? As Elody turned the pages she remembered poring over recipes with her mother, stirring the mixtures as they tried them out and the laughter in her voice as she scolded her, 'Be sparing on the butter, miss, this isn't Buckingham Palace, and it's all we've got.' The memory faded, and her communion with her mother was over, the pain of separation as strong as it had ever been.

'Can I help with anything?' She put the magazine aside and went to Mrs George.

The housekeeper gave the sauce a ferocious stir and turned to Elody.

'Miss Cole, that really wouldn't do?'

'But at home I shared the cooking. My mother said if I was old enough to work at the pot bank, I was old enough to do the chores.'

'I'm sorry, Miss Elody, but this isn't home.'

Elody bit her lip, the frustration and anger that had kept her going in the very worst of times kicking in.

'Don't you think I know it, Mrs George. What am I meant to fill my days with? Embroidery? I hate embroidery.' She got up and charged through the door with Mrs George following.

'I'm so sorry, that was thoughtless, but if her Ladyship found you working in the kitchen, we'd all be in trouble. You'll be returning to the Greenfield Works soon I daresay?'

'According to her Ladyship, I won't be returning anywhere, and now I'm not even allowed to help you.'

Mrs George put her arm around her shoulders.

'What am I meant to do?' Elody pushed her hands into the pockets of her pinafore. 'Last night Hester looked me up and down, like I was summat the cat dragged in. It's my mother's best dress, but it's still all wrong, and as for Mr Archie...'

'There now, duck. I can whip you up something in no time, fit for a queen it will be. Tomorrow is my day off and you and me are going shopping. How does that sound?'

'You can't, Mrs George.'

'There is one thing my mother taught me, Elody Cole, there is no such word as can't.'

Mrs George was as true as her word. Jacob brought the car to the side of the house, opened the door, and they stepped inside.

'It was him who lent us the car, Lord Derrington,' the

housekeeper told her, patting her smart brown hat. 'He's a good man for sure, and a fair employer. A rare breed, Elody.'

Elody gazed from the window, contemplating the little-known godfather who lapsed into silence over dinner and went for long rides on his own. 'He doesn't say much,' she murmured, waving to the gatekeeper as they passed.

'Before the war he was full of life, but when Giles, his eldest son died, he went into his shell.'

'I didn't know.'

'Why should you, duck, it was a different house back then. Everything changed when the poor boy died. And as for Lady Ursula, what mother wouldn't grieve but— Did you know Mr Archie wanted to be a writer, or a poet or some such thing, but now … He never wanted to be the heir, told me so himself.'

Elody was silent, letting her opinions adjust.

'In those days there were house parties, shooting weekends, you should have seen it. Lady Ursula was happy, and the staff – I had three cooks and there were eight gardeners outside. Now there's just me, Agnes and a few girls inside. Tim Peabody tries to keep a handle on the garden, but how can he when he's on his own.'

'That explains everything …'

'And it's not been easy for you, I imagine.'

Elody swallowed and when she spoke her voice was low. 'I've lost everything and everyone, my father to the war, Mum to lead poisoning, and when Walter fell in the canal, my aunt took him away.'

'You poor love.'

'She's a housekeeper in London, but not in a place like this, more …'

'Middle class,' Mrs George finished for her, sniffing in a satisfied sort of way. 'One of those houses built for the newly rich, I imagine.'

'I don't have an address for him. I've been through my mother's letters, nothing.' She looked across at her. 'I miss him so much.'

'You've certainly had more than your fair share of sorrow, lass, but I reckon you and your cat have come to this house for a reason. Mrs George is going to look after you both and that is for sure.'

The rest of the day passed too quickly. They had lunch in the Lyons tea room, then off to the drapers to buy material. Mrs George was not to be thwarted.

'Now this blue silk brings out the colour of your eyes, and the flowered material would be good for a pinafore.'

'Mrs George you can't. I have my mother's savings, I'll—'

Mrs George gave her a look.

'Don't deny me, I haven't had such fun in years, not since before Mr George died. I've money put aside and what am I going to do with it? You can't take it with you, that's what I say.'

'No children?'

Mrs George's eyes clouded. 'I do have a son, Harold his name is, but I never see him. Making his way in London he is, but if I'm honest I don't know what he's getting up to.' She shook her head. 'In every sort of trouble for all I know.'

'I'm sorry.'

'Don't be, duck, but allow me to do this for you.' She squeezed Elody's arm. 'I'd rather spend it on you than allow his mucky hands to get hold of it.'

Chapter Ten

Mrs George started the dress immediately.

'I'm not going to rest until it's done,' she said, pinning a paper pattern onto Elody. 'It's going to be easy, mind, no lumps and bumps in the wrong places like me.'

Elody laughed.

'So, you're obviously agreeing, lass?'

'Never, Mrs George.'

Rhea who had taken up residence in Mrs George's chair looked up and stared.

'What are you looking at, cat?' Elody accused, and Mrs George chuckled.

'She's watching the transformation from pottery girl to queen.'

Two days later the dress was finished and Elody waited in front of the fire in Mrs George's sitting room.

'The new softer silhouette,' she explained, unpinning the muslin cover. 'It's in all the magazines and very fashionable. I'm rather pleased with it, if I say so myself.'

Elody touched the low neckline, the skirt overlaid with lace.

Mrs George held it while Elody stepped into it, drawing it up her slim body, doing the buttons at the back.

'Now to the mirror.' She propelled Elody along the corridor

while the staff moved past carrying trays filled with cutlery, glasses, and crockery necessary for dinner that night.

'You keep your eyes to yourself, Jacob Shaw, and you Millie, stop gawping and get on with your work.'

Elody hardly recognised the girl in the mirror. The dress fitted snugly around her chest and swept over her hips. It was elegant and sophisticated, something a proper lady would have worn.

'Well, I'll be—'

'Don't you like it?' Mrs George looked anxious.

'I am transformed.'

Jacob Shaw coming back from the dining room with an empty tray whistled. 'Jesus, Mrs George, our little Miss Elody doesn't half brush up well.'

'She is not our little Miss Elody, and just you remember that, Jacob Shaw.'

Elody was ready for dinner, and with an hour to spare she went downstairs. She'd seen the library from the garden, but she had never been inside. The room was empty when she entered, a fire crackling in the grate, but it was the bookcases that made her sigh. There were books, miles and miles of them waiting to be read. A lifetime of books. As she wandered round the room, pulling out one volume then the next, she remembered her mother's words after Walter had left.

'No use lying in your bedroom all day, blaming yourself, I'm taking you to the public library.' She had kissed the top of her head, taken her hand. 'One day you'll see him again, of that I'm sure, but for now books will fill the empty place in your heart.'

And she was right, from the first moment Elody walked down the corridors of Burslem public library, she had been intoxicated by books. Perhaps it was the very act of opening the cover, aware that a magical experience was awaiting her. She only knew that for a short time she would forget the new pallor in her mother's cheeks, Walter's departure. She would embark on an epic journey beneath the sea with the mysterious Captain Nemo on his submarine *Nautilus*, or with Lemuel Gulliver to Lilliput. She would join Sherlock Holmes, her favourite sleuth, on the moors, Shakespeare at the Globe theatre. There was always a new adventure, something marvellous to fill her mind. Her mother would find her on her bed, a book close to her nose, squinting in the half light.

'Elody Cole, look at your lamp burnt down, paraffin costs money, and you're lucky I've saved you some tea.' But Ada had never been cross, she was relieved that her daughter was coming back to her, and she was proud of her learning.

Elody looked at one title then the next. There were different bindings, different languages, volumes of maps, others of birds. She pulled out a large folder of botanical prints by the eighteenth-century artist Redouté. Could this possibly be an original, she wondered, remembering her mother tearing a page from a magazine to copy a particular rose.

Time had no meaning for Elody, she was absorbed in the realm of books.

When Hester found her, she was sitting cross-legged on the floor, a first edition of *Twenty Thousand Leagues Under the Sea* in her lap.

'You're here. We're all waiting for you.'

'Waiting for me?' she queried, the real world returning fast.

'Daddy hates people being late, didn't you hear the gong?'

As she struggled to her feet, she was aware of Hester's critical gaze.

'A dress made by Mrs George, I see.'

Elody smoothed the rumpled skirt, her confidence seeping away. Did she believe a dress could make her feel secure? She waited for Hester to pass and followed her to the dining room.

'You're here,' it was Lady Ursula's voice, clear and sharp.

'Yes, ma'am, I mean Lady Ursula.'

Then came Lord Derrington. 'We don't have many rules here, Elody, but we do have one, please don't be late for dinner again.'

Archie stood up as Elody walked across the room. Her oval face was flushed, her bottom lip trembling, but she moved with a grace he hadn't noticed before. He looked away, resisting the sudden urge to reach out and touch the curve of her waist, her hips, the blue silk where it met the pale skin of her chest, the swathes of abundant hair. She was pretty, not a classic beauty, her eyes were a little wide and her mouth too full, but she was certainly arresting.

'You look most presentable,' he murmured as she sat down beside him.

'Are you mocking me, sir, because I'm not in the mood.'

'I would never be frivolous with a compliment, Miss Cole.'

Archie followed her gaze to a painting. He remembered sitting for it, the three of them sprawled on the floor, Giles about eleven at the time, while he was eight and Hester seven. The poor frustrated artist had threatened to leave because they wouldn't keep still. He winced, at the pain cutting through him like a knife as he remembered Giles winking at him to make him laugh.

'I assume the little boy playing with the toy train is you,' Elody murmured, shaking him from his thoughts, bringing him back to the girl at his side.

'We had no idea what lay ahead.'

'That has to be a good thing,' she replied, the knowledge of their mutual grief passing between them.

Though the conversation was brief, Archie was aware of the inflections in her voice, the colour of her eyes, tawny with golden centres beneath arched eyebrows and heavy lids, her scent, jasmine with warm undertones, but there was something else intangible, faint but familiar to Archie – the scent of books.

Throughout dinner he was conscious of her beside him, but

he could also see his mother glancing down the table at him, observing him. He felt diminished beneath her cold gaze.

'Archie, Shaw tells me he is taking you to the doctor in the morning. Is it your asthma, dear?'

'I'm perfectly fine, Mother,' he replied, wondering why she chose to belittle him in public; it was a habit of hers. Perhaps she hated him because he had survived, and her beloved Giles had died? But he should have gone to fight, could have. He was convinced his failed medical was due to his mother's machinations and not his health. When he had been in front of the army medical board his lungs were as clear as a bell. Now in the eyes of the villagers, the pottery, the estate, and even himself, he was a coward. He lapsed into silence, little realising this was taken as a slight by the girl beside him, unaware of everything except his own humiliation and pain.

Chapter Eleven

Elody was immersed in a copy of *Paradise Lost* when Lord Derrington walked into the library. He came towards her.

'Please don't get up. Ahh Milton, good choice, you really are well read. Tell me, Miss Cole, do you believe Milton has affinity with Satan or God?' He moved beyond her to the bay window, the hint of a smile on his slim face.

'Is this a test, sir?'

'I am intrigued as to your opinion?' He had laughed then, his eyes crinkling at the corners and the embarrassment of last week's rebuke was forgotten.

'If it is not a test, then I believe Milton admired Satan. He is certainly the main character in this story. The fallen angels and their leader, Satan, are our protagonists, the unfallen angels and indeed God the Father the Son, Adam and Eve are all supporting players.'

'Excellent, Miss Cole, you are a bright girl and I look forward to more lively discussions. Now, I won't interrupt you further, see you at dinner tonight.' He took his copy of *The Times* from the library table, but at the door he turned.

'I imagine it's a blow not being able to work, but there's enough in this house to keep someone of your enquiring nature amused; you could start with the map room upstairs.'

Elody watched him leave, longing to tell him that it wasn't enough, the days dragged out sliding into each other. While he went to work with Archie, Hester disappeared after breakfast to continue her studies in French. It wasn't nearly enough; she wanted to fulfil her promise to her mother and fight for change, and she wanted to be back at the Potteries with her friends. There was Florrie, her best friend since childhood, Dawn with a sharp tongue and kind heart, and sweet Bridie Brookes who had married the meanest man in the Potteries when she was just sixteen. But most of all, she missed her mother, her father and Walter. As she closed the cover, Milton's world retreating fast, she remembered Christmas in Louise Street, setting out the manger with Walter, hanging her mother's home-made bunting over the mantlepiece. She touched the locket at her throat, recalling Walter handing it to her on Christmas morning.

'Aunty Ada gave me the money.' He had given her a gap-toothed grin. 'But I got the best price from the pawnbroker, he said I was a right little dodger!'

Elody had hugged him, before opening the locket to look at the photos inside. How secure they all seemed back then, smiling into the camera, how sure of the future, but how wrong.

She left the library and wandered down the passage. Through the schoolroom door she could hear Hester and the tutor, Mr Medley, conversing fluently in French. Hester's voice was lightly flirtatious, but her accent excellent. She passed Mr Simkins holding a candelabra as he made his way to the silver room downstairs and Millie who was humming as she polished the banisters.

'Want to give me a hand?' She winked at Elody. 'From the size of this staircase I could be here all year.'

'Chance would be a fine thing.' Elody managed a grin.

'Well, aren't you the lucky one,' she replied.

But Millie was wrong. As Elody went to fetch her coat she remembered the precise moment she had learnt of her scholarship to the Burslem School of Art and the glorious year that followed. Then she was truly lucky.

Her mother had been standing in their narrow hallway, one hand on the banister, the other holding a letter.

'I'll not have you miss this opportunity,' she had said. 'However tough, I'll not, Elody.'

'What are you saying, Ma?'

'It may be difficult to step out of our class, but if anyone can do it, you can.' She started to count on her fingers. 'You'll need books, uniform, decent paintbrushes, then there are the sketch pads and you're walking out of those shoes ... but Mrs Clarke wants me to do some weekend cleaning and Mrs Simms, that will bring the extra money we need. There's also a fund from the church in situations like these.'

'Ma, tell me!'

'You've got it, Elody, the scholarship!' and Elody had charged into her mother's arms, laughing with excitement until reality returned.

'But you already work your socks off, I'll not let you finish yourself for me.'

'Hard work never killed anyone, and I'll do it for my girl.'

Elody sat down on the bench, her back resting against the wall. She could almost feel the excitement of those mornings, as she ran to the coal store, heaving the coal into the hod before making up the fire, feeding the chickens then charging down the pavements past the butcher, the ironmonger, Mr Moss the bookmaker, to the red-brick building on Queen Street, in the centre of town. She recalled the students crowding through the wide double doors, hanging up their coats, their breath steaming the air and the wonderful anticipation of the hours ahead filled with lectures, discussions, talks from famous artists and potters of the day. It had been stimulating, enlightening, they were sponges eager to learn.

And there was her first day at the Potteries, handing her certificate to Mr Asland, the light in his eyes as he handed it back.

'A distinction is it,' he had said. 'I remember when you came with your Mam to the pot bank when you were just fourteen, and you begged to try your hand at the wheel. I knew then as I watched the clay take form, we had a designer in our midst.'

'You did, sir?'

'Aye, but it's a paintress first, my girl.'

'Just give me the chance, Mr Asland, and I'll make you proud.'

Afterwards he had introduced her to the pot bank, one workshop at a time. She observed the hollow-ware pressers, the dippers, the paintresses at work. She had clamped her hands to her ears in the slip house as blungers thrashed away at the raw porous clay.

'You'll get used to it, girl,' Mr Asland reassured her in his blunt Yorkshire way. And she had laughed, excitement bubbling in her chest. 'It's a magnificent noise, sir, just a little loud,' and he had shrugged his shoulders as if she was mad. She had got used to the dust that powdered her hair and left a film on her skin and got up her nose, and the smell of clay and coal and sweat.

Soon she was a master at weaving through the alleyways between the long buildings, avoiding the children who ran this way and that, and the placers, who didn't look as if they could carry a bag of flour on their heads let alone a clay saggar filled with pottery, as they took them to the ovens for the firing.

She was doing up the laces on her outside boots when a thought came to her. She'd been instructed to keep away from the pot bank, but what if she fought for women's rights from Thorncliffe Hall? She pulled on her coat, wrapping it closely around her and went into the cold. She could leave safety in the workplace to the unions – still make a nuisance of herself, push for better conditions, but her battle would be for equal pay and opportunities for women. She reached the lake, walked the perimeter, a knot of excitement tightening inside. She would write to Lady Astor, her mother's heroine. If anyone was able to promote her cause, it was Nancy Langhorne Astor. She plucked a seed-head from the flower bed. Her idea was, at this moment, a tiny kernel, but she would make it germinate, grow. She ran inside, threw her boots into the rack and hurried to the library. Taking a piece of headed writing paper from the roll-topped desk, she sat down to write. This would make Lady Astor listen, she thought, adding her best script to the pristine sheet. A letter from a resident of Thorncliffe Hall, would make her notice. This would be a way of getting her ear.

Dear Lady Astor, she began, chewing the end of the pen.

I have admired you greatly from afar, and knowing you are a champion of the female sex I am asking you to take up the cause of women in the Potteries, hardworking, talented women who have been subdued by the patriarchal system, wronged. Though the safety guidelines are continuously breached it is women's equality I am addressing today. We need better pay. It is probably a futile aspiration to believe we will ever be on the same footing as the men, but surely we can go some way to correcting that wrong!

You have faced prejudice and inequality, but you have swept away the opposition. You have put up with small mindedness within the seat of government and you opened the gates for other women MPs. Now I am asking you, no begging you, to help me to help women in the Potteries and other industries where we have no say.

Yours very sincerely
Elody Cole.

She put the pen back and reread the letter, a smile crossing her face. It was flattering but not obsequious, the sort of letter a lady of substance would write. She would send it to the House of Commons in Westminster, the seat of government. Lady Astor was an advocate of women's rights, she couldn't fail. Finding a stamp, Elody fetched her bicycle and cycled to the post. No one could know she was writing to the House of Lords.

Chapter Twelve

Winter kept its grip on Thorncliffe Hall, the lake freezing over for the first time in years, the wind whipping beneath the doors, tugging at the curtains, lifting the ash from the smoking fires. On one of these mornings Elody hurried through the great hall, pulling her shawl closer, and went upstairs. At the top she turned left on the landing instead of right. It was dark in the passage ahead of her, the smallest glimmer breaking through a skylight but there was no sound. She paused, looked back the way she had come, nobody was there. She was inclined to return to the noise and activity downstairs, but her godfather's words had tempted her, she was once again the child longing to learn. When her hand closed around a switch and light flooded the corridor, she sighed, her lips parting, for hundreds of photographs lined the walls. There were images of shooting parties, garden parties, political gatherings. The figures were posed, frozen in time, but they told a story of life before the war. There were men in tweeds seated in front of the house, shotguns at their sides, dogs lolling at their feet, women in large hats in the rose garden, an image of Queen Victoria and a former Lady Hamilton seated in the Blue Parlour. The Queen's head was bent over a tapestry, her hostess was pouring tea. She moved from one photograph to the next wondering what it was like to entertain royalty, imagining life at the Hall back then.

She moved on down the corridor entering one bedroom then the next. There were four poster beds with embroidered hangings, a music room with a harpsichord and a violin case propped against a chair. She found the map room and entered a different universe where every inch of surface was covered in charts. She gazed from the heavens on one wall, to the oceans on another. As she climbed the short wooden steps and came face to face with every country in the world she thought of Walter. Her heart was racing as she traced a path from England to France through Spain, her ruler gliding over the Sierra Nevada mountains, across the Mediterranean Sea to Morocco, her imagination roaming from one country to the next. As she lingered on the forty-eight states that made up America, she remembered clearing the table in Louise Street to accommodate the atlas she had bought from the second-hand book shop in Stoke.

'Look,' Walter had exclaimed, jabbing his finger on New York. 'I'll live there, one day, trust me I will. You can become rich in New York, and I want to be rich, Elody.'

'Who told you that?' she had said, prodding him.

'My teacher at school. It's a melting pot it is, people from different nations with different religions and beliefs. You start at the bottom and work your way to the top. Easy, it is.'

'Nothing is easy, Walter.'

'It can be if you know how.'

Elody climbed down the steps and leant against the wall, her hand pushed against her eyes. One day she would find Walter, they would go to America, and they might not come back.

Finally, she closed the door and continued her exploration. When she discovered a box containing a piece of embroidery with the initials VR, her hands started to shake. It was the sampler in the photograph. Queen Victoria's photograph.

With time for a last room before lunch she navigated her way along yet another long corridor to the old nursery and pushed open the door. To her astonishment the enormous doll's house was the perfect replica of Thorncliffe Hall. As she read the card propped against the front she exhaled. '*This is the property of Ursula, aged eleven, daughter of the tenth Earl of Hamilton. Keep out!*' But Elody couldn't keep out, she examined the miniature tables and chairs the wardrobes and rugs, the wooden dolls dressed in servant's livery. All except one. This little figure had fair hair and grey eyes, she was unmistakably a young Ursula Derrington sitting in her usual chair.

Elody backed away, one step at a time. Ursula was guarding her own little kingdom; strangers were not allowed. But why was she on her own, isolated in the huge house, were there no other children? For a brief moment she felt sorry for her.

Elody was on her way downstairs when she rattled the door at the end of her corridor. It was locked. It was the only door that had been locked that day.

Elody came into lunch stimulated by her travels, but her optimism was quickly dispelled by Hester who was holding a brown envelope, the corners curled. Her chin was lifted in a superior sort of way.

'For you I believe, it came in the lunchtime post. You may be good at your letters, Miss Cole, but I could not say the same about your friends.'

Elody's eyes narrowed.

'My friends may not have the benefit of a fine education, but they do have manners ...' She turned her back on Hester and walked to the other end of the room.

After lunch she ran upstairs and tore open the envelope.

Dear Elody, Florence had written.

Mother says that I shouldn't tell you I miss you, but I'm worrying myself half mad. Tell me they are being kind to you, that you are not too lonely.

Work is busy as ever, but it's not the same without you. I had the colic last week, so I was taken to the handsome doctor on Bluestone Avenue, it's nothing to worry about, he said, so it was worth it just to see his big brown eyes! Come back and visit if you can, but perhaps you have forgotten your old friend.

Elody returned the letter to her pocket and went outside. The wind was blowing, stinging her cheeks, making her eyes water, but she had the need of it. Her mother had always boasted that she was better at climbing trees than playing with toys, sending her to their allotment in Dolly's Lane if she was mad.

'Go let off steam, love, pull some carrots, and come back when you've got it out of you.' And today she needed to pull carrots, she needed Florence Wright and she was desperate to get back to the Potteries.

Elody had a piece of Mrs George's leftover Christmas cake in the pocket of her coat, and a flask of hot chocolate when she set out for the moors.

Her arms were folded as she trudged across the lawn. Archie had changed his place to sit beside Hester at dinner, and he had left for work without a word of greeting. Had she done something wrong, she wondered, was her only ally angry with her, but was he really an ally? He had passed her a note under the table only the week before, making her want to smile, making Hester's taunts bearable.

'My sister is only grumpy because you are getting all the attention!'

He had even pulled her aside after supper. 'My mother doesn't mean to be unkind, it's the loss of Giles you see.' But they weren't exactly friends. Friends were accrued over a period of time; kindred spirits and you couldn't call Archie that. But he had been nice to her and now he was ignoring her, and she wasn't sure why.

Elody was heading for the gate at the bottom of the garden into the park when something rustled in the hedge nearby. The noise was distinctive, a breaking twig, undergrowth disturbed. She stopped, listened, her eyes searching, but nothing moved in the dense foliage. The moment of unease passed, and she strode on, past the statue of Minerva, beyond the overgrown amphitheatre, the semi-circular rose beds now choked with weeds, until she reached a rusting padlocked gate. It was here that Lord Derrington's spaniel found her, and together they broke away from the boundaries of the house, the oppressive atmosphere and within half an hour they had clambered over the wall, the only barrier that separated the parkland from the moors.

Ahead of her were the heather covered hillsides leading up to the Roaches, the jagged gritstone crags, formed by the slipping sliding layers of mud and rock many thousands of years before. It was to this wild and magical place that she had come with her father and Walter on their last adventure together. She remembered Walter's excitement as they scrambled up the hillside over boulders and rocks before starting the long walk along the escarpment.

'I'm not tired,' he had pronounced when her father offered to carry him. 'Grown boys are never tired.'

As the first drops of rain fell onto Elody's upturned face, her heartache eased – out here on the moors, she could feel them nearby, she could see Walter's determined expression, hear his childish, happy voice. She could almost stretch out her hand, touch her father's leather jerkin, his stubbled chin.

That night as she sat at the dinner table, listening to the clatter of silver on plates and the murmur of voices, she could feel her father's love surrounding her. 'Don't you take no stick, girl,' he would have said. 'Did Hester get a scholarship? Never. You have more brains in your little finger.' As she looked across at Hester, she no longer cared about her opinion or her Ladyship's. Archie could be as standoffish as he liked because the moors had saved her. Memories of her father and Walter had strengthened her. She ran her hands over her blue silk gown. She wouldn't be intimidated, it was the prettiest dress she had ever owned, and she would enjoy the wearing. She was Elody Cole and proud of it too.

Much later when she went to her room, she locked the door. She may not be frightened of the Derringtons, but the mannequins she had to pass, stuffed into a huge glass case, that was another thing entirely.

Elody slept well and the following morning she went down the back stairs to the servants' quarters to see Rhea and Mrs George. She was already in the room when she noticed Lord Derrington sitting in front the fire, an empty plate on a table beside him.

He jumped to his feet.

'Miss Cole.'

'Lord Derrington.'

He wiped his hands on a napkin, his face flushing.

'I have reflected on my judgement last week and though we have talked since, I have failed to apologise sufficiently. It was uncalled for and unkind, I hope you will make allowances for my churlish behaviour.'

'Sir, you are generous, and your apology is accepted.' She smiled suddenly. 'You know it was my mother who taught me to love books.'

Lord Derrington laughed. 'She always had a book in her

hand.' For a moment he was silent and then his eyes returned to Elody.

'Did you know there are some rare first editions, Dickens, Shakespeare, and other truly remarkable books, even a copy of Seneca's Tragedies printed in 1484. You have much to enjoy...'

'I have found the English translation; I'm not yet reading Latin.'

He laughed then, running his hand through his thick hair and she knew in that moment, her mother had once loved this kind and sensitive man.

'My dear Miss Cole, I'm sure you will conquer Latin quite soon, you really are an extraordinary girl.' He shook his head as if lost in a distant memory. 'Anyway, forgive me I really mustn't keep you any longer.' He was on his way to the door when he turned back.

'My goodness, Mrs George, those oatcakes were delicious, the first I've had in years and definitely the best.'

'Oh sir, what silliness you talk.'

'Unfortunately, Lady Ursula doesn't approve of them, but what if I were to sneak down here occasionally?'

Mrs George beamed. 'Your Lordship is welcome in my little sitting room any time at all, and I'll make sure I have a ready supply.'

When he had gone Mrs George sank into a chair.

'Well I never, in all the years I have been in this house, he hasn't come to visit, and there he was in my chair. Lord in heaven I didn't think to see this day.'

'I'd give my right arm for an oatcake, Mrs George.' Elody sighed.

'You wait there,' she instructed. 'Don't you move.'

A few minutes later Mrs George was back with two oatcakes filled with cheese, still warm from the hot plate.

Elody took a bite and closed her eyes.

'We used to get them from Mrs Henderson in Louise Street, she sold them from her front room window. How I've missed them, Mrs George.'

Rhea was licking the crumbs from Elody's plate when Mrs George cleared her throat.

'Oatcakes were not the reason his Lordship was here. He instructed me to make two more dresses. "We can't have her embarrassed, Mrs George, and that blue dress suited her well." He tried to give me money for the making of it, I refused, but he has insisted on paying for this commission. He's a good man, Miss Cole.'

'But I'm in his house, taking his hospitality.'

'He said he let your mother down a long time ago and he would try and make it up to you.'

Elody went onto the moors the following day, and the day afterwards. No one in the family challenged her.

On Saturday she packed her brushes and paints and headed for the kitchen. It was the first time she had touched them since her mother's death.

'I've made you a packed lunch.' Mrs George handed her a parcel wrapped in greaseproof paper. 'No good walking on an empty stomach. And you'd better tell me where you're going, because it's my belief them rosy cheeks aren't garnered in the shelter of the park.'

'*Hen Cloud*,' Elody replied, depositing the cat in her out-stretched arms. 'If it weren't for you, Mrs George, I'm not sure anyone would notice at all.'

Elody had reached the top of the looming outcrop when the sun came out. She found a ledge and with her boots dangling over the edge, she gazed out over the unending landscape of hills, crags, water and stone. She could see the light moving over the heather, the colours brightening, changing, shifting, and the spaniel Clay flushing a grouse, hundreds of feet below. She whistled, the dog looked up and charged up the narrow path to join her. After tethering him in safety behind a large rock, she took out her pad and paints. In her imagination her mother was beside her, she could almost hear her words. 'Well done, love, you're getting on with your life and one day you'll change the world.'

It was late when Elody began the journey home. Her sketchbook was full, and her mind teeming with ideas. She would create her own range of pottery even if she was breaking Lady Ursula's rules. The designs would incorporate some of the exotic animals from the illustrated books in the library and wildlife she had observed on the moors. The possibilities were endless – leopards, foxes, snakes, she would paint them all. She was nearing the entrance to the park when she saw a man striding across the moor towards her. Her alarm dissipated when she realised it was Archie.

'So you're back.' He shone a torch in her face. 'You've caused a lot of trouble, what the hell have you been doing?' he glared at her.

'What do you mean?'

'I have just told the household you're missing.'

'Missing?' she snapped. 'Am I not allowed to walk?'

'Not when it's getting dark, you could have been lost on the moors. And by the look of it you've been doing more than walking.' Before Elody could do anything to stop him, he had grabbed her sketchbook.

'Don't!' Elody's hand was on his coat sleeve, but he turned his back on her.

'They're mine, leave them alone.' She was too late, he had

already opened the cover and was shining the torch on the sketches inside.

His face softened. 'These are good, Miss Cole, excellent in fact. But that doesn't exonerate you.'

'Excuse me?'

'We have a duty to keep you safe.'

'A duty to whom, may I ask? I could have been attacked by a wild hound, or... or sucked into a bog, for all you lot would care.'

Archie started to laugh. '*The Hound of the Baskervilles* is one of my favourites too, Miss Cole.'

A strand of hair had escaped Elody's hat and now clung to her neck. Archie had an instant desire to pick it up, curl it around his finger, but she had marched past him, her nose in the air. He inhaled, catching the scent of peat and rain on her skin, and on her clothes. There was something refreshing about her, unusual, he couldn't get her out of his mind. At the house, he took off his coat, hung it on the wooden peg, and it suddenly came to him. Despite her personal tragedies, there was a vitality about her, a sense that she was very much alive.

Later, in the silence of his bedroom, his thoughts unwittingly returned to Elody. She was well read, amusing and a talented artist. He had been startled by the beauty of her drawings, their unique quality. He imagined her designs displayed at the Diligence Works; each piece illuminated on its own stand. But he didn't run that department, he was in charge of sales. It wasn't a role he had chosen but when Giles died, it became obvious he had to forget any previous aspirations and enter the business immediately. Once the war ended, the orders dried up. Crockery heading for the officers at the front and sanitary ware for the hospitals was no longer needed. Archie realised it was imperative to re-evaluate their designs to appeal to the post war market. It took him a while to convince his father of the necessity for advertising campaigns, but their success and his way with customers, soon had the order books filling up.

At present their customers were in the lower-income bracket looking for attractive, affordable china, but when he had seen Elody's drawings something had triggered inside him. Her designs would appeal to the aristocracy, the wealthy merchants. He had felt a spark of excitement as he imagined an exhibition incorporating her pieces, buyers clamouring to purchase them, Elody at his side. But what did he really want of her he wondered, pacing the room his hands behind his back, what was his interest? Was it her work or her unassuming loveliness? But it could never be, Elody Cole was a working girl from a different world.

He sank down on the bed, his eyes lingering on the fort constructed by Giles, the papier mâché dinosaur, all the childish things he had refused to let go. How different life would have been if Giles had survived. He looked up when Hester came in. She went straight to the fort, her back towards him. He could see the rigidity of her spine, her slim white fingers tracing the curve of the fort walls, the towers and turrets, obviously remembering when Giles had made it for him.

Archie had been so close to Hester once, two children a year apart, inseparable beings with their own language, and then he had deserted her, going off to school without a second glance, not even writing to her. Hester had never forgiven him, and she had lavished all her love on her eldest brother Giles. When he died, Hester was adrift, but the rift between the two younger siblings seemed too wide to cross.

'Are you all right?' he asked.

She turned around. 'If you call having to watch Father's latest charity case invade our home all right, then I suppose I am.'

'She has no one, it's the least we can do.'

'You obviously like her, I've noticed you making sheep's eyes at her whenever she appears.'

'Did you come into my room to be rude?'

She sat down on the bed beside him. 'No, sorry I just wanted...'

'What, Hester?'

For a brief moment Archie thought she might talk to him, confide in him and they could be friends again.

'Oh, I don't know...' She glanced at him and he could see the anguish in her eyes. Then her face closed. 'Nothing, Archie.' She stood up and went to the door. 'Father says don't be late for dinner, apparently he has some news.'

Chapter Thirteen

That night Elody had a bath in Waterloo. Why the bathroom had been named after a battle she couldn't imagine, and indeed why every room in the house was called Shell or Winter or Petersham. Did the Derringtons have a house in Petersham? she mused, sinking beneath the water, or perhaps an ageing aunt lived there. In Louise Street, there was just the parlour, the kitchen and two small bedrooms, but it was different, the workers didn't have time or the money for luxuries. As the water cooled, she turned on the hot tap with her toe, exhaling with pleasure as it flowed down her legs over her skin, caressing every inch and curve of her body. One day she would have her own bathroom with hot and cold water. For an instant she was reminded of bath time back home, the tin tub pulled from the cupboard every Friday and put in front of the stove, Walter going first, squealing that he didn't need a bath and was as clean as a sixpence, his laughter when her mother tickled his toes. Then her turn, the water a little grey and sudsy, her mother topping it up, soaping her back. She bit her lip knowing she would gladly exchange every bit of luxury for just one more bath time at home.

She dressed slowly, remembering the conversation with Archie. He was light-hearted one moment, arrogant and rude the next. Often an expression would come into his eyes that she didn't understand, was it longing, sadness? She really wasn't sure. She was thinking about him as she descended the wide staircase and entered the Blue Parlour, even as she examined the technique in a small but exquisite painting of flowers. Archie was a conundrum and she had never met the like of him before. She was so caught up in her observation, that she didn't see the handprint at first, it was only when she turned that it caught her eye. There it was on the glass pane of the window. For a moment she was still, she could hear her breath rising and falling. She moved towards it slowly, tentatively, touched the imprint of the small fingers, the chubby palm. She put her hand against it, measuring it against her own. It was the game she had always played with Walter, the handprint game. A sob rose in her throat as she remembered pressing her hands onto the glass, followed by Walter, knowing they would get into trouble, but doing it all the same. She jumped as Hester entered the room.

'You have just met the Thorncliffe ghost.'

Elody didn't move.

'He comes occasionally, perhaps because you're new here. Making himself acquainted.'

'It is a child's hand, it's the game I used to play with Walter.' Elody nearly choked on the words.

'Drowned in the lake we are told, now he has come back to haunt us.'

Elody pushed herself back against the wall, feeling the heat rush to her face. 'Have you really got nothing better to do?' She finally found her voice and it was hoarse, strange in her ears. 'Do you enjoy feeding on other people's misery?'

'I'm sorry, I was only joking, I didn't mean to be unkind. I didn't think…' Hester spoke the words quickly, her eyes to the floor.

'Well perhaps you should think a little more.' Elody ran from the room.

*

Lord Derrington was having a glass of champagne when Elody entered the dining room. She observed the empty bottle on the side.

'Miss Cole,' he instructed, 'you shall sit next to me, Archie on my left, Hester beside your mother.'

'But, Daddy...'

'Hester, do as I say.' His eyes followed her as she flounced to the other end of the table and when everyone was seated, he raised his glass.

'I'm celebrating a large order, from America,' he announced. 'And I'm really quite enthusiastic about it. It's worth at least three hundred pounds. Ursula, you will be able to have that—'

'Andrew, we do not talk of money in front of guests,' Ursula interrupted. 'In fact, we do not talk of money at all.'

'But Miss Cole is no longer a guest, Ursula. She's living in this house as one of the family and I'm sorry if money is a dirty word, but it's my money that keeps us here.'

Elody stared at her plate while Ursula lapsed into silence.

'For heaven's sake, Ursula, you should be celebrating. This means we can stay in your precious Thorncliffe Hall. As you never fail to tell me, it is after all, *your* family home.'

The rest of the dinner continued, and they were filing from the room when Archie caught Elody's arm.

'I hear the ghost has returned, Miss Cole.' He leant towards her, his voice low.

'Are you trying to frighten me? Because you are failing miserably.'

'Why are you trembling, then?' He grinned and Elody could feel her anger flaring.

'I can't imagine why you take every opportunity to belittle me.'

His smile fell away. 'That was not my intention, I assure you.'

Elody could see the sincerity in his eyes and the tightness in her stomach unfurled. 'Perhaps I'm being a little irrational.'

'A woman irrational, never!' He smiled and this time she knew he was teasing her.

'Once again, please forgive me, Miss Cole.'

Everyone had retired for the night when Elody returned to the Blue Parlour.

The handprint had gone, but her troubled mind would not rest.

Where was her beloved Walter? She sat in an armchair by the fire, staring into the glowing coals, the time slipping away from her.

Ten years earlier

Elody was standing on a wooden crate, staring through her window into the perpetual twilight of a pottery town. From here she could see beyond the rooftops, and rows of terraced houses, beyond the Sneyd colliery pithead, and the slag heaps where she and Walter played. Further even than the shordruck that was distinctly out of bounds, to green fields and trees, where the air was clean, the coal dust whipped away by the wind. She couldn't quite see the moors, but they were in her thoughts, wild and untamed.

She was distracted when her mother called, her voice carrying up the stairs. 'Work won't get done with you staring out the window, love.'

'Coming.' Elody stepped from the box and ran down the narrow stairs. Her mother was scrubbing the sink when she found her.

'You haven't filled the range as you promised. The coal's in the hod, so hurry now.'

'Yes, Mother.'

'You'll look after your little cousin, mind? And give him his lunch, there are herrings in the cupboard that need to be eaten.'

'Are you going to the pot bank?'

'I have some thoughts I want to thrash out with our Mr Asland.' She glanced at Elody's feet. 'Do up the buttons on your boots, girl, you'll fall on your face.'

'Walter hates herrings.'

'If he's hungry he'll learn to like them pretty quick.' Ada Cole wiped her hands on her apron, untying the strings. She was smiling as she bent to kiss her cheek. Elody inhaled deeply, loving her mother's scent, the feel of her soft skin.

'You smell good.'

'It's the one we made together last summer; jasmine remember?'

'Course I remember.'

'*Of* course, don't forget you're a lady.'

She giggled, the thought of her being a lady!

Her mother grabbed her coat from the rack and pulled it on over her black skirt. Even with those dull clothes she looked handsome, her dark hair hanging in a thick plait down her back.

'I'll be back at three. Your father's shoeing at Lord Stafford's yard, twenty horses at least, so if you need anything Mrs Owens is next door.'

Elody scowled, she hated Mrs Owens.

'Don't look like that, Elody, she isn't so bad.'

'She is so, she's a crochety old bag.'

'Elody, you mind your tongue, it will get you into trouble one of these days.'

The door closed behind her and Elody was now in charge. Walter, who was playing with his wooden train on the kitchen floor, looked up when she went in.

'I hate Mrs Owens too. She said she was going to drown our kittens in the canal. You won't let her will you, Elody?'

'Never, Walter.'

'What if they go in her garden?'

Walter was talking about the three wild kittens who lived behind the coal shed.

'You must tell them not to.'

'Aw, Elody, they won't understand.'

Elody had squashed up the herrings with mashed potatoes and Walter ate every scrap. Feeling pleased with herself she took her cousin to play in their small back garden. Two kittens came to greet them from their position outside the chicken coop, but the third, a tabby with a white splash down his nose, was nowhere to be seen.

'She's drowned him, Elo,' he cried, his face wrinkling up as the tears came. He pushed his small chubby fists in his eyes. 'Mrs Owens has drowned Biscuit, I know she has.'

Elody pulled him towards her. 'Hush now, Walter, let's just go look for him.'

They looked and looked, in the coal hole, the potting shed where her mother kept her tools for the allotments, behind the low wall where she stored her compost, even amongst the chickens, but the kitten was nowhere to be found.

Walter was wailing in anguish now.

'I want Biscuit, he's my favourite.' They actually had no idea whether the kitten was a boy or a girl.

'Can we go to the pot bank? Aunty Ada will tell us what to do.'

Elody could see the logic in this, they would most likely meet her on the canal path because it was now well past two.

'C'mon then, if it gets you off my back. But first a glass of water, you will be all dried out with those tears.' When Walter's shoulders had stopped heaving, she helped him on with his coat, pulled a thick jersey over her pinafore and they went down the front steps.

Elody could see Mrs Owens peering through her net curtains. She pulled up the sash window.

'You going out?'

'We're on our way to the pot bank.' She wanted to mention the missing cat but the look on Mrs Owens' face stopped her.

'You go straight there, child,' she instructed. 'Your mother told me to keep my eyes on you.'

Their progress down the narrow street was slow, they were stopped first by Gabriel Jackson on his way back from his shift at the colliery.

'You're looking as if something has upset you,' he announced, touching Walter's cheek.

Walter naturally told the story again, never taking his eyes off Mr Jackson's sooty face.

'Don't you worry, son, kitty will be fine.' The miner patted his head before trudging off towards Tellwright Street.

'He's awful dirty,' Walter remarked, rubbing at his cheek and Elody could hear Mr Jackson's loud guffaw.

Everyone loved Walter, not only for his cheeky personality, and mop of dark curly hair, but his character was bright and sunny when he was not distressed about a missing cat. Next came Mrs Preedy from the cake shop on the corner of Wycliffe Street, who bustled out of the shop and put an iced bun into the boy's hand.

'Not a word to your aunty or you'll get me into trouble,' her chins wobbled as she spoke.

'Can I eat it now?' Walter asked.

'If Elody doesn't chase me around the houses first.'

Walter giggled and by the time they had reached the canal, the bun had gone and Elody was holding onto his sticky hand. The sun had come out, softening the chimneys, blurring the harshness of the industrial town.

They reached the pot bank, but when Elody looked for her

mother, she wasn't yet there. Only the foreman and the packing men were out in the cold.

'You going to stack the barge, Mr Asland?' she asked, pulling Walter along.

'This ware is for London,' he told her as the men unloaded the cart. 'Now, if you'll excuse me, Miss Elody, it needs to be finished afore it's time to clock off.'

'Miss Elody,' Walter teased. 'You're a Miss now.'

She poked him in the ribs. 'And just you remember, little boy.'

'I am not little, I'm six.'

'To me you are—' Elody didn't get any further.

'I can hear meowing, Elody, I can hear . . .' Walter looked up at her, his head cocked, his eyes flashing with anguish, and before she could stop him he had slipped his hand from her grip and was running to the canal side.

Time stood still for Elody. She ran towards him, her arms going out to him as he swayed on the edge. She tried to reach for his coat, but it fluttered away. She could see his white face as he toppled, the fear in his eyes.

'Elo,' he screamed and then he was falling, his head thrown backwards, and Elody was jumping in after him. She could feel the breath leave her body as she hit the icy water. She thrashed with her arms, but she couldn't swim. She could feel the water pulling her, tugging at her skirts, dragging her down to a dark place. When she surfaced, gasping and thrashing, she looked around for Walter, but he wasn't there.

'Help,' she screamed. 'Help,' but water was in her nose, her eyes, choking the life from her. She fought with every ounce of her strength, until at last she gave up struggling and her arms floated wide. Her last thoughts before she lost consciousness were of Walter.

Elody didn't see Will Asland dive in after her, nor did she feel his arms beneath her shoulders as he towed her to the edge, or the different hands hauling her up, as he and Mr Partridge went in search of Walter. Later she learnt they never gave up on him, diving repeatedly until they found him. Ironically it was the closing of the lock gates that saved Walter. As the water level rose, he was washed against them, his head only partially submerged, and when he was pulled out, turned on his side, and slapped repeatedly on the back, a good part of the Trent and Mersey Canal gushed from his mouth.

Reliving the accident had exhausted Elody. She put the guard in front of the fire and went upstairs. The past was done, she would get on with the future, with her plans. She would not have her life derailed by a handprint in the glass, it must have belonged to a child on the estate, nothing more.

But Elody couldn't sleep, images flashed before her, Walter pulling away from her, the moment she saw him fall, Walter crying out. Fear trembled through her body like wind through grain and she clutched at the sheets to stop herself screaming. She remembered Aunty Jean coming to collect him, standing on the doorstep, her lips pursed in a thin line.

'I can't leave him here any longer, Ada,' she had said. 'You left him to the mercy of a child.'

A row had followed, her mother indignant and hurt. 'We've kept him when it suited you, and now you'll take him away, just like that. What about Walter's needs?'

'I hardly think you're in a position to tell me about his needs, your daughter nearly killed him. My son is coming with me.'

Elody had gasped, Walter was her little cousin, her very best friend; she would protect him with her life.

'Surely she doesn't think that,' she had wailed as Aunty Jean packed his things into a suitcase upstairs.

'This isn't about you, she has a new job where she can take

him and though she never wanted him till now, she does have a right to her son.'

Elody put her pillow over her head, trying to block the memory of Walter leaving but she failed. She could see him standing in front of her, one bony elbow over his mouth.

'You'll come to London?' he had muttered.

'You know I will.'

'And then you'll live with me?'

Elody had put her hand on his shoulder. 'And then I'll live with you, and it will be as it has always been.' But Elody had known she was lying. 'Maybe you'll get bored of me,' she had said, keeping her back rigid, scrunching her eyes up tight to stop herself from crying.

'Never.'

'Come now,' Aunty Jean had interrupted, picking up his small suitcase. 'Stop blathering, Walter, say goodbye to your cousin, and your aunt, we need to be on our way.' She had given Elody a long, hard look of disappointment.

'No,' wailed Walter, charging into Elody's arms.

'Don't let her take me, please, Elo,' but Elody was helpless. She held him, burying her face in his brown curls, inhaling the last smell of him.

'You be good now,' she muttered.

'No never, I'll be so bad she hates me,' he gulped, his eyes liquid pools.

'I'll come, Walter, I swear on my life. One day we'll go to America, I promise you. Now you have to go with your mother.' She kissed his forehead and ran out of the parlour to her room upstairs. Slamming the door behind her she crumpled in a heap on the floor. It hurt more than Gran dying, more than anything she had ever experienced before. Her world had broken into shattered fragments and she didn't think she could take any more.

Chapter Fourteen

Present Day

A tear spilled onto the fragile paper and Marina brushed it away. She was now tied to Elody by an invisible thread.

'That poor little Walter,' she whispered. 'What happened to him, I have to find out.'

She folded the paper knowing everything had changed. She had an affinity with the girl from the past, Marina was no longer bearing her grief alone.

She had started supper when Hugh came into the dining room.

'Sorry I'm late again, the accounts meeting overran.'

Marina hadn't spoken to Hugh for the last twenty-four hours, drawing away from him when he put his arm around her waist in the bed they shared, letting the gulf of isolation grow between them. It was not the time to be angry.

'I began without you ...'

Hugh sat down in the chair opposite her and closed his eyes, as if gathering his energy or courage, she really wasn't sure.

'I walked back from the agency, this afternoon.'

'Cold?'

'Not really.' Silence.

'The thing is, Marina, the more time we leave the gardens untended, the worse they'll become.'

'You mentioned it before.'

'I know but ...'

'And you want me to bring them back to life?'

'Would you mind? I really haven't the time.' Hugh was chewing on the corner of his fingernail, his shoulders slumped. What was going on in his head? Marina wondered. If only he confided in her, articulated his feelings instead of excluding her from his life.

'Yes, Hugh, I'll see what needs to be done.'

'Everything needs to be done.'

Later, as Marina watched Hugh watching the nine o'clock news, she reflected on the change in their relationship. Before Francesca died, they were the best of friends. They talked together, made time for each other. She remembered curling up on the sofa in the Florence apartment playing Scrabble, taking the pieces from the small pink pouch, arguing over words in English and Italian, the laughter they had shared. They went to the cinema, art galleries, concerts. They even had flu together, Hugh dosing her up with lemon juice and honey helped along with a generous slug of brandy. She recalled the move back to the farmhouse to await Francesca's birth, Hugh painting in the orchard, picnics on a large tartan rug, and the day she had crept up behind him, and he had chased her through the wildflowers, catching up with her, his voice filled with wonder as his hands circled her belly. 'The baby's kicking.'

'Like a warrior,' she had replied.

Those days had gone, but as she looked around the Blue Parlour, the same room the Derringtons had played out their lives, she could feel a spark of energy in her fingertips. Elody had arrived at Thorncliffe having lost everyone close to her, entirely alone. And yet she had not let tragedy stop her, she had fought for what she believed in, she had done extraordinary things. Hers was the story of a woman who had striven and succeeded despite her humble beginnings. She was an inspiration to those around her and, Marina realised, touching Hugh's forehead with her lips before going upstairs, she was becoming an inspiration to Marina herself.

She switched on her bedside light, picked up the little coffee pot, took off the lid and held it in her hands, knowing this was where Elody's hand had been, this was the clay she had held and moulded. Her coffee pot had been made by Elody Cole.

Chapter Fifteen

The Past

Archie was on his knees in the hall dressed in his white tie and tails when Elody came down the stairs for dinner.

'Is this a normal pursuit?' she asked, trying to keep the amusement from her voice.

'Hardly,' he uttered, looking up at her, his eyes glittering. 'My brother's cufflink, it's gone down some bloody hole.'

'Well then,' Elody replied, moving towards him, 'I shall have to help you find it.' She gathered up her dress and knelt on the floor at his side, sliding her hands over the boards, the stone hearth, searching until her fingers closed around the tiny enamel cufflink lodged behind the fire irons.

'Got it!' She held it up, her voice elated.

'You have?' Archie looked so grateful, so utterly vulnerable.

'Indeed.' For an instant Elody longed to hold him, to brush aside his pain, instead she laughed, lightening the moment. 'And now I imagine I should put it on you since you're obviously not capable.'

'Definitely incapable.' Archie was smiling now, his features composed as she leant towards him. She could feel the warmth of his hand as she joined the two starched edges of his cuffs together, his breath on her neck as she slipped the link through.

'I'm now indebted to you, Miss Cole,' he murmured, in control once more as he helped her to her feet.

'I hope you have a nice evening,' she said at last.

'The best bit of the evening has already passed,' he replied, holding onto her hand longer than necessary. Then he had gone, racing through the door, late for his engagement with Felicity Billington.

Elody had taken a walk around the garden after lunch the following day and was drying Clay's paws when Mr Simkins put his head round the boot room door. He glanced first at Elody then at the dog.

'There is a person to see you, Miss Cole.'

Elody's jaw tightened. In Mr Simkins' book, a 'person' was someone of the lower order.

'Did this person say who they were, Simkins?'

'I'm afraid I didn't ask, Miss Cole, but I have left *her* in the Great Hall.' His face softened. 'She looked a little agitated, I'm afraid.'

Elody dropped the towel and followed Simkins. It took a moment to see Mrs Wright standing beneath the head of a giant stag. She hurried towards her.

'It's not Florrie? Tell me she's all right?'

'Yes, no, not exactly.' Mrs Wright was fiddling with a hair pin, her eyes darting. 'You couldn't come and visit, could you, duck? She's not good, and insists on going to the pot bank to earn her wages, but what use is money if something happens to my girl?'

'Of course, but how did you get here, Mrs Wright, it's my reckoning there is a deal of walking in those shoes?'

'The bus got me to Leek, and my feet took me the last three mile.'

'You rest here,' Elody patted a large wing chair, 'I'll go and find Lord Derrington. Mr Simkins will provide you with a nice cup of tea.'

'My eyes will be shut afore you know it.'

'That's a good thing, Mrs Wright.'

Elody stopped outside Lord Derrington's office, and at her knock he opened the door.

'Miss Cole, what a nice surprise, I was going to ask if you'd found the map room to your liking?'

'Yes, sir, absolutely, but Florence is sick, and her mother's in the hall.'

'Florence?'

'As good a friend as one could have.'

'And you need to go back to her?'

'I do, sir.'

'Well then you must, I'll square it with Lady Ursula, Shaw will take you both to Burslem in the car.'

Relief flooded through Elody, Mrs Wright couldn't walk another inch let alone three miles. She glanced around her; aware this room was different from the rest. Here the chairs were for comfort and a little shabby, paintings covered the dark green walls. On the desk there was a photograph of two young men, each mounted on a grey gelding. They were laughing into the camera, the reins loose around the horses' necks, and they had taken off their caps revealing their glossy hair. Elody didn't need to be told one of them was his lost son Giles.

Lord Derrington observed her for a moment. 'Miss Cole?'

'They look just the ticket, sir.' She moved forward and touched the glass, her gaze lingering on their faces, as if she could reach back through time to the moment the photograph was taken.

Lord Derrington coughed. 'Aptly put, they were indeed just the ticket. The young man on the right is my son, the other, his best friend, Charles Sartorious, both gone I'm afraid.'

'I'm sorry for your bereavement.'

'And I'm sorry for yours, Elody. We've both suffered but we have to get on with it, I suppose.'

It was the first time he had called her by her Christian name and Elody felt warm inside, a slight sense of belonging. She faltered a moment, tracing a pattern on the Turkish carpet with her shoe.

'Elody?'

She looked up her cheeks flushing. 'There is something I've been meaning to ask you, it's been troubling me that much.'

'Yes?'

'Why did you bring me to Thorncliffe Hall? Lady Ursula isn't happy about it, she's made that perfectly clear. I'm not...?' Her heart was racing, the blood pumping in her ears. 'You see, it has puzzled me from the moment my mother told me you were taking me in. Why me, when I've never met you before, even though you were my godfather. Why someone you didn't even know?'

Lord Derrington's eyes were soft.

'My dear Elody, I believe you're asking if I'm your father. Much as I would love the honour, I can assure you I'm not. Your mother was my dearest friend and I let her down. This is my way of making it up to her.'

'What did you do that was so bad?'

'I reneged on our friendship, the most important thing in the world, I walked out on it because I was told to.'

'That's a pity, sir.'

'I can see you would never do that, and your constancy makes me ashamed.' He picked up a pen from the silver tray. 'Shall I let you into a secret? I've been bossed around by women my entire life and very soon that's going to change.'

He smiled, his face relaxing. 'Now off you go to Florence, but don't stay away too long.'

'Does Lady Ursula think I'm your daughter?' Elody blurted. 'It would explain her attitude, me coming here against her will.'

'Quite probably, though in her heart, she knows it's impossible. If you don't mind, we'll keep this conversation between ourselves, I've been most indiscreet. Do you promise, Elody?'

'On my honour, sir and thank you for letting me go to Florence.'

A smile pulled at the corner of Lord Derrington's mouth. 'And if I didn't, I surmise you would still go. I suggest you leave before my wife sees you.'

He strode past her to the door, opening it wide. 'Is there anything else that I can do for you, young lady?'

Elody paused, looked up into his face, there were a thousand things he could do, he could give equal pay to women for starters. He could abolish the monstrous practice of '*good from oven*' where potters were only paid if the piece survived the intense heat of the ovens. Her head spun with things she could say, instead she shook her head, that time would come. 'If you'll excuse me, I'll get along.'

'What is wrong with her?' he asked at last.

Elody raised her head and looked him in the eye. 'Plumbism probably, it happens in the Potteries.'

He put the pen in his pocket and for a moment they stared at each other, until his glance fell away. 'Good day to you, Elody, and good luck to your friend.'

The car had stopped outside the small, terraced house at the end of Louise Street, when Jacob Shaw pulled aside the glass panel separating the back of the car from the front. 'I'll not be opening your door, it might cause too much of a stir.'

Elody chuckled. 'You're right there, Jacob Shaw.'

'But you might be wanting this, it arrived in the lunchtime

post – I reckoned it might be private.' He handed her an envelope with the Palace of Westminster postmark on the front.

Elody drew in her breath. 'Jacob, you're a saint.'

He looked back at her, a grin on his handsome face. 'Don't you be getting yourself into trouble, mind.'

'Me?'

'Just a hunch, Miss Cole.'

'And don't you be worrying that head of yours, Jacob Shaw.' She folded the envelope into her pocket and stepped from the car. Mrs Wright took her arm and together they walked to the front door.

'The whole street is watching, love,' Mrs Wright whispered. 'This will give them summat to talk about.' Elody could see Mrs Danes twisting her head as she scrubbed her front step at number forty-three, and Mrs Higgs standing with her arms crossed from over the fence. A little boy skipped down the road.

'Elody, Princess Elody,' he sang. 'Can I have a ride.'

Elody laughed. 'You can have no such thing, Peter Sykes. Now you run back home, what would your mother think?'

'Aw, Elody, you are a spoilsport,' he cried.

Mrs Wright indicated with her head as they went inside.

'She's upstairs, love. She can hardly speak, yet she insists on returning to work in the morning. I don't know what to do.'

Elody took the stairs two at a time.

She lifted the latch on the bedroom door, the sour smell of sickness invading her nostrils. How many times throughout her childhood had she stayed in this room with her friend, their heads resting against the brass bedhead, sharing dreams.

She moved across the narrow boards, her eyes adjusting. In the far corner she could see Florence, her back turned away from her. As she came closer, the girl shuddered and Elody knelt on the floor at her side, running her fingers over her forehead, through her damp hair, the knot of dread growing inside her.

'Mother?' Florence moved her head, her eyes trying to focus.

'No silly, it's me, Elody.'

'Elody?' Florence turned over. 'What are you doing here? Not in that posh house with the...?' Her words tailed off.

'Had to see you, though I'm not sure why.' Elody forced a smile to her face.

'They chucked you out, I knew they would,' Florence pushed herself up on her elbow as she tried to make a joke.

'Nope, not yet anyway.'

'Tell me about them,' she whispered. 'I'd like to be distracted.'

Elody sat on the bed beside Florence, her forehead puckering as she thought about the Derringtons.

'Lord Derrington hasn't got a bad word to say about anyone, and Mr Simkins the butler, thin as a pin in his black tailcoat, who should have been dead these ten years past, but beneath the cold exterior he has a heart of gold.' She paused, looking down at Florence. 'But Lady Ursula has a poker up her bum, and Hester the daughter makes me mad.'

'And I bet you've told her.'

Elody laughed. 'I haven't been silent.'

'Tell me more about upstairs.'

'It's an unhappy house, Florrie, all of them creeping around each other, not sure who's going to make some snippy remark.'

'It's seven years since the end of the war,' whispered Florence, 'and we're still living with it in our heads. Look at Father, he doesn't move from his chair.' She sighed and Elody took her in her arms, feeling the fragile bones jutting through her skin.

'Mother's got you to check up on me, I know it.'

'She has not.'

She lay on her side, fixing her gaze on Elody. 'I'm going back to work tomorrow, and naught can stop me, I'm the only earner and we need the money.'

Elody kept her voice calm. 'Then I'm staying with you. You aren't getting rid of me that fast, Florence Wright.'

Much later, while Florence tossed and turned beside her, Elody took the letter from the pocket of her skirt and tore it open. Even in the poor light from the oil lamp, the words were clear.

Dear Miss Cole,
I was delighted to receive your letter, if you would care to meet me in my office in the Palace of Westminster, we can discuss this further. Having checked my diary, I have an hour to spare on March the 5th. Would three be convenient, Miss Cole?

Elody lay on her back clutching the letter to her chest. Would that be convenient? Oh yes, it most certainly would. 'London,' she whispered the word out loud. She had never been to London.

'What's up, Elody?'

Florence had pushed herself up in bed and was staring at the letter.

Elody giggled. 'Well, it's like this, Florrie, I wrote to Lady Astor at the Houses of Parliament and …'

'So how are you going to get to London, Elody?' Florence asked the following morning.

Elody wrinkled her nose. 'Train, I suppose.'

'And money, you need money to get to London.'

Elody thought of the florins in her bag. 'I've got some of that.'

'Lord, Elody, so you're really going to do it, like Emmeline Pankhurst and them others before us?'

'There's more that needs doing, Florrie, much more. Through-out the war we kept the pot banks going, doing the same jobs as the men, but on half the pay. It's not right, not fair. I for one am not going to take it anymore!'

'Ma always said you were different from the rest of us, but London, Elody...'

Elody lay back down and the two girls gazed at the ceiling.

'I'll manage, Florrie.'

'You will,' she replied.

Florence didn't go back to work that day or the day after, she stayed in bed while Elody tried to distract her with stories of Thorncliffe Hall.

'There's Agnes the cook, with bosoms that would keep her afloat if the ship went down, and the gamekeeper Digger Smith. I came across his cottage when I was walking Clay in the woods. I nearly jumped out of my skin because there he was with his lurcher Jake, saying not a word. Like statues they were, Florrie, honest to God.'

'What happened?' gasped Florence.

'For a second, I thought he might take out his big old gun and shoot the both of us, but he laughed, Florrie, and the lurcher bounded over. He's kind of nice but I wouldn't want to meet him on a dark night, he keeps jackdaws and crows strung on a line.'

'I'm not sure I'd want to meet him at all.' Florence shuddered. 'Anyway, tell me about the son, you've been that quiet about him.'

'Archie... sometimes he's agreeable and at others he's full of himself. He got out of fighting, his lungs or something, but they sound pretty fine to me.'

'Do you find him handsome?'

Elody prodded her. 'You behave yourself, Miss Wright, you know he's walking out with Felicity Billington—'

'Tight-arsed Miss Billington!'

'There's an understanding between them.' Elody's voice was

light, but inside she was remembering the touch of Archie's hand, the heaviness in her chest as he ran down the steps to the car.

'And you, Elody?' Florence's voice brought her back to the present.

'I'm getting there, Florrie, but I miss home, Mother, Father and Walter. Sometimes I think my heart is ripped in two, all of them gone.'

'Not Walter.'

'One day I'll find him, Florrie.'

'If he doesn't find you first. It broke his poor little heart, your aunt taking him away like that.'

Elody sighed.

'Don't forget I'm here, Elo.'

'You'd better be, Florence Wright.'

On Thursday morning Elody opened her eyes and stretched her arm across the mattress. Florence wasn't there.

She leapt out of bed, charging downstairs. Her friend was in the doorway dressed in her coat.

'Where do you think you're going, giving me the slip?' She pulled her cardigan around her nightdress. 'It's freezing out there, Florrie, are you mad?'

'Knew you'd make a fuss.'

'Fuss? Mother of God, Florence Wright! If you're going, I'm coming too, and you'll bloody well wait for me.'

Within seconds she had thrown on her old pinafore, thick woollen stockings, lace-up boots and grey jumper her mother had knitted for her and ran down the stairs after Florence. Mrs Wright was standing in the hallway.

'Take care of her,' she said, handing Elody a brown paper bag filled with sandwiches. 'That Reggie Billington doesn't give a ha'penny for his workers, when I think about your poor mother!'

Elody swallowed.

'And make her eat if you possibly can.'

'I'll do that, Mrs Wright.' They exchanged a look and Elody followed Florence outside.

For a brief second Elody thought of Lady Ursula's instructions to stay away from the pot bank. She dismissed them just as easily, whatever happened, she would look after her friend.

It was a fifteen minute walk to the pot bank but it took them twenty-five and Florence looked exhausted by the time they headed towards the branch canal. Elody took her by the arm.

'Are you sure you want to do this; go back to work, I mean?'

Florence shook her off. 'I wouldn't be doing it, now would I?'

'But, Florrie.'

'This is the way it's going to be, if I don't work the family will go hungry and there'll be no coal for the fire.'

The throng of men, women and children increased as they entered Navigation Road, some peeling off to the crate making factory in Malkin Street, others heading for the Greenfield works. It was an unattractive range of buildings, Elody thought, as they came near – a rum sort of place, from the soot blackened brickwork to the smoke belching bottle ovens, but despite the ugliness, there was an energy about the pot bank that brought a flutter to her chest.

'Stop dawdling, Elody Cole, or I'll be getting my cards before the day has started.' Florence's mood had changed, and she grabbed her friend's hand, pulling her beneath the brick archway where a green sign with gold lettering announced the name of the owner, Reginald Billington, down the outside passageway, past the boiler house and the engine house, until they reached the external staircase to the workshops upstairs. As soon as they entered the painting studio, colleagues surrounded Florence, enquiring after her health, but they looked with suspicion at Elody.

'Surely you're too high and mighty to be working at the pot bank.' said Dawn, her friend of many years.

'She's still the same Elody,' scolded Florence. 'It's hardly her fault her mother died, and rich folk took her in.'

'It's nice to see you, Elody,' Bridie Brookes came forward and gave her a quick hug before blushing pink.

'Aw Bridie, I've missed you. How's Hilda?'

The girl seemed to grow taller, and her eyes shone. 'She's doing well in school, Elody, fancy that. Frank says girls shouldn't be learning, but I'm right proud.'

'So you should be, Bridie.'

Dawn shuffled her feet. 'We thought we would never see you again.'

'Do you think it was my choice, Dawn Rogers?' Elody rebuked her. 'Just think on it.'

She ran her eyes over Dawn, noticing the thickening waist, the swell of her stomach beneath her pinafore.

'Yes, Elody, I'm pregnant again,' Dawn murmured. 'And this time I'm going to hold on to it.'

The group dispersed when Mr Asland limped into the room, his stick tapping on the uneven boards.

'Back to work, girls, do you think this is a garden party? And you, Florence Wright, I told you not to come back until you're well.'

'I'm healthy, I promise you.' Florence pulled her brushes from her satchel, her gaze lowered.

'I don't want you having a funny turn on us again, I'll be watching you, trust me I will.' He turned to Elody. 'I suppose you think you can walk in here and have your old job back.'

'No, sir, she spluttered. 'I wouldn't expect anything of the sort, I'm here to mind Florence.'

'I don't need minding,' grumbled Florence.

Mr Asland cast an eye over both the girls, unable to conceal his amusement. 'I'm not a pushover, you know.'

'No, sir,' they said.

'But I'm sure we can find something for you to do. And take that smile off your face, Florence Wright, or I'll not be giving your friend the station next to you. It's the leaf pattern this week, with which I believe you're familiar and no airs and graces in here, Miss Cole.' He was halfway across the room when he turned.

'I'm so sorry about your mother, Elody. She was a good woman, one of the best. I try to improve things, but it's them at the top. If they're not willing to pay for it, there's nothing I can do.'

As Elody looked at the slight Yorkshireman, with the receding hairline and narrow frame, she knew he was telling the truth. She owed him a debt of gratitude that she could never repay. Despite his injuries sustained at Gallipoli, he had been the one to jump into the canal after Walter, he was the man to whom she owed her life.

It wasn't long before the two girls were painting the delicate leaf patterns around the edge of their plates.

'You take care of that brush,' Florence scolded. 'Mother give it me for my birthday and it's worn exactly to my taste.'

'Licked more like,' Elody grumbled, finishing a rim.

She put another stack in front of Florence and took the finished work to the ware board to wait for the final firing. As the hours slipped by, she was aware of the dust settling on her eyelashes and her clothes, the spatters of paint on her arms. When she went to the privy outside, she despaired. Reggie Billington continued to ignore the government guidelines, there were still no facilities, no hot water and soap to wash the toxic materials from their hands.

Elody did her best to look after her friend, thinking up her own set of rules.

'A short walk down the canal, you need to work up an appetite and get some colour in your cheeks,' she instructed Florence. 'Don't give your sandwiches to the pigeons, eat them yourself.' But that was the problem, Florence wasn't hungry, and she didn't want to eat. When she tried to lick her brush, Elody dived for it. 'Don't, Florrie, what are you playing at?'

'I need to get a fine point,' she complained.

'Sod the fine point, Florence, the lead will kill you,' Elody responded, and under her breath she added, 'If it hasn't already.'

It wasn't that Elody didn't think about her upcoming trip to London, but by the time she had got Florrie home to Louise Street and she had helped Mrs Wright with the chores, she was downright drained. By the third of March there was no getting away from it.

'Will you cover for me on Thursday with Mr Asland, Florrie?' They were sitting on the steps at the back of the house. 'Tell him something that won't get him into difficulty if he's asked. You know he worries about us all.'

'I'll tell him you have the gripes.'

'He'll worry more.'

'I could say you've gone back to Thorncliffe Hall.'

'But that wouldn't be true.'

Florence laughed. 'None of this is true, Elody. I know you have a special fondness for Mr Asland, him saving you and Walter, but don't worry, I'll not let you down.'

'If it wasn't for him neither of us would be here.'

'He also admires your work. When you left, he said it was a blinking shame because your talent was exceptional.'

'He said that?'

'He did, Elody.'

The following day, Elody was finishing a plate when Reginald Billington sauntered into the studio, his hands pushed in the pockets of his tweed coat.

'Morning, girls, working hard, that's what I like to see.' His voice was smooth, but his eyes were small and hard as pebbles. Elody glanced at Florence.

'Aren't you Ada Cole's girl?' He approached Elody and even from a distance she could smell his aftershave, see the dressing in his black hair.'

'Ada Cole was my mother.'

'Attractive just like her.' He came closer and Elody's fist curled as he looked her up and down. Before she could stop herself, the words were out.

'And like my mother I don't take kindly to compliments from married men.' She could feel the girls around her stiffen as they waited for the explosion. Seconds passed and suddenly he laughed.

'You are a feisty one, just like her. I enjoy a challenge, Miss Cole.' He clapped his hands.

'Back to work, girls, don't pay any attention to me.'

As he walked away, he put out his hand to squeeze Maud Leech's round little bottom, but she skipped out of reach.

His footsteps were ringing on the cobbles outside when the girls started to giggle.

'What just happened?' Dawn's shoulders were shaking. 'I've never seen the like of it.'

'I couldn't help myself, the man's odious.' Elody wrinkled her nose.

'Disgusting,' Maud agreed, wiping her eyes. 'My mother says he has more offspring than you can shake a stick at and none of them acknowledged; he's a bad one Reggie Billington.'

'You be careful,' said Bridie Brookes. 'He'll remember what you said.'

Florence was frowning. 'What were you thinking, Elody? You've made an enemy and he's stronger than you.'

*

It was four o'clock when Elody was instructed to go to the showroom by a young lad who clattered up the stairs in over-sized boots.

'Ah, Elody lass.' Mr Asland looked up. 'Your godfather's waiting in the car outside, hurry up now, don't keep him waiting.' He lifted a vase with a fluted edge from a stand and turned it around. 'Jed Leech made this before he left for the front. Hard to imagine a big man like that making something so small and delicate. He never came back... the best thrower we ever had, a good man was Jed.' His gaze was unfocused until at last his eyes cleared and settled on Elody. 'You still want to be a thrower, Miss Cole?'

'More than you can imagine, Mr Asland.'

He smiled then, a sweet, warm smile. 'Your dad would like the woman you've become.'

Elody was leaving the room when he called after her. 'I've heard you stood up to him, but he has a long memory has Reggie Billington, so just you take care.'

A light rain was falling when Elody went outside to the car. She tapped on the window and Lord Derrington stepped out.

'My dear Elody, I've come to remind you your home is Thorncliffe Hall.'

'I know, sir, just give me time.'

'Your friend, how is she?'

'A little better, but she insists on coming to work.'

He glanced at her paint-spattered hands. 'I gave my word to your mother, so please don't stay away too long.'

Thursday came and Elody took the seven o'clock train from Porthill to Stoke, changing onto the London line. She arrived at Euston at one, stepping onto the platform, her stomach fluttering with nerves. There were people everywhere, office workers, bureaucrats in bowler hats, women with children in tow, newspaper boys, scurrying through the steam. When she finally left the concourse behind her and reached the entrance, she leant against a pillar, her pulse racing. There was more traffic than she had ever seen, bicycles, pedestrians weaving amongst the mayhem, horses and carts. She was tempted to take a taxicab from the rank outside, but that would have been a waste of her limited finances. As she ventured to the pavement, tears pricked at her eyes. She had been foolish to believe she could navigate a city she had never been in before. Forcing herself to remain calm she approached a smartly dressed woman who was leaving a chauffeur-driven car.

'Excuse me, ma'am, I'm sorry to bother you, but I need to get to the Houses of Parliament, and I'm not sure of the way.'

The woman gestured to her chauffeur. 'Thank you, William, can you collect me on Friday, I'll be on the four o'clock train?'

She turned back to Elody. 'Poor girl, you're obviously a stranger here.'

'My first time in London.'

'Oh my, it's a busy place, so do take care. I would ask William to drive you, but he has an errand to run for my husband, now let me see. If you head south-east on Eversholt Street and in Wellesley Place turn...'

By the time the woman had finished her instructions, Elody's head was spinning.

'It's not difficult,' she finished, 'and if you get lost, ask any cab driver, they're most accommodating. Now if you will excuse me, I need to catch my train.' She disappeared into the crowd and Elody set off on her way. An hour later after only two wrong turns she made a left in St Margaret Street and stopped on the pavement letting the pedestrians flow past. Ahead of her the Palace of Westminster glowed in the early afternoon light. There were pinnacles and turrets on a scale she had never seen before, exquisite stonework as fine as lace and a magnificent clock tower. Now she couldn't wait to see inside.

At two o'clock precisely Elody took her lunch box from her handbag and sat on a bench by the river surveying the seat of power. At two forty-five she threw the remainder of Mrs Wright's sandwiches into the river for the ducks, and crossed the small park to the entrance gates.

'I've come to see a Member of Parliament,' she said to one of the two policemen, keeping her voice steady.

'Do you have an appointment?'

'Certainly.'

He grinned at his associate 'I'll need to see confirmation, miss.'

Elody thrust the letter in the policeman's hand. 'Lady Astor at three, will that do, gentlemen?'

'Right, miss.' The policeman was no longer condescending. 'If you go through that door, walk through Westminster Hall and wait in Central Lobby, Mr Price, her secretary, will come for you.'

Elody crossed the draughty hall and went up the stairs. When another policeman looked at her suspiciously she glared back and marched through the room. She sat down on one of the stone benches, stood up again, her frustration diminishing as she inspected the gothic arches, the carvings, the intricate patterned floor. She was examining a statue when Lady Astor's secretary found her.

'Miss Cole?'

Elody inclined her head. 'That's me, sir.'

'I can see you're admiring the work of Pugin, possibly the greatest British designer and architect of the nineteenth century. Do come this way.'

It seemed they walked for miles, the secretary pointing out features along the way.

'This wallpaper is hand-blocked; we're extremely proud of it. I don't imagine you've seen anything this splendid before.'

Elody kept her voice level. 'Indeed I have, sir, the church in Cheadle may not be as large, but it's a superb example of Pugin's work. Perhaps you've been there?'

'Cheadle … I didn't know …' He fiddled with his glasses and Elody's irritation grew. Just because she spoke differently, didn't mean she was ignorant. They finally stopped outside a door with an elaborate gilt handle and the secretary turned around, his eyes bright with amusement.

'It's my guess you don't need my advice, but I'll give it anyway. I suggest you get straight to the point with Lady Astor, because you won't have long. Good luck and good day to you, Miss Cole.'

Elody was hovering near the doorway when a tall, elegant woman in a black dress came towards her, looking much younger than her forty-six years. 'Lord, you're just a child,' she exclaimed.

'Indeed, I'm not, I was nineteen on my last birthday.'

'Well, I admit, you're not what I was expecting, a young girl who writes so eloquently.'

'You mean I have an accent. If I may, ma'am, so do you, the only difference is yours is American and mine from the Potteries.'

Lady Astor laughed. 'My dear young woman, I am completely reassured. But here's my question, Miss Cole, you've told me what you want to achieve, you have not told me why.'

Elody gulped. This had caught her on the hop and at once a surge of emotion rushed through her. She raised her shoulders, allowing herself to breathe before she started to speak.

'When I was ten, my mother took me to a meeting she was chairing. All women it was, talking about disparity in pay, and the treatment of women in the Potteries. She stood at the front, and as she spoke something ignited inside me. I realised in that moment I would have none of it. One day I would do something, I would fight to put us on the right footing. In the years afterwards, she encouraged me to hold onto the dream. We would have done it together, but she died of plumbism a few months back, and now I'm doing it without her.' For a brief second she could feel her voice wavering. She took another breath. 'You'll be aware of the growing dissent in the pot banks, and in the workplace generally. We have worked just as hard for our wage packet, and we don't drink it away at the end of the week. We want what is due to us.' She looked up at Lady Astor, her eyes sparkling. 'So that's why am here.'

'Brava, Miss Cole. I agree with every word you're saying, I'm sure you'll be aware of my attitude to alcohol.'

'Indeed, Lady Astor, the Intoxicating Liquor Bill prohibiting the sale of alcohol to children under eighteen. An extraordinary achievement of yours.'

'Again, congratulations, charm those you hope to get on your side. You'll go far in this world. Your desire for change matches my own but it will be an uphill struggle. You understand there will be massive resistance.'

'I have no doubt.'

'I have the privilege of being the first woman to take my seat in Parliament, although some would question whether it *is* a privilege.' She smiled, showing even, white teeth. 'When I stood up in the House for the first time and asked questions affecting women and children, I was yelled at for ten minutes. But I'm still here, and we'll have a go, Elody Cole. I can make no promises, but I give you my word, I will try.' Lady Astor's eyes rested on Elody once more. 'And now I imagine you want to know how this will work.'

'If you wouldn't mind explaining the process, this is not an everyday occurrence for me.'

Nancy laughed. 'I feel sure that one day it might be, Miss Cole. So this is what will happen.'

Elody's eyes remained glued on her.

'I'll make a speech in the House about equal pay and opportunities; naturally I'll get shouted down. Then I'll make another. Next, I'll draft and introduce a Private Member's Bill in the Commons, where it will have its first reading. The name of the Bill will be read out and ordered to be printed. That is just the introduction, nothing more. Then comes the second reading, a big debate about the principles of the Bill, and it's at this point the MPs will say whether they agree with it and if not, why.' She smiled wryly. 'Which in our case will probably be everything. This is when they have a chance to state what they would like to see in the way of amendments. And on it goes. However, Elody, if I may call you that, I have to warn you, I very much doubt the Bill will get very far this time. It's early days for women, but we can use it in our campaign, and we can introduce it again in the next session of Parliament and in the one after that. It will be noticed; attitudes will eventually change. We're making strides.'

She looked at her watch. 'Forgive me, I have another appointment in five minutes, but this has been most enjoyable and illuminating. I'll write to you when I have some news.' They were nearing the door when she spoke. 'Can I ask you something, Miss Cole, you wrote the letter on Derrington writing paper, may I ask why?'

Elody laughed. 'Lord Derrington is my godfather. I live with them, I thought you might be impressed.'

'My dear Miss Cole, it was the content of your letter that impressed me, not the crest at the top.'

Mr Price was smiling as they walked back along the corridor.

'That obviously went well, Miss Cole, I can always tell.'

'You can?'

'Her Ladyship's posture, you see.'

Elody really didn't see, but she happily accepted his words.

They were halfway down the stairs when she opened her bag and rummaged inside.

'Is everything all right, Miss Cole?'

Elody found the scrap of paper and shut the bag with a click.

'While I'm here,' she started.

'Yes, Miss Cole?'

'Actually, I'm looking for someone, my little cousin, he lived with us until my aunt took him away.'

'And you want to find him, quite understandable.'

'She's a housekeeper in London.' She swallowed. 'I thought you might know of a way?'

Mr Price chuckled. 'I do love a challenge, Miss Cole. It's quite possible we can find him if you have the name of your aunt's employers and indeed the house.'

He led her into his office, took a thick book from a shelf, and sat down at his desk.

'A telephone directory.' He tapped the cover. 'Everyone who has a telephone will be in here. Do you know we're having the first public kiosk in London next year. And what is the name of her employers?'

'Elody could hardly contain her excitement. 'Mr and Mrs Bradbury. They live at Mulberry House, somewhere in Hampstead, but that's all the information I have.'

Mr Price leafed through the directory and then again. Finally he looked up at her.

'I'm sorry, Miss Cole, nothing I'm afraid, but the directories are updated twice a year.'

Elody returned to Burslem and Florence, flying into the bedroom they shared.

'You wouldn't believe it.' She threw herself down beside her, the metal springs creaking.

'Wouldn't believe what?' Florence pretended to be immersed in a book, but Elody grabbed it.

'Florence Wright, don't you want to know?'

'Course I do,' she giggled. 'I've been that testy all day.'

'She's going to give it a go, Florrie, she said she'd put it to the House, equal opportunities for women.'

'Oh my Lord, your ma would be so proud.'

'She warned me there will be resistance, the men won't like it in the least, but even if this gets nowhere right now, we can try again. Mother always said if at first you don't succeed, try, try, and . . .'

'Try again!' yelled Florence, giving it all that she had.

Chapter Sixteen

Though Lady Astor's compelling words were lodged in Elody's memory to replay at night when she couldn't sleep, there was Florence to consider, who tossed on the mattress beside her. There were the designs that unwittingly came to her mind, and she still had to fulfil her promise to Lord Derrington that she would return to Thorncliffe Hall.

Elody had finished her workload for the day and the plates were drying on the board when she pulled out her pad, designs spinning in her head. There were vases, teapots with long grace- ful spouts, their form, delicate and playful, jugs with striations on the handles, decorated with leopards weaving through the jungle, the foxes she had seen in Tittesworth Wood. Time passed quickly and she didn't notice Florrie pack away her paints.

'Come on, Elody.' Florence was blocking out her light.

'I was ready actually,' Elody grumbled, leaving her pad on the side. She followed Florence taking a worried glance back. No one would steal it overnight, now would they?

The following morning Mr Asland was waiting for them when they arrived. 'I'd like a word with you, Miss Cole.'

Elody hesitated.

'Now, Elody.' When he had limped away, Elody searched

the studio for her sketch pad. 'I should have put it away,' she moaned. 'If I'm given my cards, who'll keep an eye on you?'

'Chance would be a fine thing,' Florence retorted, then relented. 'Don't be ridiculous, Mr Asland is that glad to have you back, I reckon it's something good.'

Florence was right and as Elody entered the office, Mr Asland pointed to the sketches covering the entire surface his desk. 'Forgive me for removing them, but I was intrigued.'

'I'd finished for the day, sir ...'

'They are good, very good. And before you ask, you may try your hand at the wheel, do you want to start with the jug?' He tapped the page showing a leopard wrapped around the waist of a curvaceous little jug. 'That one, Elody when the lads have gone home.'

At six o'clock Elody and Florence filed down the rickety stairs and into the throwing shop.

While Florence read a well-thumbed copy of *Woman's Weekly* magazine, Elody roamed the room. She picked up a discarded vase, noticing the imperfections, put it down, and scrutinised the items waiting on the boards. One day it would be her pieces drying out before going into the greenhouse in preparation for the biscuit firing, her designs. Finally, she sat at a wheel and put her foot on the treadle, remembering again the first time her mother had brought her to the studio.

Mr Asland had been handsome then and fit, but that was before his leg had been blown to bits in the war.

'All set up and ready to go,' Mr Asland had said, depositing six balls of clay at her side. 'Wet your hands, centre the clay as I taught you, then let the magic begin.' Even now Elody could remember her excitement as she'd cupped her hands around the clay and put her foot down on the treadle, making the wheel spin round.

She jumped when Mr Asland pushed open the door and the image faded.

'Here's your clay, girl, I won't stand over you, it'll only distract you. Florence, come with me to the showroom, and I'll make us a cup of tea.'

On her fourth attempt Elody was happy with the jug and went to find him.

As she entered the showroom and gazed at the ware displayed, she realised he had given her an opportunity nigh on impossible before the outbreak of the war. Back then, there were designated jobs for women and others for men. The war had broken down the barriers, the women taking on all the tasks. But at the Greenfield works, turning pots was once again exclusive to the male workforce, and they wouldn't take lightly to her.

Elody held her breath as Mr Asland stood over the jug, then walked around it, his chin in his hand.

'If you don't like it, I can always change the—' She got no further.

'I'm thinking next you should try the coffee pot, and perhaps the sugar bowl with the lid, are you up to it?'

'Course I am.'

'Same time tomorrow, Miss Cole.'

Elody stayed late the following night and the night after that, while Maud walked Florence home.

She was attaching a spout to a jug she had made the day before, when Reggie Billington entered the studio. 'Miss Cole, still working?' Elody's legs turned to stone.

'Yes, sir.'

He advanced towards her. 'I hear you have talent, as well as audacity; I could always help a bright girl like you.' He came so close she could see the nick on his neck where he had cut himself shaving, the stubble on his chin. She was gripping the jug so hard, the spout fell off, and shattered on the floor. 'I don't need your help,' she muttered. 'I don't need anything from you.'

'I could raise you up in this business, give you your own studio.'

Elody backed away, humiliation and shame making her cheeks flush red. She hadn't encouraged him, so why did she feel this way. She drew back her shoulders and stared him in the eye. 'Mr Billington, I am grateful for the opportunity, but I assure you the only way I will rise in your business is by my talent as a potter.' When she reached the door, she walked down the steps. She wouldn't give Reggie Billington the benefit of seeing her afraid.

When she told Mr Asland, he sighed. 'I'm not leaving you alone in the pot bank, I don't trust him one jot, Miss Cole.'

'But you can't stay late for me.'

'I can do my paperwork here, it's no difference.'

'But your wife . . .'

'There is no wife.'

Elody swallowed remembering the gossip. His wife had walked out when he had returned from the trenches only half a man.

Elody had been back at the pot bank for two weeks when she took a newspaper cutting from the pocket of her apron.

'Who's up for the meeting at the Sea Lion in Waterloo Road tonight?' she asked, passing it on to Florence who passed it on to Dawn.

'What kind of meeting?' Maud got up from her station and wiggled her hips.

'Not that kind for sure,' Elody grinned. 'It's the Potter's Union monthly, we need to keep our ears to the ground.'

Everyone crowded around her while she spread the cutting on the table.

Tilda Kennard, a tissue printer from a workshop across the way, came into the studio. 'Couldn't help overhearing and I for one will come. I know it don't apply to some of you young ones, but I've been printing for nigh on ten years with my Fred, apart from his war work down the mine. Lucky to hang onto my job afterwards, but it's only because I'm a damn good printer.'

'And you're on half the money!' Dawn Rogers chipped in. 'Bloody disgusting it is.'

Tilda placed her hands on her hips and glared at the girls. 'And do you know what really riles me, the entire wage packet still goes into Fred's grubby hands.'

Elody, fired by Tilda's energy, thumped her fist on the table. 'The union wants our subscription money because we make up a major part of the work force, but they still favour the men. It's a patriarchal system and it's time for change.'

'Who's a paid-up member?' another paintress asked.

Tilda winked at her. 'I soon will be. I sneaked some of the wages from Fred's pocket when he was drunk.'

The girls moved closer while Elody rummaged in her handbag, finally pulling out her mother's membership card. She held it up for all to see.

'I'll go in her name,' she declared, her eyes shining. 'I'll continue her work!'

'So you should.' Tilda's face was red now and she was sweating. 'Your mother, rest her soul, gave her life to this industry as did my Aunty Gwen.' She pointed her finger at Elody. 'You're right, it's time we did something about it, and I don't mean the conditions, I mean our rights, women's rights.'

Elody felt the blood rush to her head. 'So, who's coming with us?'

'I'm coming,' shouted Dawn. 'It'll be the devil's own job to keep me away.'

'I've been an apprentice gilder for nigh on six bloody years and I am as good as anyone, better if you ask me, but I'm still paying for my learning. Daylight robbery it is,' said Gina who had just entered the room to join in the debate.

'Robbery,' the girls echoed.

As Elody tried to focus on her work, her brush dipping in and out of the paint, the small rosebuds appearing on the bowls, she could hear Lady Astor's last words, as they stood together in the doorway of her office.

'You need energy to get things done, Miss Cole, and it seems you have it in spades.'

Elody frowned. She would get things done, she had made a vow to her mother, she owed it to the women she worked with, women everywhere. Though conditions in many of the pot banks were appalling, she couldn't fight every battle, her goal was now clear. She would continue the battle for equality. With Lady Astor as an ally nothing seemed impossible to achieve. Their goals may not be accomplished in her lifetime, but by making small strides, one day women would be equal to men.

Florence was quiet as they walked home from the pot bank.

'What's wrong?'

'Nothing.'

'Well, it obviously isn't nothing.'

'The idea of a meeting brings it home to me, you know fighting for a future, and all.'

'What are you saying?'

'Oh, I don't know, Elody, I'm just being maudlin.'

Elody turned and gripped her by the shoulders. 'You are not dying on me, Florence Wright; I absolutely won't allow it. I'll hear no such talk, do you understand.'

Armed with her mother's union card which she had found in the zipped pocket of her bag, Elody and Florence left the house in Louise Street for the meeting.

They were rounding the corner into Waterloo Road when Florence cleared her throat.

'I assume you'll say something tonight.'

Elody stopped in her tracks.

'Don't look at me like that, I'm perfectly serious. Put your money where your mouth is and show us what you're made of, Elody Cole.'

The pub was full when they arrived, and they had to jostle their way through the tap room reserved for men to get to the room at the back. Potters were lounging over the counter, and despite leaving their workwear behind, they were still covered in dust. Cigarettes trailed from their mouths and Elody screwed up her nose.

'You'd think they'd clean up before coming out.'

'Don't be ridiculous,' snorted Florence. 'Most of them don't see the bathtub from one week to the next, too busy drinking beer.'

In the far corner, two men were sitting at a table in deep discussion, while taking the attendance money and inspecting cards. They were barely glancing at the members as they filed past.

Elody winked at Florence and went first, showing her mother's card. She sneaked it back to Florence and they were giggling as they piled into the hall.

'Suppose we'd been caught,' Florence grimaced. 'We'd have been thrown out.'

'Not a chance, you're in the hands of a master,' Elody smirked.

'An idiot more like,' Florence retorted, finding seats near the front.

The discussion was opened by a rotund man on a wooden podium who banged his gavel on the table.

'He must be the chair of the union meeting,' murmured Elody.

'Course he is, stupid,' Florence responded.

'Hush,' a woman behind them whispered loudly as the meeting began.

It was predictable at first, complaints about the practice *good from oven*, complaints about an accident in the workplace, then a dipper got to his feet and surveyed the room, his stubbled face unkempt.

'We get back from the war to find our trades are no longer open to us, our jobs filched by the women. I've been to five pot banks and not one has taken me.'

'Not surprised by the look of you,' Elody said, in a voice loud enough for people to hear.

'As for going to war, William Pirbright,' Tilda Kennard stood up and glared at the offending man, 'the nearest you came to the trenches was the ditch in Hot Lane!'

The man turned around until his gaze alighted on Tilda. 'You watch your mouth,' he growled.

'I'll not be watching anything, you're a lazy…'

Another woman joined in the fray cutting across her.

'We break our backs day and night for half the money.'

'Because that's what you're worth,' a voice broke through.

It was men against women now and the atmosphere was charged.

'This is going to develop into a brawl,' Florence hissed. 'Say something, Elody.' She shoved her in the ribs and Elody put up her hand.

'That woman's right, we can do the job just as well, we've proved it, but we're fed up with…' she could feel her voice trembling and coughed. 'We are fed up with the disparity between women's and men's pay.'

There was a booing and heckling from the men in the audience.

'What's your name, miss?'

Elody had to think quickly, she had her mother's card. 'Mrs Ada Cole.'

'A paid-up member?'

'To be sure.' Elody's voice was getting stronger as her confidence increased. She gazed at the sea of faces turning towards her, men ready to damn her, but she wasn't afraid. She could feel the energy building inside her. This was her calling; she had watched her mother die of plumbism, watched men cough their lungs out. She had lived through the war, suffered the consequences, but now she would fight the battle for women everywhere, she would fight for change.

'Well then, Mrs Cole, we'll put it in the minutes.'

'Is that good enough sir, put it in the minutes and forget about it?'

'Are you telling us how to do our jobs?'

'Never, sir.' There was a titter from the women. 'But I will tell you, sir, my protest isn't just about equality, your union members, men and women are dying every day. We need facilities in all the pot banks, hot and cold running water. The government gave the directives, but few of the pot banks follow them, there should be penalties, sir.'

The chairman of the meeting peered across the smoky room.

'Stand up so we can see you, Mrs Cole.'

Elody scraped back her chair and Florence squeezed her hand.

'Give it to them, Elo.'

Elody looked down at the girl she had comforted while she wretched the contents of her stomach into a bowl, her very best friend who had confessed she was dying only a short time ago. Oh yes, she would give it to them. She may be banned from union meetings in the future, but she would take that risk.

'I see it like this, sir, the union has power over the bosses,' Elody was thinking on her feet, realising how inflammatory her words sounded but she no longer cared. 'If they don't follow the guidelines, and Parliament doesn't enforce them, you should make the bosses feel it, make their businesses suffer. I am suggesting you don't just talk about it, don't wait for further misery, do something now.'

'I can see we have a suffragette among us.' His voice was strained, angry, even from a distance she could see the muscles bulge in his neck.

'We may have the vote, but we can't exactly use it,' Elody responded, in full flight now, her heart ready to burst from her chest. 'You know as well as I do, you have to be thirty years old and meet the property qualification, what sort of vote is that? Do you think any of us working girls have property qualifications? So yes, sir, I believe in rights for women and equality, if that makes me a suffragette then I am proud of that name.'

She sat down to a round of clapping from every woman in the house and booing from many of the men.

Florence and Elody put on their coats, wrapped their mufflers around their necks and went outside, followed by Tilda and Maud Leech.

'Why do men flirt so?' Maud questioned, slapping away a young man's hands.

Tilda sniggered. 'If you could call it that.'

'It may have something to do with your curves,' said Dawn, catching up with them and linking arms with Elody. When they reached the corner of Louise Street, Tilda stopped in front of them.

'Elody's right; we need to stand together and fight because if we don't, naught will change.'

While Mrs Wright prepared the dinner, Florence settled her father in the parlour next door.

'Leave him be, Elody,' she said gently when she tried to help. 'He'll stare into the fire all night, muttering to his lost friends.'

'Including my father,' Elody murmured.

'Including him.'

They returned to the kitchen where a rabbit stew was being ladled onto plates.

'You should have seen her,' Florence boasted, pouring Elody a glass of ginger beer. 'I was that proud of her.'

'I bet you were a trooper, Elody,' said her little brother Barty.

'I can imagine, duck.' Mrs Wright winked at Elody. 'You'll make something of yourself one of these days.'

Elody was exhausted but the adrenalin kept her going. She glanced across at Florence who had filled the glasses and was holding onto the back of the chair. When she winced, Elody took her hand.

'All right?' she mouthed, her heart cracking.

'Damn right I am,' she murmured. 'I wouldn't have missed that for the world.'

But she wasn't all right, Elody knew it, they both knew it. Elody ate the stew because she knew it was a luxury, but the lumps of meat stuck in her throat. What would she do if Florence died?

When her plate was empty, she glanced around the kitchen her eyes alighting on seven-year-old Dilys, a cheeky girl with flaming red hair who was helping her mother, and Jack, ten, with buck teeth and a snub nose who was chasing Barty around the kitchen.

'I'll tan both of your hides if you don't desist. If you want to do something useful, Jack, take your little brother up to bed,' Mrs Wright instructed.

'Do I have to?' moaned Jack.

'Now or it's the slipper.' Mrs Wright was smiling, and Elody felt the warmth of their love surround her. They were the nearest thing she had to family, how could she leave them and return to Thorncliffe Hall?

Chapter Seventeen

Archie was in the car with his father when they returned to the Greenfield Works the following week. Florence followed her friend from the studio.

'Go back with them, Elody, you have a chance among these people, take it, don't blow it away.'

'But everything we talked about.'

Florence lowered her voice, 'What's to stop you campaigning from Thorncliffe Hall, you can still write letters to Lady Astor, to our MP Andrew MacLaren, the unions, you're not in another country. You can still come to the meetings.'

'You don't know Lady Ursula.'

'But I know you, Elody! And as to your designs, you won't be stopped; you will always find a way.'

'Are you telling me to leave, Florrie?'

'Damn right I am. I don't want you hanging around me every minute of the day, it's hard enough feeding the family, let alone...' She dropped her gaze, refused to look her in the eye and opened the car door. 'Take her back with you, sir, she's not needed anymore.

'Go, Elody,' she insisted. 'Get away from this place.'

Elody put out her hand and then dropped it again. Florence

was cutting the ties that held them together. The indivisible bond. She drew in her breath and turned to Lord Derrington.

'If I come back, I'll need more freedom, there are things I have to do, things …' her words faltered.

'I have prevailed upon my wife, and she accepts you need to have a life away from Thorncliffe Hall.'

'Then, sir,' Elody struggled. 'Then, sir, I'll get my things.'

'And we will give your friend a lift home.'

'They've come to take me back, Mr Asland,' Elody muttered, her eyes fixed to the floor.

'And now you've come for your wages.'

'Please give them to Mrs Wright, she has more need of them.'

The foreman reached for his stick. 'You're a good girl, Elody, and your work is excellent.'

'You'll still be wanting my designs?'

'Without doubt, but Florence is right, you have to take your chances when you can.'

Elody was halfway down the passage when she turned back. 'Don't let her work if she's bad,' she begged.

'I'm not a monster, Elody. I do what I can to keep the workers safe, but if Mr Billington refuses to follow the guidelines, what am I to do? I have my job to think about, not many would employ a cripple like me.'

'Those wounds were received while fighting for your country.'

Mr Asland's voice broke. 'It was no fight, Miss Cole; it was a slaughter of innocent boys.'

'But you were a hero even before you left, sir, you saved my life.'

He looked at her for a moment and Elody could see the pain in his eyes. 'I just did what anyone would do.'

*

'You'll write, Elody?' Florence was slumped against the porch.

'I'll write.' Elody looked straight ahead and walked down the path.

She was climbing in the car when Florence stumbled after her, grabbing hold of her arm.

'It's for the best, Elody, I promise. Now get on with you before I make a fool of myself.'

Elody softened. 'I'll miss you, Florence Wright.'

'And I'll miss you.'

Then Mrs Wright came out with Barty and it was all Elody could do not to break down.

'You'll come back and see us?' the child asked, burying his face in his mother's skirts.

'I'll be back before you know it. Now look after your mother and help her with the dishes.'

'That's Dilys's job.'

'Yours too, young man.'

As the car drew away, Elody could feel the pain swamping her, the family was all she had left.

As Jacob drove them back to Thorncliffe, Archie was conscious only of the distress on Elody's face, the hurt in her eyes. They were going through the gates when he leant towards her. 'I'm so sorry, Elody.'

'But she sent me away.'

'I can tell your friend only wants the best for you.'

Elody looked down at her hands. 'Leaving her like this, know-ing—' she swallowed. 'Knowing she will probably die.'

'Parting from someone you love is desperate, but we have to believe—' he stared from the window, remembering his brother leaving for war. 'We have to keep faith, Elody.'

'I'm trying but it's difficult.'

'I know,' he replied.

Elody was prostrate on her bed when Mrs George thumped down the corridor and opened the door, her face glowing with sweat.

'These stairs get steeper every day, I could swear it – are you tired, girl, hardly surprising?'

Elody sat up. 'Not exactly.'

'Well, we're glad to have you back, that is me and Rhea, a right little madam she was.' She sank down on the cover and patted her arm.

'Tears is it? Don't tell me Florence has taken a turn for the worse?'

Elody shook her head. 'No worse.'

'Well, this might cheer you up.' Mrs George put a slim box on the bed and drew a dress from the tissue paper.

'Rhea helped me,' she smoothed out imaginary creases, 'and I had to try it on Millie. She's not the same shape as you, another few inches around her waist.' The flow of chatter didn't stop until Elody collapsed in her arms.

'Hush now, girl, your tears will get the fabric all mussed up.'

'It's beautiful, thank you.' But as Elody looked at the gown, she thought of Florrie standing in the porch, her face ashen, she remembered the speech she had made at the union, her meeting with Lady Astor, even her dreams of being a potter, and she saw them all slipping away.

'This cream silk was a real find,' Mrs George continued, 'and them little pearl buttons were from a dress her Ladyship discarded; but we don't tell her that. Come now enough of those tears.'

'I'm not sure I deserve it. I didn't want to come back, I wanted to stay with Florence.'

'You deserve it more than anyone. Tell me everything, child.'

Elody sniffed. 'All the same symptoms as my mother, and there is naught I can do. She needs to get away from the pot bank, Mrs George, it's the only chance she has.'

Chapter Eighteen

Elody entered the dining room and Archie drew in his breath. The cream silk highlighted the gold in her hair, brought out the amber in her eyes.

'You look well, Miss Cole.'

She turned, holding his gaze, until his father drew out the chair next to him.

'I hope everything was to your satisfaction on your return? Lady Derrington and I are glad you are—'

'Satisfaction? What about our satisfaction, Papa?' At once everyone turned to Hester who was rotating the stem of her glass.

'I'm sorry, Hester, but while this is my house, I shall speak in the way I choose, and it is my belief you are cared for quite well.'

Hester opened her mouth to speak then closed it again. Her mother for once was silent.

Archie dipped his spoon into the consommé, shutting out the friction in the room, recalling instead his conversation with Elody and the memories it prompted – the last dinner with his brother before he left for the front, his mother tight-lipped as she tried not to cry, Giles and Charles Sartorious keeping the conversation going, ebullient, excited. How quickly that had changed. Archie had finished his consommé when another unwanted memory surfaced. It was there, a raw wound that wouldn't go away.

It was a Thursday in 1917, two years after his brother had left for the front. He was in his office at the pot bank inspecting the samples of a feeding cup and a new lightweight urinal suitable to be shipped to the field hospitals of Belgium and France when Hester marched in. She put her hands on his desk, glanced at the ware, then back at Archie, her voice trembling with rage.

'So, you've got out of fighting, Archie?'

'What do you mean?'

'Mother tells me you've failed your medical.'

'That's not possible, I haven't heard...'

'Did you pay off the doctor? God help me, your brother is fighting in France, and you can't stomach it, you know what that makes you—'

'How dare you, Hester, I'm going to fight, I swear on—' He hadn't finished the sentence because Hester had gone, hurrying down the spiral metal stairs that led to the floor below. Somehow he managed to slam the office door behind her, leaning against it, his knees buckling, but it was too late, the women on the factory floor below were looking up, they had heard it all.

Archie remembered his humiliation afterwards, the women watching him as he came into work with disgust in their eyes. Their husbands and their sons were dying in the trenches and on the battlefields, but the boss's son was a coward. It was not true, of course; it had his mother's hand all over it.

'Do you realise what you've done, Mother, you have destroyed any respect I've earned at the pot bank, how could you?'

'I don't know what you're talking about,' she had replied, kissing the top of the dachshund's head. 'I'm sorry if your asthma has precluded you from fighting, but that is hardly my fault.'

And there was an end to it, no apology, no explanation. Nothing at all.

The dinner returned to some sort of normality. Jacob cleared away the plates and arrived with a mouth-watering concoction of meringue and whipped cream. Elody conversed with his father about the books in his excellent library, his mother commenting that actually it was her family library, and for a change his parents laughed together. The atmosphere lightened and despite Hester's bitterness, there was a semblance of life before the war.

But Archie was wound like a coil remembering the last ride with his brother and Charles, his anguish as they came near to the stables. 'I'll join up just as soon as I am eighteen, Mother can't stop me,' he had yelled.

Giles had patted Endymion's neck. 'They say it will be done by Christmas, Archie, that God is on our side, but I have this feeling…' He had picked up the reins, urging Endymion into a trot until Charles caught up with him. 'Don't look so gloomy, Giles, by Christmas those in charge will have sat around a table, redrawn some territory and we'll be back home.'

How tragically misguided Charles had been, how desperately wrong.

Simkins filled up his glass and Archie drank it in one.

For the first time, Elody didn't rush away after dinner, but lingered with the family in the Blue Parlour. She was warm from the fire, replete with food, but as she leant back in her chair, her conscience nagged her. While her friend was sick in the terraced cottage in Louise Street, she shouldn't be at Thorncliffe Hall.

Hester was playing a hand of cards with Ursula, and Archie was debating with his father when Elody went to the window. Shadows lengthened and stretched across the lawn; a cloud sailed across the moon. She could hear the predatory screech of an owl, a distant bark of a fox, night noises that had always thrilled her.

For an instant she remembered sitting on the shed roof with Walter, listening to those same nocturnal sounds, batting their hands together to keep themselves warm, giggling when Mr Higgs came home drunk again at number twenty-three. She pushed the memory aside and was about to go to bed when something stirred beyond the trees. She was alert suddenly, her face pressed against the glass.

'Are you all right, Miss Cole?' Lord Derrington looked across at her.

'Yes, thank you, if you'll excuse me.' Elody hurried through the door, but instead of going upstairs, she headed to the boot room, pulled a shawl around her shoulders and went outside. The cold sliced through her thin dress, her delicate shoes. She picked up her skirts and ran across the grass. She was nearing the lake when she saw a small figure in the distance, his coat lifting in a gust of wind. The figure turned and looked in her direction, a boy's face, pale in the moonlight, with fair curly hair, then he had gone.

She ran after him, reached a flight of stone steps and groped her way down, algae sliding beneath her fingers. Stumbling, she grabbed the handrail a cry escaping her. Instinct told her to turn back, return to the warmth and security of the house, but something was drawing her on. A small anteroom led into a long tunnel. The smell of damp was overpowering, water dripped from the ceiling and leaked down the walls. She floundered towards a glimmer of light, her wrist catching on something sharp. When she wrenched it back, put it to her mouth, she tasted the salty tang of blood. Hearing a noise behind her she turned and ran back the way she had come, but when she reached the top step, there was no sign of the boy.

Later in the warmth of her bedroom she recaptured his face, the wide forehead, the strange, unsettled eyes. Had it been a game, she wondered. Was he inviting her to join in? And who was this child who ran through the garden at night?

As she climbed into bed, pulled the blankets to her chin, her hand closed around the locket at her neck. She bit her lip to stop herself from crying. Walter had gone from her life, but the small child flying across the lawn had brought back memories of her cousin. Perhaps it was the coat flapping, perhaps it was his wild curly hair.

The following morning Elody's heart sank. The hem of her dress was spattered with mud, she had ruined her beautiful gown.

'Well, that's a fine thing, Miss Cole.' Mrs George's arms were folded as she surveyed the damage.

'Cavorting round the garden after all my hard work. I've a mind to take it off you, give it to someone who'd like it better.'

Elody took her hands. 'I apologise, I was carried away, there was this boy and the handprint in the glass and …'

'What nonsense is this?'

Elody repeated the story.

'Listen, duck, if I knew about a boy, I wouldn't talk about it, not in this house. A piece of advice, keyholes are for meddlers.'

'But I'm not being nosy, I'm …'

Mrs George took a clothes brush from her pocket. 'Lucky for you it's coming off,' she said, taking gentle swipes at the mud.

'I'm so sorry, Mrs George, it's the prettiest dress I've ever owned and …'

'Well, speak no more about it.' Mrs George smoothed the hem and gave Elody a look. 'And no more questions about the boy.' She put the brush back in her pocket and marched from the room.

Next Elody asked Millie about the child, but the reply was the same, it was quite apparent that if she knew she was not prepared to say. As Elody went to the library she was confused, it was as if the child did not exist. When Archie found her, the skin was taut across his cheekbones, his mood very different from the night before.

'I've heard you're asking questions about things that don't concern you.'

Elody felt a tightness in her chest. 'If you're talking about the child, I have a right to be concerned. Who is he, Archie, and what is he doing in the grounds at night on his own?'

'If the boy is not sufficiently supervised then that's our fault, but the rest ...' He paused, a muscle working in his cheek. 'It's nothing to do with you so please don't meddle in other people's affairs.'

'Do you honestly think—' Elody drew in her breath and stalked from the room.

The following day was Saturday, and Elody was once again in the library. She had balanced her copy of the *Sentinel* on the music stand and was reading an editorial on the women's movement in the Midlands when she felt the presence of someone behind her. She closed the newspaper and spun about.

'Reading something controversial, Miss Cole?' Archie's voice was light once more.

Elody didn't respond.

'Look, about yesterday, I'm sorry.'

'You should be.'

'As an offering of peace would you allow me to show you around?'

'I think you can see I'm busy.'

'You could read the *Sentinel* later, it's hardly entertaining.'

'Perhaps I don't feel like being entertained.'

A shadow crossed his face. 'Yes, I was rude, and again I apologise, but the sentiments have to be the same. There are some things that are better left alone. Please, Miss Cole.'

Elody fiddled with her sleeve. She tried to hold onto her anger but somehow the knot in her stomach was uncurling.

'I'm sure you've already explored the garden but there has to be territory as yet uncharted, the history is actually interesting.' Archie was wearing corduroy trousers and a cashmere jersey and despite herself Elody couldn't help noticing that the blue matched the colour of his eyes.

'Are you attempting to be nice to me?'

'Most definitely. There's a glimmer of sunshine outside, and at this time of year there's so little of it.' He gave his most winning smile.

Elody was thawing. 'Perhaps you should make your invitation more inviting.'

Archie laughed. 'Dear Miss Cole, may I presume upon you to walk with me? I think that's how my grandfather would have put it.'

'And you think with a few fine words I'll fall in line.'

'Touché, Miss Cole.'

Elody wasn't sure what *touché* meant but it sounded relevant. She wanted to refuse, but she couldn't resist.

'Only because I'm interested in the history, you understand.'

This time dressed appropriately in lace-up boots and a coat, she met Archie outside. They walked towards the lake, entering the small stone temple where Elody admired a marble bust on a slim pillar. Archie came to stand beside her.

'She has an extremely long neck,' Elody observed.

'My ancestor, the twelfth Countess of Hamilton. She was said to have been a great beauty.'

'She looks like your mother.'

'As you know from dinner recently, when my parents so readily aired their discontent with each other, the house originally belonged to my mother's family, so not that surprising. In those days they were extremely wealthy, employing Humphrey Repton to design the garden. The temple was part of his grand plan.' He gave a slightly lopsided smile. 'Come on, I'll show you the rest.' They moved on past the lake and entered a large semi-circular amphitheatre, where bindweed and thistles grew through the roses, choking the life from them.

'The rose beds were apparently the last countess's pride and joy, the amphitheatre was kept together in her memory, but war came, and now there are no young men left to tend it, and no incentive.' His voice was ragged. 'The gardener tries his best, but all this?' He shrugged his shoulders, and walked out through the gate, banging it shut behind them. They wandered on in silence until they entered the woods.

'Did you know trees speak to each other? They communicate through their complex root system.'

'You mean really talk to each other?'

'In a way, yes.' Archie's eyes were focussed again. 'If they are in danger, they let their neighbour know, they actually protect each other. We could learn a lot from them, Elody.'

'My mother always said it was us humans who made the trouble.'

'A wise woman.'

They reached a horse chestnut, the knotted boughs descending to the ground.

'My favourite tree to climb as a child, sitting up there was like being on top of the world.'

'We could climb it now.' Elody challenged.

'Now, Miss Cole?'

'Definitely, beat you to the top,' and before he could stop her, she had thrown off her coat and was scrambling up the tree, getting a foothold here, a grip there, pulling herself up until she was sitting in the branches above him.

Seconds later he had reached her. 'Move along, Miss Cole.' He bumped her along until they were both laughing.

'I see a competitive side to you I hadn't noticed before.'

Elody put her head on one side, her tawny eyes wide. 'At school I always wanted to be the first with the answers, the best, does that make me a bad person?'

'Not necessarily, just—'

'Competitive,' Elody finished for him.

Archie's voice softened as they clambered down. 'Giles taught me to climb on this very tree.'

Elody jumped to the ground and for a brief second their gaze met. She felt a jolt of recognition, before looking away.

They were passing the steps to the underground tunnel when he caught her arm.

'Don't go down,' he instructed. 'Please, Elody; it leads to an old grotto, but the roof is unstable. We were going to restore it, put in new beams, but that was before the war.'

'It should be closed up, someone could get hurt.' Elody's voice rose sharply. Now was the time to tell him about the child.

'If you keep away from it, what on earth could happen? You don't strike me as a worrier, Miss Cole.' Elody opened her mouth to speak but the words dried in her throat.

Chapter Nineteen

Though Elody didn't see the boy she sensed he was watching her. Out on the moors she turned occasionally, hearing a twig breaking, a snipe calling out in alarm. She hoped he hadn't followed her; it wasn't safe for a boy on his own.

It was here on the moors beneath a shifting sky that the sketches continued. Bowls with fluted edges filled the pages of her sketchbook, plates, jugs. When the last page was finished, she collected her bicycle and set off for the pot bank.

Jacob Shaw passed her in the drive. 'I can save you the trouble, deliver your parcel on my way to collect his lordship and Mr Archie this afternoon.'

'Thank you, but I can take it myself.' She smiled at Jacob. 'It will give me a chance to see my friends.'

Elody paused on the threshold of the painting studio, observing the broken plates abandoned on the floor, the particles of dust spinning in the air, her friends setting up their stations for the day.

Florence came over, nodded her head towards Dawn. 'Today she's the one you need to be concerned about.'

Elody walked across the boards noticing the lank hair beneath Dawn's grubby cap, the sallow skin. Alarm fluttered inside her.

'Are you resting up, looking after that baby?'

'Chance would be a fine thing.' Dawn let her hand rest on the swell of her stomach. 'But I admit, I'm so bloody tired.'

'Get that husband of yours to cook his own dinner when he returns from the mines, you have a baby growing inside you.'

Dawn gave a lopsided grin. 'Since when have you become the authority on my condition?'

'Since now,' Elody replied.

At break the girls questioned her; their previous suspicion gone. They wanted to know everything about Thorncliffe Hall.

'Is there a cook and a butler in one of them smart uniforms, and someone to make your bed?' Dawn raised her eyes to heaven. 'Oh, but I'd give my eye teeth for a steak cooked all nice and rare.'

'Aren't you bored idling in a rich man's house?' asked Tilda, surveying her from the doorway.

'I'd like to be here always but—'

'She needs to stay put, Tilda,' Florence spoke sharply. 'You don't get a chance like this every day of the week.'

'I can speak for myself,' Elody countered. The conversation was cut short by Mr Asland who came up the stairs.

'Have you finished the new designs?'

Elody handed her sketchbook to the foreman.

'When I've looked them over, I'll pass them on to the boss. If he approves, would you spend a few consecutive days?'

'You mean to get the samples made?' She shot a look at Tilda.

'The very same. I'll come back to you, Miss Cole.' He was halfway down the stairs when he called up, 'don't be concerned if it takes a few weeks to hear.'

As Elody cycled back to Thorncliffe Hall, she felt a lightness inside. If all went well she would make the samples, Mr Billington would commission them and ... She laughed, the wind tugging at her hair. It may be flouting Lady Ursula's rules, but she didn't have to know, and at this moment, she really didn't care.

Elody checked the post each morning, there was still no word from Lady Astor. It would come, she reassured herself, all in good time. She was walking near the lake when she saw the boy. This time he didn't run away. She held out her hand, her voice gentle.

'Would you let me be your friend?'

She judged him to be about nine years old, but this child wasn't sturdy like Walter, he was as fragile as a bird. Elody moved towards him, but he backed towards the willow tree, diving beneath the branches.

Elody waited. 'Do you have a name?' she asked, but he turned his face away.

When he edged closer, she didn't move. They remained inches from each other on either side of the willow cage. His breathing was laboured, and she could see the pallor of his skin.

The mood was broken when a uniformed nanny hurried across the lawn. 'Wicked child, Lucian, if you don't behave, I shall lock you in your room...' her voice trailed off.

'Excuse me, miss, just collecting my charge, always giving me the slip, you know how it is.'

Elody stood tall, her anger growing. 'I hardly think giving you the slip justifies locking him in his room.'

The nurse's eyes bulged. 'So a Potteries girl, is it! I'll not have the likes of you telling me how to do my job.' She grabbed Lucian by the hand and dragged him across the lawn. They had reached the end of the house and were disappearing round the corner when Lucian looked back. Even from this distance, Elody could see the anxiety in his face, the tension in his narrow shoulders. She wanted to run after him, for she felt a connection to the child, an instant longing.

'I'll find you, Lucian,' she called.

*

Elody waited three days for Lucian, she revisited the willow tree, the woods, anywhere she suspected he might go, she waited at the entrance to the tunnel, but did not go down. On the fourth day the sun came out and as she wandered through the garden it was as if her eyes had opened after a long winter. Aconites were stirring beneath the trees; crocuses were beginning to open, even her favourite cyclamens. As she leant down to examine the pink bud, she was reminded of a walk with Walter through the park in Burslem, her mother pointing out those first flowers, Walter's rapt face bent so close, his nose almost touching. He was only distracted when he heard the band playing nearby and shot to the steps of the Victorian pavilion.

'I'm a conductor, Aunty Ada,' he had called, waving his chubby hands as he pretended to lead the orchestra.

Elody sighed as the image faded, leaving a dull ache in her chest. Walking back across the lawn, she followed the path towards the orangery. She had no idea who the child was, or why the nurse had threatened to lock him away. She didn't understand why everyone changed the subject when she asked about him, but whatever happened she intended to find out.

She passed the disused tennis lawn, the sagging net abandoned and filled with holes. In her mind she could see them, Hester partnering Giles, Archie with Charles Sartorious. Was that a fragment of laughter, a golden moment captured before the war? She left the tennis court behind and rounded the corner, walking along the east end of the house until she arrived at a small courtyard enclosed behind a brick wall. Elody pushed open the gate, crossed the flags, and climbed the steps to a painted door. She half expected it to be locked, but it opened easily, the light spilling into the dimly lit hall. A lamp was on a table, a Turkish rug on the black and white tiles. Straight ahead of her, stairs rose into darkness. Before she could change her mind, she tiptoed upwards drawing into the shadows when she heard the woman's voice.

'Take your medicine, it will help you sleep.'

Then the child's voice, slow, hesitant, she hadn't heard it before.

'But it's not yet one o'clock.'

'Your lungs won't clog up on my watch. Take it, Lucian, or there will be no story from Mister Archie tonight.'

Elody drew in her breath, so Archie told him stories, he came to these hidden lodgings. Her mind raced ahead. What was the boy to Archie? Was he a love child concealed from prying eyes? And who was the mother, some poor girl from the village? At once her estimation of Archie plummeted, not because he had fathered a child – Mrs Webster at number thirty-five had three children by different fathers – but because the child was not acknowledged as his son. And the boy's mother, was she dead, or abandoned? She shook her head. A story did not mean parentage, did not mean ... and what was wrong with his poor little chest?

A door closed above her, footsteps disappeared down the passage, leaving Elody to continue upstairs. On the landing, there were two doors directly to her left and a long corridor that seemed to run the length of the apartment, choosing the door nearest to her, she took a deep breath and tiptoed inside.

Lucian was sitting up in bed, a book in his hand. A model farmyard was set out beneath the window and a revolving globe. A threadbare lion occupied the eiderdown and a large clock hung on the wall directly opposite his bed. When Lucian saw her, he shot beneath the covers, but seconds later he inched upwards, his curls appearing first, followed by his forehead until his face appeared from the white sheets.

'May I sit down?'

He nodded, averting his eyes.

'What are you reading?'

He pushed the book forward and climbed further up the bed until his bony little shoulders were exposed.

'*The Water Babies*,' she exclaimed. 'A favourite, would you like me to read to you?'

'Yes.' The word came out in a whisper and Elody's heart quickened.

She opened the cover and read to him, once again absorbed in the childhood fantasy. As the beautiful illustrations leapt from the page, she remembered reading it to Walter, his eyes like saucers as Tom the chimney sweep was transformed by the fairies into a sprite. When his gills followed, enabling him to breathe underwater, Elody thought of Walter struggling in the canal and her voice faltered.

'You're sad.' Once again Lucian had spoken and as she looked at the small boy, vulnerable in his white cotton vest, she longed to take him in her arms.

'Yes, I am.'

'Why?'

Though the child's gaze was lowered, she realised she couldn't lie to him, there was something disarmingly candid about him. 'Because you remind me of my little cousin Walter, and when he left, I was lonely.'

'Where did Walter go?'

'London.'

Lucian plucked at his sheet. 'I'm often lonely but not on Tuesdays and Thursdays because Drew comes at six o'clock to teach me arithmetic and English and not when Archie reads me a bedtime story, or when I'm working in the garden with Tim Peabody, and definitely not today. I've never been to London.'

Elody had heard the name Drew before, it was her mother's name for Andrew Derrington.

At just before two, Elody put the marker into the page and

closed the book. When she stood up, Lucian buried his face in the pillow.

'I'll come again.' She touched his shoulder, and he did not draw away. He turned over to look at the clock.

'Yes, Lucian. Tomorrow at one.'

'When Miss Phipps takes her rest, if you listen you can hear her snore.'

Elody cupped her hand to her ear and a loud snore emanated from the room at the end of the corridor.

Elody returned the following day, and the child was waiting for her. When she dropped Rhea on the bed, his face lit up.

'Her name is Rhea, and I'm Elody.'

'Rhea is a nice name and so is Elody. I like cats.'

Elody smiled. 'And so do I, Lucian. I'll spend an hour with you before work.'

'What kind of work?'

'I'm a potter, someone who makes pots or at least I want to be.'

'So, you don't make pots?'

Elody laughed at his logic. 'At this moment I am designing them and one day I'll make them.'

'Archie says Clay is named because of a pot.'

Elody laughed. 'The dog, I hadn't thought of it.'

Lucian pulled a worn copy of *Black Beauty* from beneath the covers and pushed it towards her.

'Archie cried when Ginger died, and when Joe mistreated Black Beauty.'

Elody smiled seeing an entirely new side to Archie. 'And you want me to read it again?'

Lucian nodded and an hour later, Elody pulled a handkerchief from her pocket and wiped her eyes. 'I'm not sure I can go on with this, Lucian, the poor horse is having the most dreadful time.'

Lucian touched her sleeve. 'It's happy in the end.'

Two days later, Elody found a translation of *Gawain and The Green Knight* in the library and took it for Lucian. 'My father loved the part where the hero went in search of the Green Knight in Lud's Church,' she told him, seeing his eyes on the book.

'Where's that?'

'It's no ordinary church, Lucian, come, I'll show you.' Lucian allowed her to lift him up on a chair so that he could see through the window, and together they gazed towards the distant hills. 'There is a track on the top of the moor, that leads to a magical green cavern, Lud's Church. He took me there and one day if you'd like, we'll do the same.'

'Promise?'

'I give you my word.'

They returned to the book and when an hour had passed, Elody stood up to leave.

'I saw you painting on the moors,' the child's words came out of nowhere and Elody drew in her breath.

'What were you doing on the moors, Lucian?'

'Following you.'

'It's dangerous on your own.'

'But you were there, Elody.'

Bluebells were breaking through the woodland floor when Elody started to take the child outside. They walked the gardens, the woods, the kitchen garden, always out of sight of the house.

'The swallows are returning,' she said one morning, excitement building in her chest. 'Look, Lucian,' and together they gazed at the fork-tailed birds swooping towards the lake.

'So pretty,' Lucian murmured.

'Did you know they migrate north through Africa, across the

Sahara and Morocco through Spain, and then the west coast of France before they reach us? That's a long way, Lucian.'

'Archie told me it takes them over a month. He's clever like you, Elody.'

Elody was still thinking about Lucian as she arrived at the pot bank first thing Monday morning. What was it about the child that made her heart turn over, she wondered? There was something so endearing about his innocence and lack of guile. She was distracted when Mr Peters yelled from a window nearby. 'Morning, duck, it's a good day for biking.'

She looked up, remembering her father's friend stopping by the forge on Saturday afternoons, both sneaking off like schoolboys to the Port Vale stadium for the latest game. 'You're right there, Mr Peters, it's my favourite time of year.'

'Your dad used to say the horses were right skittish in spring.'

Elody laughed. 'He had the devil's own job shoeing the young uns.'

'But he enjoyed the challenge all right.'

She waved and walked on cherishing the memory of her father before heading to Mr Asland's office.

'New designs, sir.' She put the folder on his desk.

'You look happy, girl.'

'I'm improved, Mr Asland,' she tapped the folder, 'this is giving me a goal.'

'Well then, I'm glad of it.'

She continued along the passage to the studio knowing it wasn't just the designs that were lifting her spirits, renewing her energy, but a little boy with wavering eyes.

Elody arrived in the studio where the girls were gathering themselves together.

'Morning, Florrie,'

Florence dropped something into her pinafore. 'Morning, Elody.'

It was on the tip of Elody's tongue to ask how she fared, but she kept her mouth tight shut; their relationship was still strained.

'All right, Dawn?'

The girl pushed her hand into the bottom of her spine and arched backwards. 'Back's killing me but baby's growing.'

'That's good, Dawn.'

They went to their stations and soon the only sound in the studio was the occasional chatter or expletive if a paintbrush slipped.

It was one o'clock and lunchtime when Tilda appeared in the doorway.

'It's my guess you're too busy creating your own range to have time for our campaign?'

'Far from it, Tilda. I've written to our local MP, not that he's replied and,' she paused, drawing in her breath, 'I had an appointment with Lady Astor, who will do what she can for us...'

'And this appointment, where did it take place?' Tilda's eyes were bulging.

'London.'

'And you didn't think to take me with you?'

'On this occasion she asked to see me. I hope there will be other occasions.'

Everyone in the studio was staring at them. Dawn was open-mouthed.

'You went to London, Elody, to the Houses of Parliament? You met her?'

'I did, Dawn.'

'Oh my gawd.'

Bridie put down her paintbrush, wiped her hands on her apron and hugged Elody.

'You really met her?' Her voice was soft. 'Oh, Elody, Florrie always said you'd go places.'

Elody looked above her head at Florence who was watching, a smile on her pale face.

'I did that,' she said.

Tilda looked as if she was about to explode.

'I should have told you, I'm sorry.' Elody went to the older woman.

'You ought to be sorry, taking all the glory.'

'It's not about glory, Tilda, it's about making a difference.'

'But nothing has happened, has it? I say we make some real trouble, make them listen.' She pushed past Elody and stood in the centre of the room.

Elody's voice was sharp. 'Violence is never the way.'

'The suffragettes weren't afraid of drastic measures.'

'That's because they had tried everything else first.' Elody looked at the brawny woman, anxiety growing in her chest. She was a loose cannon was Tilda Kennard.

Elody didn't cycle to Thorncliffe straight after work, instead she went to the book shop in the centre of town. As the door opened an elderly gentleman came towards her.

'Ahh, Miss Cole, how nice to see you. I've found you a splendid map of the world.' He went back to his desk and took a cardboard cylinder from the drawer. 'Made by the first-rate cartographer, John Bartholomew.' He pulled out the rectilinear map, unfurled it slowly, and seconds later they were poring over it.

'It's perfect, Mr Clarke.'

'I know it will serve you well,' he replied.

*

Lucian looked first at the tube, then fixed his gaze somewhere beneath Elody's chin.

'Is it really for me?'

'For you, Lucian, now help me pin it somewhere unnoticeable, perhaps the back of the toy cupboard door. Your globe is excellent but if we're to become explorers, we need to see the entire earth at once.'

'Explorers?' He breathed. 'Like Ernest Shackleton?'

'Definitely like Ernest Shackleton.'

'Did you know,' the child's eyebrows were drawn together, 'his ship *Endurance* got lost and was trapped in ice off the Caird coast and drifted for ten months. Perhaps he didn't have a map or a globe.'

Elody laughed and shook her head. 'You really are a funny little boy. Anyway, where was I?'

For the entire hour they entertained each other, tiptoeing across the floor when they had finished with the map, spinning the globe, visiting one country then the next. They travelled through Africa, India, China and Antarctica, but it was Africa Lucian loved the most.

'One day, not so far in the future, we'll be able to fly to Africa in an aeroplane.'

'Really?'

'I'll take you there. And we can visit the lions, the elephants, the leopards.'

'I would love to see a leopard with big, big spots ...' his eyes were huge as he spoke. 'And we'll soar like a bird across the oceans and continents. Think of it, Elody.' He rested his hand on the globe and as the world stopped spinning, his voice softened. 'Wouldn't it be nice if it were real.'

'It is real Lucian, all of it.'

'No, I mean if it was true and we could actually go there, a great big expedition with trunks and suitcases and I would wear a funny hat to block out the sun.'

'I will take—'

Lucian interrupted her, 'You will not, but it's nice to think about it.' His eyes had a faraway look and Elody remembered Walter's conviction that he would go to America, and inside she knew he probably would. That was the difference between them, one of the children believed they had a future, the other did not. She wanted a future for Lucian, she wanted him to have the world, but perhaps the child was right, it was a dream too far.

Chapter Twenty

Present Day

A draught of wind stirred the curtains, lifting the fragile sheets of paper, scattering them across the floor. Marina dived out of bed and was gathering them together when Hugh came into the room. He knelt down beside her, attempted to help her.

'Don't worry, its fine.' Marina could hear the panic in her voice as she hurriedly stacked the sheets together, clutching them to her chest.

'Are you OK?'

'Yes, all good.'

'What are you reading? Looks important.'

Marina exhaled. 'I found some papers.'

'Tell me more.' His voice changed.

Marina swallowed. 'A memoir written by the potter, Elody Cole – I made two copies.' Her voice was soft – apologetic she would think later.

There was silence in the room, she could hear the ticking of the clock in the corridor outside.

'And when did you find this memoir?'

'About two weeks ago.'

'And you didn't think to tell me?'

'I tried to but—'

'But what?' Hugh's face was pale, a muscle working in his jaw.

'You wouldn't listen...'

'Can I ask you a question, Marina, are they relevant to your family or mine?'

Marina could feel the knot inside her expand. '*Aspetta*, Hugh, that's not fair.'

'Frankly, what you've done is unfair, it's a matter of decency of... God sometimes I really don't understand you at all.'

Something snapped inside Marina. 'Do you even try? You brought me to your family home in a strange country, and instead of helping me settle in, you disappear to your office.'

'That's called work, Marina!'

'I know that word too, and I left it behind for you.'

'I have suggested so many things, the Artemis Centre, the garden, but you've shown no interest at all.' He left the room, slamming the door behind him, and as she sat on the edge of her bed, still holding the papers, she could hear the taps gurgling in the bathroom down the hall.

Hugh didn't speak to her the following day, leaving for work at six and coming into supper when Mrs Crump was clearing it away.

The housekeeper found Marina in the Blue Parlour, sitting against the sofa, hugging her knees.

'I'm sorry, Mrs Crump, causing all this trouble.' Marina looked up at her.

'I'm guessing he found out about the memoir.'

Marina nodded, waiting for the 'I told you so', but instead Mrs Crump sat down on the sofa and rubbed her back. 'It'll blow over, my dear, these things always do.'

'But it's not just the memoir, it's everything.'

'Take little strides, Marina, get out of this house, go and explore, get your mind off things. Stafford may not be the most glamorous town but there is a fine Tudor building in the middle, black and white it is, and a courtroom nearby, it would be good to look around.'

'And the Artemis Centre, you don't know where that is?'

'Yes, I do as a matter of fact.' Mrs Crump looked pleased with herself. 'Though it's in a secret location, that and the Refuge. My Atticus took Hugh's mother for her volunteering several times.'

'The Refuge?'

'Secure accommodation for women and children most at risk. It's what is says on the tin.'

It was past midnight when Marina came downstairs to find Hugh asleep in the chair by the fire. The television was on in the background, the newspaper open in his lap. How defenceless he looked, she thought, taking the newspaper from him, folding it up and putting it on the table at his side. He opened his eyes.

'Hello,' he said.

'Hi.'

'This is all a bit of a mess, isn't it?' he murmured.

She took his hand. 'I think...' her mouth trembled. 'I think we can get through this.'

'Marriage is about honesty and sharing, Marina. We found the coffee pot together, I bought it for you, so why did you keep this information to yourself?'

Marina shook her head, filled with self-doubt and misery. There was no point telling him she had tried and that he had pushed her away, because she believed at this moment everything was her fault.

'Will you come up to bed?'

He nodded. 'I will quite soon.'

*

The following morning, when Marina put out her hand, hoping to touch Hugh's shoulder, he wasn't there. She climbed out of bed and went to the window. Autumn was sliding into winter, the endless grey landscape broken by stark, leafless trees, a solitary bird flying across the sky. As she dressed, she thought of the first winter with Francesca, the early morning mists covering the olive groves in a froth of lace, the crisp Italian sunshine, Francesca snuggled against her chest in the crazy leopard print papoose her mother, Carla, had bought her.

'To keep your little one near you when you're walking the hills,' she had said. Marina swallowed, remembering the warmth of Francesca's body snuggled against her own, her head resting on her chest. She missed them all so very much. Davide, her remarkable grandfather, her parents, her brother Daniele, his wife, even their two exuberant and unruly children. She wanted to see them, she wanted her old life back, her work which meant so much to her. But if she returned to Italy, it meant leaving Hugh.

Later as she drank her first cup of coffee in the dining room, her thoughts returned to Elody. Despite being flung into a life that didn't really have a place for her, and a home where she didn't fit, Elody had never wavered in her focus. When she wanted to know about Lucian, she didn't give up at the first hurdle, if she wanted to create pottery she had done so. She had sat amongst her friends in Burslem as an equal and at the dining table at Thorncliffe Hall. She had continued to fight for other women and for the health of workers and she never questioned her place to do any of this, and all the while she was torn between two lives.

Marina washed her coffee cup in the kitchen and dried it vigorously. She felt stronger suddenly, motivated, she would take a lesson from Elody and get on with her life.

She found the Artemis Centre online and, as she read their profile, she realised that their beliefs, their aims, coincided with her own. They supported women and children experiencing domestic abuse, they advised them, counselled them. Surely, they could use her skills. Excitement was bubbling in her chest as she filled in the form and pressed send.

Later that morning she drove into Stafford going first to the High House, and the old courthouse nearby. It was no coincidence her route back to the car took her past a nondescript house with neither street name nor number, behind a securely locked door. She checked her mobile to see if the Artemis Centre had contacted her, she walked back and forth on the pavement outside. Before she could change her mind she rang the bell. At first there was silence, she rang again until someone shot back the bolts and partially opened the door.

'May I help you?'

'Yes, I mean, I hope so ... I know I shouldn't just turn up, but I had the address and I emailed you earlier—'

The woman's face softened. 'I see.'

'It's not what you think—'

The woman called up the narrow stairs behind her, 'Dolores, I think you'd better come down.'

Two seconds later Dolores appeared.

'Sarah, I can deal with this.' She closed and bolted the door behind Marina, glancing into the security camera. 'We can't be too careful, this being the drop-in centre. Come on, lovely, why don't we go upstairs and have a nice cup of tea.'

Marina followed Dolores up the narrow staircase to the first floor where she indicated one of the vinyl chairs.

'This is where we meet as a group, but we have two counselling rooms, and on the top floor the offices that make this charity work. We're getting too big for this house but none of us want to leave.'

Marina glanced at the pine table, the paper tree pinned to the wall with handmade messages hanging from the branches.

'*I'm worth it,*' said one, '*You are not alone,*' said another. The room exuded an air of calm.

She looked down at her hands, twisting her wedding ring.

'You shouldn't be ashamed,' Dolores's voice was filled with compassion. 'It's often more difficult for someone of your background to come forward but trust me I've seen everything in this line of work. Abuse isn't exclusive to one section of society.'

Marina cleared her throat, she had to tell Dolores the reason for her visit, there was obviously a misunderstanding. She drew in her breath.

'I think I'd better explain. I'm here to volunteer, not because I've been abused.'

'I see.' Dolores's dark eyes were kind behind her multicoloured spectacles.

'My husband, Hugh Derrington, suggested I contact you; I was hoping I could be of use.'

'You are connected to Helena Derrington-Blackett?'

'My mother-in-law.'

'She was a fine volunteer. May I ask if you've had any experience before?'

'In Florence I was a human rights lawyer, many victims of abuse were my clients.'

Dolores smiled and it was as if the sun had come out. 'I knew you weren't a local girl. Me, I come from Jamaica, but a human rights lawyer, that's quite something.'

'Thank you.' Marina's confidence was growing in the company of this warm woman.

'So you fight for justice for women?'

'Not just women, anyone without a voice, I protected the rights of vulnerable individuals, marginalised groups and the like. I took on cases that sometimes others wouldn't. My name is Marina by the way.'

'Well, Marina, despite your qualifications we'll still need to complete the usual checks, criminal records and so on. You'll have to fill out some paperwork.'

'I would expect nothing less.'

'You'll be our most over-qualified volunteer, but I'm afraid that's all I can offer you right now.'

'At this moment it's all I want.' Marina dropped her eyes and Dolores took her hand.

'People come here to volunteer for different reasons, obviously because they want to help, but often because they have their own troubles and by helping others, they find fulfilment. I've been a counsellor for twenty years and I'm guessing you've had more than your fair share.'

Marina nodded unable to speak. The floodgates were about to open but she couldn't tell Dolores, not yet.

'The work is rewarding, and you'll be a most welcome addition. Many of our clients are young women like you, but they're from many different cultures and backgrounds and the struggles they face are unimaginable. You can play with the children, talk to the women if they'll let you, help with the food bank, sort out the donated clothes. Perhaps you will come to our Tuesday morning group, that would be a very good start, but it may be a couple of weeks before we receive the results of the checks, particularly since they'll come from abroad.'

Three weeks later Marina returned and was met by Dolores.

'Welcome, Marina, now we need to get you inside.' She glanced at the security camera and secured the bolts. 'We had an incident last year when a husband followed a young mother to the centre and waited around the corner until she came out. Sarah was beaten in the street in front of her terrified child. She was one of the lucky ones, after living at our residential home for six months she finally managed to break free.'

They entered a large sitting room where women of every

nationality were gathered on the chairs. When they saw Marina, everyone stopped talking.

'If you don't mind, I'm going to throw you in the deep end, Marina.' Dolores took her mobile from her pocket. 'I need to take a call from Children's Services. I won't be long.'

She disappeared upstairs, leaving Marina at the edge of a group of children who were playing on the floor amongst piles of books and toys.

'Hello.' She knelt beside a young Asian boy who couldn't have been more than five.

He continued to push a large blue tractor back and forth across the carpet.

'Do you want to drive tractors when you grow up?'

He shook his head.

'What do you want to do?'

The boy finally looked up and his dark eyes met Marina's. 'Be a fireman.'

'You must be very brave.'

The boy glanced at a young woman in a pink sari. 'My mother says I am brave when...' He started to push the tractor again, back and forth faster and faster and Marina longed to comfort him.

'What's your name?' she asked, trying to distract him.

'I'm not meant to tell you.'

'Then you mustn't.'

He smiled at this, showing gaps in his front teeth. 'Mamma says it's safe in here, so I think it's all right... Ashok.'

'And mine is Marina.' They were interrupted when another child approached and stared at her. 'You have a funny accent.'

'That's because I'm Italian. Where do you come from?'

'Stafford, silly.'

'I am silly, aren't I?' Marina had to stop herself laughing, and for the first time in months her anxiety eased.

Soon all the children gathered around her while the mothers chatted amongst themselves.

As she engaged with them, Marina understood the skill that had gone into creating the atmosphere of security in the comfortable room. She noticed the posters covering the walls offering jobs, schools, re-training schemes and educational courses. As she glanced across at the women, she realised what a haven this must be, a place where they could learn to rebuild their lives.

She had been there for half an hour when Dolores sat down on the floor beside her.

'You're a natural at this, Marina. I hope you aren't returning to Italy any time soon.'

'My home is England now, so I imagine not for a while.'

'That's our good fortune. Would you be able to join us at our coffee morning on Monday next? We need help handing out the biscuits and cakes.' She gave a wide smile. 'I can see the mothers actually want to talk to you.'

Marina nodded, unable to speak. It wasn't like her old job, she may not be fighting for justice through the courts, but Ashok had touched a chord deep inside her, and she believed she could give something back.

Her mother reinforced this opinion in her nightly call.

'It is so good that you're doing this, *carissima*, not only for the children and their mothers but also for you.'

Later she retreated into the memoir, and Hugh into his office. As Elody's story unfolded, Marina imagined Lucian's sensitive face, his extraordinary perception, his isolation, and as she turned the page another face came into her mind, a narrow, delicate face with dark, liquid eyes. The two children came from entirely different worlds, they lived a century apart, but was that really true? Was time an illusion, nothing more?

Chapter Twenty-One

The Past

The more time Elody spent with Lucian the more she puzzled over his identity. Why was he locked away in a separate wing of the house, removed from the family, the staff and the world. It was a mystery, but one she intended to solve. When the opportunity arose, she sneaked a half-empty bottle of wine from the dining room and headed for the stairs.

She found Millie's bedroom at the end of a narrow attic passageway and knocked on the half-open door.

It wasn't the sight of the maid on her knees that surprised Elody, but the crucifix on the wall.

Millie got to her feet, her face pink.

'I brought a bottle of wine but perhaps you don't drink.'

'Sweet Jesus, Miss Cole, just because I say my prayers doesn't mean to say I won't touch a drop.'

'Well then, bottoms up!' Elody filled two beakers and passed one to Millie.

'If I may be so bold, Miss Cole, why have you come to my room? I'm sure it wasn't to discover my religious leanings.'

'Because I'm curious, what are you doing so far from home?'

Millie sank onto the bed. 'Mammy wanted me as far away from Ireland as possible.'

'I see.'

'I don't imagine you do.' She looked at Elody as if assessing her.

'My father was executed by firing squad after the Easter risings in Dublin in 1916.' She put down the beaker and crossed herself.

Elody bit her lip wanting to console the girl, but held back, there was obviously more to come.

'He was fighting for a Republic of Ireland, a new order.' Millie's persona had changed, the vivacious, funny girl had gone, and this Millie had sad, dark eyes.

She looked up at Elody a spark of fire returning. 'But he helped raise the Irish flag before they got him. It's a tinder box, Ireland, the Catholics don't get the good jobs, the good anything. There are sectarian killings every day, my brothers are in the thick of it. Mammy works for Lord Munroe in a big house in County Down, so did Pappy as a butler before he got himself killed. Lord Munroe got me the position here, I suppose I should be glad of that.'

'So you're Catholic?'

'Yes, a papist.' Her tone was challenging.

'I don't care much for religion,' Elody murmured. 'I used to pray a lot, but when everyone I loved was taken away, I realised God wasn't listening to the likes of me.'

'God is listening,' Millie said. 'Even if you don't think he can hear you. Anyway, that's what keeps me going.' She held out the beaker for Elody to fill up again. 'Now tell me what you really want, sneaking up here with poor Mr Simkins' wine.' She smirked suddenly. 'You know it's Chateau Margaux, the best in the house.'

Elody's eyes widened in concern. 'I won't have got him into trouble?'

'He'll think it's Archie, poor old boy usually saves the last drop for himself!' The two girls giggled and, as Elody savoured the wine, any reticence disappeared. 'I want to know about Lucian,' she begged. 'Please tell me, Millie. What is he to this family and why is he relegated to a wing on his own?'

'I'm not allowed to talk about it, but under the circumstances ...' She looked at Elody beneath her lashes.

'We've always been fed the story he's the child of a dead cousin, but I have a feeling we've been fobbed off.'

'So, who's child do you think he is?' Elody waited.

'It's my guess he's Archie's child.'

'Archie's?'

'By a girl in the village, though it could be Lord Derrington's or Giles's, a bit of a sly one was Giles.' She looked anxious suddenly.

'You won't tell on me, Miss Cole? Lady Ursula would give me the sack for even speaking the child's name.'

'I wouldn't dream of it, Millie, on my life.'

'Probably not very helpful.'

Elody poured the last drop of wine into Millie's beaker. 'You were extremely helpful,' she lied.

As she returned downstairs with the empty bottle of wine, she realised she had gained a friend in Millie, but she was no wiser than she had been before.

Chapter Twenty-Two

Elody was wheeling her bicycle down the basement passage when a change in the air alerted her, it was only a small draught, but enough to make her look up and see Ursula Derrington illuminated in the doorway.

'Miss Cole?'

Elody's knuckles were white as she gripped the handlebars tighter. 'Lady Ursula.'

'Are you going out?'

'Yes, yes, I am.'

'And you're still working at the pot bank, despite my wishes.'

'Not exactly, but I have to see Florence and—'

'And what? Do you think I'm blind, Elody? You're so ungrateful, so unappreciative of what we've done for you.'

'I'm truly grateful to you both, but my friend is dying of plumbism, and I know in your heart you wouldn't have me desert her now. As to work, it's my lifeblood, it's what makes me forget my mother is dead, my father and everything that I once had is gone. If you send me away,' she paused to take a breath, 'that is your choice, but I cannot change who I am.'

Ursula stepped aside and Elody walked through the double doors into the courtyard beyond.

*

Ursula returned upstairs and closed her bedroom door. How could it have got to this, she wondered, leaning against it, letting herself slip to the floor. She bent her head to her knees, hating both herself and Elody Cole. She remembered the day Elody's mother came into her life. She had gone to see Andrew, her prospective fiancé, at his ugly house in Porthill. As she turned the corner into the stable yard, she had seen them together, a tall woman with dark hair and pale skin. Andrew's hands were on her shoulders, and he was looking into her eyes.

'Please know this, Ada, I will carry you in my heart, but this has to end. I am so sorry.' Andrew had noticed Ursula then, his face blanching, but he hadn't run after her, he had stayed with Ada, using his handkerchief to wipe her tears. And now here was her daughter, in her house, reminding Andrew of all he had lost.

She sat at her dressing table and looked at herself in the mirror. 'God forgive me,' she murmured. 'But it's not all my fault Andrew loved someone else.' Later, as she walked downstairs, she thought of the child concealed in the lodgings next door. What kind of woman was she and why couldn't she change? But she knew the answer; despite the self-loathing, she had found no way to stop the cycle of bitterness and humiliation, no way to be kind.

Elody arrived at the pot bank in a reflective mood. At first, she had been in awe of Lady Derrington, now she felt only pity. She recognised too well the anguish on her face, the misery in her eyes. She remembered rescuing a fox caught in a poacher's snare; Ursula Derrington reminded her of the fox. She had no doubt she would hurt her again, because that's what you did if you were trapped and scared.

As Elody walked along the narrow passageway to the outside stairs, she realised she was caught between the old life and the new. There was Thorncliffe on one side and the Potteries on the other. Once she was only aware of the small streets where they lived squashed together like flies, the pot-bellied chimneys throwing sparks and flames into a pink tinged sky. The town hall, the library, the corner shops, even the chapels were the centre of her universe, but now she knew what it was like to throw open the windows and breathe the clean fresh air, to sleep in a soft bed with a feather mattress, and to turn on the tap and have hot water gush out.

Now she knew Thorncliffe Hall.

She settled next to Florrie, took up a stack of plates and was painting a rose, when Dawn leant across and grabbed her arm.

'I feel a little sick, do you suppose ...?' Elody ran her hand over her friend's flushed forehead, felt the quivering pulse and her stomach flipped.

'Dawn, we need to get you home.' Elody was surprised at the calm in her voice, the resolve.

'Yes, yes, home,' Dawn uttered, pushing away the table and staggering towards the door. But it was too late for home, because Elody had seen the blood blooming on her skirt. Dawn has seen it too.

'Help me, Elody,' she whimpered.

'I need you to lie down, Dawn,' she instructed, helping her to the floor. 'Bridie, have we any towels and we need some water.'

But there were no towels and no hot water. Dawn's cries were to no avail. As Elody held her hands, cradled her head, Dawn lost her fourth baby. She cleaned her up with petticoats donated by the girls and water from the well outside. As she lifted the tiny foetus and put it into a bucket, adrenalin kept her going.

'We need to bury him by the canal,' she suggested to Tilda who had come to help, 'and Bridie please say a prayer.' She wiped the blood from her hands, tears pooling in her eyes. 'That poor little boy,' she whispered to Bridie. 'God help us, what will become of Dawn?'

With Bridie's assistance they supported Dawn down the street.

'It's all right, everything will be all right,' Elody murmured as they took one tortuous step then the next, but it was a lie. Dawn, who had wanted a baby above everything, was a victim of the callous and unprincipled bosses who knew only too well about plumbism – what it did to your womb and to your body so you couldn't hold onto babies, they had seen it all before.

They got Dawn into her house, put her to bed and with money given by Mr Asland, Elody charged down the road, turning the corner into Lawton Street and the doctor's surgery. 'Please,' she cried, running inside, shaking off the receptionist who tried to stop her. 'You have to help my friend.'

'But I cannot leave my patients.'

'If they have to wait for half an hour, they'll live, but my friend will bleed to death. You have to come with me now.'

The receptionist tried to grab her, but Elody shook her away. 'Please,' she begged the patients who were sitting in chairs outside. 'You wouldn't want my friend to die?'

'Go,' an old lady instructed the doctor. 'We can wait.'

'Hurry now,' said another. 'You can't have the girl's blood on your hands.'

The doctor climbed the narrow stairs, his bag beneath his arm. 'She's lost a baby, I presume?'

Elody nodded, her fists clenching.

'She's a paintress?'

'It's obvious, isn't it? They're killing us one by one but it's not just the women. Why is it all about profit and money, at the risk of our lives?'

He shook his head, his grey hair sparse on his pink scalp. 'Sadly, greed is the root of all evil.'

'Something has to be done.'

'It will take a stronger lass than you, I'm afraid.'

Elody looked at him. 'On that you are wrong, sir. I've seen enough, I'll no longer stand by.'

Later, when Dawn was sedated, the doctor sat on the bed at her side.

'You mustn't try again; it will kill you next time.'

'No,' she moaned. 'No, I want a baby, please.'

'I'm so sorry but there's nothing I can do.'

Elody held Dawn's hand until her husband came back from the mines, and she told him, taking the smile from his soot-covered face, putting despair into his eyes.

Elody didn't return to Thorncliffe that night, she went to a union meeting with Tilda. She needed no encouragement to put up her hand.

'You,' the chairman of the local branch pointed her out and she rose to her feet, anger driving her on.

'My mother died of plumbism because of the conditions in the Potteries, because of the lead. My friend is sick, and Dawn Rogers lost her fourth baby today. When is this going to end and the pot banks held to account? When are we going to be safe?'

'As you are aware,' the chairman was speaking directly to Elody, 'many of the pot banks conform to the guidelines, but there are plenty that do not. We're trying to put pressure on them, but...' He raised his hands and dropped them to his sides. 'As we all know, there are owners who only care about profits.'

Elody stood her ground, her voice strident. 'I've said it at the last meeting, get the government to close the Potteries that don't conform. Stop this waste of life. We mean something, we have to.'

This time the men at the meeting didn't mock her.

'I assure you we will do all we can.'

*

Elody was walking back along the street, exhaustion washing over her when Tilda caught her coat.

'Just because you've had your say about conditions, it doesn't alter our position,' she challenged.

'It doesn't, Tilda, changing the lives of women, that's our main priority. I had to speak out especially for Dawn and for all the men, women and children who suffer in this brutal trade.'

Tilda's face started to soften. 'The poor lass, but our fight is no longer about Dawn it's—'

'I don't need you to be telling me, Tilda.'

Tilda's eyes flashed. 'Being on first name terms with Lady Astor counts for nothing, don't you be forgetting that, Miss Cole.'

Chapter Twenty-Three

Thorncliffe was becoming familiar to Elody. She could tell the way the wind was blowing by the creaking of the panelling, the sigh of breeze beneath the heavy oak doors. Years later she only had to close her eyes to conjure the smell of beeswax and lavender, even Millie's voice, like an echo in a long tunnel, Digger Smith walking through the garden, shotgun 'broken' open for safety, tucked beneath his arm, his lurcher Jake beside him. But it was the sound of Lucian's footsteps running across the gravel towards her, his eyes lighting up but never quite meeting her own, it was his frank questions that made her feel at home.

Elody was thinking about Lucian as she crossed the lawn after a day at the Potteries. She looked up, her eyes grazing his window. For a moment her heart lifted, for the child was there, his hand against the glass and then he was gone. Moments later a small movement made her spin around.

'Hello, young man,' she murmured, her voice soft.

Lucian shuffled his feet and stared at the ground.

'Where is Miss Phipps?' she asked.

'Washing,' he responded.

Elody wasn't sure whether that meant she was washing herself or clothes or even the dishes. 'Come on, Lucian,' she said. 'We don't have much time.'

She put out her hand and she could feel his hesitation, feel her own longing for physical contact with this little boy. When she felt a small palm in her own, her throat constricted. She looked down at him.

'You really are a special boy.'

'Special.' Lucian rolled the word on his tongue giving a tentative smile.

'This evening we'll go to Africa. You're a lion, and I'm an elephant and we've become best friends.'

'But that's not possible.'

'No buts, this is only pretend.'

Their time together wasn't enough for Elody, and she squandered precious moments glancing across the lawn, expecting to see Miss Phipps stomping towards them, but in the end, she gave herself up to the pleasure of being with Lucian. When he was tired of being a lion, he threw a stick for Clay, distracted only when a leaf fluttered through the air towards him.

'It's my leaf now,' he cried, holding out his hands, his face lifted to the sky. 'My leaf, Elody.'

Afterwards they sat on the bench at the head of the lake and while Lucian observed the ducks, Elody pulled her sketch pad from her satchel.

'You told me you could draw, Lucian?'

'Archie says I have excellent technique.'

'Show me.' She held the pad and Lucian took it, first examining her completed sketches. When he came to a drawing of a hare, he screwed up his nose.

'The ears are too short.'

Elody laughed and handed him a piece of charcoal. With a few deft strokes the ears were longer.

'So now we know you're an exceptional artist, draw something of your own.'

Lucian put his head on one side and Elody followed his

gaze to a pair of Canada geese that were coming to land. She was so caught up in the beauty of the graceful movement, the ripples hardly disturbing the water, the way they dipped their necks leaning into each other, that she didn't see the boy put the charcoal on the paper, the rapid arrangement of lines, but when she looked down, she gasped. The two geese were perfectly represented, with their distinguished black heads and elongated necks, even their striking white collars were rendered with superb accuracy.

'This is extraordinary,' she murmured.

'Canada Geese,' he replied.

They were walking back to the house when the nurse hurried across the lawn towards them. Elody automatically tightened her grip on Lucian.

'Excuse me, miss, may I ask what you think you're doing, running around the garden with my half-wit charge? Just wait until I inform her Ladyship.' She made to grab Lucian's arm, but Elody held onto him.

'Do you normally speak to house guests in such a way, Miss Phipps, or indeed a child?'

She could see the bewilderment in the woman's eyes. 'House guest? You're not...?'

'No, Miss Phipps, I'm not a maid, perhaps I'll inform my godfather Lord Derrington that you've insinuated such a thing.'

'No please—' the nurse's voice was pleading.

Elody's hands were shaking. 'I suggest that if you wish me to hold my tongue, you'll be more lenient with Lucian and indeed kinder. My godfather has made it quite clear that I can visit the child when I choose,' she lied, raising herself to her full height. 'And if I were to inform him of your negligence and indeed your cruelty, I believe that might be the end of your employment, Miss Phipps.'

'Yes miss, it won't happen again. Come on, Lucian, it's time for your bath.'

As the pair walked away, Elody pushed her hands into her pockets and went inside. She bumped straight into Hester.

'You look happy, Miss Cole.'

'Do I?' Elody questioned, laughter bubbling inside her.

Hester looked impatient. 'Whatever it is that's making you so cheerful, you might share it around.'

'Am I not allowed to smile, Hester?'

'There has to be a reason,' she persisted.

'It's a lovely day, Hester, that's all.' Elody continued upstairs. The last person she would tell was Hester Derrington.

When Elody reached her room she threw herself on the bed. The anger that had propelled her through the confrontation had gone, leaving her weak with suppressed laughter. What a charade it had been but how brilliantly she had played her part. She had terrified Miss Phipps with her ultimatum given in her best Sunday-school voice, and from the look on her face, she would never be cruel again.

Elody was right; everything changed after that. Miss Phipps began fussing over Lucian but from the look on the child's face when she ran her hand through his hair, he didn't like it at all. Elody spent every moment she could with Lucian, but no one in the family questioned her whereabouts. Ursula believed her to be at the pot bank, as for Archie, if he knew, he never mentioned it and Hester wouldn't care.

Every day was a new discovery for both of them. She sang to Lucian, teaching him her childhood songs and in return he taught her to play Rummy, invariably winning. Years later she would remember each charming and triumphant expression as he laid down his hand.

As Elody got bolder, she took greater risks, wrapping Lucian up, taking him onto the moors, to explore.

'That's a snipe, Lucian, and that,' she looked at a small bird with a red breast, 'is a—'

'Whinchat,' Lucian interjected. 'Archie gave me a book on birds.'

Elody hadn't spoken to Archie for days. He was always at work or going out in the evening to one party or another. According to Millie he'd been seen twice at the theatre with Felicity Billington.

'Wouldn't it be grand if they were to tie the knot, a wedding at Thorncliffe?'

Elody stared through the open window. 'Wouldn't it be grand,' she finally replied.

Chapter Twenty-Four

Lucian was dressed in flannel shorts, a thick woollen jumper and a pair of gardening gloves when Elody arrived at his lodgings.

He wiggled his fingers in the air. 'Tim Peabody gave me the gloves,' he told her.

'He did?'

'For gardening.'

'I see.'

'He needs my help this morning and I thought you could help too. You can borrow my gloves if you want.'

'You keep them, Lucian.'

Lucian was trotting in front of Elody as they went down the path towards the kitchen garden.

'Tim knows more about gardens than anyone,' he assured her, looking back. 'In fact, he knows more about most things. He could tell you how long it takes for each different seed to germinate, or the healing properties in flowers and herbs.'

'What a clever man.'

'He's able to work out the age of a tree using a piece of string, and he's made a bug garden at the bottom of the shrubbery and a hedgehog house so they can hibernate in winter. There's no living creature he won't help. Today he's promised to let us plant nasturtiums.'

'I can't wait, Lucian.'

They found Tim in the greenhouse; his big hands covered with soil.

'Morning, miss.' He nodded at her and smiled at Lucian. 'You've come for your seeds, lad, I imagine?' He handed over a packet and a seed tray filled with compost. 'Use your fingers to press a hole in the soil about three times the size of the seed,' he reminded him. 'Backfill gently, then water in well.'

'And one for me Tim?'

'Are you sure, miss?'

'Definitely.'

'Well then, here's a pair of gloves.'

For the next hour they worked in silence, just communing over seeds.

'God's work it is,' Tim told Elody, passing her the watering can. 'Plants don't go to war and hurt other beings.'

Elody smiled. 'I like that Tim, God's work it is.'

'I'm fighting a losing battle with this place, miss,' he uttered, his expression changing. 'It's just me and fifteen acres of land. Lucian helps me when he can and a great help he is, but when it's damp, it's no good for his chest.'

They finished the morning planting potatoes and, after a cup of tea made on the stove in his greenhouse, they said goodbye.

'Next week, lad?'

'Definitely, Tim.'

'What about me?' Elody asked, and Tim laughed.

'You're always welcome in my garden, Miss Cole.'

They were passing a young plantation when Lucian tugged at her sleeve.

'This is called the Peace Garden, Elody, do you know why?'

'I'm sure you're going to tell me,' Elody murmured.

'Drew planted these trees for his son Giles and all the other dead soldiers.'

'What a fine idea.'

'I didn't know Giles, but he must have been nice.'

'I'm sure he was, Lucian.'

'Do you want to pray, Elody?'

'I believe we should.'

The child looked at her. 'I don't pray much, but I do in the Peace Garden, because Archie taught me to.'

Together they stood quietly in the shade of the trees and thought of the dead soldiers and of Giles who never came back.

'I like the word peace, don't you?'

Elody was cycling to work when a car drew up beside her. Jacob opened the window.

'Would you be wanting a lift, Miss Cole, with the rain an' all? I could strap your bicycle to the back.'

'A little rain never hurt anyone.'

He winked and held up a letter. 'Same postmark as before.'

Elody grabbed the letter. 'The gods will reward you in heaven, that they will, Mr Shaw.'

At the pot bank she waved the letter at Florence and they ran towards the stable where Topper the dray horse was housed. Elody closed the door.

Dear Miss Cole,

This may not be the news you hoped for, I'm afraid.

I have made two speeches in the House of Commons, and I have been shouted down by the men. Sadly, our bill didn't even reach the voting stage so great was the opposition.

I know you will be disappointed, but we will have another

try next year and indeed the year after. That's how laws are made, we will keep going, Miss Cole.

Yours very truly

Nancy Langhorne Astor

Elody pushed her head against Topper's warm side. 'I didn't expect miracles, Florrie, even so.'

'Going to the House of Commons, making Lady Astor listen, that is a miracle, Elody! She *will* keep going, she said as much, you just have to make sure. One day inequality will be recognised, the bill will pass, and you'll be part of the making. It's people like you, Elody, who keep going in the face of adversity. You can't give up, not now.'

Elody groaned. 'I suppose I have to tell Tilda.'

'For that you'll need my support.'

They found Tilda smoking in the outside passage.

'It's not the outcome I would have liked but—' she got no further because Tilda had grabbed the letter, planting her legs wide as she skimmed it.

'I always said, them in high places wouldn't listen to the likes of you. It's action that makes them listen, Miss Cole.'

'Oh, but she listened, Tilda,' Florence's eyes blazed. 'Lady Astor is on our side. Don't undermine this achievement, she will continue the fight.'

Chapter Twenty-Five

April was coming to an end, the weak sunshine skimming across the moors giving light and life to the purple heather. On an unusually warm day Elody and Lucian were sitting beneath a dry stone wall, the Roaches rising ahead of them. Elody's arm was draped above Lucian, not quite touching, but so nearly there. The sun was on her face and her lids were heavy; she was lulled by the birdsong, Lucian's proximity, the smell of his hair ... When Elody opened her eyes, the child had gone.

'Lucian!' she cried, jumping to her feet, panic building in her chest, 'Lucian!'

It was only a moment before the child appeared behind a boulder and Elody ran towards him, sinking to her knees in the rough grass.

'Don't run away from me, my love.' She put her hands on his shoulders. 'Please.'

'I was playing hide and seek.'

'If anything happened to you.' She could hear the alarm in her voice and laughed. 'I'm being silly, nothing will ever happen to you, but just as a precaution.' She pulled a grubby piece of chalk from the pocket of her pinafore. 'You see this, Lucian, my mother gave it to me, and now I'm giving it to you.'

Lucian looked at the chalk and wrinkled his nose. 'That's a funny present.'

'It may seem so, but it was worth its weight in gold. You see it was my link with my mother if I was lost.'

'Lost?' Lucian's eyes opened wide.

'It will never happen, but if you ever get lost, I'd like you to mark the wall with a cross so that I'll be able to find you and then another. It will be like a trail that leads me to your side.'

Lucian was silent, studying the chalk. 'I could mark a tree?'

'Yes, a tree, Lucian, it's a precaution, that's all.'

'Precaution,' he repeated.

'Yes, along with whistling. If you whistle loudly enough, I'll come to your call.'

'Like a dog?' Lucian pursed his lips together and Clay charged to his side. Elody poked him in the ribs, and he giggled, darting away from her, until they were running across the moors, scrambling up the hillside to the ridge that led to Lud's Church.

'Have you had enough?' Elody called as they crested the escarpment, but he shook his head.

'I want to go to Lud's Church and see the Green Knight.'

'That's a long way, Lucian.'

'But I'm warrior, look at me.' The child stood with his hands on his hips and Elody laughed. 'Warriors need lunch, they also need to gather their strength.' She took a pack of sandwiches from her satchel and gave one to Lucian.

'You know he may not be there,' she observed, taking his hand afterwards.

Lucian lifted his clear blue eyes and looked into the distance. 'But he may be, Elody.'

They walked for half an hour climbing over boulders and rocks, but Lucian didn't complain. Occasionally he marked a cross on the wall.

'We may get disorientated.' He said the word slowly, enunciating each syllable.

'Now that's a good word.'

'I found it in the Oxford English dictionary,' he replied.

In an isolated forest on the top of the ridge, where the trees were bent and formed by the wind, they found the head of a deep chasm, Lucian moved closer to Elody.

'Lud's Church,' she murmured taking his hand. 'You really want to go down?'

Lucian nodded and together they descended the unhewn steps, enclosed by two vertical rockfaces, concealed by moss, liverworts and ferns. 'This is where I came with Walter.' Elody helped him over a large boulder.

'Why did he go to London?'

Elody lifted him over the last rock until he was secure on the shingle floor and held him for a moment. 'He fell in the canal.'

'But he didn't drown?'

'No, but my aunt was angry with me. She took him away, Lucian, she said it was best for him.'

'But it wouldn't have been best for him, would it, Elody?'

'I didn't think so, Lucian.'

Lucian touched her arm. 'I won't go away.'

They were coming to the end of the rock passageway when Lucian caught her sleeve. 'If I say the poem, do you think the Green Knight will come to us?'

'You could try, Lucian.'

And as Lucian's clear voice rang through the cavern, Elody believed anything was possible.

> *Great wonder of the knight*
> *Folk had in hall, I ween*
> *Full fierce he was to sight*
> *And over all bright green.*

Elody had saved a story for the journey home and, as they walked along the ridge, she told him about the Lollards who had worshipped there in the fifteenth century.

'They looked for the loneliest place to hold their services.'

'Why?'

'They were mistreated because of their religious beliefs; because they were different.'

'I'm different, Elody.'

'You are special.'

'My mother didn't want me because I'm different – that's why she left me.'

Elody leant down until their faces were level. 'Who told you that?'

'It's true, isn't it?'

'I'm sure your mother didn't leave you.'

'Everyone does in the end.'

They arrived back at Lucian's lodgings an hour later; the child was tired, but there was a light in his eyes. It faded when Archie stopped them.

'Miss Phipps take Lucian,' he instructed the nurse, who was hovering at his side, then he rounded on Elody.

'It is one thing to kill yourself, quite another to put the child at risk.'

'I would never put Lucian in danger.'

'You lied to Miss Phipps.'

'I told her Lord Derrington is my godfather, which is true, he at least would appreciate someone spending time with the child.'

'You think you can do as you like? Where the hell have you been?'

Elody's cheeks were flaming. 'You treat Lucian as if he doesn't exist, are you ashamed of him?'

'And you can't keep your nose out of other people's business.'

'He is obviously your child and yet you hide him away.'

'My child?'

'If he isn't, tell me for God's sake. I need to know, Archie!'

'I would—' Archie's words tailed off.

'Where I come from people may be poor, but they have compassion. You're pathetic Archie Derrington.' Elody rushed from the room, slamming the door behind her.

Archie kissed Lucian's forehead and went to turn off the light.

'Why were you cross with Elody? She is always nice to me.'

Archie sat on the edge of the bed. 'It's not that simple.'

Lucian yawned. 'I had such a nice day, we went to Lud's Church, and she told me about the Lollards and the Green Knight, I like her a lot, do you like her, Archie?'

'I do, Lucian, now goodnight.'

'Then you mustn't be angry with her, I persuaded her to take me, Archie. She said it was too far, but I wanted to go.'

Archie ruffled his hair. 'I know, little man; I would have done the same.'

Archie went into the Blue Parlour and fixed himself some whisky, his hands shaking. He wanted to weep for the life the beautiful child deserved and would never have, for his own shame compounded by the look of disgust in Elody's eyes. He drained his glass and crossed to the window, looking out onto the terrace beyond. He had longed to explain so many times, tell her everything, but that was impossible, he had given his word.

Damn his imperious mother he thought, watching a sparrow drink from the fountain. Damn her machinations with Felicity Billington. Their relationship had been engineered by her ambition for the marriage of the two Potteries. But he had been weak and had allowed it to happen; and now he had to stand by Felicity. Giles had always behaved like a gentleman and whether he liked it or not, so would he.

While Archie sat next to his father at dinner, Elody moved to the other end of the table.

'You are unusually quiet, Miss Cole,' Ursula commented. 'Did you have an exhausting day at work?'

Elody looked up, aware of the sarcasm in her voice. 'I wasn't at the pot bank today but thank you for your interest.' She lapsed into silence, longing to leave the room, the house, be away from all the intrigue and lies, but she couldn't leave, not now, she couldn't leave Lucian.

Archie caught up with her as she hurried along the corridor after dinner.

'I'm sorry my words were unwarranted—'

'The child lives on his own in the bachelor wing, he is eight years old and has no friends. He's left to the mercy of Miss Phipps and if anyone shows him some human kindness you get mad.'

'I know your intentions are good but—'

Elody cut him off. 'Don't patronise me, my intentions are normal. This family... you're all so buttoned up, you don't say what you think. There are so many secrets and Lucian's existence is testimony to that. There seems to be no love or empathy in any of you.'

Archie's eyelid flickered. 'There you are definitely wrong, Miss Cole.' He moved away from her, stopped at the foot of the stairs. 'But you're right, you must have access to Lucian. I will tell Miss Phipps.'

'But why is he hidden away?' Her voice was louder than she meant, harsher.

'My mother—' He started to say something and stopped. 'There are things that are better left unsaid.'

'Unsaid? We're talking about a child's life.'

'I know you think badly of me,' he said at last, 'but let me say one thing, the child is sick – he's unlikely to reach adulthood.'

'I'm not blind, but there are specialists.'

'We're not demons, the best doctors from London have examined Lucian but all your administrations will not change the outcome. I suggest you don't get too fond of him, Miss Cole.'

Two days later, Archie caught her arm as she was going into the library. She shook it off.

'Please don't run from me, Elody.'

'I'm not running.'

'I have something to tell you.'

'I'm not sure anything you have to—'

'There is an internal door to Lucian; it's never locked.'

Elody turned. 'Why are you telling me this now?'

'It's the least I can do after…' He seemed uncertain suddenly, all the polish gone. 'I don't want you to think badly of me, I would do—' The conversation was cut short when Ursula swept down the passage towards them.

'Archie, I wish to discuss the annual family picnic in May. Miss Cole, if you feel uncomfortable, you don't have to attend.'

Elody flinched. 'Be assured there is no need to include me.'

'You're talking about a picnic in over a month's time,' Archie's voice was sharp. 'While Elody is living with us, she's part of this family.'

Ursula's eyes narrowed. 'Miss Cole is hardly—'

'Mother,' Archie interrupted, 'Elody has no other family.'

Ursula opened her mouth to speak, shook her head, and marched into the Blue Parlour, banging the door behind her.

As Elody walked away she was confused. Archie had fought for her; he was trying to make amends.

*

The door was life changing for Elody, enabling her to slip in and out of Lucian's lodgings with ease. She went to his room when the child was sleeping, watched the rise and fall of his chest. She was able to tell by the merest flicker of his eyelid whether he was at peace or if his dreams were turbulent. Occasionally she gathered him in her arms and rocked him to sleep.

She was at the pot bank nearing the end of a day's work, when she put down the plate she was working on and gathered up her things. Something was wrong, she was sure of it. She glanced across at Florrie and Dawn; this time it wasn't her friends who needed her, but the child at Thorncliffe Hall. Running along the passage she collected her bicycle and didn't stop pedalling until she reached the herbalist on the corner of Bluestone Avenue.

'For a little boy, Mrs Knox, something to help with his breathing.'

'How little?'

'Eight but his lungs are weak.'

'Wild thyme, oil of cloves, root ginger and willow herb.' Mrs Knox squinted at the jars behind her. 'I'll add burnt orange peel and a touch of mustard seed – good for bronchitis.' She muttered to herself while she gathered the remedy together. 'Make a poultice Elody and put it on his chest, helps draw out the muck and will bring him relief.' Then she fetched a small bottle of oil and added it to the package. 'Add a few drops to boiling water, put a towel over his head and encourage the lad to inhale the steam.'

After taking the money she squeezed Elody's hand. 'You all right, love?'

'I'm all right, Mrs Knox.'

'You have a good heart, Elody Cole.'

*

That night when Lucian was at last asleep and his breathing regular, the room pungent with the smell of herbs, Elody opened her eyes to find Archie watching her. She took her arm from around Lucian's shoulders and settled his head on the pillow.

'It's not witchcraft, I assure you.'

'Are you suggesting I think you're a witch?' Archie was smiling. 'But if anyone can work a little magic, Miss Cole, it's you.'

Chapter Twenty-Six

Elody refused to treat Lucian as an invalid, she believed fresh air and her devotion would cure the child of his ailments, and it seemed for a while she was right. When Elody wasn't at the pot bank, she filled a rucksack with paints and a picnic which seemed to comprise mainly of chocolate, and they returned to the moors.

They were sketching together on a bluff overlooking the grassland below when she glanced at Lucian's pad. The boy had captured the movement of a bird in flight with extraordinary accuracy, each tiny feather was rendered with startling beauty, and in his drawing of a fox he had caught every sinuous line of his body, every ruffle of fur, but unlike the fox in her sketchbook, this little creature had wings.

'A flying fox.' She looked closer. 'Like mine but different, it's charming Lucian.'

Lucian popped a piece of Fry's Chocolate Cream into his mouth. 'Actually, my drawing is better than yours.'

That night as she lay in bed, she smiled into the darkness. Lucian's directness still caught her off guard, but he was right, his fox was better. It was mystical, more refined. She put on her bedside light and reached for her pad, quickly sketching a pitcher with a delicate neck but with a swell to the body, sufficient to contain Lucian's charming little fox. There was something uplifting about the animal flying through a night sky, something naïve that would catch the imagination after the misery of the war. She wanted Lucian's drawings to be part of her new collection, she wanted him to create these extraordinary drawings for her range. The more she thought about it the more inspired she became. Now she would ask Lucian.

'You know I am a potter, Lucian?' she began, choosing her words carefully as they wandered through the garden picking dandelion clocks and blowing the seeds to the wind. He nodded and held out the fragile stem.

'It's your turn, Elody.'

'What would you say if my wish was for a range of china, the Lucian range. I would design the pieces, we could make some samples, and your beautiful drawings would decorate the surface.'

'You would need a wheel to make the china.'

Elody realised that Lucian was one step ahead of her.

'I admit it is an obstacle...'

'What is an obstacle?'

'Something that gets in the way.'

Lucian picked another seed head and looked up at Elody. 'Then I shall wish for a potter's wheel.'

Archie was reading in the Blue Parlour when Elody came in.

'Am I disturbing you?' she said.

'Definitely not, though I'm convinced you're not here to ask me about my day.' Elody could hear the amusement in his voice, the slight irony. 'Perhaps you've come to discuss *War and Peace*? When I saw you had chosen it, I took it as my recommendation, though I doubt that too.' He tapped his fingers on the cover. They were like Hester's fingers, Elody mused, tapering and long.

'You'll be aware that your mother banned me from the Greenfield Works.'

'I had heard.' Archie was looking at her, one eyebrow raised.

'And I ignored her, but I can't apologise—'

'Go on,' he encouraged.

'The thing is, I have a favour to ask.'

'I see.'

'I'm creating a range, and I need to make the samples and—'

'You must think I'm blind, Elody,' he interrupted. 'Of course I know what you've been doing. I saw some of the designs in your pad remember. If it was up to me, I would employ you at the Diligence Works.'

'You would?'

'Unfortunately, that would be one step too far for my mother, but give it time, Elody.' He held her gaze. 'You obviously need a wheel, I presume that's why you're here, and some painting materials for Lucian.'

'He has so much talent.'

'He is an exceptional artist.'

'So what do you think?'

He laughed. 'I'll see what I can do, Miss Cole.'

The only person to comment on Elody's recent cheerfulness was Hester who came into the boot room when Elody was taking off her coat.

'Oh God,' Hester muttered. 'Always bright, always smiling.

'But it's a fine morning.'

'Has no one ever told you it's not fine until after ten o'clock.' Hester yawned and turned to go.'

'It's not obligatory to be miserable all the time like—' the words were out, and it was too late to stop them.

'Like me, Elody.' Hester stopped in the doorway and faced Elody. 'Is that what you were going to say?'

'I'm sorry, I didn't mean to be rude, but my mother said you should make the best out of life whatever your situation.'

'Good for your mother, Elody, but if I may suggest your situation at Thorncliffe must be better than before?'

Elody flushed. 'It depends what you perceive by better; if you mean I only have to turn on the bathroom tap for hot and cold water to run out, then I'm fortunate, but I have to face your taunts every day so no, it can't be better.'

'Excuse me, I'm sorry that you do not appreciate my humour or our hospitality.'

Elody cleared her throat. 'Humour? Really, Hester, what is wrong with you? Do you think your unhappiness gives you the right to be unkind?' She picked up her shoes and left.

'As usual I got that one wrong,' Hester shrugged to her retreating back.

Chapter Twenty-Seven

Elody was already in the dining room when Hester slid into her chair, avoiding her mother's gaze.

'Have you mislaid something, Hester?' Ursula's voice was cold. 'You are fifteen minutes late.'

'No, Mama.'

'Perhaps you've been looking for this?' Ursula tapped a finger on the sheet of paper at her side. Hester blushed, started to say something then got up as if to leave. Her mother's voice stopped her.

'Sit down, Hester.'

Hester sank back in her chair and stared at her plate.

'Were you going to tell us that you had applied for a job as a chorus girl?'

'I don't know what you're talking about.' Hester swallowed hard.

'I believe you do.'

'Please, Mama, not now.'

'Do you think that is a suitable profession for the grand-daughter of an earl?'

Archie started to laugh. 'A singer, Hester. Good for you.'

Ursula glared at him. 'How dare you, Archie?'

'Anyway, it's not for the chorus—'

Ursula interrupted her, giving vent to her vitriol.

'I hardly think you have the necessary attributes. You'll have to show your legs, and do we even know if you can sing.'

'Perhaps you would, if you had bothered to listen,' Hester muttered beneath her breath.

'What did you say?'

'Nothing, Mother.'

A tear slipped down her cheek, but the attention was diverted from Hester as Elody pushed back her plate.

'Excuse me, Lady Ursula,' she said, her voice clear in the silent room. 'The application was mine.'

'Yours, then what was it doing in Hester's room?' Ursula's head swivelled to face Elody.

'I wanted her to look after it, she agreed, and before you ask, I can certainly sing.'

Lord Derrington who had been quiet until now started to clap. 'Well spoken, Elody. Really Ursula you have said quite enough. Whoever the form belongs to I cannot see the harm in it. And dear Hester, though I can't remember seeing them in their entirety, I am convinced you have very fine legs.'

Ursula didn't wait for Jacob Shaw to pull out her chair, she stood up and glared at her husband.

'Why you think it is a fitting occupation for anyone in this household is beyond me. Remember you're now a gentleman, Andrew!' She nodded at Jacob and left the room.

Hester followed shortly afterwards and ran in a different direction. The door into the garden closed with a bang and Elody made to go after her.

'Leave her be, Elody,' Archie murmured. 'She'll get over my mother's insult, it's not as if this hasn't happened before.'

Much later there was a knock on Elody's door, followed by Hester's muffled voice.

She padded across the floor to reveal Hester in her nightgown, her hair in a long red braid. Elody stood aside.

'Sorry to disturb you but I wanted to thank you and indeed to apologise,' Hester stammered. 'Not enough I know.'

'There is no need.' Elody looked up and their eyes met. 'I couldn't let your mother humiliate you, it wasn't fair.'

'But I haven't been very kind.'

Elody was tempted to say she had been quite the opposite. 'No one's acting as they would in normal times.'

'You make me ashamed. Instead of treating you with compassion, I've done everything in my power to make you uncomfortable.'

Hester sat down at the dressing table and fiddled with a brush. 'You have gifts I could never aspire to, Elody, you light up the room when you enter, whereas I'm dull and unkind.'

'You could never be dull. You have a sharp tongue to be sure, then so do I.'

Hester giggled. 'You realise there was a terrible flaw in your story, how could you have possibly filled out my form?'

Elody shrugged. 'It does seem a little far-fetched, your mother certainly didn't believe me.'

'But she didn't dare call you a liar!' Hester put down the brush. 'I admit I've been jealous of you, and I'm truly sorry. Apart from your looks, there's something intriguing about you, wild and untamed. Even your speech is difficult to ignore.'

'Now *you* are being rude.' Elody was smiling.

'No, this time I'm not. You draw people to you like a moth to a candle, you are most unusual, Elody.'

'I shall take that as a compliment.'

'Definitely, and I'm not good at compliments.'

The girls laughed and it was the beginning of a thaw, it would take weeks for them to be friends, but it was a start. They talked about the theatre and the excitement it held for Hester away from her constricted life.

'I want to do something challenging,' she admitted, making a temple of her long white fingers. 'I want to do something that will take me away from here.'

Elody nodded. 'It seems we both need to do more in this life. I, for one, will never be a slave to a man, nor will I be bound to the kitchen sink.'

Hester's eyes lit up. 'And neither will I,' she agreed.

Chapter Twenty-Eight

Elody had finished breakfast when she found the brown envelope on the silver tray in the hall. She opened it quickly.

If you were able to spend two consecutive weeks at the pot bank to make the samples, it would suit us well. Mr Billington has suggested the week commencing Monday the 25th and if all goes according to plan, your future as a potter looks secure.

Sincerely Harold Asland.

When she handed the letter to Lucian, he screwed up his nose. 'In my calculation that is 6720 seconds at the pottery when you won't be with me.'

'I'll make it up to you, I give you my word.' She tapped his nose. 'Stories every evening, perhaps I could stay the whole night if Miss Phipps isn't looking.'

Lucian giggled 'When she's snoring!'

'Definitely.' As they walked the path behind the lake, Elody made a promise to herself that this extraordinary little boy would never slip away from her, she would never let him down.

They had reached the pavilion when they bumped into Hester coming out.

Lucian dragged on Elody's hand and tried to turn around.

'You know Hester, Lucian.'

He looked up at Elody. 'She always avoids me.'

Hester pretended she hadn't heard. 'I'm hiding from Mother, Lucian.'

'Why are you hiding?'

'Because I've been practising my audition piece.'

'What's that?'

'It's a test to see if I'm accomplished enough to sing in the theatre.'

'And are you?'

'I rather doubt it, Lucian, at least my mother doesn't seem to think so. Now, if you'll excuse me, I have to go.'

'I can test you if you like.' Lucian fiddled with the toggles on his coat.

Hester hesitated, then she smiled. 'Come with Elody to the Temple at five tomorrow and I'll be there.'

Unfortunately, when Elody arrived to collect Lucian the following day, Miss Phipps was waiting.

'The lad is a mite pale and off his food.'

'Have you taken his temperature'? Elody's voice rose.

'I was about to, I thought—'

Before she had time to finish the sentence, Elody had gone, flying along the corridor, ripping back the bed sheets and placing her ear against Lucian's chest. When she heard the bubbling, wheezing symphony of noise, she called out to the nurse. 'Bring me warm water and some towels. Now, Miss Phipps, we need to get his temperature down.'

An hour later Lucian was sleeping quietly, and Miss Phipps was darning socks in the chair.

'If anything changes you will get me, you understand?' Elody glanced at her watch. 'Anything at all.'

'Mr Archie said that—'

'I don't care what anyone said, you will find me, Miss Phipps.' Elody ran across the lawn, but when she reached the Temple, Hester had gone.

At dinner she chose a place next to her, but Hester turned away.

'I'm sorry, Lucian is unwell,' Elody apologised. 'I was unable to leave.'

Hester's expression softened. 'If that is the case then...'

'That is the case, can we try again?'

Two days later Elody was able to hear Hester sing. It was raining as the girls ran across the lawn to the Temple.

'We don't have to worry about Mother.' Hester shook the drops from her coat and sat down on the marble bench. 'The merest suggestion of bad weather and she stays inside. And how is Lucian?'

'A little better, but still in bed.'

Hester looked at her hands. 'I imagine you think I'm awful.'

'I don't understand why that wonderful little boy is shut away, why you all avoid him except Archie and your father.'

Hester's face reddened. 'You'll think I'm weak, and you're right, but my mother made me promise to keep away from him, to act as if he didn't exist.' She grimaced. 'Apparently, he's the illegitimate child of Seymour Derrington, a distant cousin.'

'And do you have a distant cousin called Seymour Derrington?'

'Not that I know of, but he conveniently died in the war. At first, I believed the child was Archie's, but I don't think so. I had a terrible row with him about three months after Lucian arrived. He begged me to go to Mother with him, said we should stand up to her together, but I refused... I didn't want any more confrontation, any more unpleasantness.' She bit her lip and got to her feet, stopping in front of the bust of her ancestor.

'I've always thought this statue looks like Mother,' she mused. 'Cold and unreachable.'

She turned back to Elody. 'Archie said he was ashamed; it was of no consequence whose child Lucian was, he should live as one of the family … like you, I suppose.'

Elody met her gaze. 'Like me, Hester.' For a moment she was silent, absorbing all the information, reassessing everything she had heard.

'I overheard Jacob saying Giles left something of himself behind, but the timing's all wrong, and he was so decent, Elody, not the type to get a girl pregnant.'

'Your father?'

'I doubt it, he's hardly romantic.'

'Supposing he was Giles's child, surely your mother would keep him at her side?'

'His illegitimacy wouldn't fit with her image of a perfect family.' Hester's laugh was harsh. 'Perfect family indeed, we're the most flawed family I know.' She dropped her eyes. 'It wasn't always like this. Mother was affectionate with Giles, but she lost everything when he died.'

'She still had you and Archie.'

'Giles was her favourite. I have tried to please her, make her like me but she doesn't even see me.' She rubbed at a spot of dirt on the statue. 'She was very beautiful you know; I'm told the entire male population of Staffordshire was in love with her. They were the perfect couple. Can you imagine, Papa was the life and soul of the party, but it was as if a light switched off in his head when my brother died. He was floundering on his own, little realising he could have turned to me.'

'I'm so sorry.'

'That's why I hated you. Father seemed better when you arrived. You bring people to life, even Archie.'

'But not your mother!'

Hester laughed her eyes lighting up. 'Well, you've certainly brought her to life but not in the right sort of way!'

She stood up and shook her head as if banishing the subject from her mind and from the conversation.

'I wanted to be a nurse, but that didn't suit Mother, now I'm about to do something even less acceptable.'

'Well, let me hear you sing before I return to Lucian.'

Years later Elody had only to close her eyes to recall Hester's voice, sweet and low, and her face that lit up with an inner beauty.

> *After you've gone and left me crying,*
> *After you've gone there's no denying,*
> *You feel blue, you feel sad,*
> *You'll miss the only pal you've ever had.*
> *There'll come a time, now don't forget it,*
> *There'll come a time, when you'll regret it*

When she reached the end, Elody was silent.

'Well, was it all right?'

Elody cleared her throat. 'You don't need any help from me, Hester.'

'Really?'

'You'll give the world something beautiful, something to be happy about. I can see your name in lights, Hester Derrington.'

'Except it won't be Hester, it will be ... something romantic.'

Elody thought for a moment, a smile pulling at the corner of her mouth as she remembered the name of the heroine in a book she had read. 'How about Chantal Blanchet?' She drew out the syllables.

'Chantal Blanchet.' Hester drew back her shoulders and pursed her lips, trying to look French.

'Or Kat, because you're slinky and mysterious. I can see you stalking the stage, looking at the audience with your feline eyes – yes, it has to be Katarina, Kat for short.' Soon they were both laughing and for a brief while, all the hurt, the misery was forgotten, and they were able to behave like ordinary girls.

They were walking back to the house when Hester cleared her throat.

'I have something to ask you.'

'Yes?'

'I probably should have invited you before, but would you care to join me in my French lessons? Mr Medley is a good teacher, and you'll get going in a flash.' She smiled and Elody felt warm inside.

'I would love to, but soon you'll leave Thorncliffe Hall and there'll be no time for the French tutor.'

Hester glanced at her and she was laughing. 'There will always be time for Mr Medley.'

Chapter Twenty-Nine

Elody arrived at the pot bank and was greeted by Mr Asland.

'I've made a place for you, in the throwing room, but don't expect the men to be happy about it, Miss Cole.'

He opened the door for her and as she inhaled the pungent scent of warm, wet earth she glanced at the five men bent over their wheels and then back to Mr Asland.

'I'm not expecting happiness from the likes of them.'

Mr Asland shook his head and smiled. 'Mr Billington is never one to miss a business opportunity, if he likes the samples.'

'I'll not let you down.'

'I have high expectations of you, Miss Cole.'

Elody put on her pinafore, filled a bucket with cold water, and settled herself on the wooden stool, aware of the charged atmosphere in the throwing room.

'Taking our bloody jobs,' Spit Goodwin muttered from the wheel at her side. 'A woman's job is bringing babies into the world, cooking and washing.'

'Aw, Spit, you know as well as I do, Mrs Goodwin does all that and more. Mother told me she has the best allotment in Dolly's Lane, and she sends out sewing. You've a lot to be grateful for.'

'I'll give you that,' he muttered with the suspicion of a grin.

'She's a good woman is Mrs Goodwin. But,' he growled, 'her place is still in the home.'

They argued a while longer, but Elody could see Spit was beginning to enjoy the altercation. Each sample she turned, he examined carefully, walking around it, muttering, but she could see the growing respect in his eyes.

On the last evening when she was about to leave, he doffed his cap.

'Humph. Not bad for a girl, I suppose.'

Elody was packing her satchel when Tilda caught up with her.

'I was a little hasty about Lady Astor. It was a good thing you did, Elody.'

Elody frowned; this was an about turn for Tilda Kennard.

'This is our crusade, a women's crusade, I'm behind you, Elody.'

Elody looked at her closely; was she being genuine, she wasn't sure, but she could do with her help, she was a strong woman was Tilda Kennard.

'Our aims are the same, but not the way we wish to achieve them. I'm not interested in violence, Tilda.'

'I've been thinking on it, Elody, and we can try it your way.'

'It's my way or nothing.'

'Your way, Elody, and if you agree I'll organise a meeting, get the women together.'

Elody nodded. 'That sounds like a good idea.'

Elody and Lucian now spent every hour they were together outside. When they weren't painting or walking with Clay, Lucian lay on a rug, his head on the cushion next to hers. Elody told him stories, but sometimes they just looked up at the sky.

'I like the sky, don't you, Elody? It's so big and we're so little.'

'I like it too, Lucian.'

'It calms me, Elody,'

'Me too, Lucian.'

When Elody offered to take him to the well dressing ceremony at the nearby village of Endon, he declined.

'You know I wouldn't enjoy it, Elody, all those people...'

'Well then, I'll tell you about it instead.'

As they sat in the shade of the willow tree, she told him of the Celts who had started the custom of dressing the wells in May with beautiful flowers.

'To thank the gods for giving them water,' she explained.

'And after the Celts?'

'Came the Roman, Saxon and Norman invaders. It was later abandoned by the early Christians who believed it was a pagan ceremony, but luckily the tradition wouldn't die. It started again not far from here at a village in the Peak District called Tissington. Do you remember we read about the Black Death?'

The child nodded.

'This village escaped the wave that swept through the country so in gratitude, the ceremony started again.'

'But there is no more Black Death so why do we still bless the wells?'

Elody laughed; Lucian saw things with a clarity she had never met before.

'Because water gives us life, Lucian.'

'I like that, Elody,' he sighed and closed his eyes.

Later she asked Hester if she would go with her.

'I've heard of it,' she admitted, 'but it's not something Mother encouraged.'

'You've been shut away in your ivory tower.'

Hester laughed. 'Well then, I shall unbraid my hair and climb down.'

At the last moment Archie and his father joined them.

'I haven't been since I was a young man,' Lord Derrington admitted, stepping into the driver's seat of the car. 'I hope you don't mind.'

As they neared the village of Endon the roads were blocked by horse drawn carts, pony traps and the occasional car.

'Your mother wanted to be well dressing queen, Elody, but the honour was restricted to the village.' Andrew turned to the girls in the back.

'She never really got over it!' Elody replied with a smile.

'And did you want to be a queen?' Archie whispered in her ear.

'What little girl doesn't want to have a beautiful white dress and wear a crown of flowers in her hair.'

'They didn't know what they were missing,' he said, so that only she could hear.

When the car was finally parked, they joined the throng making their way towards the well. The band was playing and as the parade arrived, Elody remembered her father carrying her on his shoulders to glimpse the queen and her attendants.

'What happens now?' Archie shouted over the din.

'When the crowd is silent,' she gave him a look, 'the vicar will bless the well.'

On their way back through the village, Elody noted every detail for Lucian. The well decorated with a floral tapestry dedicated to St Frances, the stalls selling food.

Lord Derrington bought the girls some candy floss, slipping his arm through Hester's.

'Don't tell your mother,' he warned.

While Hester and her father wandered off to find the jugglers, Archie and Elody moved to the village green. The children were dancing around the maypole weaving their brightly coloured ribbons.

'Did you know the maypole is a fertility rite meant to symbolise the union of the masculine and feminine?' Archie murmured in her ear.

Elody looked up at him. He was so near she could smell his cologne, see the lights in his hair.

'I did not,' she stuttered, allowing him to wipe the sugar from her chin.

'It seems you can still learn something from me, Miss Cole.'

Later, she challenged him to 'Toss the Sheaf' with the other locals, and he took off his jacket and rolled up his sleeves. Archie's was not the highest bale of straw over the bar, but he was certainly the most handsome contender.

They were leaving the village, when Andrew glanced in the mirror at his children.

'I've never taken you to my childhood home, I would like...' he tailed off.

It was Archie who spoke first. 'Then it's about time, Father, I've always speculated about our Derrington roots.'

'Your mother would rather forget them, I'm afraid.' He smiled wryly.

'Please may we go?' Hester pleaded.

'And you, Elody?'

'Most definitely.' Elody could hear the lightness in her voice. The Grange was where her mother had met Lord Derrington, this was where they had become friends.

Andrew turned off Porthill Bank into an avenue with wide verges and pillared entrances.

'The houses are quite splendid, Papa.' Hester was leaning from the window.

Andrew chuckled. 'What you really mean is opulent. But you have to understand, Hester, the area was developed for manufacturers and pot bank owners on their way up in the world. These newly rich industrialists wanted something showy to prove they had arrived. My grandfather built The Grange, and my parents lived here till they died. Your mother preferred to entertain them at Thorncliffe; it wouldn't do to bring you here!'

He steered the car down a gravelled driveway, that opened into a wide forecourt. In front of them was a solid red brick house, with a colonnaded portico and a stone balustrade around the roofline.

'You can't just enter another person's property.' Hester protested as he drew to a stop.

'I don't believe the occupants will mind, it still belongs to me.'

When Andrew stepped from the car, everyone followed.

'Why have you kept the house? It's all so mysterious, Father.'

'Because our old housekeeper Mrs Johns still lives here, I rented it to tenants who would never turn her out.'

Elody's gaze rested on her godfather as he revealed yet another side of him.

While Archie and Hester went off to explore the garden, she wandered towards the stables.

'Humbug,' she read the nameplate aloud.

Andrew caught up with her. 'My first pony, he was bad-tempered, but I loved him with all my heart. The first time I laid eyes on your mother was right here. Your grandfather had come to shoe the horses and she was in the trap. She couldn't have been more than eight and she ran straight up to me. "Why would your grandad want to build such an ugly house." I was a little affronted at the time and informed her that my family were rich, while her grandfather was a blacksmith.

'"He may be a blacksmith, but he's also the best, that's why your father pays him six pence extra to drive our pony all the way here." That put me in my place, I can tell you.' He touched the nameplate. 'We became inseparable. She had a wonderful sense of humour, but she was plain speaking, just like you.'

'What did you talk about?'

'Books, poetry, paintings, what she wanted to do with her life. At such a young age she thought everything was open to her.'

'Did she talk to you about opportunities . . .' Elody faltered. 'You know, equal opportunities for men and women.'

'On that subject we could never agree, Elody. Come, let me show you the ladder we used to climb to reach the tack room roof. On one occasion my foot went through the tiles and all hell was let loose.' He looked away. 'They were such good times, but at some point, they had to end.'

'I see.' Elody was irritated suddenly. 'My mother was as good as anyone, Lord Derrington, she—'

'She certainly was, Elody, 'Andrew interrupted. 'That's not what I meant. As I've said, our backgrounds weren't so different, it just happened that my grandfather was a farmer and found a seam of coal beneath his land, so started off life in the coal business. Realising there was money to be made in the Potteries, he took out a tenancy on a small pottery in Burslem, moving to a bigger factory as their production grew. Finally, in the 1880s with the advent of steam power, they built the Diligence Works. Sadly, my mother had chosen to forget the small farm where I was born: she had big plans for me and my friendship with your mother was discouraged. Believe me, it's a decision I've regretted. All the money in the world, the status, doesn't buy happiness, Elody.'

'And your title?'

'Services to Industry. I daresay Father gave the government a pound or two and the connection with my father-in law didn't hurt.'

The conversation ended when Archie and Hester joined them. Hester was laughing.

'Have you seen the swing in the garden? Was it yours?'

'There was also a tree house, but it must have fallen down long ago.'

'An old lady's looking at us from the top floor, Father,' Archie interrupted. 'Could it be your Mrs Johns?'

Andrew looked up at the window, a smile lighting his face.

'If you'll excuse me, I'll drop in to say goodbye.'

Elody was quiet on the way home, there was so much information to digest. She imagined two children scampering up the steps onto the roof, hiding behind the chimney pots, discussing books, poetry, arguing about equal rights.

That night she dreamt her mother was sitting on the edge of her bed looking down on her. *I told you Drew was a good man, Elody. One of the best.'*

When she awoke, she tried to hold on to the image of her mother, but it slipped away. It was true, Andrew Derrington was a good man, Archie and Hester were her friends, and yet her struggle was against the very world they belonged to. She was betraying their trust, but despite everything she knew she had to go on. As she switched off the light, she realised her mother had sent her to Thorncliffe knowing her godfather's opinions, knowing she would have to oppose him to achieve her goals.

Chapter Thirty

Elody was having breakfast with Lord Derrington, when Jacob Shaw brought her a letter.

'This came for you, Miss Cole.'

Elody's hands were shaking as she read the contents. She could feel Lord Derrington's eyes on her.

'Your friend?' his voice was gentle.

She nodded.

'Shaw will take you now.'

Elody left the table and hurried upstairs. She passed Millie on the way.

'All right, miss?'

'It's Florrie.' She looked over her shoulder, charging into her bedroom, throwing everything into her bag. 'Why did you go back to work, Florrie?' she mumbled, doing up the catches. But she knew the answer, the family needed the money and Florrie was the main provider. People took risks where she came from, knowing the consequences.

'Five minutes, Jacob,' she called down to him. 'There's something I must do.' By the time she reached Lucian's room she was panting.

'I have to go away, but I'm coming back soon,' she explained to the stricken child. She pulled her pocketbook from her satchel and took out a feather that was pressed inside.

'We found this on the way back from the Roaches, do you remember, Lucian?'

He turned away refusing to look at her.

'The tail feathers of a Peregrine Falcon. It's my most treasured possession, and I'm giving it to you to keep it safe. Can you do that, Lucian?'

He didn't reply.

'It's very important that you understand.'

'I don't.' He whispered.

'My friend is sick, I have to be with her, but I'll come back, I give you my word.'

The child looked up. 'I told you, everyone leaves in the end.'

Elody had been in Louise Street two days when Mrs Wright came up the stairs. She knelt at her daughter's side, clasping her hand as the latest seizure subsided.

'There's an ambulance outside,' she soothed, changing her underclothes. 'They're taking you to hospital, they'll make you better, I know they will.'

Elody got to her feet and pulled back the curtains.

Mrs Wright's eyes were shining in the dim light. 'Could this give her a chance, could they mend her?'

Elody chewed on her lip, met her gaze. Should she tell her the fit had been a long one, the symptoms worse. 'They could,' she replied.

While two men manoeuvred the stretcher into the back of the van, Mrs Wright passed a small bottle to Elody.

'I found this in her cupboard, do you know what it is?'

Elody took off the stopper and sighed. Laudanum, the bottle Florrie hid in her pinafore, the addictive drug that masked the pain. It was suddenly clear.

'Just herbs, Mrs Wright.'

Mrs Wright was weeping as the driver closed the door. 'We'll take good care of her,' he promised. 'She'll have the best treatment available.'

'I believe she's addicted to laudanum,' Elody murmured in his ear. 'The doctors will need to know.'

Mrs Wright was sitting on her front step when Elody left her.

'You'll keep me informed,' she urged.

'You know I will, Elody, and if Florrie...'

'There will be no if, Mrs Wright.'

Afterwards she went to Mr Asland's office at the pot bank.

'Did you organise the hospital for Florrie,' she asked. 'Did Reggie Billington pay for this?'

'I dearly wish I could own to it, Miss Cole, all these girls sickening and dying for nothing, but please know I'm praying for your friend.'

Mr Asland seemed diminished suddenly, his shoulders drooping. Motes of dust were spinning in a shaft of sunlight, a board creaked, there were footsteps in the passage outside, normal everyday things while Florrie was fighting for her life. Mr Asland's sentiments came from the heart, but her friend would need more than prayers.

She was heading for the door when his voice stopped her.

'I have something for you, Elody.' He stood up and limped to a bank of drawers pulling out a large leather-bound folder.

'The Master Potters at Wedgwood, Doulton and other grand works, they all have pattern books. I thought you might like your own.'

She looked at her initials engraved on the front; ran her fingers across the gold letters. This was testament to his faith in her. She watched him turn the first page. 'Perhaps the designs for your ware could go on one side, the artwork on the other,' he said gently.

'Like a real Master Potter?' she said at last, her hands shaking.

'Just that, Miss Cole.'

Lucian's eyes were open when Elody crept into his room. He sat up immediately.

'I thought you wouldn't come back,' he whispered.

'Have you looked after the feather?'

He nodded.

'Then you must have known I would never leave it behind.' She gently prodded him until a smile touched his lips.

'Where is Rhea?' he asked.

'So, it's the cat you missed, not me, well to think...'

Lucian climbed out of bed, crawled along the quilt, and threw himself into her arms.

Elody sat with the child, burying her face in his hair, breathing in the scent of dandelions and shampoo, then she kissed his forehead, and he did not draw away.

'As long as there is breath in my body, I will never leave you, Lucian.'

When Elody came into the Blue Parlour, Hester was waiting for her.

'How was she, your friend?'

Elody's voice choked. 'If she survives, it will be a miracle. And if she doesn't, what will become of the rest of her family? It's her wages that puts the food on the table.'

'I'm sorry.'

Elody dropped her gloves and sank onto the sofa; she had never felt so tired.

'What about Florence's father, can't he provide?' Hester lit a cigarette.

'He's an invalid who lives in his own private hell. I would never try to undermine your grief, you've lost your precious brother, but at least your family is cushioned from reality, by all this.' She looked around her. 'Forgive me for being blunt, but if you could see the poverty and hardship, you would understand.'

'You're right, I've been lucky in one way, but in another—' she paused, her silence filling the room. 'My mother hasn't exactly supported me emotionally.'

'In that way Florence has riches beyond compare and so did I.'

Hester was sitting on the garden bench overlooking the lake when Elody found her the following morning.

'Do you want to go for a walk?' Elody asked.

'What, spoil my new haircut?' Hester patted the short bob. 'Thank you, but no!' Elody sat down beside her, noticing the letter in her hand.

'What you said yesterday made me think, Elody. You're right about being cushioned from reality, but it was never my choice.'

She handed Elody a letter. 'Read it please, Giles wrote it just before he died.'

'Are you sure?' Elody hesitated.

Hester nodded. 'It's important to me, Elody.'

As Elody looked at the scribbled signature at the end, the blob of ink, she believed she was trespassing into Hester's private world.

14 August 1918

Dear Hester,

I promised I would always tell you the truth, however painful; well, here it is, my beloved sister: I fear I will not be coming home.

I am currently in a field hospital in Amiens, and kind Nurse Bly is taking my dictation. I know your own nursing ambitions were thwarted by Mama, but for once I agree with her. I am at peace knowing you are in England, safe at Thorncliffe Hall.

You may be aware, Charles Sartorius, dearest friend of my youth, has been taken from me in the Dardanelles campaign. We went through school together, holidays, all those golden summers at Thorncliffe Hall. I foolishly hoped that one day you would marry him, and he would become part of our family — it is not to be. This war has stolen an entire generation, and for what, a few acres of mud. Forgive my frankness, but I know you would expect nothing less so now I shall tell you what happened to me.

We were making a big push from Amiens, and I was escorting a team of draught horses, taking ammunition to the front. The heat was relentless, Hester, there was no shade, no cover to protect us, so when a wheel became wedged in the rutted track, the Bosch dropped everything they had on us. As you can imagine it was carnage. I was attempting to free the poor trapped beasts when a German sniper picked me out. Miraculously Endymion survived unscathed and was taken back to the picket line, but I was not so fortunate. Why we engage in battle is a mystery known only to man, but to force animals to join us on this crusade of death is now beyond me. I beg of you, Hester, please make sure he comes home.

I understand you will find this letter unbearably difficult but remember you will be in my heart wherever I shall be. Know that I am ready for my end, but please live life well and live it for me.

Always your devoted brother, Giles.

Elody folded the letter. 'I am so sorry,' she murmured.

Hester sighed. 'It's not an excuse, but ...'

Elody squeezed her hand. 'However heart-breaking, you have

Giles's last thoughts, his wishes for your future. We had nothing from my father, just the telegram.' She brushed her hand across her eyes. 'He volunteered as a blacksmith because he wanted to protect the horses. "Someone's got to look after them," he said. "Mark my words, it will be a bloodbath out there."' Her voice choked. 'And he was right, Hester, but I try not to spend my life looking backwards. It's difficult, I know, but we have to look to the future.'

'But you've lost everyone.'

'My cousin Walter is out there and one day I'll find him.' Elody stood up and dragged Hester to her feet.

'Come on. I know you hate walking, but for now it's just what you need.'

Chapter Thirty-One

'But he was not always alone, because years afterwards he became a man and married. But that is a story for grown-ups.'

Elody finished chapter five of Rudyard Kipling's *Mowgli* and closed the cover.

'See you tomorrow, little one.' She kissed Lucian's forehead, and his eyelids fluttered closed.

'Tomorrow, Elody, five o'clock,' he murmured, spreading out the syllables El-O-Dy.

'Definitely five o'clock.'

She was about to close the curtains when she noticed Lord Derrington striding across the lawn; he looked up and, before she had time to dive behind the curtain, he gave a small salute, and walked on.

He was turning the corner into the stable yard when Elody ran across the grass, catching up with him as he entered the tack room.

'I was with Lucian.' The words were out.

'I know.'

'Have you always known?'

'Always, Elody.'

Relief flooded through her, Lord Derrington didn't mind. She wanted to hug him but that would have been a step too far.

'Are you going for a ride?' she asked.

'I believe so.' There was a wry smile on his face as he glanced at the racks of saddles and bridles mounted on the panelled walls.

'Yes, yes, jodhpurs, boots, stable yard, a probability.'

'I imagine you must ride, Elody, your father and grandfather both blacksmiths?'

Elody breathed deeply, the smell of leather and saddle soap, unbearably familiar.

'Only bareback, taking the pony to the field after they came back from work.'

'Then you'll have an excellent seat. Why don't you join me?'

'Me, sir?'

'I have told you not to call me sir.'

'No si ... no, Lord Derrington.'

He laughed, lines creasing around his eyes. 'Ask Hester to lend you some kit and suggest she joins us. Don't look so alarmed, Elody, I'll instruct Page to tack up Hermione, the quietest horse in the yard.'

Elody was back within fifteen minutes, wearing Hester's jodhpurs and hacking jacket.

The jodhpurs were hitched up with a belt, and the jacket was at least a size too large.

'She's having a singing lesson,' she panted.

'Ah that,' he chuckled. 'Isn't her audition quite soon?'

'Next week, and if I'm not mistaken, you had a hand in her lessons.'

'Possibly, but better keep that from Lady Ursula.'

Elody was trembling as Robert Page led the mare to the mounting block. 'You're a bit pale,' he murmured.

'I'm absolutely fine.' She glared at him. 'But there are two reins on either side.'

'It's called a double bridle, Elody,' he grinned.

With the groom watching their departure, they progressed from the yard. Elody was frowning as she tried to shorten the reins.

'You'll soon get the hang of it,' Andrew reassured her.

Elody didn't believe him, the reins were a muddle, and the saddle chafed her legs. 'Whoever invented stirrups had his head on backwards,' she muttered beneath her breath.

'I think you'll find them useful,' he responded with a smile.

They were nearing the agent's house, when he pointed his whip to a fenced-off area.

'Endymion, Giles's horse,' the lightness had left his voice. 'He is buried there.'

'Hester said you brought him home.'

Andrew threw his leg over the horse's back and jumped down, slipping his reins over the fence. Elody followed. They entered a small enclosure, hidden by overhanging trees.

'When I heard they were going to shoot the horses, I realised there was no time to lose.' He sank onto the edge of a large gravestone and put his elbows on his knees. 'It was November, the month the war ended, and the rains had come. I got there just in time; Endymion was in one of the first batches to be shot, I could hear the gunfire. Can you imagine all those precious horses destroyed after everything they'd done? I can tell you I gave the colonel a piece of my mind.' He shook his head. 'Forgive me, I've said too much.'

'No, please go on.'

'I brought Endymion back with me and Hermione, the mare you're riding. I wish I'd been able to save more, but there was no room on the boat.'

'My father enlisted so he could protect them,' Elody murmured, 'not to see them slaughtered when the British had no more use of them. In some ways I'm glad he didn't have to see it.'

'I listened to their reasoning,' Andrew turned to Elody, his eyes blazing, 'but it wasn't good enough for me.'

'Tell me what it was like, out there.'

'Beyond anything you could imagine. When I saw the craters left by exploding shells, the mud, the wire, Elody, miles of it, I broke down.' He cleared his throat. 'And what has it all achieved?'

He ran his hand over the words inscribed in the headstone. *'Endymion, charger, warrior and loyal friend.'*

'Endymion was so thin,' he uttered. 'Pining for his master, they'd been through so much together. He only lasted a year; a heart attack the vet said, but in reality, he didn't want to live after Giles had gone. If anyone thinks horses don't understand loss, they're wrong.'

Elody picked some daffodils from beneath the tree and laid them on the stone. 'He's at peace now, and if we're to believe my father, horses have the same right to heaven, and he's with your son.'

They were on their way back to the yard when they let out the reins. Everything was different on a horse, Elody recognised, patting Hermione. You could see further, and from an altered perspective. She was observing a kite wheeling above her when Andrew cut into her thoughts.

'The boys went to war with enthusiasm, little understanding what was in front of them. Many of them, including my son, exposed the sheer madness through their poetry. Giles sent me something written by a fellow officer from Shrewsbury, Owen his name was.'

'Do you have any of Giles' poems?' she asked.

'I do actually.' Lord Derrington swallowed as if the very act of telling her was breaking his heart. 'It was found in the pocket of his battledress. A friend he served with gave it to me, I keep it on me always.' He put his hand in his pocket and drew out a fragment of paper. 'One day this will fall to bits, but I have to keep it nearby.'

'Would you read it to me,' Elody asked.

He returned the paper to his pocket. 'I don't need to read it, Elody, I know every word.

> *I dream of home and bed,*
> *Clean sheets, pyjamas, mother's kiss,*
> *And these vile scenes are in my head.*
> *I long for simple things like this.'*

He had finished the last verse when his voice broke. 'Enough, Elody, I'm about to make a fool of myself but thank you for listening.'

Elody swallowed, the stark words, the simple rhyming technique had touched a chord in her heart.

'It has been a privilege to hear it, thank you.'

'Will you join me again, Elody? Perhaps Archie will come. And by the way you ride as if you were born in the saddle.'

Elody laughed and the anguish of the last half hour dissipated.

'Now that, Lord Derrington, is the biggest whacker I've ever heard.'

Elody had taken off her saddle and given Hermione to the groom, when she found Lord Derrington in the stable brushing his mount.

'There is something... something I want to ask, and it concerns Lucian. Who is his father, Lord Derrington?'

Andrew put down his brush and leant against the horse. 'For reasons I cannot explain, I'm bound to secrecy. Believe me, I love Lucian with all my heart, and I'll do anything for him. That's all I can say.'

*

Andrew was walking across the lawn when he looked up, searching for the familiar face at the window, the blue eyes staring down at him.

Of course, Elody wanted to know whose child he was, she had every right, but he couldn't tell her.

He was distracted by tapping on the window, Lucian's face, and every other thought dissolved. He ran through the courtyard, taking the stairs two at a time, and entered the small kitchen. He felt a surge of joy as the boy pushed back his chair and stopped a foot away from him, his head on one side.

'Are you joining us for tea?'

'Yes,' he smiled. 'Most certainly, Lucian. Perhaps Miss Phipps will lay another place. Five minutes for my eggs and plenty of butter on the soldiers please.'

Miss Phipps left them together in the quiet room. Andrew could hear the ticking of the clock down the hall, the birds singing outside. He watched as Lucian dipped his soldiers into the yolk, solemnly taking one mouthful then the next. When he had wiped his mouth with his napkin, he looked at Andrew.

'Are you going now, it's not arithmetic today?'

'No, Lucian, I would like you to read me a story, if you don't mind.'

As they entered Lucian's bedroom, he picked up the teddy bear he had given him shortly after his arrival and he was filled with shame. *He* had allowed Ursula to relegate the boy to a wing on his own.

He sank down in the nursing chair, cherishing the familiar ritual of Lucian climbing onto the bed, pulling his copy of *A Midsummer Night's Dream* from the shelf.

'I shall start from the bit where Titania falls in love with Bottom because it's my favourite.'

'My favourite too,' he replied.

Andrew's eyes closed and as Lucian's clear voice rang through the air, his mind returned to the night in 1917 when Lucian's destiny was set in stone. He had been working late at the pot bank, trying to forget that Giles was at the front, that his eldest son was putting himself in danger every moment of the day. It was about ten o'clock when he heard voices in the office down the hall, it was probably Mr Digby's wife, he speculated, coming to fetch him home. He walked along the passage, pushed open the door but as his eyes adjusted, he realised the two shadowy figures twined together were not the foreman and his wife. One of them was his secretary, Jane Pole, the other his son.

'Giles,' the word was strangled as he switched on the light. He put out a hand to steady himself, finding the edge of the filing cabinet. 'Thank God, you're safe ... But your letter said you were at the front?'

Jane pulled away, did up her blouse, and ran from the room; he could hear the sound of her heels clattering down the iron stairs.

He went towards Giles, the words forming in his mouth. He was trembling with emotion.

'What's going on, I don't understand?'

'I didn't tell you.' Giles closed the distance between them, held his father briefly in his arms. 'I couldn't. I had twenty-four hours leave and I had to see Jane. I can't explain everything now, but I love her. You must have noticed something when we worked here together ...'

'I just thought you got on with her, as we all did. Giles, she's married, she's my secretary.' Andrew's voice was shaking.

'Her husband is a monster.' Giles ran a hand through his unkempt hair and in that moment, Andrew noticed the lipstick on his chin, his face grey with exhaustion. 'I had to see her, she is ...'

'What Giles?'

'She is carrying my child.'

Andrew stepped backwards as if he'd been hit, confusion and despair muddying his thoughts once more.

'A child? But why... why didn't you tell us?'

'How could I, Father, Jane is everything Mother hates, she would consider her unworthy – she's married, pregnant with my illegitimate child. If I'd confided in her, she would have contrived to end this, maybe even banished her son.'

'I can't believe that, even of your mother.'

'I think you can, she's worn you down to such an extent you'd probably go along with whatever she dictated.'

'That's hardly fair.'

'To the outside world you may seem content – *the golden couple* – but you can't fool me. All those parties, people coming to stay, the truth is you don't like being on your own together. You've given up on happiness within your marriage, but I know I can be happy with Jane.'

'But if Frank Pole hears of this, he'll kill her.'

'When I get back from the front, we'll find a way and I *will* marry Jane. This isn't some sordid affair.'

'And if you don't get back?' Andrew's voice broke.

'If I don't, she has to be protected.' He took his father's hands. 'Swear to me that you won't tell anyone. I need to return to the front knowing you'll care for Jane and the child if anything happens to me.'

Andrew nodded, unable to speak, and his son's face lit up. 'You of all people know how wonderful she is, how kind. We will be so happy, Pa.'

Andrew exhaled, he had given his word to Giles and as he had predicted, he met his death at the front less than a year afterwards. When the child was born, he had paid Jane's expenses, nothing more than a good employer would do. She had continued to work for him, but it was an unwritten rule that the relationship was never discussed. When she died very suddenly of flu everything changed. Lucian came to Thorncliffe unannounced, brought by his grandmother.

'You have to take Lucian; I can't afford to bring the little 'un up and he's at risk if he stays.' She looked back at the cart where the child was crying. 'He's your son's boy and I know you'll take up your responsibilities. Please, I beg of you, do this for Giles.'

He had watched the cart roll away while the distressed infant struggled in his arms.

He recalled the row with Ursula, her hatred and bitterness spilling over when he tried to explain.

'Whatever you're going to say, I won't believe you. I know the truth, so I don't wish to hear another word.'

'But you're wrong, Lucian is your late son's child, your grand-son. You have to hear me out.'

'I always thought you were weak, but I find you're also a liar. And to bring him into my home. You have humiliated me, and dishonoured the name of our dead son, so you will listen to me. From now on, Lucian is the offspring of a dead cousin, choose any name you please. This is the line for our children, and what few friends we have left. He will be a distant relation, nothing more. Tomorrow he'll be moved to the East Wing and that's where he'll remain. I've put up with too much, Andrew, but this is the end. You will move out of my bedroom; from now on ours will be a marriage in name only.'

He had tried again.

'Don't you see Giles's child could help heal the pain of your loss? You could give your love to Lucian.'

She had slapped him, her face contorted with rage, he could still remember the sting.

'How dare you, Andrew? You're pathetic but I *will* have your word.'

He had given his word, but he had never stopped trying to convince her of the truth: Lucian was their grandson.

Chapter Thirty-Two

Present Day

Marina arrived at the Artemis Centre at eleven sharp and was let in by Dolores.

'We're so glad you're here,' she exclaimed. 'Ashok is already upstairs. I think you made quite an impression; his mother would like to speak to you.'

Rani Kumar was petite with a heart-shaped face and black eyes that were never still.

'I enjoyed talking to your son.' Marina sat on the bench beside her. 'Ashok is a special boy.'

'Perhaps he felt safe.'

'Possibly because I'm Italian, an outsider.'

'But you aren't like us.' Her voice was sharp. 'You may be foreign, but you're affluent.'

'Forgive me, I didn't mean …' Marina looked at her hands.

'Dolores says you're a lawyer, you have a voice. You weren't forced into a marriage, taken from your country, flown thousands of miles.' She draped her sari over her shoulder. 'My husband rapes me and he gets away with it, I'm his property, nothing more.'

Marina knew she would gladly put the man behind bars, lock

him up and throw away the key. At law school the students were advised to remain impartial, but she believed if you cared for the victim, you would fight harder.

'It should never happen.'

'But it does happen. If I suggest I'm going to leave him, he threatens to kill us both and burn the house down while we're inside. Excuse me, it's been nice talking to you, but I must see to my son.' She got up and went to Ashok, encouraging him to leave.

'No, Mama, we've only just got here, why are you upset?'

Marina could see Rani's mouth turning down in defeat. She had seen it all before. In the past she had been able to do something, fight for the injured party through the courts.

She knelt on the floor beside her. 'Forgive me, I've asked too many questions.'

'No, I was carried away. One day he'll finish me and then what? What will happen to my son?'

Marina spoke to several of the mothers that day, and many had the same story, a husband who took out his frustration and misery on his wife, because he could.

She handed out shortbread and cake and Jess Blake, a tall girl with multiple piercings and dyed pink hair, took a box of éclairs from her backpack.

'My Josie here,' she pointed to her daughter, a miniature version of herself, 'she loves them, so I brought them for all the kids.' She shrugged her shoulders and the women giggled.

Marina sighed. 'Can I pretend to be a child?'

The women giggled again, and soon everyone was chatting and there was a feeling of warmth and solidarity amongst the group. Josie handed the éclairs around, the children grabbing them. She stopped in front of Marina.

'There's one left for you,' she grinned, the freckles on her nose merging.

'What about yours?'

'Mum says it's all about sharing.'

'Well then,' said Marina, breaking the éclair into two and taking the smaller part for herself. 'Your mum is extremely wise, and you're extremely generous.' She popped it into her mouth, the entire company watching her.

Marina didn't want the morning to end, she met two counsellors who were holding private sessions in the meeting rooms, and Wendy in charge of collating all the data from her office upstairs. When it was time to leave, Dolores suggested she came again.

'Will next Monday suit you?' She gave a wide smile. 'They have all taken to you, I feel you must have children of your own...'

Marina hesitated. 'I...' She shook her head and followed Dolores to the door. She still wasn't ready, not for a while.

At dinner that night, Hugh was reading an official-looking paper with House of Commons Library printed on the top.

'Did you have a good day?' Marina asked him.

'If you call a good day having a case of bovine TB at Longton. The cow was obviously slaughtered and if any others test positive, they'll have to be culled too.'

'I'm sorry, Hugh.'

'So am I. Sometimes I wonder why anyone wants to be a farmer. Everything can be lost so quickly and in the case of Mr and Mrs Wood, the animals mean so much to them.'

'But it wasn't the entire herd?'

'They'll still have to endure months of testing with this hanging over their heads.' He returned to the papers. 'Bovine TB statistics,' he groaned. 'Whoever thought this would be my life.'

For a moment Marina wanted to tell him to sell the house, his wellbeing was more important than an estate in Staffordshire, but he would think it was her happiness she was talking about, her needs.

She fetched a bottle of wine from the sideboard and poured them both a glass.

'I took your advice, Hugh.' Marina could see his mind was elsewhere. 'I've been to the Artemis Centre twice now and I've started to volunteer.'

'That's good, Marina.'

'I met this little girl called Josie who came to the refuge with her mother, and she shared her chocolate éclair with me. I know it doesn't sound much but it was ...'

How old was she?'

'About ten, I suppose.'

'I see.' He speared his fork into a potato and Marina knew he was thinking about their daughter, about a lifetime missed.

'*Stai bene*, Hugh?'

'No, Marina, I'm not all right. Sorry, I ...' He left the room and Marina could hear his footsteps on the stairs, the dressing room door slam.

She finished her glass of wine. 'Neither am I,' she replied.

Marina had been to the centre several times when the incident happened. She was chatting to Dolores in the office when the phone rang. Dolores picked it up and reached for her pad.

Marina could hear a child's voice on the end of the phone.

'Please help me,' the girl cried. 'Dad's giving mum a beating, says she did his washing wrong.'

'What's your name, my lovely?'

'Josie, Josie Blake.'

'Don't worry, Josie,' Dolores soothed. 'Help is on its way.'

She held the receiver away from her. 'Call 999,' she instructed Marina. 'Report a violent crime, and when you have them on the line, can you find Jess Blake's address in that big grey file.' She returned to the call, her voice low and reassuring.

'And where are you, Josie?'

'I'm locked in the bathroom and he's banging on the door.'

While Dolores kept Josie on the line, Marina located the file, found the address and reported a violent incident in Sinclair Avenue. In the background she could hear Dolores soothing Josie, she could hear the child's sobs.

It was five minutes before Dolores finally put down the phone. When she spoke her voice was drained. 'At last help has arrived.'

Marina scheduled a meeting with Dolores the following day. She made her own coffee from the machine; there would be no more tea.

'What happened yesterday set me thinking Dolores.'

'Violence happens every day, lovely. It was no exception.'

'You could do with my help.'

'We could?' Dolores was smiling.

Marina's face was suffused with pink. 'Yes, Dolores.' Marina's courage was increasing with every word she spoke. 'I've looked into it; I can be a McKenzie friend, give free legal advice, help with court applications, I know I can't advocate, but I can provide support throughout the process.'

'We do call on them often, free legal advice is a great bonus.'

'But many aren't qualified like me, they haven't fought through the courts. I can use my skills to help people like Jess and Josie, I want to help set women like Rani Kumar free.'

Dolores put her hands together and smiled.

Chapter Thirty-Three

The Past

It was Saturday and Elody was engrossed in an editorial on the current economic hardships in the mining towns, while Hester practised her chords.

'Lucian hasn't heard your audition piece.' She put down her newspaper. 'It would mean a lot to him.'

Hester, who kept looking towards the door in anticipation of Mr Medley's arrival for their French lesson, shut the piano.

'Yes, shall we say—' Their conversation was interrupted by Piers Medley who tripped over the dachshund as he came through the door.

'I'm sorry, young ladies,' he panted. 'My bicycle had a flat and I had to run up the drive. Miss Cole, are you familiar with French?'

Elody found she did not have the same aptitude for languages as she did for pottery, but Hester was equally distracted, showing more interest in the teacher than in her verbs. When the lesson ended, Elody left the class before Hester, giving them time on their own.

She was on her way to see Lucian when Hester called out.

'The Temple at three?'

Elody and Lucian were crossing the lawn behind the shrubbery when Hester caught up with them. She went to shake his hand, but he stepped backwards.

'We mustn't keep Hester waiting,' Elody nudged him. 'She has to leave for her audition at four.'

Lucian looked at his watch. 'That gives you ten minutes to sing and twenty to change, leaving you thirty minutes for tea and cake.'

'You have it all worked out, Lucian, and you're right,' Hester's voice was warm. 'I should begin immediately; I would hate to miss my tea.'

They had reached the Temple when Archie appeared through the drizzle.

Lucian let go of Elody's hand and charged towards him.

'A little bird told me you were practising your audition piece, Hester. You had the sweetest voice as a child.'

Hester's eyes lit up. 'I'm surprised you remember.'

They sat down on the stone bench and as Hester took a deep breath and her voice floated through the air, Lucian leant against Archie.

She finished and for a second there was silence.

'Goodness,' Archie uttered first. 'You sing like an angel.'

'You have a pretty voice,' Lucian agreed, 'but so does Elody.'

Everyone turned to Elody. 'I didn't know you liked to sing,' Hester spoke softly. 'But then I never enquired.' The two girls looked at each other.

'Neither did I.' Archie was staring at Elody.

'My name is melody without the *M*,' Elody's voice was low. 'At least that's what my mother used to say.'

'Melody without the M,' Lucian repeated.

'Will you sing for me again, Hester?' Lucian asked as they walked back through the shrubbery.

'Would you like me to?'

'I think so.'

'Will you sing for me?' Archie leant towards Elody.

She could feel her heart racing. 'Maybe,' she replied.

On Hester's return from the audition, she came into Elody's room.

'Are you asleep?'

'Not unless I sleep with a book in my hand and the light on,' she teased. 'Sit down, Hester, and tell me how it went.'

Hester perched on the edge of her bed. 'I was pretty nervous to start with, but the pianist was nice and went through a couple of chords. When I gave her my music, she said it was the perfect audition piece, after that I was fine.'

'But what did they say? Tell me for heaven's sake.'

'*We'll be in touch?*' Hester put on a deep voice and the girls laughed.

'In my opinion Hester Derrington, your future is assured.'

Hester got up and danced around the room. 'Do you really think so?'

'I do, and if you've finished cavorting around my bedroom, I want you to tell me every single detail, from the moment you stepped from the car.'

Chapter Thirty-Four

On the morning of the family picnic, Elody leant from the window, peering into the leaden sky.

'The festivities will definitely go ahead,' Hester commented, applying dark kohl along her eyes. She pointed a smudged finger at Elody and grinned. 'But don't worry, you'll like them. Cousin Nigel may be pompous, but he's kind and so is his father Uncle Bertram the current Lord Hamilton. You'd never believe he's my mother's brother. And there's our cousin on the other side, Harry Derrington. He's working at the pot bank and really wants Archie's job.'

'And what does Archie think to that?' Elody's retort was sharper than she intended.

'He finds it amusing. He won't get it unless Archie bolts, but I can't see him doing that, not if Felicity Billington has anything to do with it!'

Elody shut the window with a bang. 'You're right, I'm not looking forward to this, your mother doesn't want me there, and my accent will embarrass you.'

'I rather like your Staffordshire vowels; in any event I'm getting used to them.'

Elody made a face. 'And you call that a compliment?'

'My kind of compliment,' Hester replied.

Hester was on the way to the door when she glanced over her shoulder at Elody. 'I'll look after you and you'll be absolutely fine.'

Lucian was bent over his globe when Elody entered his bedroom. He observed her for a moment, his gaze steady.

'You look nice,' he said at last. 'Where are you going, you don't normally wear a pretty dress.'

Elody laughed. 'Why thank you, Lucian, it seems I'm getting backhanded compliments from everyone today.'

'What's backhanded.'

'Compliments that are possibly agreeable and possibly not.'

'Mine was agreeable. But you haven't answered my question.'

Elody hated telling him, but he would find out soon enough. 'Today there is a picnic in the Temple, and I've been invited.'

'I'm never invited.'

'I'm sorry, Lucian.'

'I heard Miss Phipps say that I'm odd, is that why, Elody? She said I never look people in the eye, and I have obsessive behaviour.' He twisted his fingers together. 'I don't like looking at people, it makes me feel funny inside and I've looked up obsessive.'

'You are an extraordinary child.'

'That makes me odd.'

Elody wanted to weep but she knew there was no convincing Lucian. 'I'll come back after the picnic,' she assured him. 'Would you like that?'

'Will you read me a story?'

'Without doubt,' she replied.

Hester was as good as her word, introducing Elody to her cousin Nigel who had ruddy cheeks and a cheerful personality, her uncle Bertram, and the assembled relations.

'My goodness, Aunt Ursula,' Nigel held the umbrella for her as they walked across the lawn, 'you have this charming young lady living under your roof, you must be delighted.'

'We are obliged—'

'We are indeed lucky to have Elody with us,' Andrew cut in. 'She's brought some light into our lives after ... Is that not true, Hester?'

Hester laughed. 'To my shame I was mean to Elody, but I believe she has forgiven me.'

'You could never be unkind.' Nigel took her arm.

'I can be absolutely beastly, it's the red hair, I'm afraid.'

'Well then,' Nigel teased, 'I shall take the greatest care not to get on the wrong side of you.' They all laughed, and Elody glanced at Hester. 'Thank you,' she mouthed.

They arrived at the Temple where Mr Simkins, Jacob Shaw and Mrs George were waiting with a fire burning in the grate and two tables laden with food. As soon as the guests had taken their seats they were served.

'Surviving, Miss Cole?' Jacob Shaw whispered as he passed her a plate of poached salmon, lightly glazed chicken and Mrs George's speciality, stuffed quail's eggs.

She looked up at him. 'I'm actually fine,' she replied. And to her surprise her words were true. The Hamiltons, who apparently lived in a more manageable house near Lichfield, seemed determined to make her feel at home.

'I've never seen such hair,' Lady Hamilton stated, putting down her fork and commenting on Elody's luxurious locks. 'I was at an exhibition at the Royal Academy last week, the pre-Raphaelites you know, and it's quite clear you sat for Rosetti's Lady Lilith.'

'It wasn't me, I can assure you,' Elody stuttered.

'Indeed, if it were, you'd be an old lady by now,' she chuckled.

'Forgive me, I was only teasing. But you are quite as gorgeous, isn't she, Archie?'

Archie coughed. 'I admit I don't know the painting, but as to Miss Cole resembling it, I have absolutely no doubt you're right.'

Elody could feel her cheeks burning. Where she came from it was blunt talking only, with no time for frivolity, and it was strange to be the centre of attention.

The subject moved on and the talk was about music, and the enormous new mansion built by a business magnate five miles away in spite of the recession.

'When I've made my fortune, I shall build something equally impressive,' it was Harry Derrington. 'Recessions come and go, houses do not.'

'And how will you make your fortune?' Elody's face was a picture of innocence but her conversation with Hester still rankled.

Harry blushed and Lord Derrington winked.

'Got his eye on the main job, haven't you, Harry, but I'm not dead yet and there's Archie to consider.'

'I didn't for a moment mean...' the young man was flustered. 'I just thought that—' he ran out of steam, and helped himself to another bread roll. The conversation moved on to the Hamiltons' new foxhounds.

'Their bloodline is superb,' Nigel proclaimed. 'Got some of the Beaufort champion dam, Rarity in 'em. Do you hunt, Miss Cole?'

'I do not.'

'Miss Cole may not hunt, but she's a capable rider,' Andrew Derrington confirmed.

Elody looked up, her confidence growing. 'I can stay on a horse if it's steady, if not, you would have to pick me off the floor.'

'And what an honour that would be. Uncle Andrew, find me a bucker if you will.'

His father, Lord Hamilton, laughed. 'Nigel whatever next, apologise immediately.'

'Certainly not,' he replied.

'Not only can Miss Cole ride,' Archie interrupted, 'but I have it on the greatest authority she can also climb trees.'

He was smiling across at her.

'A bit of a tomboy, I'm afraid.' She looked up and their eyes held for the briefest moment. It was only the flash of white in the trees that distracted her.

'Will you excuse me.' She pushed back her chair and hurried from the Temple towards the house, doubling back to slip behind the rhododendrons. She found Lucian throwing sticks in the lake.

'You shouldn't get too near the water.' She knelt down beside him, careless of her dress.

'Why not?'

'Because you could fall in.' Her voice was strangled. 'Please, Lucian.'

'I was watching you with all those people. I wish they would go away.'

'They will soon.'

'Then will you come and read my story?'

'I promise you, Lucian.' She took his hand and led him back to his wing, her heart breaking.

The family had assembled for supper, when Ursula drew Elody aside.

'May I remind you the Hamiltons are my relations, Elody, perhaps you will remember it another time.'

Chapter Thirty-Five

Ursula Derrington had noticed the change in her son, in fact she had seen a shift in everyone's disposition since the girl arrived.

She looked into the dressing table mirror, noticing the frown between her eyes, the lines etched from nose to mouth, *lines of bitterness* she called them, and it was true, unhappiness had changed her, making her ashamed of the person she had become. For a brief moment she remembered holding her firstborn son in her arms, looking into his tiny face, the rush of emotion. Giles was her compensation for a loveless marriage. God had given her a son, but just as easily he had taken him away.

She could feel a tightness in her chest, her husband disliked her and her surviving children were indifferent, and now Elody Cole, the daughter of Andrew's only real love was making people happy where she could not. She rested her head on the polished surface, how had it come to this, how had *she* come to this? But she knew the answer, her life had ended the day Andrew came into the library.

'My dear Ursula,' he had said, leading her to the sofa. 'I've something to tell you, and you need to sit down.' Ursula only had to look at him to know the truth, but not Giles, not her precious boy?

She was distracted when Millie, who had doubled up as her lady's maid since the last girl left, knocked on the door.

'Here is your dress, all nice and pressed, your Ladyship. Shall I help you into it and do up your hair?'

'You're late, Millie.'

'Sorry, but I had to get it done, I know how fuss... how you like things.'

She was helping her into the delicate silk dress, doing up the buttons at the back when she pushed away her hand.

'For heaven's sake, Millie, your clumsy fingers have caught a strand of my hair.'

'Sorry, milady.'

'Just be more careful, your salary was increased when you became my maid, it would be a shame if you were to lose the position.'

'The only shame is that you don't fall down the plughole,' Millie whispered beneath her breath.

'Did you say something, Millie?' Ursula looked at the girl in the mirror.

'Me, milady? Nothing at all.'

With the routine finished Ursula went downstairs for dinner, observing Hester's happy smile, and her husband's good humour. She stabbed at a piece of veal. Why couldn't she make Andrew laugh in that way? When she thought about it, she had never really made him laugh at all. She remembered meeting Andrew at a dance, and her father's words afterwards.

'You can marry your penniless Alexander Munroe, if you wish, but there will be no fine carriages nor cars and no servants. You'll be living in a draughty, crumbling house in Ireland, mortgaged to the nines. The Derringtons may be trade, but they're rich. You'll have everything you need, and more.' In her weakness she had agreed, letting go of her one true love and ruining all of their lives. It was Alex Munroe who had written to her about

Millie – her family was caught up in the Troubles and it would be a kindness to get her away. She had said yes immediately; Millie was her link with her past and Alex. Naturally everyone believed it was decent, benevolent Andrew who had taken Millie in, but they were wrong: this act of charity was hers.

She was finishing her sorbet when she caught the direction of Archie's gaze, the widening of his eyes when he looked at Elody. She drew in her breath; she hadn't bargained for Archie liking the girl. Well, she wouldn't allow it, couldn't let it happen. The girl's mother, had taken Andrew's heart; Elody was not going to take her one remaining son.

Chapter Thirty-Six

Elody was on the way back from the moors, Lucian's hand tucked in her own when Archie waved from the terrace.

'Archie!' The child broke away and ran towards him.

'Has Elody been kind to you?'

'Elody is always kind.'

'And have you been painting?'

'Oh yes...' Lucian ran behind Elody and undid the satchel pulling out a bundle of art paper. He gave the bundle to Archie.

'Today we saw two Meadow Pipits, a curlew, a hare and a rabbit; you see I've drawn the rabbit here, and the pipit. We found a broken egg; I've drawn that too. I counted the speckles, one hundred and ten.'

'Excellent, Lucian.'

'I know.'

Archie looked at Elody above his head and winked. 'What would you say, Lucian, if we read you a story together tonight?'

'You mean Archie and Elody?'

'That's precisely what I mean. But I'm not sure what to read,' Archie teased.

'*The Owl and the Pussycat*,' Lucian retorted. 'I like it when you put on your silly voice.'

'So you think my voice is silly?' Archie rolled his eyes at Lucian.

'Very.' Lucian ran ahead and when they arrived upstairs, he was holding a battered copy of Edward Lear's stories. 'Can Rhea listen?' he said to Elody. 'You know it's her favourite.'

Elody was dispatched to fetch the cat and returned to find Archie and Lucian sitting on the bed, their heads together as they looked at the pictures. Archie beckoned to her and patted the cover beside him and for a brief while they were cocooned together in the small bedroom, the night light glowing in the corner as the sky grew darker. As Archie read the story, Elody watched the expressions moving across his face, his hands as they turned the pages. She listened to the inflections in his voice. When she took on the role of the pussycat, she was conscious of his eyes on her. He had reached the end, when she took Lucian by the hand and they danced by the light of the moon, swaying around the room, waving their arms.

'More,' Lucian cried. 'More, more, Elody.'

The hour passed too quickly. How she had misjudged Archie, Elody thought as he passed Rhea to her.

'Rhea tells me she wants to do this again,' he said softly, his hands brushing her own.

'Well then, we shall.'

That night as she lay in bed, she recalled the way Archie spoke to Lucian, the tenderness in his eyes as he looked at his drawings. Was it paternal pride, she wondered, recalling the intimacy of the evening, the three of them together in the shadowed room. She ran her fingers up her arm, remembering the thrill of Archie's touch on her skin, she recalled the scent of his cologne, the wave in his dark brown hair.

She sat up in bed and switched on the light. What was she thinking of? Not only was Archie taken, but he had a mother who would rather die than let him get involved with a penniless potter. More importantly, she had her own goals, her own dreams and she would never let a man get in the way, especially a man like Archie Derrington.

Chapter Thirty-Seven

It was customary for Lucian to be waiting when Elody arrived at his lodgings, but on this occasion, he was not.

'Gone,' said Miss Phipps.'

'Gone where?'

'Little bugger was looking for Rhea when he saw the vicar, and there was naught I could do. Lady Ursula will be mad if he bothers her.'

Before she could say another word, Elody had sprinted away. She was heading for the drawing room when Lucian's voice came through the door. She crept closer, saw the vicar holding a cup of tea, the boy standing in front of him. Ursula Derrington was sitting in her usual chair.

'I think Rhea's trying to get to Africa.'

'Is Rhea a member of your family?'

A small smile crept over Lucian's face. 'She's a cat.'

'I had several cats when I was a missionary in Africa.'

'A missionary?'

'Teaching the word of God, young man.'

Lucian's eyes darted to Ursula then back to the vicar. 'Do you know that Africa is the second largest continent in the world after Asia. It covers about one-fifth of the total land surface of the earth but contains only about ten per cent of the world's population, which I find very interesting, because there are a lot of people in England and comparatively speaking, we're very, very small! I'm Lucian by the way.' He stopped, and Elody could see the vicar was smiling.

'In all my years in ministry, I've never met such an enlightened young man. How old are you, Lucian?'

'My birthday is on the third of October so that makes me eight and three quarters.'

'And where did you get all this knowledge?'

'Elody brought the Encyclopaedia Britannica from the library. I can tell you about the indigenous peoples, and elephants. People kill them for their beautiful tusks. So pointless, don't you think? Did you know if elephants get stung on their trunks they can die?' He drew in his breath.

'Tell me, Lucian, who are you, and why have I never met you before?'

'I don't actually k—'

'Another time, Lucian. Forgive me, Vicar, it's time for the child's tea.' Ursula had got to her feet and propelled him from the room.

'How dare you allow the child to disturb me like this,' she hissed at Elody when the door was closed behind them.

'Excuse me?'

'You heard, Elody. Now take Lucian back to his lodgings where he belongs.'

Lucian trudged along the terrace with Elody.

'What did I do wrong, Elody and why does the tall lady hate me? I was only talking to the vicar, and he seemed to be interested in Africa.'

'You did nothing wrong; I could tell he loved talking to you.'

But on this occasion Lucian wouldn't be consoled. He curled himself into a ball on the bedroom floor and rocked to and fro.

'The vicar asked me who I was, but I didn't know.'

He started to cry and Elody wanted to hold him but he pushed her away.

'Just leave me alone, Elody, I need to be alone.'

Elody rubbed his back then went into the kitchen where Miss Phipps made her a cup of tea. She started to speak but Elody held up her hand. 'Please don't say a word.'

When she finally returned to the bedroom his sobs were subsiding.

'Do you remember anything about your mother?' she asked.

He sniffed, looking up through his tears. 'Sometimes I think I can hear a lady saying nice things to me, but I don't know if it's real or a dream and I don't know where I came from and why I'm here at all.'

'Oh, Lucian,' she murmured, and at last he allowed her to take him in her arms.

'But I do know you,' he whispered. 'Because you have a nice voice and you smell of flowers except when you come home from work and you smell like the mud in Tim Peabody's garden. You bite your nails and Miss Phipps said you should never bite your fingernails, and you've lost everyone apart from Walter, who fell in the canal and his mother took him away. I'm sorry if I was naughty, Elody.'

'You are never naughty, my darling little boy.'

Lucian's first recollections of his mother were also his last. They were vague, hazy indecipherable, but that night when he shut his eyes and a voice floated towards him, he knew it wasn't Elody.

'Mother?' he whispered

'Lucian, please...'

Please what? he wondered, turning on his night light, trying to force the cobwebs from his memory, but nothing would come.

Normally he could remember events with extraordinary clarity, but not this.

He screwed up his eyes until stars floated in front of him. Suddenly he could recall a man shouting, and he was afraid, he could hear his words.

'I'll give you sorry.'

He drew his legs to his chin afraid the man was coming for him, but there was something else, an old lady taking him from the house.

'You have to come with me, Lucian, you're not safe. Come with me now.'

Though Lucian realised these events had happened years before, he was still shivering with terror. He climbed out of bed, slipped through the door at the end of the corridor and ran along the passageway. All the doors were the same, but one had a ribbon tied to the handle, a pink ribbon, it smelt of flowers, and Elody.

He turned it slowly, let it creak open, and crept across the floor to the bed. He could hear Elody's quiet breathing, see the rise and fall of her chest. He climbed up next to her, regulating his breath until it was in harmony with Elody's, and fell into a deep and dreamless sleep.

Chapter Thirty-Eight

Elody was curled amongst the cushions in her favourite corner of the library, obscured from the world by an embroidered curtain and a pillar of books. When the door opened, every muscle in her body tensed. Ursula entered with Archie and Otto, they were deep in conversation and the only one to recognise something amiss was the dog who trotted towards the curtain, his head on one side.

'Miss Phipps has threatened to give in her notice,' Ursula complained.

'Are you surprised? You were rude to her.'

'That woman is under strict instructions to keep Lucian from this part of the house.'

'Did you frighten the child?' Archie accused her.

'It's my house, and I'll not have him running around like some demented—'

'Sometimes you're positively cruel, Mother.'

'He was looking for the blasted cat and started rambling on to the poor vicar about Africa, it was embarrassing for both of us.'

Archie was pacing the room, his hands behind his back. 'I hardly think that's true, as he informed me we have a prodigy in our midst. Except Lucian isn't in our midst, is he?'

'The vicar's a gullible old man,' Ursula pointed out.

'You should apologise to Miss Phipps.'

'Don't be ridiculous, Archie, in any event it's opportune, the boy needs to go into a home with medical equipment. We both know the time has come.'

Archie had stopped by the window and was staring into the garden. 'Come on, Mother, his days are limited, his lungs are getting weaker, he must be here where he belongs.'

'He will be amongst people of his own kind.'

He turned to face her. 'Now we're really getting to the point. You find him an embarrassment.'

'That's quite enough.' Ursula's eyes were flashing and there were bright spots of colour on her cheeks.

Archie's voice was lower, pleading. 'He's more content than I've ever seen him. If Nurse Phipps insists on leaving, I'm sure Elody will find someone to replace her.'

'All you seem to talk about is that girl. You must put any ideas of the potter out of your head, Archie, for pity's sake, she is . . .'

'What, Mother?'

'All right, she's working class.'

'Papa wasn't exactly an aristocrat,' he retorted. 'Neither is Felicity Billington, but her money speaks for her, doesn't it? If I recall, that's why you married my father and now you'd have me repeat your mistakes.'

'How dare you?'

Elody put her hand to her mouth, stifling a gasp.

'With regard to Elody, put your mind at rest, Mother. "The potter" as you call her, just lives in this house, and I can assure you there's nothing more.'

Elody dropped her head to her knees, shutting out their words. She could hear chairs scraping, Archie coughing and then it happened, Otto caught hold of the curtain and started to pull.

'Otto, stop that,' Ursula ordered. But the dog continued to drag the curtain until it began to slide along the rail.

There was shocked silence as Elody dropped her legs over the seat, and stood up, the dog yapping at her feet.

'What on earth are you doing?' Ursula's tone was reproachful. 'You know what they say about eavesdroppers.'

'I was hardly eavesdropping.'

Ursula looked at her watch. 'If you will excuse me, I need to get on. Otto, come.' She swept from the room, leaving Archie and Elody alone.

'I didn't know you were there.' Archie's words were strangled.

'I just live in this house, how inconvenient for you.'

'I'm so sorry,' he uttered, moving towards her. 'I didn't want my mother prying into my affairs.'

Elody thrust her book into his hands. 'I wasn't aware we were having an affair! My God, how stupid to have believed you were my friend.'

She fled outside, crossing the garden to the stable yard and Hermione's stall, and buried her head in the mare's coat. How could her vanity blind her to the truth? Archie was weak and snobbish; flirting was a game to him, nothing more. She remembered the look on his face, the touch of his hand only the night before. It meant nothing to him, she realised. Nothing at all.

As she walked back to the house, she looked up at Lucian's window. She would never let them put him in a home, not as long as she lived and breathed.

Chapter Thirty-Nine

Elody didn't go to dinner that night and the following morning she cycled to the pot bank, releasing some of her pent-up anger as she pedalled the hills.

Dawn was back at her table when Elody pushed open the door.

She glanced up. 'You look sweaty.'

'So would you, it's nigh on twelve miles from Thorncliffe.'

Elody crossed the floor and took her hands, turning them over, scrutinising every bit of them.

'You're a doctor now?' Dawn grumbled.

Elody ignored her. 'Any tingling?' she asked.

Dawn shook her head.

'Do you mind if I look at your gums?'

Dawn opened her mouth and Elody peered inside.

'There's no blue line, Dawn.' She hugged her friend. 'But you must be careful, scrub your hands, keep yourself clean and don't—'

'Lick the sodding brush,' Dawn replied.

Elody went to the window and threw it wide.

'And we need to get some air into this studio, even if it's a smog-ridden, soot-ridden killer out there, it's better than in here.'

As Dawn glanced outside at the lowering sky, the chimneys belching thick black smoke, the suggestion of a smile crossed her face. 'Are you sure?'

'If we can't clean up the air outside, we must keep it clean inside. That means wetting the floor and brushing it, we don't want this dust clogging up our lungs.' She fetched a bucket of water and set to work with a mop and broom.

Half an hour later, the floor had been mopped and swept and Elody was exhausted. She sank onto Dawn's chair. 'We need to do this every day,' she addressed the women. 'And if I'm not here, you bloody have to, I don't want this place killing you, one by one.'

Elody missed dinner again, finding consolation in Mrs George's sitting room downstairs.

'Are you all right, duck?' The housekeeper dropped Rhea in her lap. 'You'd tell me if something was wrong?'

Elody buried her face in the cat's warm coat. 'I'm fine, Mrs George.'

But she wasn't fine and on Saturday morning, she packed her satchel, put on a coat and went outside. She was halfway across the lawn, when Hester caught up with her.

'You look as if you're in a hurry.'

Elody buried her hands deeper into her pockets and strode on.

'What's wrong, Elody, you've missed dinner two nights in a row.'

'Nothing that concerns you.'

'I was only trying to help.' Hester was turning to go when Elody caught her arm.

'Your mother intends to send Lucian away.' There was a tremor in her voice, the misery of the last few days surfacing.

'Father wouldn't let her.'

'Archie said . . .' she tailed off.

'What did he say? Elody what's going on? Archie didn't come to dinner and Father left before coffee was served.'

'I was in the library; they didn't know I was there...' She got no further.

Hester held on to her. 'You can tell me as we walk.'

'But you don't like walking.'

Hester smiled. 'You're right, but I'm showing you how utterly thoughtful I am.'

Elody sniffed. 'That's disputable,' she replied.

They were making their way towards the gate at the bottom of the garden when Clay spotted a spaniel and charged towards it.

'I do apologise,' they could hear the disembodied voice of the French tutor somewhere nearby. Seconds later he appeared with a young woman at his side.

'My sister and I have permission from your father, such a lovely garden, Miss Hester, but I didn't anticipate—'

'Come whenever you wish,' Hester interrupted. 'We were heading for the moors and would love you to join us. Walking is my passion, Mr Medley.' She tucked a strand of hair behind her ear and glanced at Elody.

Elody's misery was temporarily averted. 'Oh yes, rain or shine Hester drags me outside.'

The young woman, who was a carbon copy of her brother, put out her hand. 'I'm Hannah, and this is Ralph.' She patted the dog who looked affronted by Clay's continued attentions.

'He's rather better behaved than Clay,' Elody murmured.

'Actually, he is a she; I just liked the name.' She broke into peals of laughter and Elody found herself smiling. 'And as for the dog's behaviour, I've had too many years bossing naughty children in school.'

'So, you're a teacher like your brother?'

'I teach English at a government school in Stoke, unlike Piers who has a comfortable life as headmaster of the village school.'

'I thought he was a tutor to all the—'

'Gentry,' Hannah finished for her. 'His tutoring is pin money, but he enjoys it.'

'I think Hester does too!' Elody nodded at Hester who was gazing up at Piers with open admiration. The two young women smiled at each other.

'And what do you do, Elody?' she asked, stepping out beside her. 'I can't quite see you as a gentlewoman doing needlepoint?'

'I'm a potter by trade, but Lord Derrington is my godfather. Don't ask me how, it's too long a story!'

'I would never be so rude, but I had worked out you were from the Potteries.'

'Heavens above, my accent gives me away!'

They scrambled up Hen Cloud, sheltering from the wind behind a large boulder.

Hannah took a camera from its leather case.

'I need a photograph, right here with this splendid view,' she said. 'Piers, would you mind?'

The three women stood self-consciously together, Hester holding her hair in place, Elody's arms crossed, Hannah's fine profile turned towards the view.

'My sister's convinced these photos will be of interest to future generations.' Piers clicked the shutter.

'And they will,' she replied.

A lively discussion followed on the merits of amateur photography leading onto the more serious topic of education.

'So many children leave school unable to read or write, it's my aim to change that.' Hannah glanced at Elody.

'You may gather my sister is a girl of conviction.'

'Don't apologise for me, Piers,' she retorted, eyes flashing. 'The Education Act may have raised the school leaving age to fourteen, but so many pupils never appear.'

The conversation continued as the two women climbed down

the hill. Elody revealed her desire for reform at the Potteries, she even told Hannah of her mother's death.

'I don't often talk about it,' she admitted.

'I feel honoured that you've taken me into your confidence.'

Elody smiled, the tension inside her releasing. 'Perhaps because you're a teacher.'

'It's a meeting of minds, Miss Cole.'

They had arrived back at the garden when Hannah invited Elody and Hester to the village hall for a gathering the following weekend. 'It's very local, not what you're used to.'

'We'd love to come, wouldn't we, Elody?'

'Absolutely,' she replied.

They were taking off their boots when Elody nudged Hester in the ribs and lowered her voice.

'You like Piers, don't you?'

'I don't know what you're talking about.'

'You do, absolutely.'

Hester brushed the hair from her damp cheeks. 'Away with you, Elody Cole!'

Elody was talking to Hester in the Blue Parlour when Archie came in. She turned her back as he approached.

'Hester, would you mind if I spoke to Elody?'

Hester glanced at Elody.

'Alone,' he reiterated.

'Well, excuse me, Archie.' Hester raised her eyebrows and left them together.

'I don't know what you have to say to me?' Elody faced him. 'I'm aware of your mother's plans for Lucian, my only hope is that you'll stand up to her ... like a man.'

Archie flinched. 'Trust me, he won't be going ...'

'I learnt a lot about you, Archie,' Elody interrupted. 'But let me assure you, the only thing I care about is Lucian's welfare.'

'I'm so sorry, my mother—'

'There's nothing to be sorry about, as you say I'm a girl from the Potteries, and as for blaming your mother! There's something you should know, Archie Derrington: keep your pleasantries for Felicity Billington! If you were the last man on earth, I wouldn't be interested in you.'

The gong for dinner sounded and Elody put down her glass and left the room.

Saturday came and Hester was throwing everything out of her cupboard when Elody walked in.

'I have nothing suitable to wear,' she moaned.

'You mean for an occasion at the village hall!' Elody glanced at the rug, littered with clothes.

'I can see you're irritated,' Hester pleaded, 'but I want to get it right.'

'Where I come from this would be considered excessive.'

'It's true but—'

'You want to look nice for Piers.' Elody relented, picking up a mid-calf skirt from the floor and a blue silk blouse. She passed them to Hester. 'You can wear a cardigan if you're cold.'

After being plied with homemade cake and cups of tea, at six o'clock precisely, a bottle of sherry came out for the women and beer for the men. Hannah dragged the girls around, introducing them to one local then the next. To Elody it was reminiscent of a church meeting in the Methodist chapel hall, to Hester it was a new experience.

'I'm ashamed, they seem to know about me, but I know nothing of them,' she murmured.

Elody gave her a look. 'It's never too late to start.'

Hester threw herself into the evening, chatting to everyone. She was particularly taken with a tenant farmer who told her about his pigs.

'Your grandfather, Lord Hamilton, now he liked the Tamworth, but I told him to give the Gloucester Old Spot a try, and he did, miss, and I said to myself, now there's a sensible man. He may be an earl, but he takes advice from a man who knows his pigs.'

The two girls were deep in conversation with old Lady Hamilton's maid, when Piers came up behind them.

'Will you excuse me, Mrs Sykes, but Miss Price is anxious to meet these fine young ladies before she leaves.'

'I think you mean she's anxious to meet Hester,' Elody contradicted, and Piers smiled. 'I admit everyone's fascinated by the young Miss Derrington.'

They followed him across the room to an armchair where an old lady reclined, her knees covered in a crocheted blanket. He leant towards her and raised his voice.

'Hester Derrington is here to meet you, Miss Price. She's accompanied by Lord Derrington's ward, Elody Cole.'

The old woman chuckled. 'You don't need to shout, I may be blind, Mr Medley, but I'm not deaf. Come closer, girls, so that I may touch you.' She put up her hand, lightly running her fingers down Hester's profile.

'You don't look like your mother, but you're a fine-looking girl; I used to do her pigtails and she'd like them just so, even at five.'

'That sounds like my mother.'

'Oh yes, she certainly knew her mind. Does she still hunt?'

'She gave it up when Giles died,' Hester explained.

'Such a waste. I met Master Giles you know, she brought him down to see me, a charming little boy.' She sighed. 'She was a fine rider, your mother, the best seat in Staffordshire. And you,

276

dear,' she turned her face towards Elody, 'his Lordship's ward, eh?'

She caught one of Elody's curls. 'I bet it's one to wash.'

'Well, it dunner need rags, Miss Price.'

Miss Price started to laugh. 'And for sure here's some Potteries dialect. My entire family worked in the pot banks except me.'

While Piers took Hester to meet some other locals, Miss Price and Elody were exchanging stories of their past. Before they knew it, it was seven.

'It's been a pleasure talking to you. We'd better get back to the house, or Lady Ursula will have something to say.'

'And I wouldn't be in your shoes, Miss Cole.'

As they had imagined their reception at supper was hostile.

'Where have you been? It's so inconsiderate to be late.' Ursula looked up as the girls hurried into the dining room. 'My soufflé is entirely ruined. And, Hester, why are you wearing those abominable clothes?'

'You bought them for me, Mother.'

'If I did, it was for charity work, not for dinner in the hall.'

'Charity work? Since when did you ever do—'

'Hester,' her father warned.

Ursula cleared her throat, her jaw tightening. 'Am I to put up with this rudeness, Andrew? Your daughter has become insufferable of late. And I wonder why?' She glared at Elody.

Andrew continued with his soufflé. 'I'm really not in the mood for an argument, Ursula. Perhaps another time.'

Chapter Forty

Rain was falling outside the windows, spattering onto the leaded panes when Elody took the envelope from the silver tray. The writing was unfamiliar and it wasn't from Florrie or Mr Asland, and it definitely wasn't an olive branch from Archie. She chewed on her lip, angry with herself for even thinking it might be. She was nothing to Archie Derrington and he was less than nothing to her. She turned it over, examined the thick, blunt writing, who could it possibly be?

> *Dear Elody,*
> *I imagine you're not coming into the pot bank this week, being a holiday and all, so I am sending this letter. If you are agreeable, I have found a venue for our meeting. The Olde Crown, Middleport Rd, Monday the tenth of June at seven p.m..*
> *Yours truly,*
> *Tilda Kennard.*

Elody stood up and paced the room. Tilda's letter was exciting, but it filled her with anxiety. The battle lines were being drawn, but the more entrenched she became, the more her conscience nagged her. She was fighting the very people who had given her a home. Her thoughts see-sawed back and forth, one moment believing she couldn't betray Lord Derrington, the next moment realising she couldn't betray herself. Outside the window Tim Peabody was scuffing a bed with his hoe despite the rain, and Millie was running through the puddles with her laundry basket. It was normal life at Thorncliffe Hall, but her plans were far from normal.

Later, when the sun had broken through the cloud, she cycled down the drive to the school house and Hannah.

'What am I to do?' she asked as they walked together round the garden. 'I have a dilemma either way.'

Hannah picked a rose from one of the well-stocked beds and held it to her nose.

'What's important, Elody? What will make a difference to people's lives?'

'We both know the answer, but what about Lord Derrington?'

'Think of the good you could do; the transformation you could bring. You have to stand up for what you believe in.'

'But it's become so difficult—'

'My brother and I have this charming schoolhouse on the patronage of the Derringtons, but I have to follow my conscience. I have to say what I feel is right.'

'But I live with the Derringtons. Am I really the person to be doing this?'

'Elody your mother died of plumbism, that's why you're in this situation. She wished for a society where women were equal with men, you'll be carrying the banner for her.'

Elody was quiet for a moment. 'My grandmother was a suffragette and Mother part of the Women's Freedom League in Wolverhampton, but it's still hard.'

'Of course it is.'

Elody looked at her. 'And you, Hannah, are you part of it?'

'I'll be behind you every step of the way.'

The evening for the meeting arrived and Elody dressed with care, choosing her mother's skirt and pin-tucked blouse. She put her grandmother's suffragette rosette in her pocket.

'Going somewhere nice?' Mrs George asked as Elody collected her bicycle.

'Hannah has asked me to tea.'

'You watch your step with that one, I've heard she's got some modern ideas. Come here, love.' She took a pretty pink astrantia from the trug she was carrying and tucked it in her hat. 'Now you look a picture.'

Millie came up behind them. 'Dressed up for a young man, I'll be guessing.'

Mrs George tutted. 'Millie Doyle, your thoughts will get you into trouble one of these days.'

Elody met Hannah at the war memorial and together they cycled to Burslem chaining their bicycles behind The Olde Crown. As they made their way through the women gathering outside, Hannah nudged Elody.

'Isn't this a Port Vale supporters' pub?'

Elody grinned. 'When the FA banned women from playing football in '21, they didn't think we'd be holding a women's rally in this very pub.'

'Well then,' smirked Hannah, 'I'll take a picture to mark our defiance and I'll send it to the Sentinel!'

Elody held up her grandmother's rosette, Hannah took the cap off her camera, and the shutter closed.

When everyone was assembled in the back room, the doors closed.

'Today,' Tilda announced, 'we're going to discuss our future in the industry. This meeting isn't about conditions in the pot banks, for the present we'll leave that to the unions, it's about equal pay and, trust me, tonight there's not a man in sight, apart from the bartender, and if he's caught blabbing, I wouldn't be in his shoes, or his underpants, if you know what I mean.' There was a titter around the room.

'Most of you are members but, despite everything, the union isn't listening. It's time we took this into our own hands, we need to make our voices stronger. For those of you who didn't hear our spokeswoman last month, she's college-educated and a fine speaker.' There was a murmur of approval.

'Let me introduce you to Elody Cole.'

Elody stood up, searching for a familiar face in the crowd. Her eyes locked on Dawn who smiled at her reassuringly.

'Am I right that we all want the same thing?' she began.

'Yes,' the women murmured in assent.

'Well then, we're speaking from the same page. But you will want to know why me? Why a girl half some of your age. I'll tell you now. When my mother died of plumbism I made a promise to myself that I would be part of change, I would make it right for her, and now is the time. The War Cabinet report on women in the industry was an attempt to address the inequalities in pay, but did it help us?'

'No,' yelled one woman.

'So what are we going to do about it?' Elody paused, gazing around the room at the expectant women's faces.

'Strike,' someone shouted from the back. 'Bring the industry to its knees, then they'll listen.'

'Show them we're fed up with being lied to,' another cried.

'We must start with diplomacy, but if that fails ...' Elody let the words hang in the air.

'I had a meeting with Lady Astor, our first woman MP. She will be fighting for us, but it may take years. We must begin our own battle now. I believe we should start with posters making clear our demands; if nothing else, we'll get their attention. The bosses all dine together so word will get around.'

'If that fails,' Tilda interjected, 'we will go further. The government report concluded we're not equal in strength and our place is in the home, we're not worthy of the best positions or equal pay. But I say, who manned the machines when the men went off to war? Who did their jobs? We were capable then, we are capable now.'

'If they refuse to listen,' Elody could feel her heart beating, the blood coursing through her veins, she was in full flight now, fighting for Dawn, for Florence, for her mother, for every woman in the room, 'they leave us with no other option, we'll come out on strike. Are you in?' She pointed her finger at the crowd.

'We're in!' everyone cried, clapping and cheering. As the meeting ended and the women clamoured around them, Elody was elated. The fight had truly begun.

Chapter Forty-One

Hester looked up from the newspaper as Jacob approached. 'Clue Jacob, *Break in the word*, nine letters and it starts with an h.'

Jacob put his tray on the sideboard and started to count on his fingers, grinning smugly. 'Got it.'

'Well?'

'Hyphenate, Miss Hester.'

Hester filled in the crossword and frowned. 'How do you do it, Jacob? It's really not fair.'

'Brains and beauty, Miss Hester, and talking of letters.' He held out an envelope. 'Morning post and in my reckoning it's—'

Hester grabbed it. 'Oh, my Lord, Jacob, what if I don't get in?'

'You will, Miss, and may I have the honour of telling them below stairs?'

Hester tore open the envelope and started to laugh.

'Yes, Jacob, you can tell everyone except my mother.' She grinned wickedly. 'That's a pleasure I'm saving for myself.'

Ursula was at the desk in the Blue Parlour when Elody came in and flung herself into a chair. She immediately shot to her feet. 'I didn't see you, I'm sorry.'

Ursula looked across at her and realised she hadn't the energy to be unkind.

'I'm trying to sort my letters.' She picked up a handful, and let them drop through her fingers. Suddenly she was weary, all her energy drained. She leant her elbows on the desk and lowered her head, misery washing over her in waves.

'Giles's letters.' She raised her head, her eyes meeting Elody's. 'I have them, every single one. And mine to him, they came back with his things.' She bit her lip to stop her tears, but the storm was too great; her shoulders started to shake, and she was sobbing, great heaving sobs that wracked her body.

Elody crossed the distance between them and hovered behind her. 'I'm so sorry,' she soothed, putting out her hand, but Ursula drew away.

'Most undignified, forgive me.'

'You could never be undignified, Lady Ursula, and as to the letters, how wonderful to have them, to hear your boy's words.'

Ursula looked up. 'I thought of putting them into an album so that he's never forgotten, so that future generations would know of my son.'

'I think that's a splendid idea, Lady Ursula.'

'You do?' Ursula's face was hopeful suddenly, then her shoulders drooped.

'But his writing isn't easy to read,' she qualified.

'Perhaps you could type them out,' Elody suggested. 'Have the letters on one side of the page, and the transcript on the other, an actual book.'

'But I don't type.'

'I'm told if you can play the piano you can type. There's a typewriter in the office.'

Ursula shook her head. 'No. I couldn't, it would be impossible.'

Elody knelt at her side. 'A project helps, trust me I know. It's almost seven years since your son died, seven years of grieving. Now you could do something to help treasure his memory, but it will also help you to live your life.'

Ursula sat there long after Elody had gone. The girl shamed her; she was compassionate when she didn't deserve it, and wise. She remembered Hester's application to the theatre, Elody had stood up for her, lied for her; it was a bad lie, she remembered, but she had shown courage, while she, Ursula Derrington, had tried to humiliate her own daughter. She recalled the day in the library and the misery on the girl's face when the curtain had slipped aside. How could Elody be nice to her, when she had been so vile?

Perhaps she could change, she thought, tidying the letters into three piles. It was extraordinary, but there was something about Elody that made her want to change. For years she had held on to her anger and grief, she had believed everyone was an enemy, and yet this penniless girl had shown her there could be another way.

She looked at the letters, a glimmer of hope building. Perhaps she should try Elody's suggestion, show future generations how war had not only destroyed a generation of young men, but also the people they had left behind.

Chapter Forty-Two

Ursula glanced around the dining room table. Hester was slipping a note to Elody, Andrew and Archie were discussing the recent disappearance of the explorer, Percy Fawcett in the jungles of Brazil, but as usual no one was speaking to her. It was hardly surprising, Ursula thought, dissecting her potato into tiny pieces. She had isolated herself from the family, enclosed herself in a world of anger and grief. But today something had moved inside her. Elody was right, sorting Giles's letters had given her a purpose and she would transpose them into a leather-bound book. She smiled remembering Mr Simkins hurrying into the Blue Parlour trying to disguise his amusement when he saw the typewriter.

'Are you all right, milady, I thought I heard—?'

'No, Simkins, I am not all right, this is the most devilish machine ever made, but I'll learn to type if it kills me, and yes, Simkins, the cursing was me.'

'Well done, milady.'

'For cursing, Simkins?'

'Definitely not,' his mouth was twitching. 'But you never did give up, even as a little girl.'

She had started to laugh and so had he.

'What would I do without you, Simkins?'

His eyes had watered just a little. 'You will manage very well, I'm sure.'

Ursula looked up to find Andrew watching her, she gave a nod of acknowledgement, a small smile. He raised his glass and for just a second there was a truce between them.

What have we done to each other? she wondered, what had she done to the children? And why was she thinking like this now and not before. She knew the answer, Elody had come into their lives like a whirlwind, but in her unsophisticated, artless way she was showing them how to be kind. She glanced at Hester, despite her veneer of sophistication, she was a brittle unhappy child still mourning her brother Giles. Instead of trying to help, she had abandoned her. Now Hester would leave the family home, go on the stage, and she had driven her away. Her gaze moved to Archie, handsome, urbane, but inside she knew he was an anxious young man. He would never forgive her intervention when he tried to enlist. But that was the one thing she didn't regret; he could hate her all he liked, but she had saved his life. Her gaze fell on Andrew, despite his polished exterior he was as unhappy in their marriage as she was. He probably deserved better, she thought, pushing her plate away, she had killed him emotionally but what had he done to her, bringing Lucian into the house, his child, keeping him nearby? Of course, Giles wasn't his father, she reflected her anger rising again. That was a ruthless lie told by Andrew. But she wasn't fooled, she could never be fooled. What Andrew didn't know was that she had proof.

Chapter Forty-Three

Present Day

When Marina was at the Artemis Centre her mind stayed at the centre, Thorncliffe Hall was left behind. The women's struggles were pressing and immediate, they needed all of her.

Jess returned to her husband, then came back, battered and bruised.

'Why?' Marina asked her. 'After everything he's done to you?'

'It's not that simple, Marina, the bank account is in Dan's name, everything I earn goes into it. And as to Josie's school, she likes it and there's not much else for her.'

'I understand, of course I do but—'

'There's the fear thing, Marina. Can you imagine what it's like wondering if they'll come after you? Laila, a girl I met at the drop-in centre, was killed by her partner the day she was due to leave him.' Jess looked down and Marina noticed the circular burn on her arm.

'Dan did this to you?'

She nodded, 'A cigarette. The bastard believes the more he wears me down, the more passive and afraid I'll be.'

'Everyone here will support you.'

'If he ever hurts my Josie, I'll kill him myself.' She gave a small grin. 'Then I suppose you'll have to defend me!'

Marina hugged her, knowing she would take any exam in order to help Jess Blake.

A few days later Dan hit Josie. That was when Jess left him for good.

Chapter Forty-Four

The Past

'Miss Cole.'

Elody looked up from her easel and squinted into the sunlight.

'Yes, Jacob?'

'Sorry to disturb you, but Mister Archie asked me to retrieve you both from the kitchen garden.'

She glanced across at Lucian who was putting the finishing touches to an oil painting.

'And what does he want?'

'I'm not allowed to say, miss.'

'Perhaps he should ask us himself,' she retorted to the chauffeur who doubled as a footman and now added messenger to his job description. 'Sorry, Jacob, that's unfair. Would you tell him we'll be with him shortly?'

'But he said I was to deliver you myself.'

'I'm not a parcel, Jacob.'

'No, miss.'

'Oh, very well.' Elody took a last satisfied look at her canvas. She had depicted the apricot trees espaliered against the high brick wall rather well, she thought a little smugly, but when she looked at Lucian's interpretation of the cultivated area of kitchen garden, the breath caught in her throat. The child had captured the magic entirely, the clematis and sweet peas rampant on trellis obelisks, the gravelled paths bordered with lavender. There were carrots, marrows with delicate yellow flowers. Everything was represented, the doorway hidden by roses, the wrought-iron archway, even Tim Peabody planting runner beans.

'That's wonderful, Lucian.' She put the top on her paints. 'But we'll have to leave it for a moment because Archie wishes to see us.'

Lucian began his own process of cleaning his brushes which took several minutes and when he had finished, he smoothed his smocked overall, took off his straw hat and ran a hand through his hair. 'I'm ready, Elody. Do I look nice?'

'Very nice, Lucian.' She linked arms with the boy, and they followed Jacob down the path, through the narrow slip of orchard where the chickens roamed freely, past the laurel bushes screening the area from the formal garden and on towards the house.

From the basement window Archie watched the small procession cross the lawn. Elody was leaning towards Lucian, her back in a gentle curve. They were talking quietly, intimately, the sunlight making a halo around them. Jacob Shaw was in front, but they seemed lost in their own private world. It was a beautiful image, one he would hold in his heart in the bleak times ahead, one he wished he could create again. Soon they were lost from view, and he waited in the studio, his stomach knotted with nerves. Would this earn some forgiveness? he wondered, glancing at the potter's wheel, the jars of paints, the heavy art paper they used. Would this show his measure of atonement, his effort to make amends?

He stacked the paper again, altered the position of a jar and was waiting when they arrived. He nodded to Jacob, who left them alone.

'Lucian, I have something to show you.'

Lucian went towards him.

'Would you trust me and shut your eyes,' he suggested.

Lucian frowned. 'I don't think so, Archie.'

Archie smiled. 'Very well, little man, perhaps Elody will join us?'

Elody knew what she would find but it still brought a lump to her throat. The footman's sitting room was now a charming studio with a table, two chairs – the smaller for Lucian – shelves filled with jars and brushes, even a sink beneath the window and buckets to wet the clay. The wheel was slightly apart from the rest, with a view of the world outside. Archie had thought of everything.

'I hope you like it, Lucian. Now you can make pots and paint them, and the table is just the right height.' He was looking over the child's head at Elody. 'I'm afraid as yet we're lacking a kiln, but I've set up an account with Carters so you can order the glazes and paints you require.'

'You have no idea what this means to both of us.'

'I had hoped this may begin to put things right and I know you're anxious to continue with your range. I thought...' He hesitated again. 'I thought this might help.'

'Does your mother know?'

'She won't trouble you, nor will Miss Phipps, who's been persuaded to stay.' He lowered his voice. 'There will be no more talk of Lucian being sent away.'

They were leaving the room when she looked up at him. 'I'll pay you back. Every penny, you'll see.'

'Your friendship is good enough payment for me.'

Elody changed for dinner into her cream silk dress, put on her shoes, threaded a ribbon through her hair. Archie's kindness had changed things in one sense, but not in another. She couldn't pack up her dreams. But as his face came into her mind, his confidence stripped away, she longed to throw caution to the wind and fling herself into his arms.

Chapter Forty-Five

Lord Derrington finished his scallops, put down the small silver fork with the mother of pearl handle and addressed his wife. 'Since she's not here, I can only assume Hester is rehearsing?'

Ursula cleared her throat. 'She went out this morning and said she wouldn't be with us for dinner, she didn't give a reason and to be honest I didn't ask.'

'Perhaps if you showed some interest, you would know more about your daughter.' Andrew wiped his mouth with the corner of his napkin. 'And Archie, do we know where he is?'

'He's taken Felicity to Buxton. Sir Thomas Beecham is conducting at the Opera House.' Elody watched a tiny spider scuttling across the wall. Her mother always said you shouldn't wash dirty linen in public, but the Derringtons obviously didn't know about dirty linen. Their voices droned on and she tried to shut them out but failed.

'Really, Ursula? I wasn't aware that Archie had a taste for opera.'

'I don't imagine he has, but Felicity is a cultured girl despite—'

'Despite her father being in trade? Are you sure she's up to your impeccable standards?'

'Her mother is a Pinkerton.'

'So that makes it all right?'

'If they were to marry, both Potteries would be joined – think of the benefits.'

'I see no benefit in a marriage based entirely on expediency; you and I both know that to our disappointment, Ursula.'

Elody swallowed the last scallop and raised her head. They were speaking as if they were on their own.

'Will you excuse me,' she said. 'I'm feeling unwell.'

'I'm so sorry, Elody. Jacob, will you escort Miss Cole?' Lord Derrington was on his feet helping her from her chair.

Once outside the room she left Jacob and ran towards the lake. She had no attachment to Archie, but she wished he was with anyone but Felicity Billington! She remembered the first time she had been aware of her coming down the passage at work. She was wearing a suit with a long jacket, nipped in at the waist and a cloche hat, accentuating her luminous skin and waving black hair. All the girls had seen her. 'My, she's a looker,' said Dawn. 'And those clothes, they must have come from Beatties at the least.'

'No,' said another, 'they're custom made.'

Everyone acknowledged her as she passed but she had merely peered down her finely chiselled nose.

Elody looked up to see Lucian racing towards her in his nightgown.

'I saw you from my window.'

'Sweet child.' She wrapped him up in her shawl. 'You should have been asleep. Your feet will get cold.'

'If someone has made you unhappy, I'll challenge them to a duel.'

'I'd rather you didn't.' Elody couldn't help but smile. 'Come on, dearest little boy, let me return you to your room.'

As she walked him back across the lawn, she believed the only person who would never let her down was Lucian.

*

When Elody was working from home, Lucian learnt to throw pots.

'This is most enjoyable,' he observed, his face solemn as he sat behind the wheel. 'Drew said I've become extremely good at maths.'

Elody laughed. 'And you're modest, now put your hands around the clay, centre it, and put your foot on the treadle. Do you see it's starting to turn?' Lucian nodded, and a few seconds later the clay wobbled, Lucian giggled, and had to begin again.

Those weeks were infinitely precious to Elody. At night she would lie in the warmth of her bedroom, the window open to let in the breeze and she would picture his dear little face scrunched in concentration as he tried and often failed to make the clay behave. She remembered his jubilant smile when he completed his first pot.

'See, I've done it,' he said. 'But it's not like drawing. I think I can paint better than you, and you're a better potter than me.'

It was on her windowsill now, the lumpy little unglazed pot.

Lucian slowly mastered the art of potting, but he was right in his assessment and the delineation of work became clear. Soon, scores of beautiful drawings covered the pages of the book. There were the images for the decoration of the front of each piece, the back, images that would wrap around the body of the work, and he copied the samples themselves. She had written the name of each in italic script.

'When Mr Billington puts this into work, I'll have to increase my days at the pot bank,' she explained to Lucian. 'It's for you and me.'

'But how can it be for me, when you're not here?' he asked with childish logic.

'The pieces will live forever, Lucian.'

'You mean after I'm dead?'

Elody drew in her breath. 'Long after we've both gone.'

295

'But I'll go first. I overheard Doctor Bly saying TB had made my chest weak and I'd never reach twelve. I looked it up and it's caused by the organism Mycobacterium Tuberculosis.' He said the words slowly and Elody flinched, imagining the virus moving through his fragile body.

'Perhaps my mother had the disease and passed it onto me.'

Elody held onto him and he didn't back away. She was drowning in her grief. Not Lucian, not her darling little boy.

'It's all right, Elody,' he said, drawing away at last, 'I'm not sad, Archie said God is kind to good little boys.'

'And you are good,' she murmured.

He looked at her then, his blue eyes huge in his pale face. 'There aren't many people who will mind, Archie and Andrew, and Tim Peabody I expect, but you will mind most of all.'

Chapter Forty-Six

Mr Asland was leaning against the wall when Elody arrived at the pot bank. He straightened slowly.

'Are you well, sir?' She climbed from the saddle.

'It's nothing I can't live with.' He limped through the archway towards her. 'Still a bicycle, instead of the fancy car?'

'Still the bicycle, Mr Asland.'

He laughed. 'One day you'll have your own car, Miss Cole, but perhaps we should start with your own range.'

'My own range?'

'Yes, Miss Cole,' he interrupted. 'Mr Billington has finally commissioned your range.'

Elody was humming as she worked.

'Not sure what you've got to be happy about,' Spit Goodwin grumbled, his spare frame casting a shadow over her wheel.

'Everything all right, Spit?' She looked up at him.

'The weather's messing with the clay, three of my jugs returned from the oven broken. It's not a good day at all.'

Spit couldn't have been a day over forty but from the lines on his face, the drooping shoulders, he looked well beyond his years.

'Kids all right, Spit?'

'Mrs Goodwin had to stay in with Joey who has spots all over him, and our Katie has a cough that keeps me up at night, so no, Miss, they are not all right.'

'I'm sorry, Spit.' She touched his arm with her wet hand. This was not the time to tell him her news.

Later, as she bent over the wheel, a delicate jug forming beneath her hands, her mind strayed from the magic in her fingers to the events of the night before. It was the first time Felicity had been invited to bring her parents to dinner at Thorncliffe Hall and a momentous occasion in the household. Mrs George was in a right fluster ordering everyone around, including Elody.

'You'll wear one of your best frocks, duck,' she had said. 'Miss Billington is that sophisticated, we wouldn't want you to let yourself down.' Elody had worn her cream silk, but she had felt provincial when Felicity came into the room. She recalled the introduction to her mother and her initial humiliation, but her surprise at the unexpected turn of events that came afterwards.

'Your face looks familiar?' Mrs Billington had shaken her hand. 'I know where I've met you, wasn't it Annabel Fraser's Christmas party?'

'I doubt it,' Felicity interjected in a lowered voice. 'She's a paintress at Papa's works, nothing more.'

Throughout the first course Elody was aware of being assessed, but even before Agnes's trifle was served, she was clearly dismissed as irrelevant.

Jacob was clearing the plates when Ursula trained her eyes on Felicity.

'Archie tells me you're fond of reading, Felicity. As you may be aware we have a fine library.'

Elody swallowed. Was this her introduction to every guest?

'Indeed, I enjoy the classics, and am particularly fond of Shakespeare, Lady Ursula. Actually *Hamlet* is one of my favourites. I don't imagine you're acquainted with Shakespeare, Miss Cole?'

Elody had looked up aware she was being spoken to. She could see the superiority in Felicity's eyes and couldn't help herself.

'*Hamlet* is definitely one of his greatest plays – it deals with all the elements that still drive us today, grief, betrayal, love or indeed lack of it, and family. Wouldn't you agree, Miss Billington?'

'Yes, indeed,' she faltered. 'I'm merely surprised someone of your education—' She trailed off.

'What you really mean is lack of education.' Elody was aware of everyone watching her.

'But many of the girls at the pottery can't read.'

'If that's the case, I'm not one of them.'

Ursula started to say something, seemed to think better of it and began again. 'Actually, Felicity, Miss Cole here is our resident expert on Shakespeare. Perhaps after dinner, Elody, you'll fetch our volume of *Hamlet* from the library and explain Shakespeare's use of soliloquies. For my part they leave me totally confused.'

Lord Derrington raised his glass to his wife. 'We would be most obliged.'

Elody looked up to find Archie watching her. Was he angry with her, she had wondered. Amused? She really wasn't sure.

She remembered him sprinting after her as she went up to bed.

'Elody, I have to talk to you.'

'Yes, Archie?'

'I'm sorry Felicity was patronising.'

'I'm used to it.'

'But you were magnificent.'

Her voice when she finally spoke was low. 'Why are you with her? Of all people, why Felicity Billington?'

'Because…' he hesitated. 'She's a good distraction from…'

He had stopped then, the shutters coming down. 'I'm sorry. Goodnight, Elody.'

As she continued upstairs, she was filled with a thousand emotions, none of them wise.

Elody carefully removed the jug from the potter's wheel. Tomorrow she would set the jug on the lathe and, using her sharpest tool she would refine the edges and make a pattern of ridges on the rim. As she placed it on the table, she smiled. Somewhere at the bottom of the bitterness, Lady Ursula was trying to be kind.

She picked up another ball of clay and the process began again. She was stretching her back when Spit looked up from his wheel.

'I've heard your news.' He hesitated before speaking again. 'And I reckon you deserve it.'

'Aw, thank you, Spit.' Elody pushed back her chair and hugged him hard. 'You don't know how happy that makes me.'

Spit's face turned the colour of beetroot. 'It was a compliment not a proposal of marriage, and be careful, girl, you're messing with my pot.'

Elody laughed. 'It's my belief, with five kiddies, you're already spoken for.'

He raised his eyebrows and grinned.

'Here, Pip,' he called to the turner on the other side of him. 'Come and look at this jug, not bad at all.'

Soon Pip was assessing her jug, along with the others in the studio, and a turner from the workshop next door. By the afternoon word had sped around the factory and a regular trickle of workers had come to see her ware.

She was unchaining her bicycle when Mr Asland stopped at her side.

'It seems you're already making a name for yourself.'

Elody grinned. 'This is just the start of it, sir, you'll see.'

'I have no doubt of it, Miss Cole.'

Elody was sitting with Lucian later, his window was open, the sweet scent of summer filling the room. The child's blonde head was bent over a book, his finger following the words. '*It was the best of times, it was the worst of times, it was the age of wisdom...*' he looked up at Elody. 'This is going to be sad.'

Elody placed a wisp of blonde hair behind his ear. 'You're right, but it's a story of heroism and how love can change a man.'

'I love you, Elody, will that change me?'

'You are perfect, just as you are.'

He looked at her then. 'I think you're perfect too, Elody.'

But as Elody switched off his light and went to bed, she believed she was far from perfect.

Her love for Lucian was complete, but her feelings for him, her growing affection for the family, could not deflect her from her cause. She had made a promise to herself and to her mother, and she would carry it through.

At lunch break the following day Elody called a meeting in the packing room and a date was set for the first phase of the plan.

'Ladies,' she said, standing on a wicker crate, 'it's posters first, afore we get to the hard stuff. Every pot bank entrance will be plastered with them. Would the night of twenty-fifth of June be suitable, please raise your hands?'

'The answer is yes, definitely yes.' Bridie Brookes's hand was up, and she was gazing at Elody her blue eyes filled with awe.

'Hubby ain't taking me to the Riviera any time soon,' Dawn called out, 'so there might be room in my diary.'

'Pipe down, Dawn,' said Bess, a handler from the workshop downstairs.

'And where will we get the posters?' Maud asked, waving her half-eaten oatcake in the air.

'We have to print them, duck, they don't print themselves,' Tilda rebuked her.

'But we can't use the printing press here!'

'And why not?' Tilda's eyes were challenging. 'Bridie, your husband works in the office, couldn't you get his key so we can use the press?'

Bridie smoothed her hands over her pinafore. 'I'm not sure to be honest, Tilda.'

'We would get the paper and I know how it works,' Tilda persisted. 'We won't leave a trail.'

'If Frank finds out...'

'But he won't.'

'No, Tilda, we can't do it here.' Elody's voice was firm. 'I'll not put Bridie at risk, there's a printing press at the Diligence Works, I can get in. Archie... Mr Derrington will have a key.'

'And how will you get said key?' Tilda looked flushed.

'I'll find a way.'

Elody was packing up her things, when Bridie put her hand on her arm.

'I'll get Frank's key, he'll be down the pub tomorrow night drinking our wages, we can make the posters then.'

'No, Bridie.'

'Look, I can see how difficult this is – you living with the Derringtons.'

'I admit it's not easy, Bridie, but my course was set long before my mother placed me with them.'

'We'll do it here.' Birdie looked determined. 'Frank will be that drunk by nine, so I'll meet you tomorrow at ten.'

Elody was halfway down the stairs when Bridie came after her. 'I don't trust Tilda Kennard, so just you take care.'

Elody changed after supper and returned to the pot bank, finding her stash of paper beneath the studio boards.

The task, though not straightforward, was mastered with Bridie at the keyboard setting the type on the printing press, while Elody checked the line. Two hours later, tired and elated, the girls switched off the light and crept from the room.

Monday came and nothing seemed amiss. Bridie took her lunch break with Elody and they sat by the canal eating home-made biscuits from her battered tin.

'Sometimes I think I'd like to get on one of them barges and float away,' she mused.

'And what about your girls?' Elody pointed out.

'There's the problem with that.'

The pot bank was closing for the day when Elody checked in the painting studio, but Bridie wasn't there. She looked in the privy, the packing room, she called her name. When she heard a cry from the office, she started to run. Bridie was cowering in the corner, Frank standing over her. There was a thud as her head hit the wall. Elody charged across the room and threw herself at his back.

'Get off her, you coward!' She clawed at his face, pulled at his hair, but he batted her off like a fly. His hands were around Bridie's throat, and he was choking her when Elody sank her teeth into his ear. He spun around, freeing Bridie, and tried to catch Elody as she sprinted away.

Her heart was thudding in her chest as he advanced across the office, throwing aside a table, sending the typewriter crashing to the floor.

'I'd watch it if I were you, Frank. Stop this before more trouble's made for you. Mr Asland knows I'm here.'

Frank's head shot up. 'It's your fault, you and that Kennard woman, putting ideas into Bridie's mind. Equal rights, I'll give you equal rights. You deserve a bashing you do, along with Bridie.' He pointed a finger at Elody. 'Using my precious Linotype for your bloody posters, you could have me sacked and where would your friend be then?'

'I don't know what you're talking about, Frank Brookes. How could we use your press when the room remains locked after hours, and you have the only key? I don't know where you get these notions, but they're pretty unsound to me.'

She could see the confusion on his coarse features, the doubt in his eyes.

'And if you lay a finger on Bridie again, I'll use my influence at the Diligence Works to make sure you don't get a day's work in a pot bank ever again.'

Frank shook his fist at her and retreated, slamming the door behind him.

When he'd gone, she took some salve from her pocket and went to Bridie, peeling back her fingers, spreading the cream on the marks around her neck. 'He's a brute, Bridie, and it's not as if he hasn't done this before.'

Bridie flinched, curving towards her. 'It used to be every time the drink was in him, now he'll find any excuse. He even beats me in front of the girls.'

Elody screwed on the top, her blood boiling. 'And the worst part of it, Bridie, it's not against the law.'

'I have to put up with this, because if I don't, he'll kick me out and keep the children. I take it because of them.'

Elody held her as she cried. 'You have to get away from him.'

'And where would I go? I don't have a godfather with a

sodding great house, there is nowhere else.' She picked up her bag. 'Thank you for trying to help, Elody, but I have to get home.'

As Elody bicycled back to Thorncliffe, she railed against a world where women could be beaten, where abuse went unpunished, and children suffered as a consequence.

Chapter Forty-Seven

Archie was taking a short cut to the agency on an errand for his father when he heard the murmur of voices coming through the studio door. He walked along the passage and leant against the wooden frame, watching the scene inside. It was like a Dutch painting, he considered, two people at work in a quiet interior, yet it wasn't only sunlight drifting through the window; energy flowed through the air. Lucian's head was lowered, his brow furrowed as his pencil flew across the paper in continuous fluid curves. Elody was leaning over the wheel, her hair piled on her head, her back away from him, her bare arms covered in slip. Her foot was on the pedal, her hands circling the clay. There was something sensuous about her: proud, beautiful, Athena, the goddess of pottery.

They were completely unaware of him and as Elody wiped her forearm across her face, removing the drops of moisture from her lips, he was mesmerised.

He moved away, but the image of Elody's neck above her white chemise remained. As he walked along the back drive to the agency, his thoughts returned to Felicity. When he had first met her at the dinner organised by his mother, he'd been attracted to her. She was glamorous, well-educated and had seemed amusing at the time. It was true, joining the two

Potteries would bring considerable wealth to both families. She was everything his mother had intended for him, but he wasn't in love with Felicity. He had gone along with it, like so many of his peers, and there was an understanding between them, but when Elody came into the house all that changed. He couldn't deny his feelings any longer, Elody had altered everything. His mother had taken away his right to fight in the war, but was he strong enough to fight her for Elody?

Elody was having tea with Mrs George and Rhea, when the older woman lifted the iron, bringing it down with a thump on Archie's shirt.

'He – that is, Mr Archie – is taking Miss Billington to the opening night at the Hippodrome.' She glanced at Elody.

'I see,' Elody said, but she didn't see at all. She hadn't been asked to Hester's opening night. In fact, she had hardly seen Hester since rehearsals started the month before.

It seemed all the Derringtons had the power to hurt her, all except one and that was Lucian.

Three days before the performance Hester sailed into her bedroom.

'Where have you been?' Elody muttered, unable to keep the resentment from her voice.

'I've been so busy; you know how it is.'

Elody didn't, but held her tongue.

Hester pirouetted in front of her. 'So what do you think? You can tell me the truth.'

Elody smiled. 'You look grand, that's what I think.' And it was true. In a few short weeks Hester had changed almost beyond recognition. She was wearing long drop earrings and her dress, a silk tunic that fell from the hips, stopped just below the knee.

'Mother thinks these hemlines are ghastly, but I really don't care.' She pulled an invitation from behind her back. 'For the opening, the mayor is attending along with several critics from London.' Her face was radiant, and Elody's humour was restored.

'So are you coming?'

'I wouldn't dream of missing it.'

Hester fiddled with Elody's powder puff, scattering dust onto the dressing table. 'Would you mind attending as Piers' partner?'

'Ahh, the ulterior motive.'

'Don't be like that, I want you there beyond anything, but Piers would be one blow too many for Mama.'

'Is she coming?'

'I doubt it.' She sat down, resting her chin on the spire of her long white fingers, her eyes lowered. She looked vulnerable suddenly and Elody knew she couldn't refuse.

Elody was immersed in a study of Josiah Wedgwood's experimentation with glazes, when there was a knock on her door. She didn't at first hear it.

'Are you in there, duck?'

Elody climbed from the bed, the real world returning fast. 'Sorry, Mrs George, I was debating on whether to fire a bowl at a higher temperature, using...' She opened the door to find the housekeeper leaning against the wall, her chest heaving.

'I'd forget about the ware for the time being,' Mrs George panted. 'You need to get yourself changed.'

'And you shouldn't be charging up the stairs.'

The housekeeper's face was smug as she brought a hanger from behind her back. 'When I saw Miss Hester all togged up for the rehearsals, I thought to myself, we can't have Miss Elody out of tune, pardon the pun, so I used my discretion on this last dress from your godfather. There's a jewelled headband to match – the assistant in Beatties said they were all the rage.'

Elody let the swathe of shimmering silver silk glide through her hands. She examined the bow on the side, the covered buttons, the tiny stitching and dropped to her knees at the housekeeper's side. 'You didn't have to do this.'

'I know you find Miss Billington a little...'

Elody could feel the knot of anxiety tightening, the fluttering of nerves when her name was mentioned, 'alarming?'

She nodded. 'I thought this might help.'

Elody put it on, letting Mrs George do up the buttons on the side, then she did a twirl, halting in front of the pier glass. The back was daringly low, a whisper of chiffon covering her pale skin. The front was simple with the tiniest of straps; it was altogether the most beautiful dress she had ever seen.

Next came Millie who combed and teased her abundant hair into a chignon and placed the headband on her forehead.

'Lawd, look at you,' she murmured. 'When I leave here, I'm going to set up a salon, I'm that good at styling.'

'And what man is going to fund you, Millie Doyle?' Mrs George asked.

'Haven't found him yet, but I will,' she replied.

Archie was waiting in the lobby when Elody opened the door. She had borrowed a white fox stole from Hester and, in her new dress, she felt confident suddenly, sophisticated. She could definitely face the world.

'Good evening, Archie.' She could hear the intake of breath.

'Elody, you look... different.'

'I rather hoped you'd say something complimentary – up to the minute, glamorous, but different?' She laughed, wondering who was speaking. Could this be the same Elody Cole?

'Are you driving with us or with Mr Medley?' he asked, scrutinising her face.

She laughed. 'Piers is taking the bus, so I've arranged to meet him inside the entrance. Forgive me, on this occasion I'll have to come with you.'

'I would suggest your gentleman friend should join us, but sadly there's no room in the car.'

'Piers?' Elody could feel the laughter bubbling in her chest. 'He isn't that sort of friend.'

Archie looked uncomfortable. 'I didn't mean to pry.'

'He is not that sort of friend. And Felicity?'

'I shall meet her at the theatre.'

'I see.'

'What do you see?' he asked, probing her, the tension palpable between them.

She shook her head and looked beyond him to Lady Ursula who was gliding down the steps.

'Nothing,' she murmured, 'that matters now.'

Seated next to Archie she could feel the warmth of his body through the thin silk of her dress, she could smell the hint of lemons in his cologne. Occasionally she was thrown against him, and she did not draw away. When they arrived at the Hippodrome, Lord Derrington helped her from the car.

'You can hold your head up high, Miss Cole, you look splendid.'

He put out his arm for his wife, who took it, surprise registering in her eyes.

Despite her conflicting emotions, Elody was quickly lost in the joy of the evening.

Hester's was not the leading role, but she sang two solos, and with her face illuminated in the lights, her voice hauntingly low, the audience was spellbound.

'If only Giles could have been here.' Lord Derrington leant towards her from the seat above. 'He would have been so proud.'

'We have to believe he's proud, Lord Derrington, something so beautiful transcends earthly bounds.'

Throughout the whispered exchange she was aware of Felicity's razor-sharp gaze.

Afterwards in the foyer, while most of them discussed a new young potter, Clarisse Cliff, who was already making waves, Felicity drummed her fingers on a pillar looking bored.

'Archie, I hope you're not going to talk about your favourite subject all night.'

'And what is my favourite subject, Felicity?' Archie's voice was cold.

'Oh, you know, darling, pots.'

The moment was saved by Hester who flew in, throwing her slim arms around her father.

'So, what did you think, Papa?'

'You were superb, my child.'

'Mother...'

Ursula Derrington hesitated, a soft glint in her eyes. 'I admit to a certain admiration.'

'Really?'

'You were more than passable, Hester, I was actually proud.'

Throughout the conversation, Elody was an observer. She saw laughter spill from Archie's mouth, the sibling love that had been buried for years, the look of awe on his face.

'Gosh, old girl, I'm not sure what to say.'

Hester laughed. 'Is this your way of congratulating me?'

'I believe it is,' he replied.

Elody stood back, witnessing the beginning of harmony within the family, the rebuilding of bridges... but she also recognised the blunt edge of jealousy in Felicity Billington's cold blue eyes.

Chapter Forty-Eight

Present Day

It was the beginning of December and Francesca's birthday, a year since she had come into their lives, over six months since she had gone. Hugh didn't go into the agency, instead he collected a tree from a nursery in Leek.

'I've bought this as a memorial to our daughter.' He showed the *Sorbus Cashmiriana* to Marina. 'Apparently, in the spring it will be covered with delicate pink flowers, the leaves will turn russet in autumn.'

'Matching the lights in Francesca's hair,' Marina murmured, looking up at him.

'Exactly, and I thought if you agreed we'd plant it in the Peace Garden, I used to go there a lot as a child.'

That afternoon, Hugh dug a sizeable hole in the ground and together they lowered the tree inside. When the roots were covered with soil, and the clusters of creamy white berries stirred in the breeze, Marina read an essay she had found in the desk in the Blue Parlour. It was written by Archie Derrington, after his brother's death in the Great War.

These trees will live on long after we have gone, the roots will reach out to their neighbours, they will connect and nourish each other, exchanging nutrients, working together. They will not create war but live in harmony and peace with the natural world. Be kind to these trees and they will protect you.

Marina passed the essay to Hugh, a sense of tranquillity enveloping her, the words were a fitting tribute to their little girl.

Another week passed, the first frost arrived, there was ice on the drive, but despite everything, things didn't get better with Hugh.

Marina continued to volunteer at both the Refuge and the Artemis Centre. But she now had another role, attending her first session in court with Rani Kumar, acting as her McKenzie friend.

'I'll be able to give you advice on points of law or procedure and any issues you may wish to raise. I can't speak for you,' she instructed the traumatised woman, 'but I'll be at your side.' When Rani was granted a non-molestation order, that also protected Ashok, Marina was elated. She would no longer be under the control of her husband and would be able to start a new life. But it was more than that, Rani had stood up for herself in court, after years of abuse she now had the courage to set herself free.

'But I couldn't have done this without you,' she said, standing on the steps of the court, her pink sari a splash of colour against the grey sky. 'Your compassion gave me the strength to speak out, and you offered me the greatest gift of all, hope.'

As Marina drove home, she thought of her words. It was true, the loss of Francesca had made her more empathetic, capable of understanding every nuance of women's suffering. Suddenly being Italian was no longer a barrier, it was an opportunity. She would fulfil the criteria necessary to practise in England, she would begin again. She parked the car, went upstairs, and ran a bath in Waterloo. As she sank beneath the water, she realised that despite being in a strange place that wasn't quite home, she could be a phoenix helping those who needed her, and it was thanks to Elody Cole. She was speaking to her through the pages of her memoir, even through her pottery. She had shown her she had the option to do whatever she wanted, making a difference was up to her. It would be hard and sometimes she would fail, but it was her own choice to try.

But this new insight didn't help her with Hugh. Day by day she recognised his deterioration into self-doubt and misery, but he wouldn't talk about it so there was nothing she could do.

'You're burying your emotions, Hugh,' she suggested one evening. 'Perhaps it would be good to confide in someone, if not in me.'

'Why on earth do I need to spill my emotions,' he had snapped at her. 'I'm not the kind to unload to a shrink at the first opportunity.'

'I think boarding school did this to you.'

'Did what, Marina?'

'Being sent away so young, particularly after your mother—' she stopped mid-sentence.

'What about my mother?'

'Mrs Crump said she left shortly after your father died.'

Hugh's lips were white. 'It's none of Mrs Crump's business, nor is it any of yours.'

Marina was determined to continue. 'Perhaps her absence from your life caused you so much trauma you're unable to speak about it.'

'It was all a long time ago and I don't see how it has any bearing on the present, on us! I don't believe in digging around in the past, it's best left alone.'

'But...'

He pushed on, ignoring her, 'I consider myself lucky. I had a fortunate childhood, living in this house, being sent to good schools, travelling with Jeremy, I've nothing to complain about. And for your information I only boarded for a year, so you can forget your psychological trauma bit.'

'But it must have been hard to be separated from her at such a young age. I'm trying to understand, Hugh, I want to feel close to you again. I want to understand why we don't seem to be able to reach each other. I hardly know Helena and I feel it could be helpful to have a sense of your past relationship with her.'

Hugh stood up. 'I'm sorry but you're going too far. If you will excuse me, I'm no longer hungry.'

'Perhaps she—'

'You know nothing about my mother so don't go there, Marina.' He had turned his back on her and her words just slipped out.

'You're so full of self- pity, Hugh, as you English are so fond of saying, snap out of it.'

'What? Like flicking a switch? Fuck off, Marina.'

The clouds gathered and finally broke after an argument following a phone call to Italy. Hugh had come in from work, and instead of calling her mother back, Marina continued talking. When she finally put down the phone, Hugh was fixing himself a drink on the kitchen counter. She could tell he was angry by the tight set of his mouth.

'That's the third time this week you've completely ignored me. It would be nice to be acknowledged when I return from the agency. I get the feeling everyone's important except me.'

'That's not true.' She leant forward to touch him, but he brushed away her arm.

'You spend hours talking to your mother, your brother, your

father, and if your grandfather didn't hate the telephone, I dread to think—'

'*Mi dispiace*, I was discussing our plans for Christmas.'

Hugh's voice was level. 'Perhaps you should forget Christmas.'

'What do you mean?' She could discern the panic in her voice. 'I have asked my family to stay and your mother.'

'Do you really wish to celebrate at a time like this? And for your information my mother hates Christmas.'

'But my family, I need to see them.'

'Your family are great but they're quite—'

'Yes, Hugh?'

'Overwhelming, noisy . . . Italian.'

'If you hadn't noticed, your wife is Italian.' Marina's voice was quiet, deadly. She was filled with a sense of outrage and shock.

'I'm sorry that's not what I meant.'

'What did you mean, Hugh?'

'Perhaps we should be on our own, have time to think of Francesca.'

'All I do is think about our daughter. I trailed across the globe for you, uprooting myself from my family when I needed them most, and you deny them now. Christ, Hugh, how selfish is that?' She threw up her hands. 'I was stupid to have believed this would work. After all I'm an Italian and you're an upper-class Englishman with issues.'

That night, as she lay in the darkness, she remembered the man who had enchanted her in Florence, the impulsive, passionate Hugh who had dragged her from the famous Via de' Tornabuoni where she was window shopping, into the Church of Santa Trinita in the square along the street.

'Every country has masterpieces,' he had said, putting in a coin, so the dim light of the Sassetti Chapel was replaced by a luminous glow. 'But this, Marina, this glorious Adoration of the

Shepherds moves me in the way no other can. The harmonious composition is an embodiment of purity and beauty. Do you see the quality and depth of light that remain in the five-hundred-year-old pigment?' He had one arm around her shoulders, the other pointing to the panel.

Marina had studied the altar piece and she had been moved by it, but it was the joy on Hugh's face, the energy that made her heart swell.

Afterwards, they walked out through the heavy church door into the bright sunlight, and he had caught her hand as they ran down the steps.

'This country, your country, makes me feel alive, Marina. I could be here every moment of my life and see something new, something that fills my soul. Your country speaks to me in a language I'm not yet fluent in, but I could spend years learning.'

The day had ended as it should have done, in their bedroom, Hugh unbuttoning her shirt, unhooking her bra. Where was the Hugh that loved her country now?

Chapter Forty-Nine

The Past

The first phase of the plan was carried out, and the following morning there was consternation in the pot banks.

'Who's done this?' Reggie Billington called a meeting of the workers in the yard outside. Men and women shuffled their feet on the cobbles while the sun beat down.

He held up the poster, tore it into pieces and threw it in the canal. 'Equal pay, you're lucky to get paid at all. If I hear any more of this from you women, you're out, the lot of you.'

'Who's going to do the hard work then?' Dawn whispered.

'Who said that?'

Reggie's eyes were bulging as he scanned a group of fettlers, among them, Patsy Wainwright. 'Was it you?' He pointed her out.

'No, sir.'

'This subversive rubbish has been plastered over the walls of the pot banks. If I find any of you were involved, there will be consequences. And you men,' he was scowling now, his heavy brows drawn together in a frown, 'get some balls the lot of you and keep your wives under control.'

Elody opened her mouth to speak, but Bridie pulled her back. 'Not now, duck, you'll have your day.'

At Thorncliffe the event was discussed with irritation.

'It's not a good time to do this,' Andrew said at dinner, while dissecting his sole. 'Many in the industry have gone under and the Diligence Works only just survived the war.'

Elody longed to ask him who got them through the war, but she held her tongue.

'Perhaps there's never a good time,' said Archie, 'and they could be right.'

'Archie for heaven's sake.' Ursula raised her eyes. 'If everyone was as soft as you, we wouldn't have a factory at all.'

Word filtered through the pot banks, whispered outside the privies, in the corridors. Notes exchanged hands. The march would take place on the thirtieth of September.

The die was cast, but the march was a ticking time bomb to Elody. With several new designs tried and tested in the studio at Thorncliffe Hall, and a range of drawings supplied by Lucian, she endeavoured with little success to push it to the back of her mind.

One evening, she showed the pattern book to Mr Asland along with a charming new jug.

'I knew you had it in you,' he murmured, admiring the painted leopard, with feathers sprouting from his head. He turned the jug on its side. 'And the way the creature is pacing through the vegetation, it's admirable, Miss Cole.'

'Thank you for your faith in me, but it's also the work of my assistant Lucian.'

He smiled. 'Ah, the elusive young man. Will you please inform him we're ready for an exhibition, but the collection will need a name.'

'The Lucian range,' she replied.

*

He had gone and Elody was standing in the empty studio, the pieces she had created with Lucian, drying on the boards. There was no doubt she was proud of their achievement, but anxiety clouded her pleasure. An ominous foreboding filled a place in her heart. She opened the pattern book once more, and she could hear her mother's voice, '*I told you college would set you up right, my love, and it has.*' But as she walked back down the stairs, she couldn't forget their vision for equality, and she knew she would have to choose.

The exhibition was organised for the penultimate day in July, eight weeks before the march.

'I suppose you won't be joining me, Lucian,' Elody asked as she was about to turn out his light.

'I don't think so.'

'So you wish to remain an enigma?'

Lucian dragged the dictionary from the bedside table and started leafing through the pages.

'E-n-i-gma, *a mystery, a riddle, a puzzle,*' he looked up at Elody, 'so I'll be the mysterious figure, who nobody sees.'

Elody prodded him, then she took him in her arms. The child was perceptive and insightful, and she loved him with all her heart.

'If you want to come, just let me know, my dearest little boy.'

On the morning of the exhibition, Elody was in Lucian's room at dawn. She kissed him on the forehead.

'Are you going to wish us luck?' she asked.

'We don't need luck,' he murmured. 'One day our designs will be known around the world, even America.'

'Who told you that?'

'You did.'

Elody smiled. 'We'll spend all of Thursday together.'

'That's forty-eight hours away.'

'Go back to sleep, you funny little boy.'

Elody unpacked the samples in the showroom downstairs. '*If you don't have dreams, you have nothing, Elody,*' her mother had said. And it was those dreams that had brought her to this attractive red brick showroom with the specially made stands, and an exhibition dedicated entirely to the Lucian range. She was running a duster over the pieces when Felicity Billington walked in, immaculate in a nautical dress with a sailor collar and a blue bow.

'It seems you're doing well, Miss Cole.' She picked up a coffee pot, took off the lid, then a bowl, turning it upside down. 'It will be good if you're successful, will it not?'

'I hope it will be profitable for the Greenfield Works,' Elody murmured, her fingers laced tight, though they were itching to return the bowl to its rightful place on the stand.

Felicity laughed. 'No, dear girl, I mean it would be good for you. I assume you won't be staying on at Thorncliffe Hall.'

'I'm sorry?'

'When Archie and I are married.' She looked at Elody as if she was stupid. 'You must have known?'

'I did not,' she stuttered, looking into the face of the girl who had patronised her, undermined her and who she knew hated her. She forced herself to remain calm.

'When did he propose?'

'He hasn't yet, but it's a mere formality.'

'Aren't you a little premature if he hasn't asked you?' Elody regretted the words as soon as they were out, there would be repercussions she was sure of it.

Felicity came closer, her face taut. 'Miss Cole, your future depends on us, so I suggest you show some respect to the future Lady Ursula.'

Elody had conflicting feelings about Ursula Derrington, but she hadn't written her off quite yet. Anger bubbled inside her.

'Can I ask why you're telling me this now?'

'I thought I ought to warn you, Elody. Forget any feelings you may have for Archie. He may seduce you, but you would be a conquest, a little game for him, nothing more.'

Elody exhaled, her restraint dissolving. 'You and your clever words, but for all your money you'll never have his love.' She stepped forward, looked her in the eye. 'It will be a marriage of mere convenience, nothing more.'

What happened next would remain burned in Elody's memory.

Felicity's mouth was working, and Elody thought she would explode. 'Damn your stupid exhibition and this wretched little bowl.' She let the bowl go, but Elody dived for it, catching it just before it hit the floor.

'And damn you, Elody Cole.'

The exhibition commenced at six, and as the room filled with selected members of the public, the mayor and several other dignitaries, Mr Asland prompted her.

'Now, that's Mr Pretty, lives in Port Hill but he owns a china emporium in Manchester and another in Leeds, and the gentleman coming towards us is our Member of Parliament for Stoke.'

'Andrew MacLaren,' Elody murmured, knowing exactly who he was.

'You've done well, girl.' Mr Asland ushered yet another reporter to her side.

The journalist, a fresh-faced junior with a confident air, took out his pad. 'Mr Whitby from the *Sentinel* at your service, and I take it you're the lucky potter, Miss Cole?'

'Lucky?' Elody queried.

'Working alongside the men, you must be right proud.'

'That's not exactly how I would have put it, Mr Whitby.' The conversation was cut short when Reggie Billington joined them, sweating profusely in his tweed suit.

'We give our girls opportunities at the Greenfield Works, Mr Whitby, as you can see.'

'You're obviously an excellent employer, sir.'

'I do my best,' he replied.

When the journalist had gone, Reggie caught Elody's arm, all pretence of good humour gone.

'You'll come to my office in the morning, nine o'clock sharp. I want a word with you, girl.'

Elody knew she was in trouble, but the excitement of the evening had cushioned her from reality. He wouldn't sack her, she thought, putting the samples in the cupboard, not with all those orders to fulfil, the editorials in the press. He was a businessman, was Reggie Billington. Before she switched off the light, she picked up the small willow box Mr Asland had given her, the jug she had made inside. This she was taking home for Lucian.

Elody was hardly through the door when Archie strode down the corridor towards her.

'What did you say to Felicity?' he asked, his jaw tight.

Elody was tired and emotional; she had taken enough. 'Is it any business of yours?'

'I believe it has plenty to do with me, you've caused more trouble than most people do in a lifetime.'

She was turning to leave when he caught her arm. She shook it away.

'Come with me to the library, Elody, unless you wish the entire household to hear.'

Elody didn't move.

'I think you owe it to me. Please,' he finished.

Elody followed him through the door, remembering their confrontation in the library a few months before.

'Everything was fine until you came along. What do you want from us, Elody?'

'I'm sorry, but I won't listen to this.'

'What did you say to her?'

Elody's anger bubbled over. 'Your fiancée accused me of trying to get between you, that I would be another conquest! As I have said before, Archie, I'm not interested in you, and I never will be.'

Archie was standing directly in front of her, only inches away. She could sense his pent-up anger, but there was something else in his eyes and it was mirrored in her own. He moved closer and Elody was rooted to the ground. Her mind was telling her to leave, her emotions rendered her immobile.

'Felicity is right, you are getting between us. Tell me to leave now, and I'll go, Elody.'

When Elody remained silent, he put his hands around her waist and kissed her. Without meaning to she was kissing him back.

He took her face in his hands looked into her eyes. 'Have you any idea what you're doing to me?'

'Don't,' she whispered, shaking her head, pushing him away. 'Please don't make fun of me, Archie.'

A tear slipped down her cheek and he wiped it away with his thumb.

'What about Felicity? What about your engagement?'

'There is an understanding ... we're not engaged.'

'Isn't that the same?'

'It is not, Elody. I've never proposed because I couldn't bring myself to do so, not since you arrived.'

'But it's cruel to lead her on, make her believe—'

'Cruel to Felicity Billington,' he interrupted. 'The toughest woman this side of Spitsbergen?'

'I don't know where that is,' she mumbled, feeling hysterical laughter rising inside her.

'It's an island north of Norway, about as far as you can go. What is it about you, Elody? Why do you make me mad, then deliriously, wonderfully alive? To be honest, I thought I could marry her – I hoped that marriage to Felicity, children, a settled life, would quell my demons. When you came along, you changed everything.'

'And someone like me couldn't make you happy?' Elody's jaw thrust forward.

'That's not what I meant. Why are you always cross with me?' He laughed suddenly, his face relaxing. 'The trouble is, however hard I try, I can't get you out of my mind.' He lifted up her chin and she could see what he wanted in his eyes.

'No, Archie, not like this, not now.'

He lowered his hands. 'Forgive me, I would never take advantage of you.'

'There's too much going on in my life.' Elody's voice had dropped so Archie had to lean closer to hear. 'This isn't the time for either of us, I have to leave.'

She glanced around the room, imagining Archie making love to her in the library, the moonlight pouring through the shutters, surrounded by her beloved books. Though every sense in her body begged her to stay, she knew she had to go.

Somehow Elody managed to drag herself upstairs. She threw herself onto the bed, fully clothed, accepting that she longed for Archie, wanted him... but she couldn't let this derail her path. She had been right to walk away.

Chapter Fifty

Heat funnelled down the passage as Elody waited outside the office. She wiped her hands on her skirt, her previous confidence diminished. Felicity was the light of her father's life, and she, a potter in her father's works, had the temerity to cross her. She flinched as a voice bellowed her name, then she stepped inside.

Her employer's hands were palm down on the surface of his desk and it was a moment before he raised his head.

'Do you realise how much this has cost me, Miss Cole?' he spat. 'Everything I have invested in you, the money for the exhibition, the wine, to say nothing of the cost of creating the range.'

'I'm truly grateful.'

'Ha,' he laughed. 'I'll show you grateful, if you were to stay on, you would pay me back every penny, but since you are to leave, your pieces will stay behind.'

'Leave?'

'Yes, leave, you scheming little whore. Did you think you can stay on after this?'

'But—'

'I can see you're intent on destroying my daughter's chances of becoming the future Lady Derrington. Well, it won't happen, our Potteries will be united, I will not allow you to ruin our plans.'

'It was hardly my—'

'You are a troublemaker, Miss Cole.' He cut across her, venom in his dark eyes. 'Mr Asland will escort you from the premises, now get out.'

Elody retreated from the office to the passage outside. She would recall later leaning against the wall, cradling her head in her hands, her dreams in tattered ruins. Everything she had worked for was collapsing around her. Perhaps she should have remained silent, curbed her tongue, but where was the integrity in that? Felicity Billington had insulted her in every conceivable way. And what about the collection? All the blood, sweat and tears, her creations, Lucian's. Her head was spinning but she could see the inevitability of it all. If Felicity married Archie in the future, she would be given her cards; if she did not, the outcome was the same.

She was climbing the stairs to get her things when Mr Asland caught up with her.

'I don't know how to say this,' he muttered, 'but I have instructions from Mr Billington you are not to see the girls.'

'I can't say goodbye?'

'I'm so sorry, Elody.'

Black soot billowed into the sky, clouding the pot bank in darkness, but Elody's mind was suddenly clear. Reginald Billington wouldn't have her ware. He would not keep any of it. She returned to the showroom, turned the key in the lock and glanced around the empty shelves. The opening night was in the past, this was now, and it had to be done. She breathed deeply gathering her resolve and walked to the cupboards taking out the pieces one by one.

Every precious plate she had designed with Lucian, every bowl, she unwrapped and threw on the floor. With fascinated horror she watched the fragments scatter, Lucian's beautiful artwork destroyed. She had nearly finished her task when Reggie Billington banged on the door.

'Stop that immediately,' he yelled, rattling the handle. 'I'll come after you and any family you have left, trust me I will.'

Elody continued in her task until every piece of china was smashed beyond repair, then she opened the door.

'You bitch,' he yelled, grabbing hold of her, swinging his fist into her face. 'You dirty bitch.' There was a blinding flash, a thud as fist met bone, her head spun as she staggered backwards into the wall. She could feel her knees buckling as his fist came again, but she had no strength to move. Suddenly a huge man was in the way, Arthur Shadbolt, the gentle giant from the packing room.

'I think that's enough, sir,' he said, holding his arm. 'It's my belief you're not meaning to do this, being a kind man and all.'

Reggie Billington looked up at him, confusion in his eyes. His arms dropped to his sides, and he walked away. Moments later a car roared down the road.

Much later when the workers were at lunch, Elody climbed on her bicycle.

'Are you all right, Miss Cole?' Arthur Shadbolt asked, shaking his head. 'Not sure you should be pedalling.'

'It's thanks to you he didn't kill me.'

'You're mad,' said Dawn. 'You'll fall in a ditch and then you'll be good for nothing at all. You have to stay awhile.'

'Dawn's right.' Mr Asland limped down the alleyway towards them. 'Let me contact Lord Derrington, ask him to take you home.'

'No,' whispered Elody, 'trust me I'm fine.' But she didn't feel fine, she felt sick, and stars flew before her eyes.

'I don't trust you at all,' said Dawn. 'What kind of stunt was that, breaking all the china?' She smiled, showing her crooked teeth. 'But I have to admit it was something to see Reggie's face as he charged down the passage. If he doesn't have a heart attack, I'll be surprised.'

Mr Asland sighed. 'She'll not listen to us, Dawn. Stubborn, just like her mother.' He took the cloth bag from his arm. 'Since it seems we'll not dissuade you, I have this for you. Though it's bound to get me the sack, you shall not leave the pattern book behind.

'I can't take it; you'll lose your job.'

'My dear, you can. You've shown us what honour means, what honesty and courage really are.' He put the book in her satchel and did up the straps. 'Make good use of it, Miss Cole, and if you ever have a position for me in your next place of work, I'll be there.'

'Thank you, Mr Asland, I now have everything I need to start again, though I'm not sure where and when that will be; but trust me, if I'm ever in that fortunate situation, there will always be a place for you.'

Elody was lying on her bed when Mrs George came in.

'When I saw your bicycle on the floor, your paints scattered, I wondered what was wrong. Lord in heaven, what's happened to you?' She put her hand over her mouth and rushed from the room.

She was back seconds later with Millie. 'Mary, Mother of Jesus,' the girl exclaimed. 'We need to call the doctor.'

'No,' Elody whispered. 'No doctor, but please tell Lucian I'm a little unwell, nothing serious – he's expecting me.'

Mrs George nodded at her. 'Go, Millie, it's all right. And tell Jacob Shaw to get me some ice. A whole bucket, if you please.'

Half an hour later, Elody was propped up in bed, ice wrapped in a tea towel being applied by Mrs George.

'The skin isn't permanently damaged, thank heavens, but you have the biggest black eye, child. Who did this to you?'

'It's a long story,' she whispered.

'I like long stories,' said Mrs George.

Archie took the stairs two at a time and entered the darkened bedroom. Elody was covered by a sheet, her clothes folded over the chair, her sturdy boots beneath. He moved closer, a groan escaping him as he saw her cracked and broken lips, blood matted in her hair. How could any man do this to a young and defenceless woman? How was it possible? But he knew with a painful jolt it happened every day. He uncurled her hand which was circled around a canvas bag and brought it to his cheek, noticing the rounded fingernails a little chewed at the end, the soft feel of it in his own.

'Elody,' he whispered, fury igniting a fire in his heart, 'this won't go unpunished, I promise.' She opened her eyes, tried to focus, then they flickered closed.

'I smashed the ware.' Her words were faint, indistinct. He moved closer. 'I smashed it all, Archie. There's nothing left.'

'You can make it again.'

A tear slipped unchecked down her cheek. 'All of Lucian's work, but I couldn't leave it behind.'

'You had your reasons, Elody, and I'm convinced they must have been good.'

Elody tried to smile. 'It seemed so at the time.'

Archie left her, knowing that Elody was changing him. Yesterday he was a weak and anxious young man, today he was prepared to fight for what he believed was right.

Archie returned the following afternoon to find Elody sitting up in bed, a small willow crate on her knees. Her hair was washed, but her right eye was closed.

'Mrs George tidied me up.'

'You look…'

'Terrible.' Elody managed a small smile.

'Are you feeling any better?' Archie hovered by the bed and when she didn't reply he sat down in the chair at her side.

'It doesn't make up for any of this, but I've seen your former employer.'

'What did he say?' she whispered, brushing her hand across her cheek.

Archie remembered Reggie Billington's initial bluster when confronted, and his fear when he had flung him against the wall, hissed into his face.

'It was something about the damage done, Elody, but I believe it's more about his wounded pride. The police reprimanded him, but they pointed out that—'

'I smashed the ware,' Elody whispered for him. She winced and Archie longed to take her in his arms. She looked so vulnerable, deflated, not the strong and determined girl he knew before.

'He should be punished through the courts. I'm so sorry.'

Elody raised her head and looked at Archie with some of her old fire. 'But he won't be because the law allows this to happen.' She sighed and sank down the pillow, tapping the basket at her side.

'I brought this home for Lucian before…' her tongue ran around her parched lips.

'Open it, Archie.'

Archie lifted the coffee pot from its nest of straw, took off the lid, examining it one way then another, and when at last he spoke, his voice was filled with emotion.

'Do you know how beautiful this is, Elody? How unique?' He leant towards her, moving a strand of damp hair that had fallen over her cheek, and gently kissed her brow. 'Would you mind

331

if I showed this to my father? I give you my word, I'll bring it back tonight.'

'You can show him the pattern book too if you like.'

Archie was closing the door when he looked back at her. 'Needless to say, Felicity is no longer speaking to me, the understanding is off, thank God.'

Archie didn't go straight to his father, instead he found his mother in the Blue Parlour feeding paper into the typewriter, her brow furrowed in concentration.

'I have something to show you and I want you to keep an open mind.'

'Miss Cole did this?' she asked, handling the coffee pot, turning it this way and that.

'So what do you think?'

His mother gave a wry smile. 'I have to admit the girl is full of surprises, I haven't seen anything quite so unusual before.'

When Archie left the Blue Parlour, his footsteps were light.

His mother was changing too, and it had taken a girl from the Potteries to bring her back to life.

'What would you say if Elody worked with us, if this became part of our range?' he had suggested.

'I thought she worked for the Billingtons?'

'That news, dear mother, is for another time.'

Lucian was scrutinising the globe when Elody entered his bedroom the following morning. 'I thought if you wanted, we could go to America,' he murmured.

'You did?'

He turned around, his gaze taking in her face, running down her entire body to her feet.

'Who did this to you, Elody?' he gulped, his little fists clenching.

'I fell over.'

Lucian touched the swollen skin, her broken lip. 'Someone has hurt you.'

'I'm all right now.'

'I'll fight them, Elody, a duel.' He buried his face in her side. 'I knew you were hurt, I told Millie she was lying.'

'No more duels.' Elody put the crate on the bed. 'But I have this for you, open it and see.'

Lucian held up the little coffee pot.

'Ours, Elody.'

'I haven't stamped it yet, I wanted you to do that with our initials, EC and LD.'

Chapter Fifty-One

Elody spent every moment of her recuperation with Lucian. Now it was the child who read to her, made up stories, brought flowers from the garden and plaited them into garlands while she rested on his bed.

'You've made me better, now I'm making you better,' he said, a large ox-eye daisy trailing through his fingers.

Elody would have given her soul to have made him truly well, for today there were dark rings beneath his eyes and his chest was rattling like a drum. She drew him into the crook of her arm.

'I've made up my mind, I'll come with you to America,' he informed her.

'So what are we going to do in America?'

'We're going to find Walter and make beautiful pots and Archie will marry you because he loves you.'

'Why do you say that, my love?'

'Because he does.'

It was another two days before she told Lucian about the broken ware.

'I've done something, Lucian.'

He raised his head.

'And the something might make you sad.'

'You're not going?' Alarm triggered in his eyes.

'No, sweet boy, but I've broken our range, all of it, every single piece.'

'Why did you do that?' His look was curious nothing more and Elody exhaled, before telling him a version of the events.

'Well then,' he said when she had finished. 'We shall make it all again!'

When they finally went outside, Archie joined them with Rhea, the small band wandering towards the kitchen garden, weaving through the flower beds towards the large oak door. Inside the high walls, the sweet peas flourished on obelisk canes, and clouds of cosmos billowed beneath the espaliered apple trees. The nasturtiums planted by Lucian, provided a bright flash of colour around the marrows and peas.

'Did you know nasturtiums attract the aphids and flea beetles.' Lucian turned an orange flower towards Archie.

'I did not, young man.'

'And that means the pests are likely to leave the marrows alone.'

'Is there anything else you'd like to tell me?' Elody took his hand.

'The square on the hypotenuse is equal to the squares on the other two sides – Pythagoras's theorem for right-angled triangles.'

'Oh my,' said Archie. 'Remind me not to teach you chess.'

They sat down on a wrought iron bench, Lucian on one side of her and Archie on the other. The July air was soporific and as Elody closed her eyes, the cascading notes of a song thrush pierced her consciousness. At some point she must have fallen asleep because she awoke to find Archie looking down on her.

'There's something I'd like to discuss.'

'What is it?' she asked, her eyes attuned to Lucian who was walking along a low wall, his arms outstretched.

'You be careful,' she called out. 'No accidents, mind.'

Lucian giggled. 'This isn't a tightrope, Elody, just a little wall.' She turned back to Archie, giving him her attention.

'Before the war, we had a large crate making shop, but we have come to realise it's cheaper to buy them in. Now many of the crates and packing cases are sourced elsewhere.'

'Yes?'

'That leaves only Roger Croft working there and old Mr Hill. We obviously couldn't let them go, but we have a smaller building for them next door...' Archie shrugged his shoulders, a glint in his eye. 'The thing is, Elody, if they move, the studios will be empty, which isn't good for the fabric of the building. It has running water and a proper stove inside...'

Elody sat up. 'What are you saying?'

'Ah,' he laughed. 'I have your attention. We would have to do a bit of work clearing the stray bits of willow left by the men, they're a mucky lot if I'm honest, but the building is plenty big enough for studios.'

Elody held her breath. 'Studios?'

'Yes, Elody, your studios. You could use our bottle ovens and kilns and the workforce would be at your disposal. I've asked Father, and he is in agreement, what do you say?'

'A business arrangement?'

'A business arrangement.'

'I could use your placers, fettlers, spongers and the like?'

'It would be my suggestion that you employ your own paintresses and throwers, but we'll provide you with clay from the pug mill, glazes, all your needs. There is a connecting walkway giving you easy access to the factory buildings and indeed the workforce.'

Elody chewed on her lip. It was what she had always dreamed

of, but she wouldn't accept this opportunity without including her friends. They had supported her through the worst of times, they were family. She chose her words carefully. 'I always hoped that one day I could open my own pottery, but...'

'But?'

'There are people who mean a lot to me, good workers each and every one, they would need to come with me. First, I couldn't do it without Mr Asland, then there's Dawn, Bridie and Maud. Not Florence, she's convalescing and must never come back.' She stopped, having run out of steam and looked down at her hands.

'Anything else?' Archie was smiling.

'I'll need hot water too, I must have that to keep them safe, and if it's too long a list, I'll do it on my own, no hard feelings.'

Archie didn't ask how she would do it on her own.

'You drive a hard bargain, Miss Cole.'

'I know my ware.' She frowned, collecting her thoughts. 'No, our ware, mine and Lucian's. It's special, everyone says so. And,' she added as an afterthought, 'equal financial terms.'

'Everything you use will be accounted for and we would split the profit, how does that sound?'

'It sounds agreeable so far, but what about your mother?'

'You will find she's a realist where money is concerned, and it's my opinion there will be large financial rewards in your Lucian range.'

'And Reggie Billington, what about rights?'

'If he has any, I rather doubt he will exercise them. With word out that he beat you ... It's not a large town.'

Though Elody was longing to see the studios, it was the following Monday before she was ready to face the world.

'So how do you think I look?' she asked Lucian.

337

He put his head on one side, surveying her. 'I think you shouldn't go to work.'

'Is that because I look bruised, or because you don't want me to?'

'Hmmm, let me see ...'

Elody tickled him and he squealed with delight. 'All right, there are no more bruises, Elody.'

Archie and Lord Derrington were already at breakfast when she arrived.

'Archie tells me you're joining us at the pot bank this morning. In fact, he's told me about the events of the last few days. I'm so sorry, Elody.' He put down his cup and surveyed her thoughtfully. 'I would have come to see you, but I was told you were sick and didn't wish to be disturbed.'

'I wasn't feeling like company, sir.'

'You've had a difficult time.'

'Not with my colleagues, not Mr Asland, he's the kindest man alive. He fought for my ware, got me the exhibition ...' She put the butter knife back in the dish. 'I know you didn't want me at the pot bank, but we agreed I could ...'

Andrew laughed. 'No, Elody, you decided you were going back, and I accepted your terms. I've realised it's impossible to keep you under control. In any event, having seen the coffee pot and your remarkable sample book, there could very well be an arrangement suitable for both of us.'

'And Lady Ursula?'

'Now Lady Ursula is reconciled to the fact that Archie and Felicity are no longer walking out, she has turned her attention elsewhere.' He smiled wryly. 'She knows a good product when she sees one!' He stood up and Jacob pulled out his chair. 'I believe, Elody, you will find us rather different from the Greenfield Works.'

Jacob Shaw drove the car beyond the Diligence Works and stopped at a tall, two-storey workshop at the end of the lane.

'This is it, Elody.' Archie was out of the car before Jacob, opening the gate to let her through. 'No hurry, just have a look around.'

'And when you've seen enough, come and meet our foreman,' Lord Derrington called. 'Go through the main entrance then go right at the top of the stairs. You'll find my office at the end of the corridor.'

As the car drew away, Elody closed the gate behind her and leant against it. She observed the grass growing through the cracked concrete, the dirty reservoir used by the crate makers to soften the willow, a rusting metal advertisement bolted to the walls. But none of this mattered, a bit of work and imagination was all that was needed. She moved toward the external stairway and was startled when an old man came through the door at the top.

'Pinching my studios are you, duck?'

'I'm not chucking you out. Oh Lord, I would never do that . . . Mr Archie said he . . .'

The man's face broke into a wide grin. 'Look, duck, you're welcome to it, a dusty old place it is. Got a nice new workshop yonder.' He nodded and continued down the stairs, sauntering along the walkway to the factory next door. When Elody was on her own, she entered the studios. Sunlight highlighted the bird droppings, the broken windows, the rubbish littering the floors, but she could see beyond it to a room filled with tables, her friends painting, gossiping, their laughter filling the air. She could picture herself at a wheel creating beautiful shapes, occasionally Lucian joining her. This was the future she had dreamt of. She would be her own boss, on her own terms.

When she had seen enough, she returned down the lane,

gazing up at the red brick buildings, the smartly painted doors. A man was relaxing beneath the archway a cigarette in his hand. He stubbed it out on the cobbles, tipped his cap and sauntered inside. On the weighbridge, a lorry-driver saluted her and smiled. Did she look different she wondered; did she look as if she had come up in the world? As she skirted the outside of the pottery, she realised the Diligence Works was a well-oiled machine, the raw clay coming into the slip house, nearest the canal, and all the procedures arranged in order of production until the finished product emerged at the other end in the packing house, also near the canal. She had done her circuit, and was at the top of the outside stairs, when a grey-haired man in brown cotton overalls beckoned her from a door at the end of the passage 'Miss Cole, this way.'

Lord Derrington was leaning through an internal window looking onto the works beneath.

'I like to know what's going on.' He straightened and came towards her across the large, raftered office. 'The throwing shop is below us and the jollying shop next door, welcome to the Diligence Works, Miss Cole.'

Archie was sitting on the corner of his father's desk.

'If you do decide to take up our offer, you will need to keep on the right side of Mr Digby. Our foreman is definitely in charge, Cousin Harry is his second in command.'

The foreman tapped his nose. 'If your product is as good as I'm told, Miss Cole, then we'll get along just fine. Ask me anything and I'll do what I can to oblige, everyone calls me Digby by the way.'

'So, Elody how do you find the works?' Lord Derrington asked as they helped themselves to biscuits and mugs of tea brought in by his secretary Mrs Bond, a stout middle-aged woman with white hair.

'It's certainly very different from the Greenfield Works. You

340

have a bathroom for a start, with hot water and proper washing facilities, but—'

'Wedgwood recognised the need for hygiene one hundred and fifty years ago, I can't imagine why every pot bank doesn't follow these simple rules.' Andrew reached for another biscuit.

'Because it's about money and cost over people's lives.' Elody blushed, aware Mr Digby was watching her.

'I accept there's always room for change, but we're getting better at it, Miss Cole.' Lord Derrington's voice was animated as he defended his pottery. 'While the Victorian industrial period may have a reputation for being the worst era for the workers, with the advent of steam-power several of the perilous jobs were scrapped. Did you see our steam engine on your travels, she is a mighty beast?' He didn't wait for her answer, pacing the room with an energy she hadn't seen in him before. 'We're actually rather proud of her, but soon she'll be relegated to the scrapheap – electricity, Miss Cole,' he sighed, spreading his hands wide.

'It's called progress, Father.'

'You're right, Archie, and it has its benefits. Do you see down there, Elody, all our wheels now run by electricity. In Wedgwood's time, women and children would have been employed to manually turn the potters' wheels and indeed the lathe.'

'And little 'uns, revolving the lathe with their foot, while the turner worked! All those terrible deformities, Lord Derrington. But we haven't learnt … other dangers have taken their place.'

'At these works we are conscious of safety.'

'And plumbism, what is your record with that?' Elody looked first at Lord Derrington, then Archie. 'Sorry, but it's important to me.'

'I cannot deny there have been cases, not a lot has changed in the way pottery is made, but we are trying, Elody. I give you my word.'

'Recent legislation should have helped protect the workers.'

Archie took Elody's empty mug. 'But it seems in many of the pot banks, including your old place of work, rules are made to be broken. At the Diligence Works, we're doing what we can.'

Elody was returning downstairs when Archie ran after her.

'Sorry, but Father is defensive about this place.'

'It's not often I hear about things from an owner's perspective. Josiah Wedgwood broke the mould, Archie. Did you know he had smallpox and it settled in his leg – not long afterwards he had a riding accident and broke his shin. They had to amputate but it didn't stop him. When he couldn't use the wheel, he turned his mind to the science of colours, glazes and consistencies, to designing beautiful shapes and building canals. He was a genius. I often wonder what it was like to be young in the most remarkable period of the ceramics industry.' She turned to him, her eyes wide with excitement. 'All these resources lying under the very ground they walked on and local people like Wedgwood lighting a fire that would cause such artistry and life. Think of your great grandfather who found coal beneath his farm. It all led to this.'

She looked up to find Archie watching her.

'What,' she said, shaking her head.

'Elody Cole, you are the most extraordinary young woman.'

'I'll take that as praise,' she replied.

They were in the car when Elody summoned her most formal voice.

'Lord Derrington, Archie, I've considered your offer and will be glad of the association with the Diligence Works. I believe we will get on fine.'

Chapter Fifty-Two

With equipment borrowed from the pot bank, Elody set to work on the studios. On Saturday morning, Dawn arrived with Maud and they rolled up their sleeves. Bridie came as quick as she could with her two girls. When Elody offered them employment, the only one to decline was Bridie.

'I'd love to, you know that, but…' Elody knew what the but was and hugged her hard.

'If you ever get rid of your husband and run off with the girls, you know where we are.'

When Mrs Wright appeared in the studio with a basket of pastries, she was beaming.

'Against all odds my Florence is going to live, she's coming home!' She paused to wipe her eyes and revealed the other astonishing news. Mr Wright had been offered a job as cowman; they were moving lock stock and barrel to a cottage on Froghall Farm.

It was an emotional moment, all the women crowding together laughing and crying. When they had recovered their equilibrium, they continued scrubbing the floors, disinfecting the privy, sloshing white paint on the walls.

Before two weeks were out, the broken windows had been replaced by a glazier, the gas lamps repaired, the oven cleaned and the buildings were as good as new. As Elody sat at the table, looking at the three new wheels, the lathe, she believed she was dreaming. This wasn't reality; this couldn't be happening to her.

Dusk was falling when Archie found Elody asleep in the studio, her head resting on the table, her body obscured in shadow.

'If we don't leave soon, dinner will be over, and it'll be scraps in the kitchen for you and me.'

'I like scraps,' Elody murmured.

She was packing up her things when she brought up the subject.

'I want the women to have the same salary as the two male throwers, I want equal pay.' She was aware she was pushing the boundaries, pushing Archie, but it had to be said.

'You know it would raise tensions at the Diligence Works.'

'I realise there will be resistance, Archie, but—'

He went to the window and looked into the lowering sky. 'Don't you see, Elody, inequality is entrenched into the very fabric of our society.' He turned back to her. 'That's not to say I believe in it—'

'But we have to start somewhere, Archie, don't you see? You could be a trailblazer, a pioneer.' She went to stand beside him, her eyes shining.

'I worry that at this moment, the men would resent you: a girl, a young one at that, arriving at the pot bank, changing the rules.'

'Think of this moment as the new future; it could work.'

'I'll see what I can do, but I'd rather you give it some time.' The conversation was closed, but Elody knew she couldn't let it lie.

When she arrived back at the house, she ran straight to Lucian.

'You're late,' he grumbled, looking at his watch. She poked his tummy.

'Sorry.'

You said you'd come at six and it's five minutes to seven.'

'Everyone in my life is fractious with me today.'

'Who is everyone?'

Elody laughed, her anxiety disappearing. Lucian saw life in such simple terms. 'There is just you, Lucian.'

Later as she read him a story, Rhea curled in his lap, she realised that structure was so important in the child's life, nothing could change. Her own ambitions had to run alongside her love for Lucian.

From that day, she kept a log and showed it to Lucian on her return. He would ask questions and make suggestions, but he had never been to the studios. One afternoon, she went in search of Jacob.

'I know her Ladyship wouldn't approve, taking him out in the car, but it would only be for an hour.'

He laughed. 'You're asking me to break all the rules, Miss Cole.'

'Please, Jacob.'

'You get the lad and I'll fetch the car.'

They arrived at the studios an hour later, and Elody showed Lucian everything. He examined the jars of brightly coloured pigments, the lathe, the wheels, then she took him into the studio upstairs. The two new paintresses, Mavis Botley and Glenda Briggs looked up from the table where they were practising Lucian's designs with Dawn.

'You didn't really paint the flying fox?' asked Mavis as they gathered around Lucian.

'I did.'

'You, a little boy?'

'I know for a fact it's true.' Dawn was looking at Lucian with something akin to longing in her eyes.

'Lucian, why don't you draw something for Mavis here?' Elody gave Lucian a piece of charcoal and paper, and within a few minutes a charming rendering of the leopard with wings had appeared.

'This is for you, Mavis.' He passed her the paper, and she held it to her chest.

'When you're famous, this shall be worth a fortune, thank you, Lucian,' she said with a sigh.

They were standing outside, Elody holding tight to his arm, when a horse pulling a fully loaded cart plodded from the packing room towards the canal.

'Where are all the crates going?' Lucian asked the drayman.

'See, lad, we've just loaded Bess – you can stroke her nose if you like. These willow crates will be stacked onto the barge and start their journey to America.'

'America?' Lucian's eyes were wide.

'From here they'll go north on the canal to the Mersey. At the Liverpool ports the ware will be packed on a ship bound for America, if you ever go there, look out for it, lad.'

They thanked the drayman and were watching the crates being stowed when Lucian moved closer to Elody. 'Is this where Walter fell in?'

'Not far, so don't let go of my hand.'

They were walking to the gate when Andrew Derrington emerged from a doorway.

Elody felt her cheeks flame, but instead of looking angry he smiled at Lucian.

'Hello, young man.'

'I just ... I had to show him, Lord Derrington,' she interrupted. 'He had to see where the collection is being made, *his* collection. Don't blame Jacob, it's not his fault ...' She tailed off.

346

'Definitely, Lucian.' Andrew's hand was on Lucian's shoulder. 'It's important you should view the studios where your work will be carried out, but as we've discussed, it would be wise to limit your visits.'

Lucian sighed. 'I wish I didn't have a bad chest and was like other little boys.'

'But you're a special boy,' he said. 'And you're extremely talented and, in my opinion, quite the best boy. In any event, I have a treat for you. I was going to give it to you after your lesson tonight, but now is the perfect time.'

They followed Andrew into his office, and he took a box from his desk. 'For you, Lucian, an essential part of a gentleman's dress in Africa.'

Andrew's eyes were fixed on the child as he peeled away the paper and opened the box.

'David Livingstone had a hat like this,' Lucian's voice was barely more than a whisper.

'It's called a pith helmet, Lucian, and I was assured by the shop assistant it would be equally suitable at Thorncliffe Hall.'

Chapter Fifty-Three

Lucian was wearing his new hat when Elody returned from work.

'Africa?' she asked, holding out her hand.

'Africa,' he replied.

They stopped in the kitchen garden where Tim Peabody admired it, then they ran into Mrs George. After her initial hesitation, she patted the boy's hat.

'Oh my lord, a regular explorer.'

'Livingstone actually,' he replied.

They had returned from their travels, and Lucian ran up the stairs ahead of her. Elody could hear him in the kitchen with Miss Phipps.

'Have you seen it, Miss Phipps, the painting of the fishes?'

'Is this what you're looking for, duck?'

'I'm not a duck, Miss Phipps.'

And then came laughter. 'Of course not, Lucian.'

Lucian led her into the sitting room.

'You can look now, Elody' he said, and Elody opened her eyes. In front of her was a seascape on a luminous blue ground, but it was not only fishes covering the paper, parrots, turtles, seahorses and flowers inhabited his magical undersea world.

'Where do you get your ideas?' she asked, and Lucian smiled.

'Inside my head.'

She bent down so she was level with him. 'Thank you, Lucian.'

For the first time, he looked into her eyes.

'I'm giving you the sea, Elody, the animals and the birds, I'm giving you everything I have.'

Elody swallowed. 'My darling little boy, this is the greatest gift of all.'

Chapter Fifty-Four

Elody was instructing the newly employed thrower on the use of the pattern book, when Archie put his head round the door.

'Would you care for a stroll, Miss Cole?'

'If Albert here can spare me.' Elody took off her apron and followed him outside. A strong breeze was blowing, rippling the surface of the canal. She paused for a moment to watch a barge slowly chugging north.

'Do you ever wonder what's going to happen to it all, Archie? Whose table the ware will end up on? It could be one of them robber barons, you know the Vanderbilts or the Rockefellers, or ...'

'What do you know about robber barons?'

She looked up at him. 'Not a lot.'

He smiled. 'You intrigue me, Elody.'

'My mother used to tell me stories, lots of them, there was this big old jug on the dresser, and she made up its past – not true obviously – but the jug had seen it all. It went into the Methodist chapel sale when she died. Could hardly bring it with me, could I?'

'There aren't many stories in our house.'

'Tosh, Archie, you just have to look for them, open your mind and your ears.'

They had passed the lock when Archie cleared his throat, something he did when he was nervous.

'There's a lecture at the Royal College of Art, given by a pupil of the late Edward Lycett.'

'The porcelain artist from Stoke?'

'One and the same.' He coughed again, more loudly this time, and Elody waited.

'The thing is, Elody, you'd find it interesting and the following day you could meet the most respected buyers in town.'

Elody looked up at him, her tone soft, provocative. 'Are you protecting your investment, Archie?'

He moved closer until he was standing over her, blocking out the light.

'I need to take extreme care of my investment.'

'And would you be joining me in London?'

'I would hope so, Miss Cole.'

Elody folded the silk dress into her case, then took it out. She was a realist. Archie had never suggested marriage and even if it were the case, they needed different things. She would spend her life fighting for the future of women; he needed a well-bred wife who would smooth his passage through the world rather than disrupting it. She flinched, the pain cutting through her like a knife as she accepted her love for Archie. She buried her head in the soft silk. How could it have happened, she wondered, but she knew, oh yes, she knew all right, the moment he held her gaze that first night in the dining room, that's when it happened. She hadn't stood a chance.

She packed the rest of her clothes and shut her suitcase with a click.

Archie would never step out of his class, marry a woman like her, and she would never give up on her promise to her mother and Florence, all the women relying on her. Loving him was out of the question, it was a step too far. For a moment she remembered the feel of his lips on her skin, the scent of him, the intoxicating rush inside her every time he drew near. Yes, she would sleep with him in London, allow herself the luxury of wanton, irrepressible joy and one day in the future she might look back on the ghosts of missed opportunities, but that would be all.

The lecture at the Royal College of Art, was everything Archie had promised. Elody felt an affinity with the young man who went to America in search of his fortune, but to Elody his greatest achievement was as an experimental potter and designer.

Afterwards Archie took her for tea at the Ritz and as they entered the foyer, Elody studied the young women who wafted past, hips pushed forward.

'They have class, Archie,' she observed, adjusting her step accordingly.

'But they don't have your style.'

'Now that, Mr Derrington, is debatable.'

'Did you know the Ritz is the first hotel to allow unmarried ladies to go unchaperoned?' he murmured, guiding her elbow into the mirrored Palm Court.

'Are you flirting with me, Archie?'

'Definitely, Miss Cole.'

They were interrupted by a waiter who led them to their table.

'I see you've booked the full afternoon tea, sir, shall we start with champagne?'

Elody had finished her glass when the tiered cake stand arrived, and any attempt at sophistication fell away. 'Blimey,' she whispered, her eyes round.

'Do you want a scone, or perhaps a sandwich or one of these cakes,' Archie teased, holding out the stand. 'Or perhaps the lot – definitely the lot, I suspect.'

Elody spent the night in her sensible lodgings while Archie stayed in a nearby hotel. 'For your reputation, you understand.'

The following morning after packing and repacking the samples, she waited in the hall.

'First stop, Fortnum & Mason. The buyer is a Mrs Munroe,' Archie told her, directing her into the street, pulling her back as she stepped from the kerb. 'This is London not Burslem,' he instructed her, and she gave her most haughty look.

'I have been here before.'

The interior of London's finest grocery store was sumptuous with thick crimson carpets and gilded chandeliers. Elody glided from one mahogany counter to the next. She inhaled the scent of handmade chocolate, tea and exotic food, accepting the offer of a marzipan *petit four* from a liveried footman.

'The climbers in the 1922 Everest attempt, were provided with foie gras from Fortnum's,' Archie informed her as they stopped in a department on the second floor dedicated entirely to expeditions.

'They didn't reach the summit and seven porters died,' Elody responded.

'But it's a romantic notion, don't you think?'

Elody looked at him from beneath the rim of her straw hat and shook her head.

'I shall have to try harder to impress you. During the war, Fortnum's sent hampers to the front, and every soldier who worked here was offered his job back when he returned.'

'Now you have impressed me,' she replied.

Mrs Munroe was tall and sophisticated with cropped blonde hair, and a long string of pearls which trailed over her fashionable black dress.

'Mr Derrington has enthralled me with his description of your collection, Miss Cole, I can't wait to see it.' Her voice was languid, a little affected. She held out two perfectly manicured hands. 'The crate if you please.'

Elody passed her the crate, her heart thumping against her ribs. She watched as Mrs Munroe pulled at the straw, scattering it over the carpeted floor. She lifted out the dragon bowl first, examined it, placed it on a table, then handled the coffee pot taking off the top, before finally inspecting the small china jug. She raised her cool gaze to Elody.

'Mr Derrington hasn't exaggerated, I feel sure these will sell in my department. However,' she let the word fall on Elody's waiting ears, 'if my customers preferred a different body, would bone china be hard to achieve?'

Elody looked to Archie.

'It depends on the numbers, Mrs Munroe, Selfridges have already shown interest in our earthenware, but if your order was substantial, I'm sure we could come to some arrangement.'

'That, Mr Derrington, is the point – we would need to be different from Selfridges.'

'But we haven't yet been to Selfridges,' said Elody as they walked onto the street, immersing themselves in the noise and clamour once more.

Archie grinned. 'When it comes to business, a small exaggeration here and there...'

'I'd call that a distortion of the truth.'

'That's business, Miss Cole.'

Next they went to Selfridges, and the reception was the same. As they walked out of Thomas Goode into the afternoon sunshine, Archie lifted Elody from her feet. 'This deserves a celebration.' And celebrate they did, window shopping in Bond Street, actual shopping in Regent's Street. When Elody admired a dress in the window of Liberty's, he dragged her inside. 'You will try it on,' he insisted.

'But, Archie—'

'No buts, Miss Cole.'

As she came out of the dressing room he was waiting. 'Positively ravishing,' he murmured.

'The dress?' she asked.

'The glorious creature inside.'

He called the assistant, a woman with slim hips and a roman nose. 'Wrap it up for the young lady if you please, and add a couple of headbands, and your best silk stockings. While I'm thinking about it, can you ask a girl to bring up a bottle of your finest scent, something young and delicate, possibly Chanel.'

The assistant's exotic nose narrowed.

'If it was me, I'd be buying Guerlain's Shalimar. It's a sublime melody of iris, lily, rose. The coolness of the citrus notes leads to a floral heart ending with a—' Archie winked at Elody and asked the assistant to wrap it up with the rest.

Elody would never remember where they went for afternoon tea, all she could recall was what happened afterwards.

'I have a suggestion,' he murmured, stopping outside a shop dedicated entirely to men's shirts.

'There's a country inn near Windsor, it could be on our way home if you wished, or you could stay in your solitary room in the boarding house, it's up to you.'

'And the name of this country inn?' she had murmured, tilting her neck as he kissed her shoulder, moving the tiny strap to the side.

'It's called the Bird in Hand.'

'A good name I think,' she had replied.

And much later when they were standing in their bedroom under the eaves, the moonlight shining through the tiny paned windows he had looked into her eyes.

'I hope I live up to your expectations, Elody.'

'If you don't know what to expect, you don't have any,' she replied.

Chapter Fifty-Five

Elody hated August, it was too damn hot in Burslem, the chimneys didn't stop firing but the people did, tempers frayed while the ovens burned. But the first Tuesday in August was a good day because Mr Asland arrived.

'As expected, Miss Cole, I've been given my cards.' He wiped his forehead with a handkerchief. 'Does the offer still stand?'

'I've been waiting for you, Mr Asland, there's much to learn with little time to do it and I'm not that good at numbers.'

'There's the ordering too.'

'That too, Mr Asland.'

'And getting the products out on time.'

'All of it.'

'When do you want me to start?'

'Now, Mr Asland.'

Elody arrived back at Thorncliffe to find Archie outside her bedroom, with Jacob Shaw, their knees buckling beneath the weight of a walnut desk.

'Can I ask what's going on?'

'I found it in an antique shop in Leek,' Archie panted. 'Are you going to open the door so we can put it down?'

'You bought it for me?'

'Since you're the only person in this corridor, then yes.'

'Archie, I'm lost for words.'

'At this moment in time, I don't need words, please open the bloody door.'

Later, Elody was writing at her new desk. She had never owned a desk; in fact, she'd never owned anything like it before. She picked up the piece of card, blew on it and smiled.

Elody requests your company for a viewing of the Lucian range.
Please join me for drinks at the Studios, the Diligence Works on
the fourteenth of August at six.

She put the card in an envelope, closed the lid, and took it downstairs.

In preparation for the event, Elody and Lucian painted a backdrop of mythical creatures flying through the night sky and pinned it to the studio wall.

'What do you think?'

'Exceptional,' murmured Mr Asland.

'I'm proud of us,' said Lucian.

Ursula was unable to attend but Lucian stood beneath the artwork in his best new clothes.

'Extraordinary, Lucian.' Andrew put his hand on the boy's shoulder.

'Superb,' exclaimed Archie.

'We did it together,' said Lucian. 'Do you want a glass of wine?'

They walked across the studio to the tables set out with ware.

'It took five firings to get the colours right,' Elody explained, 'all those glazes to achieve that wonderful jewel red.'

'And what do you think of our new jug?' Lucian handed them the jug and they were lost for words.

It was Andrew who spoke first, looking at the jug decorated

with a leopard stalking through the jungle, multi-coloured feathers sprouting from his head, then at Lucian holding out a bowl decorated with his fantasy sea-world on a shimmering blue ground.

'Exquisite,' his voice was measured. 'In all my years as a potter, I've never seen anything like this.'

Elody was packing away her paints the following lunchtime, when she looked up to find Archie standing in the doorway. The light was behind him, illuminating his straight nose, his deep blue eyes. One day she would paint him, she thought, putting her head on one side, imagining the door as a canvas, comparing the canvas and model to scale.

'I thought I might take you for a walk.' He leant against the frame, lit up a cigarette. 'Elody are you listening?'

Elody shut her paintbox with a click, focusing once more. 'I have to copy an image for the girls upstairs. Perhaps in an hour, but I can't be late for Lucian.'

'Suit yourself.' He sauntered towards the gate his jacket slung over his shoulder. 'We'll go by train,' he called. 'To Rudyard Lake, if you haven't been before, it's worth it, Miss Cole.'

They took the train from Longport, getting out at Rudyard Station a short while later.

'Father brought us here as children.' Archie frowned. 'But that was before ...'

'Before Giles died,' Elody finished for him, observing the couples ambling along the footpath at the side of the reservoir, dogs pulling their owners, nannies with their prams. 'It's a fine place to walk.'

'Or row. We used to race each other down the lake, Hester always went with Giles.'

'So you and your father won?'

'Never. Giles was the strong one. He seemed invincible, Elody.' The tone of the conversation had changed, and Archie's eyes were glittering.

'I'm sorry.' She put her hand on his sleeve.

'He wrote to me when Charles Sartorious was killed. I think of his letter every day. *'I like to think of him in white flannels at Thorncliffe, or in any other clothes but a uniform.'*'

Archie picked up a stick and broke it in half. 'Giles was mortal as we all are, and he died for nothing, I think he gave up when he heard about Sartor.' He took Elody's hand, turned it over and traced the lines on her palm. 'I wanted to bring you to Rudyard Lake, somewhere filled with happy memories, to tell you I'm not a coward.'

'I've never thought that.'

'My sister believes I am, along with many of the women at the pot bank. But they're wrong. I tried to enlist, begged the medical officer but as usual Mother had her way.'

Elody took his face in both hands and gently drew it towards her, kissing his lips. 'I may have thought many things of you, Archie Derrington, but being a coward was not one of them.'

As they walked around the lake, Elody was quiet. Archie had revealed his innermost fears to her and now she would make love to him, this handsome, articulate man who had turned her heart inside out. She wanted to shout it from the rooftops, but she couldn't. She was a fool to have believed one night of passion would be enough. For a brief moment she imagined the three of them as a family – Lucian, Elody and Archie – but the image was fleeting and out of reach.

When the last couple had left the footpath, and the boats had been tied to the dock, Elody took his arm.

'I'm no longer interested in boats,' she murmured, pulling him off the path, past the empty holiday homes and weekend houses for the rich. 'At this moment, I'm only interested in you.'

'And how are you going to distract me?' he asked, his voice soft.

'Like this.' Elody smiled at him and with the sunlight dappling through the leaves, she undid her blouse, and slowly took off her skirt, until she was standing in her white petticoat and chemise. Then she took his hand and drew it to her neck.

'I could never, ever think you were a coward,' she whispered, undoing the buttons on her chemise one by one.

Later, as Elody cradled Archie's head in her lap, the breeze moving through the branches above her, she traced his profile, remembering Archie striding to find her on the moors – all Heathcliff with his brooding looks. Though she had been infuriated by what she perceived as his arrogance, she was moved by his concern. But unlike Heathcliff, Archie was kind, generous. She had observed him running through the trees with Lucian, playing hide and seek, reading to him. She remembered the well dressing ceremony, the spark that had ignited between them, walking up the winding stairs to their bedroom at the Bird in Hand as Mr and Mrs Brown. She looked down at Archie's face, relaxed now, at peace and with a sinking feeling she knew there could be no secrets from the one you loved.

'I have something to tell you, Archie.'

'What is it?' He opened his eyes, but they fluttered closed.

'Things happened, long before I arrived at Thorncliffe Hall.'

'What things?' They were open now, wide open.

'Things that made me who I am, that made me realise I can't sit back. I have to fight inequality even if it means fighting you.'

He sat up, pulled his shirt around him. 'I hope this isn't part of a plan – seduce the boss's son to get him on your side.'

He was smiling but there was a wariness in his gaze.

Elody drew away. 'I want the truth between us, nothing more.'

Chapter Fifty-Six

The Potteries reeled beneath the heat from the bottle ovens.

'Boiling Burslem,' muttered Elody, splashing her face in Lucian's bathroom after returning home.

'Alliteration,' said Lucian, having found the word in the dictionary. 'I've got something for you, but first dry your hands.'

As dusk dimmed the sky and swallows dipped and dived, Elody became the owner of a charcoal drawing of the pot bank. It wasn't gentle, but ominous somehow, as if Lucian had an eye on the future.

'It will remind you, of us, Elody, of what we've created together, and Archie.'

'Why Archie?'

'Because he's part of the pot bank.'

And he was right, wherever she went in the future the drawing went with her, pulling her back to the chimneys, to the brutal reality of Burslem but also to Lucian and Archie.

On Monday morning, Elody was working at the wheel, the drawing on the shelf beside her.

'Morning, duck.' Dawn came first, then Mavis and they went upstairs.

Elody acknowledged them but her mind was elsewhere.

She was creating scenarios where Archie would understand, he would appreciate her moral dilemma and battle at her side. Her concentration faltered, the clay wobbled, and the jug failed. She let her head fall into her wet clay hands. She couldn't bear the agony of letting him go, but she knew she had to make a choice between Archie and the campaign – that's what it came down to in the end. She could see Mr Asland bent over a ledger nearby, the two throwers at work. Archie would feel betrayed after all he had done for her, and he'd be right in his way. She wiped her hands on her apron, pushed back her hair. Though it was impossible to contemplate the thought of losing him, she knew with clarity that made her sick with misery, lose him must.

She looked up to see Tilda Kennard in the doorway. She could feel her cheeks burning as if Tilda could see into her mind.

'Lawd, this is a good set up, duck.' She glanced at her knowingly. 'Is there somewhere we can speak?'

Elody nodded.

'So,' she said, sitting on the low wall, away from the Diligence Works. 'Have you grown beyond us, Elody? Do you still wish to break boundaries and forge new narratives, because I'm not seeing it?'

'I have to make a living, Tilda.'

'By the look of it, you don't.'

Elody was angry suddenly. 'Stop, Tilda! Enough of your doubt and accusations, my dreams haven't diminished or changed.'

'But all this? Supposing you have to give it up for what you believe in.'

Elody didn't reply.

'Remember your mother's dying wish.'

'I'm doing this in memory of my mother!' Elody faced her. 'I won't deny it comes at a cost, but I'm fighting for women everywhere.'

'Everything in life comes at a cost,' grumbled Tilda.

Elody shook her head. 'You said you were behind me, Tilda, I don't understand?'

'I am behind you, I had to be sure you still felt the same.'

Tilda was heading for the gate when Elody called after her.

'I'll organise a meeting here, Friday, seven o'clock, my studio upstairs.'

'And the Derringtons?'

'They're attending a council meeting and won't be around.'

For the first time in months, Archie felt energised and truly alive. Elody had come into his life, turning every preconception upside down. She was bright, talented and different to anyone he had ever known. What's more, he was in love with her. He was humming as he shaved; he would marry her, tell his mother to be damned, force his father to accept her demands. He had lived in a patriarchal system believing men were superior intellectually, physically. Elody was forcing him to open his eyes, showing him he was wrong. And Lucian; whatever time the child had left they would be a unit, he would have what he wanted most, a family. He did up his tie and put on a crisp white shirt, followed by the cufflinks Giles had given him. Shrugging into his jacket, he went downstairs.

'You're in a good mood, Archie.' His father handed him a newspaper. 'You may not be, after you've read this. Deflation has reached record heights; I imagine we'll have to drop our prices if we're to survive.'

Archie took the paper, glancing down the central column. Today of all days he had no wish to think of the world as it really was.

'There's a rumour of trouble in the pot bank, the women agitating again. Will you deal with it?'

Archie took a piece of toast from the silver rack and buttered it, his attention returning. 'While there's such disparity in the wages, the friction will remain.'

Andrew looked at Archie over the top of his glasses. 'If we put the men and women anywhere near an equal footing, we will never survive.'

'Isn't that a little unfair when the women kept the pot bank going through the war.'

'We can't afford to increase their salaries, not now, Archie. Haven't you noticed we're in a recession?' Andrew's voice was curt.

Archie pushed back his chair. 'I'm not stupid, Father, so please don't treat me as such, but we need to address this before it's too late.' He drank the last of his coffee and left the room, refusing to be riled. 'I'm afraid I'll be missing the council meeting on Friday,' he called. 'But we should finish this discussion another time.'

As he sat beside his father in the car, his mind strayed to Elody, the way her hair curled around her face when damp, the small mole above her lip. On Friday he would walk the moors with Elody and Lucian. As he leant against the window, he imagined holding the child between them, swinging him back and forth. Later when the household was asleep, he would go to Elody's bedroom, slip into her bed and bury his face in her warm neck. He was woken from his reverie as the car entered Burslem. Every sense in his body was attuned to the billowing fumes and oppressive heat. He fiddled with the collar of his shirt, longing to get back to the clean, cool air.

As the car stopped in Port Street, the wrought iron sign hanging over the alleyway brought the usual stab of pain. When Giles had died, the S had been removed from 'Derrington and Sons'.

*

At seven fifteen on Friday evening, Archie hurried down the cobbled lane to Elody's studio, flew up the stairs and opened the door.

'Elody Cole, I have to tell you—' the words died in his mouth. A worker he didn't recognise was standing in the middle of a circle of women, holding a banner, he could see the words, '*You have a fight on your hands*'. For an instant their gaze collided, and he glimpsed the hatred in her eyes.

Elody's back was to him, her chin lifted.

'For those of you who haven't joined us before, may I introduce Miss Cole who is spearheading our mission to bring the pot bank owners to their knees. It is people like the Derringtons who have got fat on our labour, our—'

Archie didn't wait to hear any more. As his world collapsed around him he stumbled down the stairs. The girl he was about to pledge his life to, was plotting and scheming behind his back. He would have tried to bring her dreams to fruition but not like this, not after this betrayal of his family after all they had done for her. His misery was quickly replaced with fury, and he didn't see Elody move to the front, didn't hear her defence of the Derringtons. 'They are good people,' she insisted. 'Our fight is not against individuals, we merely want the owners to understand how important this is, we want them to hear our demands for equal pay, nothing more.'

He was running down the stairs when Bridie leant forward and clutched Elody's arm. 'A man was in the doorway, I think…'

She got no further because Elody had gone.

Archie was at the end of the outside passage when Elody caught up with him.

'Archie, I—'

He turned around. 'If you tell me where you'd like your things delivered, I'll have them sent on.' His voice was curt, without emotion.

'It's not what you think…'

'It's exactly what I think. You have used me and my family – was this your plan all along?'

'No, please you have it all wrong.'

'You may stay on here, fulfil your orders, but I never wish to see your face again, do you understand?'

'May I see Lucian? Please may I say goodbye?'

'You forfeited that right when you deceived my family. Good evening, Miss Cole.'

Elody dragged herself back up the stairs. For a moment there was silence as everyone stared at her.

'Blimey,' said Dawn when the sound of his footsteps had finally disappeared.

'Tilda, what have you done?' Bridie's face was pale.

'How could I know he was standing in the bloody doorway!'

Elody fixed her eyes on Tilda. 'But you did know, didn't you?'

'Course I didn't, duck, I would never have spoken those words.'

Elody's voice was low. 'I've been kicked out of Thorncliffe, thanks to you, and I'm not allowed to see Lucian.'

Dawn took her hands.

'You'll stay with me, the attic room is all done out, that will be yours.'

'I swear on my life, Elody.' Tilda's eyes were pleading.

Elody looked from one to the other then last turned to Tilda. 'I'll run the campaign with you, but nothing more. Now I need to be on my own.'

When the women had gone, she sank to her knees on the newly swept floor. What would happen to Lucian, her precious little boy?

Chapter Fifty-Seven

Archie was late into supper and flung himself onto his chair. The flicker in his eye that had appeared when Giles died was suddenly more pronounced.

'Are you all right, Archie? You look awful.' His mother glanced up from her soup.

'Only you could observe that so quickly,' he uttered, his voice a little slurred.

'For someone who cares about their appearance as you do, it's hardly surprising. Come here, dear, and let me sort your bow tie.'

'Ursula, leave him alone.' Andrew looked at her sternly.

'I was only trying to help. And Elody, is she not here? Has success gone to her head?'

Archie raised his eyes and looked at his mother. 'The potter, as you normally call her, has left. You will be delighted to know she will not be returning.'

'Left?'

'Yes, Mother. She's organising a walkout; she's used us for her own aims.'

For a moment Ursula looked crestfallen, her shoulders drooped, then she was up and fighting. 'From the moment I saw her I realised she was trouble and to think after everything we've done for her, the ungratefu—'

'Ursula, leave the boy alone, can't you see he's upset.' Andrew Derrington put down his glass of burgundy.

'For God's sake, Andrew, am I not allowed to have an opinion in my own house?'

'Not if it's unhelpful. Archie, I suggest we have a glass of port in my study afterwards?'

Archie looked up. 'Thank you, Father,' he murmured, but all he could see was Elody's shocked face, the tears sparkling in her eyes. He could only hear one word, '*Archie.*'

Dawn was waiting when Elody arrived at the house in Tellwright Street. She led her up the narrow stairs.

'Not what you're used to I'm afraid, our Dan made the chest, but it was for—'

She pushed open the door and Elody followed. In the middle of the room, beside the metal bed was a small wooden crib.

'Oh, Dawn,' Elody murmured.

'Yeah well, no use for it now.'

Elody went to the window and looked out into the gathering dusk. 'What a pair we are.'

'What a sodding pair, I'll get you some sheets, love, just make yourself at home.'

That night Elody took paper and pen from her satchel and started to write.

Dear Archie,
If you had waited, if you had trusted me, you would have realised I could never share Tilda's views. She has her motives which are not my own. Yes, we are marching, but this is a fight for equality, nothing personal. I have the highest regard for your family. I am grateful for everything you have done for me and it has been the hardest choice to make. This is not

about me, it is about the women who watched their men die
at the front while they were working their jobs, doing the
same gruelling hours for half the pay.
    Please allow me to see Lucian, I need to explain. If not for
me, please do this for Lucian's sake.
    Always,
    Elody

    PS I will be staying with Dawn Rogers until I find
somewhere more permanent.

Elody delivered the letter to Archie's office on Saturday morning and was in the kitchen when Dawn came in from the coal house.

'Tilda dropped by when you were out, asked me to hand out the flyers. I imagine you won't be joining us?' She wiped a sooty hand across her face.

'If you don't mind, Dawn, I'll keep away from Tilda just now.'

That afternoon, Elody left her a note and cycled to Thorncliffe Hall. She couldn't wait for Archie's response, she couldn't wait for Dawn, she needed to see Lucian now. As she pedalled up the hill, panting in the warm air, she could hear his words. *'Everyone leaves me in the end.'* But she would never leave him voluntarily, she had to explain. She concealed her bicycle in the ditch, waited until it was dark and ran across the lawn. She rattled the door handle – it was locked, the ground floor windows shuttered and closed. When he didn't appear, she sat on the grass beneath their favourite tree.

'Come to me, Lucian,' she murmured, praying the child would know she was there. She awoke to see him running across the lawn.

She held onto him, wrapping him in her shawl, breathing in the familiar smell of washed hair and soft childish skin.

'I knew you would come. I waited until Miss Phipps was asleep, then I took her key. But why did you leave?'

'It's a long story, but I'll try to explain.'

He looked at the luminous hands on his watch. 'We have four hours until Miss Phipps wakes up, that gives us plenty of time.'

Before the first seam of light appeared in the sky, Elody gently woke Lucian.

'We must get you inside.'

'You will come again, Elody.'

'And you'll look out for me.'

'Every minute. And if you don't come, I'll find you.'

'Perhaps you'll create some more magical creatures for the range.'

'The magical creatures have gone.'

Hannah found her at dawn curled in a chair on the school house veranda.

She took her into the kitchen, put a poached egg in front of her and waited.

'I knew it would destroy me, Hannah,' Elody said at last. 'But I didn't imagine for one moment it would be a risk to Lucian. I wanted to look after him, keep him safe, and now they've sent me away.' She put her head in her hands and Hannah sat down beside her. 'What you're fighting for is worth it.'

'I've lost everything.'

'But you'll gain so much, Elody. Yes, there will be sacrifices, but we'll win in the end.'

Elody returned to Tellwright Street that evening, and though exhausted, she began her memoir. As the hours ticked by, the lamp burning down, she continued to write. Perhaps it was a premonition of disaster that propelled her, or the desire for clarity, but as she dragged herself to bed in the early hours, sheet after sheet of paper were covered with her fine script. The following evening it was the same and the next few nights. It was cathartic, healing, and as her tears flowed, occasionally smudging the ink, she described her years with Walter, her parents' death, the Derringtons, Archie, her desire for reform, but above all her love for Lucian. If anything happened to her, she wanted future generations to learn the truth about him, she wanted them to learn about the Lucian range.

Chapter Fifty-Eight

With the entire male population of Burslem, Tunstall and Stoke watching the football match between Aston Villa and Port Vale, at least five hundred women gathered in the back room of the Leopard.

Elody climbed onto the podium, hesitating only a second before lifting her head.

'In these parts news travels,' she started, 'and you may question if I'm still a worthy spokeswoman. I admit I wondered so myself, but then I thought of our struggles to get the vote, our suffering, and I promise you, I am capable. We're not expecting miracles, at this moment parity is probably a step too far, but we want more than we have. We have made progress, ladies, but there's still a hill to climb.' She unfurled a poster and held it up for all to see.

'For our eyes only, girls. Fix the date in your brains but don't talk about it in your sleep.

'We'll gather outside the town hall where you'll be given banners and torches. Over the following three nights we'll cover the other five towns.' She rolled up the poster and held it aloft.

'Remember, girls, James Brindley and Josiah Wedgwood

discussed the creation of the Trent and Mersey Canal in this very room. History was made, we're about to make our own history.'

Elody returned to Thorncliffe the following Friday and waited in the dark for Lucian. When he didn't come, she left a note beneath their appointed tree and retreated to the school house. Hannah was wearing pyjamas when she opened the door. 'Poor girl, you look shattered, perhaps a bath, then a mug of tea, not necessarily in that order.' She held out her arms.

'Lucian wasn't there, he won't know I came,' Elody moaned.

'Did you leave anything for him?'

'A note but—'

'Then he'll find it, Elody.'

After breakfast Hester arrived. She glanced around the kitchen, her eyes resting on Elody.

'If you want my brother,' Hannah's voice was sharp. 'He isn't here.'

'But Miss Cole seems to be.' Hester dropped her jacket on the kitchen counter and glared at Elody. 'Have you any right to be here, in a Derrington house?'

'My house,' murmured Hannah behind her. 'At least I thought it was…'

'Yes, Hester, I let your family down and I'm sorry for all of it, but there are women counting on me and I can't walk away.'

'And we mean so little?'

'Your family has come to mean so much, but I had to follow my conscience. I wanted to tell you, I needed to confide in you, but you never came home.' Elody lapsed into silence; in the end it was Hester who spoke.

'Archie has had a face like a poker for days, am I missing something, Elody?'

Elody looked up, and their eyes met.

'Oh my God, you're in love with him...' Hester fumbled in her bag and took out a cigarette. 'I suspected it from the moment I saw you together.' Her voice was soft. 'How do you have this effect on people, Elody Cole?'

Elody remembered Archie hurling abuse. There was no love now.

She finished her cigarette and swung her jacket over her shoulders. 'Will you forgive me, fittings for Noel Coward's latest hit, *London Calling*, I have to be there by twelve.'

As Elody congratulated her, she realised her brief friendship with Hester Derrington was coming to an end. The girl had found her calling and would leave her behind. She wondered if Piers would also be a casualty of her success.

Hester was walking to the door when Hannah spoke out.

'Women have to fight for what they believe in and in your own way you're making a stand. You should be proud.'

Hester's polished veneer fell away and she turned to Elody. 'I've let you down when I should have been a friend, I'm truly sorry.' She went towards her and held out her hand. Once they would have hugged each other, but that time had gone.

Elody was rinsing the dishes in Tellwright Street, when the door was thrown open and Archie strode towards her.

'It's Lucian, he's gone!'

'What do you mean gone?'

'He ran away.'

A plate crashed to the floor. 'It will be dark in less than an hour.'

'You have to help us find him.'

'If anything happens to that little boy, God help you, Archie Derrington.'

'There's no time for blame, we need to get home.'

*

A fog had come down at Thorncliffe, obscuring the figures in the forecourt, muffling their calls. Before Archie had pulled on the brake, Elody leapt from the car and raced upstairs.

'I put him down,' Miss Phipps was standing in the corridor, 'gave him Doctor Bly's medicine and afore I knew it, he was gone.'

'Medicine?' Elody rounded on Archie, her voice rising.

'One of his chest infections,' he qualified.

'And you didn't think to let me know?'

'I was about—'

'I'm going to the grotto.' Elody pushed past him, hurtling into the garden calling Lucian's name. When a lurcher bounded towards her, she knew the gamekeeper wouldn't be far behind.

'I'll check the woods,' Digger shouted. 'He may have hidden in the hollow of the big old oak. It's where I'd go, if I was a child.'

Elody flew across the lawn, reaching the entrance to the grotto where Mr Simkins was heaving at the planks, throwing them aside with a vigour that belied his age.

'All closed up, Miss Cole, but there's plenty of room for the lad to slip by.'

He was halfway down the steps when Elody stopped him. 'Stay Mr Simpkins, one of us has to keep guard.'

As she entered the dark tunnel, light from her torch flickered and bounced off the walls. Soon Digger's cries receded until she could hear nothing at all. 'Lucian,' she called, her voice echoing in the stillness. 'Lucian,' but only the statue of Neptune gazed from his throne of shells.

She ran back the way she had come. She could hardly breathe; Lucian was lost and alone. *'If you don't come, I will find you, Elody,'* he had said, and she had come, but she had been too late.

She had reached the terrace when Andrew Derrington grabbed her arm.

'Thank God you're here, Elody.'

The family and household split into three groups combing the kitchen garden, the Temple, the woods, but there was no sign of Lucian.

'I'm going to the moors, Jacob,' Elody cried, recognising the footman. 'Will you fetch Clay.' Before he could reply she had gone, sprinting through the gardens, over the stile into the parkland and the moors beyond. The Roaches loomed ahead of her, the outline of Hen Cloud. She called Lucian's name and called again. Supposing he had climbed the path, missed his footing and fallen hundreds of feet to the ground. She was about to turn back when Clay pounded across the turf towards her. She tangled her arms around his neck. 'Where is he?' she moaned. 'Please help me, Clay.'

She looked up as Archie approached.

'I'm coming with you, it's not safe on your own.'

'Do you think I care for my safety when Lucian's missing?'

'We'll find him, Elody.'

As they trudged the foothills of the Roaches, scrambling upwards over rocks and scree, Elody went through every conversation. Where would Lucian go if he was frightened and alone. She shone her torch in the scrub, the beam skimming across the rough turf, the uneven walls. Then she saw it, a white cross on the dark stone, then another further along the wall. It was where they had rested on their first trip to the moors, where she had handed him the chalk. The child had remembered her instructions. He was leading her to him.

Lucian emerged from Back Forest and blinked in the darkness. When a blast of freezing air funnelled through a gap in the rocks, spiralling upwards towards him, he knew he had reached the gorge. He folded his arms around his small frame, but the cold had spread its tentacles deep inside his bones. He trembled, wanting to return to the warmth of his bedroom, but he wouldn't give up because he was nearly there. He only had to descend the rocks, and he would find Elody. He stared into the darkness, put his foot over the edge and very soon he was climbing down, one boulder then the next, slipping, sliding, until at last he stood on the shingle floor, but there was no Elody. He pursed his lips, whistled, listened as the sound echoed around the cavern, but she didn't come.

'Elody,' he moaned. 'I thought you'd be here.'

He pushed himself into a corner, where two rocks joined. Water trickled down his neck into his clothes. He curled into a tight ball, rocking to and fro. He wanted to climb out, but he was just too tired. When finally, his eyelids drooped, the walls seemed to be alight with a thousand candles, shimmering in the darkness. The Green Knight on a green horse was galloping towards him in a flurry of bells. He called his name, put out his hand.

Lucian awoke to a fit of coughing, he could hardly breathe. There was a strange salty tang in his mouth, he hadn't tasted before. Tears leaked down his face and into his hands, but he had no strength to wipe them away. He wanted to lie in the warmth of Elody's arms, feel her cool hands smoothing his brow. He wanted to go home. But where was home, he wondered, looking upwards at the little slice of moon beneath an inky black sky. Home was Elody.

Elody knew she was getting closer to Lucian when Clay shot ahead of her, weaving through the trees. At the top of the ravine, he yelped wildly and together they descended into the darkness.

She found Lucian at the bottom of the chasm; a small figure curled beneath the dripping moss walls. Clay was licking at his face, his hands, but the child was not responding.

'My love, I'm here,' she whispered, cocooning his fragile body against her, holding his freezing hands. When his head lolled forward, she cradled it in her palms, kissing his eyes, his forehead.

'I'm here to take you home.'

'Elody,' he murmured at last. 'I knew you'd come.' But Elody had heard the rasp in his breath, the constriction in his lungs.

She lifted up his arms, stripped off his wet shirt, replacing it with Archie's jumper, then she wrapped him in her shawl.

Archie lifted Lucian, cradling him against his warm chest.

'My poor sweet child,' he murmured, holding him gently as he picked his way to the other end of the canyon for the walk back to Thorncliffe Hall.

Andrew was returning from Hen Cloud, when the small party arrived.

'Quickly we need to get him indoors. A fire's made up and Dr Bly is waiting, there's no time to lose.'

Dr Bly removed the stethoscope from his ears and replaced the blankets over Lucian. He shut his bag, and they went outside.

'Master Lucian has been exposed to the elements. Unfortunately, the chill on top of everything . . .' He looked at Archie over his glasses, his voice grave. 'I'm sorry, sir, but you have to prepare yourself for the worst.'

'But that's not possible, there must be something you can do,' Elody begged.

'I can't perform miracles. At present the child is unconscious, all we can do is wait and pray.'

Elody sat with him all night and the following day, refusing to leave his side. She sang to him, prayed to God, and on the third day Lucian opened his eyes.

'I saw him, Elody.'

'Who, my darling little boy?'

'The Green Knight came to me, I told you he would.'

'He came to protect you, my precious little boy.'

Even if the doctor couldn't help Lucian, Elody believed Mrs Knox could. Leaving Lucian with Archie, Jacob took her to the herbalist on the corner of Bluestone Avenue.

'What's the best remedy you have for Lucian?' she pleaded, explaining the symptoms. Mrs Knox rubbed her hand across her brow. After a minute she spoke.

'I'll do what I can, Elody, but from what you say, I fear it may be too late.' She carefully made up a prescription and handed her the paper bag. Then she went to the dresser and took a small bottle from the shelf. She wrapped it in tissue and tied it with ribbon.

'I'm hoping for the best, Elody, but please accept this as my gift to you, just in case.'

Elody knew what just in case meant, and as she ran outside she wanted to throw the bottle back at her, tell her that Lucian was going to live, he was coming with her to America, but she knew in her heart, kind old Mrs Knox only had the best intentions.

When she got back to Thorncliffe, she burnt the herbs, helped Lucian to inhale and afterwards she read to him.

'Can we have the scene from *A Midsummer Night's Dream*?' he whispered, looking up at her. 'You know, where Titania is kind to the donkey.' And Elody remembered tumbling around in the grass pretending to be Bottom, Lucian with a garland of flowers in his hair, the perfect Titania.

When she reached the last three lines Lucian closed his eyes.

And pluck the wings from painted butterflies,
To fan the moonbeams from his sleeping eyes:
Nod to him, elves, and do him courtesies.

'I want moonbeams, Elody,' he murmured.

'Well then, I'll get them for you, my beloved child.'

When Archie came, she was dozing on the bed beside Lucian. She opened her eyes.

'You can say what you like, I'm not leaving. If you hadn't sent me away...'

'Please, Elody.' He raised his hands and dropped them to his sides. 'You can't imagine—'

'What about Lucian? What about me? This is your fault, Archie Derrington.'

'You'll stay with him,' he uttered, his face etched with grief. 'It's what you both desire.'

Two days later, on a fine September evening, Lucian asked to be carried outside.

'No, darling,' Elody implored. 'We need to keep you in bed.'

'I want to go into the garden to our favourite place, so I can look up at the stars. Please take me, Elody.'

Elody relented and when a mattress had been laid on the grass, she carried him outside and he rested against her.

'You must go to America, Elody. Promise me?' he whispered.

'Only if you come with me.'

'I can see you there designing beautiful things, and you'll find Walter, and Archie will come,' he sighed, nuzzling against her and together they looked up into the night sky.

'Don't leave me,' Elody begged.

'I'm going to be up there in heaven, but I'm not afraid.' He lifted his hand, his fingers lightly touching her face. 'But this time you mustn't search for me.'

Elody couldn't speak, tears were flooding her eyes, her heart was breaking. Lucian, the child she had given her love to, was slipping away.

She gathered her strength and smiled through her tears.

'You're right, for you'll lead the way.'

'I like that, Elody. I'm leading the way.'

She drew his hand to her lips, could feel the blood coursing below the translucent skin, his little heart fluttering in his chest. He opened his eyes and looked into her own.

'If you're sad, Elody, you only have to look for the Polar star, the biggest and brightest in the sky. Do you remember what you told me?'

'If you get lost you can always find your way by that star,' Elody murmured.

Lucian sighed, his breath slowing. 'And I'll be waiting for you until you arrive.'

When Archie found them, Elody was cradling Lucian in her arms.

'He's gone,' she wailed. 'He trusted me, and I failed.'

'The family failed him. You gave him everything, Elody.'

'I have to prepare him, he won't have strangers. Please take him to his room.'

Elody followed as Archie lifted Lucian's body, cradling him, holding him close. His mouth was trembling as he laid him gently on the bed, so gently as if he didn't want to hurt him – but Lucian was beyond pain, he was beyond everything.

'Leave us now please,' she begged.

He shut the door and Elody listened until his footsteps had gone. She filled the basin with warm water and the lavender oil from Mrs Knox on Bluestone Avenue. She washed Lucian gently, first his hands, then his chest, his legs and his beautiful feet. It was her prayer to Lucian. She put on his nightshirt and brushed his hair, then she drew an outline on a piece of paper and put it into his hands. 'America,' she murmured, kissing his lips, her tears falling on his pale cheeks. Last, she opened the window and looked out into the night sky.

'Goodbye, my love,' she whispered. 'I'll find you by that star.'

Elody walked downstairs and into the summer night, where Archie was waiting for her.

'I don't imagine I'll come to the funeral, but please tell me where you put him to rest and don't let it be on his own.'

'You have my word.'

'And flowers, he loves flowers.'

'He'll be in the family plot in the churchyard, and I'll make sure he's surrounded by flowers.'

Elody shook her head. 'Well, that will be a first, being with his family. Perhaps it's a little too late for that.'

'Please, Elody, let me explain, I—'

'No, I've heard too much.'

'Are you going?' He lifted his eyes to Elody's. 'Of course you are, there's nothing to stay for.'

Elody was about to reply, about to let her anger fly, but what was the point? It wouldn't bring Lucian back.

'I'm going to find Mrs George,' she uttered. 'Then you'll never see me again.'

Elody walked into Mrs George's sitting room where she was sitting by the fire even though it was August. The housekeeper got up and opened her arms.

'I've heard the little lad's gone.'

Elody nodded.

'Come here, you poor wee girl.'

'I loved him more than life itself and I let him down.'

Mrs George stroked her hair. 'Hush, love, you did no such thing. He was going either way, we all knew that.'

'But why all the secrecy?' she asked, her anger igniting. 'Why was he abandoned, Mrs George?'

'Sit down, love, and I'll tell you what I know. It's a rum do it is, all of us bound to secrecy, but...'

Elody stayed with Mrs George and as the fire died in the grate and the ashes stirred, she gripped the housekeeper's hands.

'Rhea is yours, Mrs George, love her well, love her for me. The ashes said a stranger would come to you, and she will stay, but I must leave.'

'We've grown that fond of you, Elody.'

'I never fitted here. I need to go back where I belong. For all the fancy clothes, I'm just a girl from the Potteries.'

'Not any girl, you're spirited and clever and Mr Archie will be bereft without you.'

'So you knew?'

'We all knew, Elody.'

Elody sighed. 'Despite everything, I have to fight for what I believe in, and that means fighting against a system this family is part of.' She gave Mrs George a last hug. 'Say goodbye to Mr Simkins will you, and Millie and Jacob Shaw. I shall miss you all.'

Mrs George fetched a canvas bag from her cupboard.

'The frocks I made you.'

'I can't take them.'

'You can and you will. Besides, no one else would get into them.'

Elody smiled. 'You've been so good to me, Mrs George.'

Mrs George sniffed into her new lace handkerchief. 'Go now afore I get sentimental, but if you ever need me don't forget that I'm here.'

Last, Elody knelt down beside the chair where Rhea was sleeping and stroked her fur. 'Behave, cat, and look after Mrs George.'

'We'll look after each other,' the housekeeper vowed.

Chapter Fifty-Nine

Present Day

Marina had to get out of the house, away from Thorncliffe, her pain was all-consuming, and she couldn't take any more. She de-iced the car and drove around Stafford for an hour before reaching the Artemis Refuge for her reunion with Josie and Jess. They needed all of her, not the grieving Marina caught up in the life of a long-dead child. She spoke into the intercom and went inside.

'Big day, Jess?'

'Big day, Marina.'

'You'll be OK?'

'Definitely.'

'No going back.'

'Never. We're moving into our new flat and new life.' She pointed to the boxes beside her. 'Even got saucepans, courtesy of the refuge.'

'I've been thinking about you.' Marina folded her in her arms.

'You have?' Jess looked at Marina, the bumblebee tattoo on her hand nearly flying off in surprise.

'Every day I prayed you wouldn't give in and return to your husband, be taken in by yet more promises.'

'This was the last time, I swear. When my Josie is hurt, so am I. You showed me I'm not a complete waste of space, and I can look after myself and Josie. You made me believe in myself, Marina.'

'The counselling sessions had a lot to do with it.'

Jess had not finished yet. 'You, this hotshot lawyer thought I was worthy of being your friend.'

Marina had cried then and so had Jess and they had stayed in a huddle with Josie inside the security doors.

When at last they had dried their tears, Marina put her hands either side of Jess's face and looked her in the eyes.

'When I was practising in Italy, I fought for courageous women like you. You make me realise I can work towards change in this challenging world.'

'Me?'

Marina nodded. 'You and Elody Cole.'

'Who's she?'

'A long-dead potter.'

'Cool.' Jess shuffled her Doc Martens, a donation from a member of the public to the refuge. 'We need people like you to watch our backs.'

'Well, I'm going to do just that, Jess, I'm going to complete the exam necessary to practise in England so I can act on your behalf. But there is something else,' her voice was energised, a light shining in her eyes. 'I want to see the laws on domestic abuse amended, there are loopholes that need to be closed, you need to feel safe always. I'm going to fight for change.'

Jess had hugged her then. 'Awesome, and if you want any help, me and my Josie will be right behind you.'

Chapter Sixty

The Past

In the quiet of the throwing shop after the workers had left, Elody gained some kind of solace. While the wheel whirred in a gentle, continuous motion and shadows flowed and ebbed across the walls, she could feel Lucian's presence beside her. Occasionally she spoke to him, her voice breaking the silence, a profound longing unravelling inside her.

She didn't care how long she worked because there was no one to go home for and she didn't wish to get in Dawn's way.

She was sitting on the steps outside her studio when Tilda dropped by.

'I've heard of your loss, and I'm sorry.'

'Sorry Tilda?'

'Truly, the loss of a child.' She spread her hands wide. 'When my Tim died I—' She stopped and drew herself up. 'But that doesn't alter the situation. We need all of you, Elody, just as before.' As Elody looked into Tilda's coarse features she realised they had never had all of her, she had been torn then and only Lucian's death had cut her ties.

'It's just the march you're after, Tilda, you have no other plans.'

'No other plans, I give you my word.'

On the night before the funeral, Elody crept downstairs and went outside.

If any of the residents of Tellwright Street had been on their porch as dawn leaked across the sky, they would have seen Elody return from her mother's old allotment in Dolly's Lane, carrying a trug and a bunch of flowers, and Gabriel Jackson stopping to talk to her on his way home from the colliery. They could have heard his words of encouragement as he admired the charming wreath plaited from nasturtiums and carrot tops.

'It's a good thing you're doing, lass, you need to say goodbye.'

At two o'clock, Elody sat behind the church wall, her eyes closed, wondering how the sun could shine on this day of all days, how the birds could sing when Lucian was dead? She remembered drawing the nightgown over his shoulders, brushing his hair, kissing his pale forehead, observing how quickly the body had grown cold. She stood up, tears blurring her vision, steadying herself against the wall. She had prepared Lucian for this moment, the movement from one life to the next, but she wasn't ready, she could never be ready.

She was aware of the church doors swinging open, Lord Derrington and Archie carrying the small white coffin followed by the priest along the flower strewn path.

Very gently they lowered the coffin into the black, gaping hole, each taking a spade, lifting the rich Staffordshire soil and scattering it onto the casket until Lucian was covered, gone. When it was done, they stood back, their shoulders shaking.

What happened next would remain in Elody's mind for the rest of her life. Ursula Derrington entered through the lychgate, her back straight, her head bare. She moved to the graveside, knelt down on the bare earth, studied the wooden cross.

'No,' she moaned, earth falling through her fingers like corn.

'The inscription is all wrong, he cannot be Giles's child.' She rose to her feet, rounded on her husband. 'He is your son, yours.'

'The truth is written there.' Andrew's voice was muted. 'Lucian was Giles's child. Jane Pole, my secretary, was his mother.'

Ursula pushed her hand against her forehead, swaying from side to side as if she would fall. 'Frank Pole came to the house, he said Lucian was your child. I paid him money to keep him away.' Her voice was trembling, she was struggling to keep control.

'Before God and Lucian, I have never been unfaithful to you.'

Ursula started to weep, great shuddering sobs that wracked her body until at last she looked at her husband, her face streaked with dirt.

'I tried to tell you, Ursula, so many times, I wanted you to embrace Lucian into our family, have part of your son restored to you, but you took that man's word over my own.'

Ursula's hand went to her mouth. 'No,' she mouthed. 'Please God, no. It can't be true.'

'You had put Giles on a pedestal, but he was human, Ursula, that's all.'

'And Jane Pole?' Ursula's voice was quiet.

'I found them together. Giles was meant to be at the front, but he came home on leave to see her. He didn't tell us because he believed correctly, we wouldn't sanction their love – she was married, of a different class. All this grief, Ursula, this misery because of what ... and Lucian was such an endearing little boy.' He raised his hands and dropped them to his sides. 'When Jane died four years later, her mother brought Lucian to Thorncliffe. Frank had threatened to harm the child and she believed he would be safe with us.'

'And instead I was vile.'

Archie went forward and took her hand.

'Did you know, Archie?'

'I thought I did, but I got it all wrong. I was coming home

late the night Lucian arrived, I witnessed Father carrying him upstairs. He asked me to keep it to ourselves and I gave my word. All these years I believed I was protecting you, Father.'

'Oh my God, Archie, what you must have thought of me.' Andrew brushed his hand across his eyes.

'Is this really true?' Ursula looked from one to the other.

Andrew nodded, silently.

'What have I done?' she uttered.

'What have we all done, Mother?' Archie glanced over her shoulder his gaze meeting Elody's. For a moment they stared at each other, drowning in their mutual sorrow and despair until she came forward, dropped the wreath of nasturtiums over the small wooden cross and fled.

Chapter Sixty-One

Present day

Marina's hands were shaking as she stacked the papers together. She was confused, angry, the Derringtons may have begun to resolve their differences, but it was too late for Lucian. Exhaustion washed over her in waves. The child had died never knowing who his father was, he had suffered at Ursula's hands, and whatever the circumstances, Marina could never forgive her.

Taking her coat, she walked beyond the garden to the park, and for a brief moment she was back in Italy with Francesca, walking through the meadow, her daughter in the papoose, gazing around in her own private world. She recalled Francesca reaching out, opening her fingers as she tried to touch a butterfly, expressions of wonder crossing her face. She had died prematurely but unlike Lucian, in her short life she had known only security and love. Hugh had been part of that, he had helped to create their intimate, private world, but where had he gone, where had all that happiness gone? Was Hugh like Archie, was he weak, closed off from the real world? But that was unfair to Hugh, possibly to both of them.

She returned inside and without taking off her coat, she unlocked the door to the main part of the house. The long reaches of winter sun filtered through the leaded windows, casting diamond patterns on the wooden boards. She picked a sprig of dried lavender from the Delft china bowl, rubbed it between her hands, perhaps if she found a painting of Archie Derrington, she would find some answers, and the past could be laid to rest. She turned in a circle, the portraits looking down on her as she moved from room to room, she studied the nameplates, but Archie wasn't there.

Hugh was sitting in his usual place in the dining room when she went in. His chin was resting in his hand, the memoir on the table in front of him.

He inclined his head, a muscle working in his cheek. 'It's not pretty reading.'

'It's not.'

'Have you finished it?' he asked.

'No, I can't take any more just now.'

Hugh's face was weary. 'That's obviously why it was locked away. I'm sure of it. Jeremy wasn't proud of it, particularly in the circumstances.'

'What circumstances?'

'My Great Aunt Alice tried to prevent him from being with the man he loved, and before you say it, Marina, we're Derringtons.'

The following morning, Marina made Hugh a strong Italian coffee and put it on the table in front of him.

'Are we going to let Francesca's death destroy us, just as Lucian's did in the past?'

Hugh pushed back his plate. 'I can see where this is going. Lucian died a hundred years ago, for Christ's sake.'

'Perhaps nothing has changed since then. You keep all your emotions hidden away, you can't even talk to your wife.'

'Tell me more, Marina.'

'We've both changed. The memoir has highlighted how different we are. In Italy we speak about our emotions, we embrace family, young and old.' She stared at her plate, the energy draining from her. She longed to say words that would soothe and appease Hugh, but they wouldn't come.

When Hugh finally spoke his voice was flat. 'I don't know what you expect from me. Nothing I do or say is right.'

'I need you to show that you care.'

'Care, Marina? All I've ever done is care, but you ...'

'Yes, Hugh, what about me?'

He raised his hands and dropped them to the table. 'There's little point continuing, no good will come of it.'

Marina pulled at her croissant. 'Perhaps it's better if we have some time apart. We both need to find out what we really want.'

'From where I'm standing, it seems you don't really want your husband. But you're right, Marina, perhaps you should return to the family you love, to the place you belong. You've never liked Thorncliffe. We've tried. I've tried.' He shrugged his shoulders. 'I give up, Marina.'

Marina wanted to deny everything, tell him Thorncliffe was her home, that she did love him, but everything she wished to say remained inside her head.

'I'll stay for Christmas,' she told her mother. 'Finish the memoir, then I have to come home.'

'And Hugh?'

'I'm staying for Hugh.'

But Christmas was a miserable affair, they were both locked in their own grief and the distance between them now seemed insurmountable. Mrs Crump made a valiant effort but even her kindness couldn't break the mood.

'Maybe you're right, love,' she said. 'A little break is what you need, but don't forget to come back.' But Marina believed it unlikely, they had gone too far. She made arrangements with

Dolores at the centre and finally told her the truth. 'I'll do the same work for you in Italy, give advice on Skype, but the death of our child—'

'I see.' Dolores' eyes were filled with compassion. 'I thought it was something like that.'

On a grey morning at the beginning of January, Marina booked a plane ticket to Italy, packed her suitcase, then she went to find Mrs Crump. Afterwards she lit the fire in the Blue Parlour and settled down to read. She couldn't put it off any longer, it was time to learn what happened in the end.

Chapter Sixty-Two

The Past

The ware for Fortnum's was now in production, but the painting was never quite good enough for Elody.

'The dragon's tail has more curve, look at Lucian's example,' she urged, but the problem was the girls didn't have the lightness of hand, the brilliance of his eye, they could never do it like Lucian. In the end they did some of the infill work and the larger blocks of colour, but the detailed work she kept for herself.

'Give yourself a break, girl.' Mr Asland came into the studio late one evening.

'I have to get it finished, afore ...'

'Before what, Miss Cole? Ah, you really carrying on with this business?'

'If I don't go through with this, Lucian's death will have been for nothing. Don't you see that, Mr Asland?'

'At the expense of the Lucian range?'

'That's just it, he would want me to carry on, I know he would, but can I ask you one thing?'

'I imagine you're going to.' Mr Asland took off his glasses, wiping them with a rag.

'If anything happens to me, will you keep the Lucian range exclusive? Sell what you have, nothing more.'

'You trouble me with your words. You've had a rough time of it, but life is a God given gift, otherwise your father and all those boys died for nothing in the war.'

'You're a good man, Mr Asland, but do I have your word?'

Mr Asland took her hand. 'I'll make sure of it, Miss Cole.'

Elody was opening the gate to Dawn's house, when Archie caught up with her.

'Forgive me for disturbing you, Miss Cole, but I was on my way back from the pottery...'

Only the month before, Elody had made love to him on a bed of leaves, and now she was just Miss Cole.

'Yes?' she responded, seeing the hollows in his cheeks, the misery in his eyes.

'I wanted...I wanted to see if you were better.'

Better? she would never be better, a part of her had died with her father, her mother, and now Lucian.

'Hardly, sir, but go on.'

'I had hoped we could speak.'

'I will speak plainly, Archie, you kept me away from Lucian and he died as a result of it. And for what, your pride?'

'But the things that were said, were unforgiveable, so disloyal, cruel. I was about to ask you to be...'

'I denied Tilda's words, said I owed you so much, but you didn't wait...'

Archie put his hand on her wrist, but she shook it away.

'I didn't ask to be the voice of these women; it consumed me with guilt thinking I was betraying you and your family, but actually I would have been betraying myself if I didn't help them.'

Archie drew in his breath. 'Why didn't you tell me before?'

'I did, several times, but you made light of my words, brushed them aside. You live in your grand house; you have no idea what it's like to wake up hungry and cold. You can't conceive the idea of a husband receiving the family wages, then drinking them in the pub. We're fighting for what we deserve, Archie Derrington. Throughout the war we held things together for the pot bank owners. We took over the heavy work which apparently, you thought us incapable of doing, and yet you still didn't reward us. Half the wages for the same work, do you not see the injustice?'

'The men had gone to fight,' he uttered, not meeting her eyes.

'And you don't think our contribution meant something, means something now? You keep us on because we keep your kilns burning, the wheels turning. If it weren't for us women, your precious pot banks would have failed long ago. We want to be treated as if we're worth something, not slaves for the men.'

She leant against the wall, her face flushed, all the fight gone from her.

Archie drew in his breath. 'If only I had made a stronger case to my father, pushed through your request, how different our lives might have been.'

'If only, Archie... but I would have continued to fight for the other pot banks, other women everywhere.'

'I suppose there's no going back?'

'Lucian's death would always come between us; our backgrounds and our ambitions would always come between us. No, Archie, I'll make my own way, there's no going back.'

Archie bowed his head. 'Goodnight to you, Miss Cole.'

He closed the gate behind him and as he walked down the street, his back receding into the shadows, Elody's legs buckled beneath her, and she wept.

Chapter Sixty-Three

30th September

Elody left the house before dawn. There was still work to be done, a few finishing touches before the order was complete. When the paintresses appeared, she went on working. At half past eleven, she put down her brush surveying the gossamer wings that furled from the fox's back and placed the coffee pot with its companions. New fruit bowls, jugs, a dazzling assortment of ware was assembled on the board for the final firing, before transportation to London and Fortnum's. Mr Asland would deal with it, as he now dealt with everything to do with the Diligence Works. He never asked what had happened, he was too respectful for that, but he knew Mr Archie no longer appeared.

Elody undid her apron and walked upstairs, observing the girls working silently at their tables as if today they had taken their cue from Elody. She gazed around the bright airy room with the internal window looking onto the colour room next door, the pots holding different brushes, the designs pinned to the wall. For some indefinable reason she believed it would be the last of the Lucian range. Perhaps because it had been a collaboration between them, perhaps she no longer had the heart for it. She remembered drawing with Lucian on the moors, working in their studio at the Hall, Lucian's comments as the character of each piece emerged. He had told her it was magic, and he was right, but it was not just the creation of the collection, or his exquisite artwork tailored to each piece, it was being with Lucian, watching the intensity in his clear blue eyes as he painted, the pride as he looked up at her. The result was a mystery that seemed to come from the very core of both of them.

She took a last look at the coffee pot, at the colours built up layer upon layer until they sung, shimmered and glowed. Whatever else she had got wrong, she was truly proud of the Lucian range.

On her way out she stopped at Mr Asland's desk.

He put the accounts book aside. 'There are rumours you're marching tonight – just you take good care.'

'I'll do that, Mr Asland, and thank you for your faith in me. Thank you for everything.'

'Not sure why you're saying that, Miss Cole, I'll be seeing you tomorrow, right?'

Elody gave him a quick hug. 'You'll be seeing me tomorrow, my friend.'

Elody took the train to Froghall Station, cycling the last mile past the Bolton Copper Works, to the farm and Florence. She found the row of terraced cottages and rang the bell.

Florence came down the path and Elody fell into her arms.

'Jesus!' she exclaimed, holding her away. 'By the state of you, you'd better come inside.'

While Florence brewed the tea, Elody looked her up and down. 'Well, at least I won't be burying you. You're good as new.'

Florence laughed. 'Always blunt, but you're right and Father is speaking at last. He's up with the lark and there's a spring in his step.' She put her hand on Elody's shoulder. 'Tell me, Elody, what's ailing you?'

Elody stirred her cup of tea, 'I didn't tell you about Lucian,' she began.

Twenty minutes later, Florence fetched the tin of shortbread from the larder and levered off the lid. She took one for herself and passed it to Elody.

'What can I say, I get a new lease of life, and your little one's gone. That's too bad.'

'This shouldn't have happened, Florrie, but I've been split in two.'

'You wanted reform,'

'Not at the cost of Lucian's life.'

'Only a miracle could have changed his destiny, but in this life, we're rather short of miracles.' Florrie smiled at her friend. 'Remember every time you hold the china in your hands, it will bring you closer to Lucian. It will be his memorial, Elody.'

'His memorial – I like that, Florrie.'

Elody stood up. 'I have to get back, I'm afraid.'

Florrie looked at her hard. 'What are you up to, Elody?'

'We're marching tonight.'

Florence drew in her breath. 'You can't.'

'But I have to Florrie, I'm committed.'

Florence fiddled with a button on her blouse. 'There's something I need to explain.'

'It's not your father, you're not sick...?'

'No, Elody,' she interrupted. 'We are in good health; it's about the Derringtons.'

'What about them?' Elody's voice was strained.

Florence walked to the open window and looked across the cornfield, gold in the afternoon sun. 'All this, the hospital, this cottage, everything, it was Lord Derrington and Mr Archie.'

Elody's hands were shaking. She had never believed it was Reggie Billington, perhaps she had always known.

'I see.'

'We were only given the lease this week; their names were on the contract. It wasn't difficult to find out the rest.'

'Do you realise what this means, Florrie ... they must have done it because—'

'Because of you,' Florence finished for her.

Elody stood up and paced the room, coming to a stop in front of Florence. 'The Diligence Works will be on tonight's route. Tilda's out for blood, I'm sure of it.'

Florence grimaced. 'We've always been honest with each other, and I'm going to say this, I don't trust Tilda. Stop the march, give up while you still have a chance.'

'I have to go on, Florrie, I've got this far.'

'You've lost too much already.'

'The women are relying on me ... but this march bothers me. Tempers are running high ...'

Florence sighed. 'If you won't give up on the idea, give up on Tilda. Start again, Elody, with someone you can trust.'

'I have to go tonight.'

'Do this one march tonight, then get out. It'll be Tunstall tomorrow, Hanley the day after. By Wednesday the police will be waiting, no two ways about it.'

Elody stepped from the bus and joined the figures trudging up the hill in the twilight world of chimneys, pot banks and strange pink skies. At Louise Street, Tilda was waiting in the porch, a banner propped against her hip.

'I was beginning to wonder if you were coming,' she grumbled.

'I was seeing Florence.'

'Don't forget this is our chance to make a stand.' Tilda took hold of her arm, gripping it until she winced.

Elody shook her off and in the dim light she faced her. 'I'm the spokeswoman, so we do this my way, understand?'

'Your way,' Tilda muttered, taking an unlit torch from the pile, and beneath her breath said, 'always your bloody way.'

Elody put a match to the flame, took the end of the banner and stepped into the dusk with Tilda.

The lights of three hundred torches flickered as the women gathered outside the town hall. Hannah came forward, pinned the rosette on Elody's chest. 'Remember you can do this, and I'll be at your side.' As Elody looked at the expectant faces in front of her, women who were risking everything to march, she hesitated only a second.

'To a bright future that starts right now,' she yelled, and as her voice rose and carried on the night air, a simultaneous murmur grew in the crowd, until it was a chant for victory, a spontaneous, rallying call.

'To a new future for women,' they cried, punching their torches in the air.

Soon they had left the market place behind, falling silent as they filed through the narrow passage towards the high street and 'the Sytch'. Here in the dark heart of the Potteries, amongst the dank and decaying factories, they painted slogans on the walls, scattered leaflets on the mouldering floors. Their faces were solemn as they processed from one pot bank to the next. Leaving the high street, they turned left into Liverpool Street, passing the Methodist Sunday School, and the smithy that had once belonged to her grandfather. The forge was still there, and as the torchlight glinted on the shed roof, she remembered helping to load her grandfather's cart before he set out for work, how long ago that seemed. They were passing the Bulls Head in St John's Square when a man staggered towards her, throwing the contents of his tankard in her face.

'Yer conner change the natural order,' he spat. 'Get back in the home where you belong.' Elody could feel the liquid drip down her face, she could smell his sour breath. He swayed along at their side as they turned along the bottom of St John's Square, but in Queen Street he stumbled away. By the time they reached Swan Square the numbers had swelled, women slipping from side streets, warily closing front doors. When they reached the top of Nile Street, and the tripe factory, a groan swept through the crowd, then laughter as they recognised the same foul odour that assaulted them every day. They skirted the Doulton factory, reaching Parker's Brewery in Regent Street. By now several hundred women had joined the throng. Elody could feel their excitement, hear the mantra that rose in the air like a prayer, *Rights for Women, Equal Pay.* From there it was up Bournes Bank and back to Queen Street, the rumble of their feet now throbbing on the ground. On it went and on, more women joining, more insults and abuse. In Upper Hadderidge Road, a group of men heckled them, throwing rotten eggs. When they reached Amicable Street and the Greenfield Works, at the end of the Branch Canal, Elody glanced around her as if for the very first time. In the centre of the squalid cluster of factories, comprising engineering works, brush makers, crate makers, her mother had spent her working years.

When they broke through the Clay Mill Yard, into Furlong Lane, Elody's stomach grew taut. Without doubt Tilda was pushing them towards the relative prosperity of Middleport. All evening she had vowed they would avoid the Diligence Works, but when they reached Yale Street, anxiety gripped her. At Burgess & Leigh her worst fears were confirmed.

'It's the Diligence Works next, women,' Tilda shouted, the light of a zealot burning in her eyes. 'Give them what they deserve.' And Elody realised Tilda Kennard would put her own aims and ambitions above any respect for their cause. Bile rose in her throat, she had to stop her. 'Not the Diligence Works,' she instructed. 'Turn around now.'

Tilda threw her a look. 'Whose side are you on?' she challenged, and Elody could see the jealousy in her eyes.

They were halfway down the street when Elody's blood ran cold. She had been around horses all her childhood, she knew the smell of them, the stench of their sweat. Her father took his bath in the outhouse after work, before he was allowed inside. She could hear the faint ring of metal on the cobbles moving from Albion Street into Port Street.

'The mounted police are coming, we need to separate,' she yelled. 'People will get hurt.'

'Don't be ridiculous.' There was a note in Tilda's voice that alarmed Elody. 'We've only just begun.'

'We have to get back, we have to disperse!' Elody screamed, trying to rally the women, desperate to push them out of harm's way, but she was too late. A wall of mounted police approached from the end of Port Street, a menacing, powerful barricade that moved towards them out of the haze.

'Go home, women,' the police shouted. 'Get back to your houses, your husbands, you have no place here.'

Many of the women fled in terror while Tilda tried to rein them in. 'Don't let them scare you, we have a right to demonstrate, don't be afraid.'

The police came closer, the hooves were louder now, threatening.

'Bloody hell,' it was Dawn shouting, 'get back, for Christ's sake.' But it was too late, the police were cantering towards them, their powerful horses approaching with speed. Within seconds they were amongst them, scattering the women who ran in every direction. There were screams, cries of pain as women got kicked, beaten with batons. When an elderly woman fell, she was crushed beneath the horses' hooves.

Elody was dragged aside by Dawn, as a horse approached.

'Bastards,' she shouted. 'Fucking bastards,' her voice was shaking with fury as she pulled another woman to safety.

It happened so quickly Elody would never be sure who threw the torch. She saw it flying through the air over the Diligence Works' sign above the wrought iron archway, picking out the lettering on the green and gold board. Up it went higher, arching like a crescent before crashing through a window upstairs. Elody cried out, her heart pounding in her chest, and then she saw it, a light in Lord Derrington's office – her mentor was there. She thrust her torch at Dawn and, without a second's hesitation, ran across the cobbled street, hurtling over the weighbridge, past the clocking in machine. For an instant she looked back, her eyes searching the crowd until they alighted on Hannah. 'You have to let out the horse,' she screamed, 'please open the stable door.'

By the time Elody arrived at the outside stairs, the fire had reached the colour room. Explosions rocked the buildings as chemicals and pigments ignited, sending eruptions of flames and sparks skywards in a pyrotechnic display. Avoiding the balustrade, she took the steps two at a time pulling off her jacket to cover her head. She tried to open the door, but the heat had distorted the frame and it was jammed. She kicked hard and it flew open, but she was knocked backwards by the intense heat. In the distance she could hear Tilda shouting, women crying out. Every instinct told her to run, to listen to the weakness in her limbs, but she kept on going. She held on to one thought: if her godfather was there, she would get him out.

She crouched low, coughing, choking, unable to prevent herself inhaling the scorching smoke. Her eyes were streaming as she made her way along the passage, yelping with pain as her hand grazed the wall. Despite her terror she forced herself to go on.

The roof and ceiling were now alight, fragments of burning

timber falling to the ground. The wrought iron structure was groaning as it began to sag and warp, the columns buckling. Flames were licking across the floor.

Elody found Lord Derrington slumped at his desk in his smoke-filled office. She tried to stir him and failed. Ripping the curtains from the wall she doused them with water from the jug on his desk and threw the rest in his face. He spluttered, coughed, and at last opened his eyes.

'You have to help me,' she shouted. Slowly she dragged him from the chair, and they staggered across the floor, their faces covered with the wet curtain.

'We need to go faster,' she urged, supporting him as they stumbled along the passage to the outside staircase, only to find it was ablaze. She could see the people below them, men and women, mouths gaping in their upturned faces. 'Jump, you have to jump,' they screamed as the steps crashed to the ground. When a blanket was held out for them, she knew there was no recourse.

'I'm going to push you,' she said.

As Andrew Derrington fell, limbs waving helplessly, Elody thought she heard a cry behind her, a voice she knew so well. She took one last look at the people begging her to jump and turned back, running into the burning building behind.

Chapter Sixty-Four

Present day

It was dawn when Marina finally finished the memoir. Who had written the ending she wondered, scrutinising the change in script. 'Whose pen had taken the story to its dramatic conclusion? She opened the window, breathing in the cold dawn air. The fire was in the past, Elody had gone, but in her mind, she could smell the scorched timber, hear the crash of falling masonry, the chemicals igniting as the pot bank burned. She tried to quell her anxiety, but as she went to fetch her suitcase, she felt the past and present collide.

'I'm sorry, Hugh,' she whispered, going into his dressing room, watching him sleep. 'It wasn't our fault – neither of us. We didn't stand a chance.' A strand of hair had fallen over his forehead, she was tempted to brush it aside, wake him to say goodbye. Instead, she went downstairs, and sped along the drive. Sheep raised their heads and gazed at her, a solitary crow flew above her, a black silhouette against a pewter sky. She reached the family burial ground and leant over, her breath slowing – she was ready for Lucian.

She found him buried beneath the lichen-covered stones.

Archie had kept his word; Ursula was buried on one side; Andrew on the other. Lucian wasn't alone. Sinking to her knees in the damp grass, she murmured a prayer for Francesca, for Lucian and Elody Cole.

Returning to the house she wrapped the coffee pot and put it into her holdall, before going to find Mrs Crump.

'I'm ready,' she whispered.

'Mr Crump is by the car,' she responded, brushing Marina's cheek with her fingers. 'But as I said, this is your home now, so don't forget to come back.'

'Take care of Hugh.'

'I have before, and I will again. But you take care of you.'

It was half past seven when Marina descended the front steps of Thorncliffe Hall, the same steps she had come up only five months before. Failure weighed heavily in her chest. She couldn't make a go of her marriage; she couldn't even keep her daughter alive. She looked up at the house. How bleak it seemed in the raw January light, how black the stone. She thought of Elody arriving at Thorncliffe, terrified and alone. Would this be the last time she came here, she wondered, as Mr Crump put her suitcase in the boot. Was this the end?

They reached Stafford and, as she had requested, he turned the car off the road into a quiet cul-de-sac, stopping in front of a semi-detached house.

'Would you give me five minutes,' she asked, looking up at the newly painted exterior, the green front door. 'I need to say goodbye.'

She rang the bell and there was Jess, pink hair brighter, with an added streak of blue.

'Blimey, duck,' she said, gathering her in her arms. 'You'd better come inside.'

*

Hugh read through the night and as he finished the memoir his guilt was unrelenting. Though the actions of his ancestors had taken place a century before, he still felt responsible. They were his family, he carried their genes, it was no surprise Marina was angry and scared. He stepped in the shower accepting every word she had spoken was true. He had put up walls to protect himself, but those same walls held him in. It had taken a memoir from the past written by a girl from the Potteries to show him there could be a different way.

As he lifted his face, letting the warm water refresh him, he remembered Uncle Jeremy coming into the Blue Parlour after his father had died all those years before.

'Would you like to stay here?' he had asked, turning off the television, his voice gentle. 'Permanently at Thorncliffe?'

'Mother will need me, Uncle Jeremy. I must return to London, it's time to go home.'

'That's the thing, Hugh, she'd like you to stay here, just for a while, until she's sorted out her gallery.'

He could remember the crushing feeling, the panic inside, and the pity in Uncle Jeremy's eyes.

'She'll come for you soon.'

Hugh had cried himself to sleep that night and for weeks afterwards. His father was dead, his mother no longer wanted him. Every day he had asked Jeremy when she was coming for him, but as the days turned into weeks he stopped asking. The gallery was more important than her son.

Hugh didn't learn the truth until he was fifteen years old, by which time it was too late. He had told the boys at school she was dead.

'I'm so sorry, my darling boy,' she had said, sitting opposite him in a smart London restaurant. 'It's time you knew the truth.'

'What truth, Mother? You're so obsessed with the gallery,

there's never been anything left for me. I'm the son you didn't want or…' He was unable to finish the sentence.

'What are you talking about? You are my son… I have always loved you.'

'You could have fooled me.'

'I was not well, when your father died.'

'Neither was I, Mother, you abandoned me. Your career came first.'

She had tried to take his hand, but he brushed it away. 'Don't. It's too late for that.'

What came next was the biggest shock of all.

'I was at a clinic in Switzerland.' His mother opened her bag, took out a handkerchief and blew her nose.

'What?'

'I went for my safety and indeed for yours. It was voluntary but I recognised the absolute necessity of keeping this from you.'

Hugh remembered feeling dizzy, hot then cold. 'And how long were you at this clinic?'

'A year, but after that I was an outpatient in Wimbledon. I felt…' she struggled with her words. 'We felt, it was better you didn't know you had a suicidal mother who couldn't look after herself, let alone her child.'

'And after that? What about the years when you were travelling the world to find paintings, that little Chagall in Russia, the Klimt in New York?' He was so angry and confused he was clutching at straws.

'Work was my consolation, Hugh. I wanted to bring you back to London, but you were happy, settled at Thorncliffe with Jeremy. You were the son he never had.'

'And you were the mother I never had,' Hugh muttered.

'Oh, Hugh, I believed you were better off without me.'

'And you never thought to ask my opinion? To question your judgement?'

'I had no judgement, except this one thing, Hugh: I had to protect you.'

He had gone back to school but the pretence of her death continued. The damage couldn't be undone.

Hugh was getting dressed when the realisation came to him. While he had been submerged in an avalanche of grief and responsibility, losing himself along the way, his wife was using her suffering to help others.

He walked down the passage, with a firm step, resolving he would fight for Marina and find his way back to being the man she once loved. He was filled with anticipation as he opened the bedroom door. It took him a moment to notice the bed had not been slept in. Marina wasn't there.

Chapter Sixty-Five

Davide Angelini was carving a little wooden wren, when a girl walked up the worn stone steps of the Villa Durante towards his studio. She had long dark hair which swung in a familiar way and a tilt to her head that he recognised. He took off his visor to get a closer look, and as his confusion cleared, his face broke into an incredulous smile.

'Marina, is it you?' he said as a draught of cold air blew in through the door. 'Are you real?'

'It's me, Papa Davide, I'm quite real I assure you.'

'I was afraid I would never...' He stopped, his lip trembling.

Marina went towards him, leant down so she was level with his chair. '*Allora*, you are seeing me again,' she finished for him. 'Oh, *Nonno* Davide, I have missed you so much.'

'I've missed you too, but what's wrong?' He opened his arms and she embraced him, feeling his fragile body beneath his woollen jumper.

'Everything's wrong.'

'Well then, you'd better sit down and tell me about everything.'

Marina sat on a chair at his side. 'Do you remember me coming in your studio when I was little?'

He smiled. 'I taught you to carve and you did quite well.'

'I thought it was very well.'

'You always did like flattery, but what's wrong, Marina? Tell me, please.'

'I have come home.'

Half an hour later Marina leant her head against her grandfather's shoulder and sighed. 'Our grief has destroyed us, we're two strangers living in the same house.'

Davide nodded. 'I see.'

'I thought he would be strong for me, Papa Davide.'

Davide gently held her away, looked into her eyes. 'Perhaps he's unable to be strong, and your disappointment makes him feel even more insecure.'

'But I've never said that.'

'You don't have to, he'll sense it, Marina. We often look to our partners to heal us, but there's only one person who can do that, and it's yourself.'

'Why are you so wise?'

'I have learnt from years of experience.' Davide picked up a small metal chisel and continued to work on a piece of wood. 'And now you're away from Hugh, are you still angry with him?'

'I don't know. He never tells me what's inside his heart.' Marina tapped her breastbone. 'If we don't discuss our pain there's no hope for us, and where does that leave Francesca?' She pushed back her chair and went to the espresso machine on the counter, making them both a shot of strong coffee.

'Believe me, *carissima*, I know about suffering.' Davide ignored the coffee, and it was obvious to Marina his mind was far away.

'I'm so sorry, I shouldn't have—'

'When I lost both my parents to the death camps, there was such a rage inside me. I became a different person, someone that I'm not particularly proud of… it was your grandmother, Diana, who saved me.'

As they sat together in silence, Marina glanced around the studio seeing relics of her grandfather's past, the beautiful carvings he had made for her grandmother, the bronze of an eagle on a granite pedestal, the awards and accolades. She recognised his father's book of Leopardi poems, the bag of tools his mother had given him that he still used today. When at last he turned to face her, there was an intense look in his eyes.

'When you've lost so many of your family and friends, you understand the need to keep those you love close by. From what I've seen, Hugh is a fine young man, and they're hard to come by. He has human frailties, we all do, but my advice is give it another try.'

He picked up the cup and stared into the dark liquid as if he was looking back on his own life.

'Men have been conditioned to be brave, Marina, to hold in their emotions. I imagine Hugh is trying to protect you from his feelings of grief.'

'But he doesn't share them with me.'

'That's not a crime,' Davide smiled. 'I'm sure he wants to, but he doesn't know how. Perhaps you should show him what you need rather than being angry? You can't change another person's behaviour, but you can change how you respond to it.' He sighed, his shoulders sagging. 'Your grandmother taught me so much. I was damaged, Marina, but she encouraged me to trust her, to reveal my darkest thoughts, and she did the same. It was this honesty that enabled us to enjoy a lasting marriage.'

'What if it's too late?'

'You must remember that Hugh lost both his parents at a crucial age. Imagine his fear of abandonment. Get in touch with him, Marina, reassure him you're healing, but you need more time.'

Chapter Sixty-Six

Hugh was sitting in his darkened office when he made the call to his mother. He let the phone ring and when she didn't pick up, he tried again.

'Hello.' He could hear her voice, slightly suspicious, anxious. 'Helena Derrington-Blackett.'

'Mother, it's me.'

'Is everything all right?'

'Actually no ...' Hugh's words caught in his throat. 'It's Marina, she's gone, Mr Crump took her to the station this morning.'

'Why didn't you ring me before?'

'Do I ever ring you?'

Silence. 'Well, perhaps you should start. I'll catch the early train. Meanwhile I suggest a stiff gin and tonic, but don't get drunk!'

Hugh put down the phone and walked along the corridor to the Blue Parlour. There seemed to be no end to the heartbreak. First his father, drowning on a fishing trip in Perthshire, and just when Hugh was beginning to reconnect with his mother, Jeremy died. He remembered the exact moment Signor Rinaldini came into the studio where he was teaching, apologising to the class with a wave of his hand.

'You have a phone call from your mother,' he said in his gravelly voice.

All the way upstairs, the possibilities had whirled in his head. Was she ill again, or was it Uncle Jeremy?

'Hello, Mother,' he had said, dreading the words that would follow.

'I am so sorry.'

He could hear the tremor in her voice.

'Jeremy died this morning, it was very peaceful.'

The only thing he could think about was he hadn't been there. Afterwards, he had finished the lesson recalling his uncle insisting he remained in Italy after his diagnosis.

'Oh, this old thing, a touch of cancer won't stop me. One day you'll need to run this place, in the meantime, have a splendid time in Italy.' But it had stopped him and Hugh hadn't said goodbye.

Mrs Crump found him asleep in an armchair several hours later, a glass in his hand, an empty bottle at his side. He had taken his mother's advice about one thing but not the other, he was certainly drunk.

'I bet you've got a head on you,' she murmured.

'A bit,' he replied.

Hugh hadn't moved from the chair when Helena Derrington-Blackett arrived in a taxi accompanied by her terrier Jack.

He looked up, his eyes glazed.

'She found a memoir, Mother. It paints the family in an awful light; I'm not surprised she left.'

'Umm.' Helena sat down in the armchair opposite and lit a cigarette. She crossed her long, elegant legs and gazed at her son.

'You look awful,' she observed, a wry smile crossing her finely chiselled features.

'Not actually surprising.' He managed a sheepish grin. 'But despite my thumping head and your welcome presence, I must go to the estate office.' He looked at her for a moment. 'Isn't it time you gave up the fags?'

'Today I need nicotine, but you don't need to work. The estate ran without you before, it will do so again.' She stubbed out the cigarette. 'I'll sort breakfast while you have a shower and a change of clothes, it will make you feel better,' she suggested, and to no one in particular. 'It will make me feel better too...'

When he reappeared, his hair brushed, his stubble removed, she handed him a cup of coffee and a piece of toast. Afterwards they wrapped up in thick coats and went outside.

'Where are you taking me?' he grumbled.

'For a walk round the garden. Fresh air clears your mind and feeds your soul!'

When they reached the Peace Garden both of them stopped automatically.

'We planted a tree for Francesca,' Hugh began.

'Of course you did. The coppice was planted by your ancestor possibly to give clarity to the devastation that had taken place. Your Uncle Jeremy loved it and your father. It's where I retreated when...' she stopped and Hugh put his arm through hers.

'It wasn't a good time, Hugh, forgive me. Let me make up for the past.'

'You coming here today is a pretty good start,' he replied.

After Hugh had showed her the *Sorbus*, she led him to a slender tree with pale bark and started to pull the weeds from the base. 'Aspen,' she said, looking up at him. 'It was planted for Lucian apparently. When the wind blows you can hear it whisper through the leaves. The trees are associated with peace.'

'So you know about Lucian?' he murmured. 'But why have we never spoken about him before, why was I never shown the memoir?'

'As you reminded me, we don't speak frequently.' She cleared her throat. 'With everything else you've been through, Jeremy and I decided it was better to keep the memoir from you, but it seems your Marina had other ideas.'

'She's not my Marina anymore, I pushed her away.'

'She can be again, but that's up to you.'

They started to talk and it seemed they couldn't stop. They were returning to the house when Hugh picked up a stick and tossed it for Jack.

'It's taken Elody, a young woman who lost everything, to show me how stupid I've been.'

Helena glanced sideways at her son. 'Guidance can come from the most unlikely sources.'

'I was furious with Marina. I couldn't believe she kept the memoir to herself, but she obviously thought I was one of them.'

'But you're not like Andrew and Ursula, they were pushed into a marriage neither of them wanted. You love Marina.'

'I hated to see her unhappy, but I didn't know how to reach her.'

'You must fight for her, Hugh. She needs you to show how much you care. I assume she's contacted you?'

'Only to say she's arrived.'

Helena gave him a look. 'Now we've established you're both too stubborn to say what you really feel, I suggest you go to her, remind her the man she married is still very much alive.'

'Now?'

Helena shook her head. 'Give her time with her family, then bring her home. And once you've found out the ending to the story, together you can tell the world about Lucian and Elody Cole.'

Chapter Sixty-Seven

The feast of Epiphany arrived and though Marina embraced the familiar celebrations with her family, commemorating the visit of the Three Wise Men, her thoughts kept returning to Hugh.

Throughout January the frost lingered on the ground and the trees were bathed in shadows, but in February the hills above the Niccone Valley brushed winter aside. The sun rose through clear skies into dazzling mists. Cyclamens opened beneath the trees in splashes of vibrant pink, anemones, crocuses even wild orchids began to push their way through the rough grass. If Marina woke early, she would walk through the meadow at dawn, willing the elusive occupants of the woods to appear. Occasionally she was rewarded with a wild boar rooting in the rough grass, or the glimpse of a fallow deer. Over breakfast in the kitchen with her grandfather, eating her mother's home baked pastries, Davide would recount stories of his early childhood in Bolzano. Afterwards she would link up with the Artemis Centre and do individual sessions on Skype. It had become a welcome routine as they examined the legal options, what they could expect and how they would answer questions in court. Not only was this important to the women who depended on her, but also to Marina's recovery, and every day she felt stronger.

One spring morning while she sat with her grandfather on

the terrace, she took out the anthology of poetry Hugh had given her on her wedding day. 'I want to read this to you,' she murmured. 'It's called "Máiréad Linnane".'

If you are lost, I will write your name in the sand and the birds
will be finding you.
The trees will whisper your name and the wind will be bearing
you.
The moon will make a path through the wheat fields and guide
you towards me.
And I will open my arms wide to hasten you home.

When she reached the end, her eyes were shining as she remembered Hugh turning towards her in the orchard, a catch in his voice as he recited the words, and she realised with a jolt, she needed to go back to Thorncliffe, because home was Hugh.

'I can see it has stirred memories, Marina.' Davide was smiling softly. 'Why don't you send the poem to Hugh, this will be a way of telling him your love is as strong as ever.'

'What if he rejects me?'

'Lead by example, climb down from your own grievances and make the first move.'

'*Sei sicuro?*'

'I am sure,' he replied.

Chapter Sixty-Eight

Helena had returned from London for the weekend and Hugh was pouring the wine, when Mrs Crump bustled into the dining room.

'We're so pleased to see you again.' She placed a prawn cocktail in front of Helena. 'My Atticus and me, well we've missed you these past few years and I don't mind saying it.'

Helena smiled. 'Likewise, Mrs Crump.'

'I'll be honest I think your boy needs you right now; Marina having a sabbatical and all.'

'We're very much hoping she'll be back soon.'

'Oh indeed, Mrs Derrington-Blackett, I said to her, this is your home Marina and make no mistake of it. Now, if you'll excuse me, there's a surprise for your main, and I wouldn't want to ruin it.'

Helena gave a discreet look at Hugh and they tried not to smile.

They were finishing their sole à la meunière, quite a feat for the housekeeper, when Hugh put down his fork.

'Have you any idea who completed the memoir, Mother, and why it's here?'

Helen took a sip of her wine. 'It was Hannah Medley, the teacher from the School House,'

Hugh exhaled. 'That makes sense.'

'I believe she finished it after the fire and kept it until she died. Her daughter brought it shortly before I left for London. I remember it distinctly; she gave the envelope to your uncle, said it was her mother's last wishes. That's when we read it and decided to put it away – permanently.'

'Was there anything else with it?'

'Not that I know of, but we could ask the daughter, she shouldn't be hard to find.'

At that moment Mrs Crump sailed in with a plate of cheese. 'Forgive me but in a house this size …'

'Yes, Mrs Crump?'

'Jennifer Medley-Scott lives in Folly Lane not far from the school house.'

'What would we do without you, Mrs Crump?'

'Well, you know what they say, the apple never falls very far from the tree.'

The door to Folly Cottage was opened by a tall octogenarian with piercing blue eyes.

'I hope you don't mind us turning up like this,' Hugh's voice was apologetic, 'but—'

The woman interrupted him. 'I was expecting you.'

'Mrs Crump?' Hugh shook his head in mock exasperation.

'Of course, but what can I do for you?'

'We're hoping the name Elody Cole means something to you.'

'Means something,' the woman chuckled. 'It certainly does, my mother corresponded with her for years.'

Hugh could feel his heart racing. 'So, Elody didn't die in the fire at the Diligence Works?'

'Far from it, Hugh, if I may call you that. She went to America, made a new life. She wrote regularly and always sent photographs.'

'Do you have any of the letters?' Hugh waited, his mouth dry.

'I'm sorry, I cleared out her desk only last year.'

Hugh's disappointment was overwhelming. 'I see, well thank you for your time.'

They were halfway down the path when Jennifer called out. 'Just a thought, Mum's albums are in the attic, the snaps might be in them, but I haven't been up there for years.'

Hugh and Helena turned around. 'Albums?' they said in unison.

'I'm not offering to get them, but if you want—' she got no further because Hugh was striding towards her.

'Want to, Jennifer, please show me the way!'

An hour later Hugh and Helena were back in the dining room at Thorncliffe, two albums bound in green leather on the table in front of them.

'You go first,' said Helena. 'With any luck...' She tailed off, her eyes fixed on her son as he opened the cover. On the flyleaf there was an inscription.

I purchased these albums for you in Liverpool before the ship sailed,
  From your very dear friend who will be indebted to you always.
  Elody Cole

They were quickly immersed in a different time, a world coming together after the Great War. Each photograph was dated and named and as Hugh and Helena pored over them, their emotions ranged from sadness to jubilation. There was a tea party at the school house, two uniformed lads in wheelchairs laying wreaths at the war memorial, a picnic on the moors, and at last they met Elody Cole. She was staring into the camera, a defiant yet humorous look in her eyes outside the Olde Crown in Burslem.

'She looks superb.' Helena was smiling.

'She's just as I'd imagined her,' said Hugh.

They had started the second album when Hugh's hand froze.

'America,' Helena murmured. 'These must be the photos Elody sent. Hugh, this is what you're looking for.'

There was a photo of Elody standing outside a pot bank, a bottle oven behind her and another of Elody beside a young man with dark curly hair. Hugh read the inscription, his voice husky. 'A grown-up Walter, so they found each other in the end.'

The photos went on, but on the last page, Hugh read the name, the colour draining from his face. He pointed to a photograph of Archie Derrington, his arm around Elody as they posed outside a church. They were laughing as she tossed a bouquet in the air. There was another in front of a clapboard house with painted shutters. Elody was holding a baby in her arms.

'Archie followed Elody to America, he married her and they had a child.' His eyes were shining. 'Do you realise what this means? Thorncliffe, the pottery, he gave it all up for Elody.'

Chapter Sixty-Nine

The days turned into weeks and there was still no word from Hugh.

The mimosa was coming into bud, the same trees that had filled the garden with sweetness during Francesca's first months.

As Marina searched her inbox again, she remembered Hugh walking up the worn stone steps with Francesca, stopping at the top, showing his baby daughter the view. Now there was no Francesca and no Hugh. She closed the laptop. There was no point hoping and waiting, she would get on with her life.

Later, she had her daily call with the Artemis Centre. 'So, who's on the list today, Dolores?'

'Rani has her appointment with the counsellor, but would you mind speaking to Ashok. They're finding their feet but still need our support. Afterwards, there's Tonya. Her ex beats her up at regular intervals using the contact arrangements to continue his abuse. We're encouraging her to come to the refuge.'

'Surely an injunction?'

As Dolores's warm voice enveloped her, Marina felt she was doing something useful again, something worthwhile.

*

Marina was feeding carrot peelings to the hens when her grandfather came outside carrying her mobile phone.

'This rang for you, *carissima*. You might want to call back.' He shuffled off leaving Marina on her own.

'Tonya is in hospital,' it was Dolores. 'The bastard was lying in wait when she went to the shops, I thought you ought to know.'

Marina put down the phone, the familiar anger welling inside her and realised the time had come for her to leave.

'You're returning to England,' her grandfather stated, his voice flat.

'I'll stay for Francesca's anniversary, then I must go home.'

'You're right, the time has come.'

'But I hate to leave Francesca.' Marina looked at her hands.

'Your daughter will always be with you, because she's in your heart. Never forget that, Marina.'

He coughed, his eyes watering. 'Though it has been a privilege to have spent these weeks with you, my child, you have work to do in England. That wonderful charity needs you more than I do. You're married to an Englishman. I may be old-fashioned, but you should be at his side.'

Marina stood up and went to the window. 'It's the twenty-first century and there's been no significant change in the laws on domestic abuse, and rape within marriage still goes unchallenged. The charity in Staffordshire is part of a network across the country fighting for change and I want to be involved in it.'

Her face was determined and when she turned back to her grandfather, he laughed. 'You're going to be busy, Marina.'

'I had lost sight of who I am, Papa Davide, and now I must continue my work.' She smiled gently. 'With you and Elody spurring me on, I can't fail.'

'And will you practise law in England?'

'I intend to join the Inner Temple. It will involve further exams and pupillage, but then I'll be able to advocate on the behalf of women. It's not an easy undertaking but I want to return to the job I was good at.'

'And Hugh, he is part of your plan?'

'I hope so,' she replied.

Chapter Seventy

The anniversary of Francesca's death was approaching, and still there was no news from Marina.

Hugh took the late afternoon flight from London City Airport to Florence and arrived at the Borgo San Frediano, and his old workplace, Antonio Rinaldini's Atelier, in time to see his mentor for a drink.

'If you ever wish to come back, there'll always be a place for you.' Antonio put his arm around his shoulders and guided him through the door and into the street outside. 'We're short of talented artists with your skills. If anywhere can distract you, the *culla del rinascimento* is the place for you and Marina to recover.'

'The cradle of the Renaissance. I like that, Antonio.'

Hugh ambled down the narrow street enjoying the last of the evening sun, stopping to dine at his favourite *osteria* in Santo Spirito, finishing his shrimp linguine but resisting the offer of tiramisu on the house. Afterwards, he lingered in the square, sitting on the bench near the fountain, listening to the murmur of voices coming through an open window, a dog barking nearby. Nothing had changed since he had left, but he had changed. Tomorrow he would leave for the hills above the Niccone Valley, lay flowers at his daughter's grave and make a bid to save his marriage, but tonight he felt a sweep of loneliness inside. It was quite probable Marina would reject him, then what? Would he return to England, to Thorncliffe alone, or would he stay in Italy, his responsibilities be damned? It was dark when he rang the bell to the old palazzo, now divided into apartments and Signora Barbieri's familiar face appeared at the door.

'Ahh, Signor Ugh—' Signora Barbieri could never pronounce his name, 'I am happy to see you.' She looked beyond him, her forehead creasing. 'But no Marina?'

'No Marina, I'm afraid.'

'I've heard about your baby from Signor Rinaldini, *mi dispiace*.' She gathered Hugh in her arms. 'My heart it cries for you. Please, let us drink together before I take you to your old apartment upstairs.'

At six the following morning, Hugh made his way to the Basilica di Santo Spirito. It was here, in the octagonal sacristy, beneath the wooden crucifix, carved by Michelangelo, he had come for refuge when his uncle had died. Now as light filtered through the circular windows far above him into the luminous space below, he hoped that once again it would give him courage to face the day ahead.

He walked down the steps and into the outside world. In *Via della Chiesa* the baker greeted him as he pulled up his metal blind, the grocer was sweeping his store front. Even at this early hour, the Oltrarno quarter of Florence was coming alive. He jumped aside to dodge a speeding Vespa, and by the time he had reached Santa Maria Novella station twenty minutes later, something had moved inside him. He felt the budding of hope.

Hugh paid for his ticket and as the rush hour flowed past, he bought an espresso from the café, stamped his ticket on the platform and boarded the train.

Soon the tapestry of terracotta rooftops, '*campanile*' and churches gave way to olive trees, squat farmhouses, and wooded hillsides. With every kilometre that passed his apprehension grew. He paced the carriage. Marina didn't know he was coming, nor did her family, but he had to be with her to mark the anniversary, and he had to tell her his news. Archie had given up everything for the love of Elody.

At nine o'clock, he took a taxi from Camucia station to the piazza of Sant Andrea di Sorbello.

'Are you sure you don't want me to take you up?' The driver, a wiry man with at least three days' stubble on his chin, looked with suspicion at the uneven drive that wound up the hillside.

'No, thank you, I need to walk.'

The man shrugged his shoulders, took a cigarette from a packet and leant against the car. 'If you change your mind, you will find me in the bar.'

As he began the long walk up the wooded drive towards the Villa Durante, the light spilling through the dense foliage, his heart was thudding against his ribs, but he needed to be strong for Marina. He needed to keep it all together for what was to come.

Hugh saw her as he came from the trees into the meadow. She was alone outside the chapel, wearing the sprigged dress he had given her the summer before Francesca was born. Her back was towards him, but he could see the flowers in her hand. He was out in the open now, striding across the grass towards the gate.

'Turn,' he whispered, his breath quickening. 'Turn now, Marina.'

Marina looked over her shoulder and, for a brief second, she was immobile, her eyes wide, then she moved slowly, her footsteps tentative, the flowers falling to the ground as her pace quickened and she was running towards him, speeding across the meadow, and so was he.

'I prayed you would come, I was waiting for you,' she whispered, throwing herself in his arms. 'You had to come back to me.' She wound her arms around his neck. 'I thought you'd gone from my life and it was my fault.' She began to sob and as Hugh kissed her face and hair, his voice was shaking.

'I thought you didn't love me, that you would be better off here.'

'But you didn't respond to the poem I sent you. You must have understood.'

'What poem? I didn't get any poem.'

'For days, no weeks, I waited for a reply, and I thought...' she bit her lip. 'I thought I had lost you.'

'You could never lose me, Marina.' Hugh leant down so their lips were not quite touching. 'I had to be with you today of all days.'

'But can you ever forgive me for leaving?' She wiped the tears from his linen shirt.

He took her hand, held it to his lips. 'There's nothing to forgive. I was distant, unsure how to reach you, but I should have tried harder.'

'*Carissimo*, I am so sorry. I was blinded by my own grief and became obsessed with the past. I couldn't save our beautiful daughter, but I could save Lucian's memory.'

'You can still save Lucian's memory and Elody's. I have something for you.' Hugh unhitched his rucksack, took out the albums.

'What are these?'

'Hannah Medley's albums, they tell the story of Elody's life in America.'

'America?' Her eyes were wide.

'I'll show you the albums tonight and explain,' he promised, putting them back in his rucksack. 'I have an extraordinary tale to tell, but I'm hoping there's plenty of time.'

Marina smiled softly. 'We have the rest of our lives, Hugh, but first let's go and see our daughter. Today it's about Francesca, our perfect little girl.'

Epilogue

Marina was standing on the bridge looking back at the Palace of Westminster when she saw him. A tall, slim man, with dark hair, a rucksack over his shoulder.

He crossed the road and stopped in front of her, '*Avvocatessa* Angelini.'

'*Signor* Derrington.' Marina took her husband's arm and they walked along the street.

'Well, how did it go?' he asked. 'Were you able to see much from the public gallery?'

'It was amazing, Hugh, history in the making.'

'Did the Domestic Abuse Bill get through?'

Marina smiled. 'Not yet, it was only the Second Reading, there will be obstacles to overcome before it receives Royal Assent.'

Hugh smiled. 'With so many people behind it—'

'It's about time.' Marina frowned. 'Throughout the debate, I kept thinking of Elody, how she fought for women to be valued and safe. Please God, they'll soon be protected by law.'

Hugh looked at his wife, his eyes filled with pride.

'And don't underestimate your contribution, Marina, no one has been more determined.'

Marina lifted her chin. 'Slowly change will come. The Bill will help, but we still have a battle ahead to ensure a woman's right to safety. I won't stop now.'

Hugh smiled. 'I wouldn't have expected anything less.'

After lunch at a trattoria in St James, where Marina was definitely eating for two, they stopped outside the Derrington-Blackett gallery to admire the painting in the window by Chagall.

'Your mother has great taste, Hugh.'

He grinned. 'Now you know where I get it from!'

Marina punched him lightly and they went inside. Helena's assistant Sebastian bounded over to them, his fluorescent trainers at odds with his immaculate suit. He pushed his floppy blonde hair from his forehead.

'Great news, Hugh, "Still Life with Coffee Pot" sold this morning. It's going to New York.'

'*Mio Dio,*' Marina's voice was joyful. 'Now perhaps Hugh will believe how good he is, Sebastian.'

'The client is a tough businessman, but extremely discerning.'

'I'm still here,' Hugh reminded them, and they all laughed.

At that moment, Helena walked across the carpet towards them. 'So here is our celebrated artist. Well done, darling, I'm proud of you.'

Afterwards, with a promise extracted from his mother to join them for tea at the Ritz, Hugh and Marina strolled together down the street.

'Now shall we visit Mr Button?' questioned Hugh.

'Definitely,' she agreed.

Hugh went in first and was greeted by a flustered Mr Button. 'Lord Derrington, the item is beneath the counter as you requested, I'm assuming it's a present for your wife?' Shortly afterwards their conversation was interrupted by Marina.

'How lovely to see you, Mr Button. My husband insisted I stayed outside; I sense a conspiracy afoot.'

Mr Button blushed and looked to Hugh for reassurance.

Hugh nodded and the shopkeeper lifted a little jug from beneath the counter. 'As you may remember, this is by the celebrated American potter Cleo Doyle,' he said proudly.

Marina picked up the jug, cradling it in her hands. 'Wasn't it here last time we came? I'm surprised it hasn't sold.' She glanced at her husband.

'I've kept it at home; these pieces are extremely rare.'

'I have no doubt,' Hugh agreed, 'but I have something to tell you both.'

'What?' Marina looked at him quizzically.

'Wait and see, it's rather amazing.' Hugh was smiling as he lifted the rucksack from his shoulder and took out a small cardboard box.

'As we both know, Mr Button, there was once a talented potter called Elody Cole.' He placed the coffee pot beside the jug on the glass counter.

'I can assure you this piece is by Cleo Doyle.'

'That is actually the point, Mr Button, let me show you what I mean.'

There was tension in the shop as Hugh took a pink velvet pouch from his pocket and dropped some Scrabble pieces onto the glass surface. Then he began to arrange the letters until the two names, Elody Cole and Cleo Doyle were side by side.

'Perhaps if you were to rearrange them, Mr Button?'

The man looked confused.

'Do you mean like this?' Mr Button's expression slowly started to change as he moved the letters, swapping them around. 'Oh my Lord,' he murmured. 'This is quite the most marvellous moment of my entire career.'

Marina picked up the little jug, her eyes shining. 'You mean Cleo Doyle is an anagram of Elody Cole?'

Mr Button's face was flushed with excitement. 'Yes, it seems the two potters are one and the same.'

'Exactly, Mr Button. Now that we've solved the mystery and indeed the pedigree of our celebrated potter, would you mind wrapping up the jug? We'll take it home.'

Acknowledgements

Of all my novels, I believe this is the one my mother would have been most proud of. *The Pieces of Us* celebrates the achievements of women, their fight for equality and their perseverance. She was a barrister who fought for women her entire career. Thank you, Mummy, for being such an extraordinary role model. You left us far too soon.

Next, I wish to thank Jemma Baskeyfield, the company historian at Burgess & Leigh, who so generously shared her extraordinary knowledge of the Potteries and gave up so much of her time. She took me on a voyage of discovery through the Victorian premises, giving me an understanding of the past and indeed present manufacturing processes where the same equipment is used to this day. It was Jemma who showed me the remarkable journey taken by a lump of clay before it is turned into a beautiful object.

Joan Walley, former MP for Stoke on Trent North and avid supporter of Port Vale football Club, who introduced me to the real Burslem where my heroine Elody Cole would have lived and worked, and her husband Jan who made me my first ever Staffordshire oatcake.

Ian Dudson Lord-Lieutenant of Staffordshire whose family business, manufacturing ceramic tableware has been based in Stoke on Trent since 1800. Thank you for sending me your mother's insightful and charming book on the industry and for telling me about the Potteries from an owner's perspective.

Dickie James, Chief Executive of Staffordshire Women's Aid, who works tirelessly to combat violence against women and girls. She is remarkable and I have learnt so much from her. Somehow in her crammed schedule she found time to give me insight into her lifechanging work, and indeed to check my manuscript for any inconsistencies. She showed me case studies, introduced me to members of her team and to the resilient and brave women who come to the centre. I will be forever grateful.

Wonderful Shona Small who checked my Italian, which is so important, thank you.

Jonathan Marks KC, my big brother who, with many others, championed the Domestic Abuse Act and worked tirelessly to get it through Parliament. Thank you for explaining (several times!!!!) the many processes a bill has to go through before it becomes law. Your support and love has always been inspirational.

Jo Frank, my great friend and brilliant freelance editor, who I turned to when I was overwhelmed with the enormity of the task ahead and who tirelessly helped me to surmount that solid brick wall.

Hannah Medley, social worker, dog trainer and dear friend who was always ready to give me advice, mostly during our dog walks, and to give me her extremely expert opinions, and yes, her dog is called Ralph!

My thanks go to Rob Johnston, whose wife Marie-Therese was a dear friend. At her funeral, Rob read the beautiful extract from her grandmother, Daphne du Maurier's Rebecca Notebook, and so kindly helped me get the permissions to reproduce this at the front of my novel.

Lara Marks, my glorious niece for loving the idea of my novel and Medina, my sister-in-law, for agreeing with her.

Matilda Forbes Watson. What can I say but thank you. She is an extraordinary agent, encouraging, patient and wonderfully honest. She has become a Titan in the industry, and I am so privileged to be represented by her.

Nicola Finlay, with her razor-sharp eyes and invaluable honesty, who once again helped me tighten passages, cut passages and whose help I couldn't do without.

Charlotte Mursell, who did the first edit on this book. Thank you. It was brilliant, insightful and clever.

Rhea Kurien, my current editor who I must have known in another life. Thank you for your eagle eye and inspiring comments, for helping me to refine the book and refine it again, for loving the concept and believing in the book and me. Sahil Javed, brilliant editorial assistant who will one day be at the top of the industry tree.

Tristram Hunt, director of the Victoria and Albert Museum and former MP for Stoke on Trent who brought Josiah Wedgwood to life at our Literature Festival last year and whose book *The Radical Potter* was a complete inspiration. Owen Sloss, lifelong socialist and trade union representative for the ceramics industry, who gave me insight into the trade unions, and their huge role in the Potteries.

Chris Yeats, who once again put his pyrotechnical and engineering skills to brilliant use and helped me create the fire in the pot bank with historical accuracy.

My thanks to Celia McGee, arts, culture and publishing writer for the *New York Times* for her interest and encouragement. Theo Clarke MP, who checked all things pertaining to the House of Commons and who I discussed this with from the very beginning.

Henry Coram James, my wonderful son who I turned to when I needed insight into emotional aspects of the novel.

Clemmie Coram James, first draft reader extraordinaire.

Emily Ryder, my incredibly talented stepdaughter for helping me design my fictional ceramic ware.

Eddie Coram Jones, for stepping in to support my hard-working publicist at Orion.

My very dear friends Louise Harwood, Pink Harrison, Gina Blomefield. Caroline Sanderson, for coming to Italy with me in the course of my research, encouraging me always. To my patient and amazing family. Michael Doulton and Christopher Evans who opened the archives at Royal Doulton so that I could see past pattern books, and generously gave me permission to use them. What a joy. Grant and Lisa Donner and her mother Lynn Evans, who so generously provided me with photographs, books and magazines of the Potteries in the 1920s. They were fascinating and inspiring, and helped me to place myself in the Potteries at that time, thank you. Emily Ryder, my gorgeous step-daughter for helping me design my fictional ceramic ware.

Laura Horwell, a gloriously strong, independent young woman whom I know and love and whom I shamelessly copied in the making of Elody Cole. Eddie Coram James, for stepping in to lend another pair of hands to my hard-working publicist Ellen Turner.

Conroy Harrowby, my incredible husband whose family has lived in Staffordshire for generations. He has encouraged me always, listened to my incoherent ramblings in the middle of the night when I have an idea, supplied an unbelievable dictionary of words when I have run out, walked the hills with me, introduced me to Luds church, tried to teach me how to read a map (and failed), trawled libraries with me, visited potteries, canals, shordrucks. I couldn't do any of this without you. Thank you.

Credits

Caroline Montague and Orion Fiction would like to thank everyone at Orion who worked on the publication of *The Pieces of Us* in the UK.

Editorial
Rhea Kurien
Sahil Javed

Copyeditor
Laura Gerrard

Proofreader
Linda Joyce

Audio
Paul Stark
Jake Alderson

Contracts
Dan Herron
Ellie Bowker
Alyx Hurst

Design
Tomás Almeida
Joanna Ridley

Operations
Jo Jacobs
Dan Stevens

Editorial Management
Charlie Panayiotou
Jane Hughes
Bartley Shaw

Finance
Jasdip Nandra
Nick Gibson
Sue Baker

Marketing and Publicity
Ellen Turner

Production
Ruth Sharvell

Sales
Jen Wilson
Esther Waters
Victoria Laws
Toluwalope Ayo-Ajala
Rachael Hum
Ellie Kyrke-Smith
Sinead White
Georgina Cutler